The Keeper Chronicles:
Playing with Fire

J.R. Vikse

ISBN: 1479272981
ISBN 13: 978-1479272983

For my parents

who taught me to enter new worlds
by teaching me to open new books

Prologue - Part One:
The Thief
{London, England; 1882}

The gentleman stood in front of the shop's window, his brow furrowed in thought, his fingers playing nervously over the head of his cane. He licked his lips as his gaze wandered over the selection of beautifully carved and tastefully engraved wooden humidors. They were displayed behind thick, distorting glass which showed him a warped reflection of his pudgy face and the laneway behind him. The wavering clouds above were darker than the normal London grey.

The gentleman carefully turned up his collar.

Not just rain tonight, then. A storm.

A flicker in the reflection before him caught his eye. A man was igniting a coal-gas lamp on the corner of the street, his arm stretching up towards the mantle, his body perched precariously on a ladder with uneven feet that rocked back and forth as the lamplighter shifted his weight.

The flame caught and the familiar *whiff* of the lamp as it burst into brightness was a comfortable sound; the lamps would hold the night at bay a little longer. London's streets were not the safest in the world, and darkness did not make them any safer. The gentleman knew this well.

The lamplighters were late this evening. Dusk had long since settled on the city, and many of the shopkeepers were already closing up. The lane was empty of buggies, and what few shoppers were left were hastening to get home before night fell. The gentleman watched for a moment as a cluster of women, wrapped in shawls and grouped together for safety, scurried out of the lane and turned onto the busier street beyond. A burly man carrying a small barrel watched them go as well, the scar across his face eerily drawing one eye down to the cobblestone street.

Two street urchins were dodging in and out of the sparse pedestrian traffic, heading in the gentleman's direction. One was a tall red-headed boy in brown trousers and shirt, with a grey vest and cap, and the other was a thin, dirty girl with hollow cheeks in a similar costume, wearing a bowler. In their haste to avoid colliding with a young mother and her squalling child they veered suddenly towards the gentleman and bumped into him. He chased them off with his cane, waving away their apologies.

Children today. No respect.

The gentleman turned back towards the window, and after a few more seconds of consideration, he decidedly squared his shoulders and stepped towards the door, reaching into his frock coat for his wallet as he did so.

His hand found only an empty pocket.

He whirled around and caught sight of the two thin and dirty youths racing around the corner onto the busy street beyond.

"Police! They've stolen my wallet! Police!"

A nearby constable responded immediately, blowing his silver whistle to draw his subordinates' attention. He quickly began shouting directions to his comrades. Two policemen took off down the street in pursuit of the pickpockets while the constable sent two more officers through an alleyway in hopes that they could cut off the fleeing delinquents.

The shopkeeper rushed out onto the street, inquiring after the well-being of the gentleman and casting his gaze down the lane, watching the police chase down "those ungrateful guttersnipe." The gentleman brushed his concerns away and, agreeing heartily with the shopkeeper's forceful opinions, stepped quickly in and out of the shop, pocketing a small, silver cigarette case while the proprietor was otherwise engaged before heading down the lane in pursuit of the pickpockets, the police, and his pilfered wallet.

Fifteen-year-old Callum Swift heard the whistle blow behind him and urged his legs to move faster as they turned onto the sidewalk of the larger street. Bridget was racing along beside him, her practiced fingers rifling through the wallet, searching for notes, coins, or anything else of possible value. Out of the corner of his eye, Callum could see her plucking the money out and tucking it into her shirt as she ran.

Suddenly her eyes widened and without warning she sprang away into the street. Callum glanced back up at the road ahead and saw two police constables emerging from an alleyway into the wavering light of the gas lamps. They searched the crowd and their eyes landed on Callum. A cry of discovery rang out, followed by another shrill blast on a whistle.

Callum veered right, following Bridget across the busy street, now filled with the living traffic of Londoners returning to the suburbs after a hectic day in the City. Bridget had disappeared behind the spoked wheels of a passing hansom cab and Callum was forced to wind his way around hurrying animals and pedestrians alike as he jostled through the crowd.

Bridget was not making the run easy for him. She purposely pushed into people as she ran, knocking them over, dumping their goods onto the ground, creating obstacles that were meant to slow down her pursuers, and consequently Callum as well.

Callum gritted his teeth and kept moving. His legs pumped as he tore past a woman who had kneeled in the street to pick up a fallen book. He ignored the shouts of the two men whose shoulders he used to vault himself over an upturned wheelbarrow. Up ahead, Bridget raced in front of a shaggy mare pulling an empty milk truck. Callum watched her reach out her hand and slap its chest as she tore past it.

The horse reared in fear and shock. Callum didn't have time to stop and threw himself into a leap, his body rushing towards the ground. He curled himself at the last second and turned his dive into a forward roll, passing beneath the horse's hooves and scrambling up on the other side just as the animal clattered heavily to the ground behind him, creating a rearing, foaming, living barrier between himself and the police.

But in spite of his speed, the whistles behind him were growing louder as he elbowed his way through a final mass of people, emerging from the crowds at the Cumberland Gate entrance to Hyde Park.

Bridget was nowhere in sight. Callum pursed his lips. Trust her to take care of herself, and no one else.

Without stopping, he tore down the footpath towards Kensington Gardens, hoping to lose any pursuit in the wooded areas along the Serpentine. Heavy footsteps sounded loudly behind him as a pursuer began to gain ground, the policeman's path cleared with whistles and shouts, his long legs matching Callum's lengthy strides and eating up the distance between him and his quarry.

Storm clouds had gathered above the city, and Callum could see the branches of the trees waving him towards safety in the rising wind as he turned off the footpath.

"Gotcha!" said a rough voice as a hand closed painfully on Callum's collar, knocking the cap off his head with a sudden jolt. The policeman pulled Callum to a stop and wrenched the boy around to face him, drawing him up on his toes to do so.

The officer was a full four inches taller than Callum's 5'11" frame, and had the bulk of a Clydesdale workhorse. He sneered at the pickpocket, showing off a mouthful of tobacco-stained teeth.

"Not this time, my clever cutpurse! That fine gentleman wants his goodies back, and he don't mind if I have to shake you to pieces to get 'em! Now, 'and 'em over, nice and easy-like, and you won't have nothin' to fret over." The sneer widened. "And if you don't, then you and me gets to have... a conversation."

Callum panicked and swung a loose and reckless fist towards his captor, who knocked it casually aside. He continued to struggle frantically against the officer's grip, but it was useless. The man was just too strong. Lightning flashed in the sky overhead as rain started to pour down, drenching them both.

"I don't have nothing! The other one, she took it all!"

The policeman narrowed his eyes as thunder rumbled. He shook his hand, flicking off the first few drops of rain, and then rammed his fist into Callum's stomach.

Callum doubled over onto the ground, gasping. The officer loomed over him, highlighted against the blackened sky by now-frequent flashes of lightning.

"Shall we 'ave another go?"

Callum grabbed his cap from off the ground next to him and stuffed it into his pocket. He didn't answer, but started to scramble sideways, away from the policeman, his feet slipping wildly over the wet grass. The man reared back and kicked at his side, throwing him onto his back.

In the distance, the other policemen were rushing down the footpath towards them, their truncheons glittering wetly in the lamplight. The officer reached down and roughly grabbed Callum's hair, pulling him forcibly, and painfully, to his feet. They stared at one another, the policeman expectantly, the pickpocket stubbornly.

With a smile and a sigh, the officer pulled his arm back to deliver a blow directly to Callum's face. All pretence of bravery faded as Callum widened his eyes and yelled out in fear, his cry echoing across the park.

At that moment, the gas lamps went dark, the flames not *whiffing* out, but instead *popping*, each one shattering the thin, wavy glass of the lamp as they blew. The park was plunged into a sudden blackness that startled the policemen, and the rhythmic footsteps of the approaching constables were interrupted by the sounds of stumbling and swearing while the man who held Callum by the hair momentarily lessened his grip in surprise.

A moment was all that was needed for Callum to pull away and race into the trees. Loud cursing followed his escape and he kept on, pushing blindly through the underbrush until he was certain he was a safe distance from the open parkland.

Callum regained his feet and clambered up the thick trunk of a sturdy oak, and then inched his way along a top branch until he could see out.

Curiously, the lamps were lit again, their flickering light reflecting off the wet footpath and shards of shattered glass below. He could see the retreating shapes of the policemen as they gave up the hunt and hurried to get out of the downpour, dragging their violent comrade away with them.

Callum sighed and let his body relax, lowering his head onto the branch. That had been his closest call yet. He knew that Bridget would have plenty to say to him when he returned to the abandoned warehouse they used as a base. She was always hard on any of her protégés who got caught.

Useless, she called them.

Well, Callum thought, *least she got the tin. That should cheer her up. Though I'll be a basket of oranges if I ever see me share.*

Thunder rolled over the park again, and Callum carefully inched back towards the trunk, preparing to lower himself to the ground. Better to brave Bridget's wrath than be caught out in this storm.

Suddenly the sky above him lit up and a bolt of lightning shot down from the blackness, crashing into the oak and forking through the upper branches of the tree, its current racing through the cracks in the bark, making it look as though the tree was glowing from the inside out. The bolt found Callum's prone body and settled in a startling flash of brilliant energy.

When the blaze of light cleared, Callum was no longer there.

Prologue - Part Two:
The Activist
{Los Angeles, USA; 2012}

Santa Monica Place was always busiest in the afterschool hours. Packs of students milled around the main concourse; eating, shoplifting, flirting, and generally celebrating surviving another day in the American educational system. The open-air plaza was a popular hangout, especially on days like this one; high temperatures, blue skies, and not a cloud in sight.

Jingwei Li stepped back from the easel she had unfolded. It looked sturdy enough. Sometimes it fell over if nudged by a passing shopper, but she'd widened its stance today. Hopefully it would last for the summer; she had lots of work to do.

She crouched down to her backpack, pulling the back of her skirt down as she did so in a gesture of conscious modesty. She had always hated school uniforms, and didn't appreciate being forced to wear a skirt just because she was a girl. She had told her grade ten teacher that, being Chinese, she had to deal with enough stereotyping already, and didn't want to add to it. Her teacher had pressed her fingers against her temples and told Jingwei that she would take the matter up with the school board, if only Jingwei would put down the bullhorn.

Jingwei pulled that same bullhorn out of her backpack and set it on the ground next to the crescent-moon-shaped fountain pool. She placed her poster-board graphs on the easel and carefully folded her dark blue school jacket and set it on a bench, flipping her short black hair out of her eyes. Taking a deep breath, she grabbed a clipboard and pen and turned towards a passing shopper. She'd save the bullhorn for later, if she needed it.

"Excuse me. Do you have a moment to talk about the rainforests?" Jingwei spoke very quickly. She'd learned the hard way that unless you got right into it, the majority of people didn't want to stop and chat about the role of major corporations in the destruction of rainforests in the Amazon and around the world.

The shopper continued past her without a word. This was the usual response, but Jingwei didn't give up easily. In the last three days alone she had garnered more than one hundred and twenty signatures for her petition; a number more than worth a few rude passers-by, in her opinion.

Jingwei stuck her hand out to dissuade someone else from walking past her, and spent the next few hours continuing to invite shoppers to sign her petition, gaining a few more signatures. By the time five o'clock rolled around and the mall started to empty, she felt satisfied with the day's results.

She began to pack up her equipment and pulled her school jacket on. Her foster parent, Rhonda, was a stickler for her being home to help with dinner and make sure all the younger kids were ready. Jingwei was sure that Rhonda was only using her for the governmental support cheque that she brought with her. The young girl didn't get anything from the woman that she didn't have to work for; the only reason she was in a private school was because she had tested so highly that she had been entered in a sort of educational lottery, which she had won.

Every time Rhonda saw the school uniform's jacket, she rolled her eyes and grumbled under her breath about "knowing your place." Jingwei ignored the woman, and though she was sure that she had nothing to prove to anyone, sometimes left the jacket lying around the house, accidentally on purpose.

The easel was folded up and Jingwei was kneeling on the ground, stuffing the bullhorn into her backpack when a shadow fell over the clipboard on the bench and a hand reached down to grab it.

"Hey, Jingwei. What's the petition for?"

Jingwei lifted her head and felt her heart flip-flop in her chest. Hunter Wells was standing within the crescent shape of the fountain holding the clipboard in his hands. Hunter Wells was the most popular boy in school. He was hot, and funny, and an amazing athlete. And Hunter Wells was talking to *her*.

A group of his friends was standing a few feet farther back, staring strangely at Jingwei as she remained frozen, crouched next to her backpack on the ground with her neck craned up to look at the boy standing above her. She realized this and quickly stood up.

"It's to save the forest. For rain. I mean the rainforest. To save it."

Jingwei mentally kicked herself. She was sure she was blushing. She hated blushing.

Hunter didn't seem to notice as he smiled down at her. "Sounds cool. Can I sign it?"

Jingwei scooped up the pen and thrust it towards him, pressing it against his chest and holding it there. He raised an eyebrow and gently pulled it from her hand, then glanced over his shoulder at the other guys. They all took their cue from him and stepped up to sign the petition too.

Once each of them had signed, the boys spread into lounging positions around the fountain, one lying on the bench that bordered it, another sitting on the ground with his back to the low glass wall that surrounded it. The last boy handed it back to Jingwei with a wink. They rest were littered out around the fountain now, as Jingwei looked down at the clipboard in her hand.

"Thanks guys! It's great to have teens interested in–" Jingwei broke off to a chorus of guffaws from the boys.

She looked up at them, her face burning with fury.

They had all signed names that were formed from crude anatomical slang.

Even Hunter.

Jingwei didn't think twice. She stepped up to Hunter and swatted him on the shoulder with the clipboard.

"You think that's funny? I spent all day getting those signatures, and now the whole paper is useless!" She hit him again. "You think you're *soooo* clever, impressing your friends, but you're just an immature jerk!"

Hunter had raised his arms against the onslaught and looked surprised at her anger.

"Hey, Jingwei, it was just a joke. Calm down!"

"Calm down? You calm down! I'm perfectly calm! You want to see me when I'm not calm?! Trust me; you don't want to see me when I'm not calm!" Jingwei's voice had raised itself into a shriek.

The last few passing shoppers began to glance over at the group of youths by the fountain, their attention drawn by the rising noise and scuffling. Hunter grabbed at Jingwei's arms to keep her from hitting him. She began to struggle even harder.

"Let me go!" Jingwei was shouting now. She lifted her foot behind her.

Hunter recognized the signs of a knee to the groin and immediately released her arms and pushed her away from him. Jingwei was surprised by her sudden freedom and stumbled backwards into the bench. She sat down hard on the stomach of the boy who had been casually lounging there, laughing at her. He let out a startled breath and reflexively pushed her off him, and she fell.

Into the fountain.

Jingwei landed with a tremendous splash. Water flew everywhere, soaking the boys completely.

Jingwei floundered for a moment and then gingerly sat up and looked around her. She had miraculously missed the metal pipes that stuck up randomly through the pool to spit water into the air. She looked out at the boys.

Every drop had landed on one of her attackers. The bench, her backpack, the easel, even the ground around the fountain had remained dry, save for the pools that now began to gather under the soaking boys.

The stunned boys looked down at their dripping selves and then around them, taking in the unbelievable dryness of the area. Their eyes grew even wider as they looked at Jingwei, who stood up in the centre of the fountain.

Jingwei was completely dry.

She was looking at her clothes, holding her jacket sleeve up in front of her in disbelief. She slowly turned to see the soaking boys and the dry surroundings, and her hand started to shake.

This isn't possible.

Hunter took an uncertain step towards her. "Jingwei–"

"No! Don't come near me!" Jingwei almost slipped and fell again in her haste to jump out of the fountain. She abandoned her belongings as she hurriedly side-stepped around the dumbstruck boys and began to rush towards the exit.

Hunter turned to follow her. "Hey! How did you do that? You aren't even wet!"

Jingwei didn't turn around. She didn't answer. She just kept moving, her mind working in overdrive.

How?!

Hunter started to run behind her. "Hey! Stop! Come back here!"

Jingwei took off. She raced across the plaza and up the escalator, taking the steps two at a time. She stumbled when she reached the second floor and, looking back, saw Hunter gaining on her as she made the switchback turn. She bolted up the next escalator, not missing a step this time as she jumped off on the third floor, and then sprinted through the empty food-court and entered the open-air parking lot just metres ahead of Hunter.

He stopped at the entrance and stood panting as Jingwei's motion stuttered to a halt fifty metres away in the centre of the rooftop parking structure.

"There's nowhere to go," Hunter called out as he took a step forward. "Now, tell me how you did that."

Jingwei retreated from his advancing form. "I... I *can't*..." As she backed up, her leg grazed the bumper of a luxury car, setting off its alarm. Startled, she turned away from Hunter for a moment. He saw his chance and made a break for her.

Jingwei heard the footsteps and swung back around, realizing her mistake. Hunter grinned. She had no way out.

He was still three car-lengths away from her when the lightning bolt flashed down out of the cloudless sky.

Hunter was blown back onto the ground, his head knocking with a heavy *thunk* against the concrete floor. He shuffled backwards on his elbows in shock as the pounding rumble of thunder swept over the parked vehicles, setting off more car alarms.

Hunter threw his hands over his ears and stared blankly around the lot for a few moments until his eyes cleared.

There, where Jingwei had been standing only seconds before was nothing but a large, black scorch mark.

Chapter One:
The Unfamiliar

Callum opened his eyes. He was lying face-down in the dirt. He could just see his left hand beside his head; its fingers were curled and dug harshly into the ground. Smoke was rising from his skin.

He forced himself to roll over and sit up and instantly regretted it. Sharp pains stabbed at his stomach, a gift from the nameless policeman and his wicked kick. Callum groaned and looked around, blinking.

He wasn't in Hyde Park anymore.

The carefully manicured green grass and vigilantly protected trees of the park were gone. Callum was now sitting on a vast plain that dipped and rose gently for kilometres in every direction. The ground was covered in a grain-like plant that rose about a half-metre into the air, except for a circular area around Callum, which was burned to a crisp.

Lightning.

Callum forced himself to remain calm and thought back. He remembered stealing the wallet, then running from the police. He remembered the way his heart was pounding just before he was nabbed, and the way it skipped a beat when all the lights went out. He remembered crawling through the underbrush, and then climbing the tree, and then his fear had been replaced by relief, and then...

Callum struggled to his feet and took a deep breath. He coughed. The air was thick. He could feel it on his skin, he could roll it over his tongue. It felt like he was breathing underwater, or breathing in a thick, tasteless smoke. It wasn't terribly unpleasant, but it certainly didn't feel normal.

Nothing about this place felt normal.

Where am I? Callum thought. *And how did I get here?*

Smoke was still rising from his body, but he didn't appear to be burned. Callum forced himself to ignore this for now, as he seemed to have bigger problems. He turned and looked into the distance, trying to get his bearings. The only break he could see in the tan-coloured field was an enormous mountain range in the distance. It rose high into the air, higher than anything he had ever seen, before being absorbed into the large white clouds that drifted above the plains, but it was a long way off.

He completed his turn, seeing nothing more than endless, rolling prairie. The smoke from his crater moved murkily in the air, flowing slowly upward through the thick atmosphere. Strangely, Callum didn't see a sun anywhere. The air *itself* glowed, spreading a luminescence across the plains as far as the eye could see. Yet, even without the sun to guide him, Callum still somehow knew that the mountain range behind him was to the east.

Blimey. That's not on.

Callum tore his eyes off the horizon and took a quick self-inventory. His rain-soaked clothes had survived whatever had happened and were almost completely dry, but his ribs were badly bruised. At least they didn't feel broken. He pulled out his cap and put it on.

A light wind started a ripple in the stalks next to him, and a few sparks and embers that had until now remained docile on the outskirts of his crater were carried into the tall grains, starting new little columns of smoke. Callum leaped forward and started slapping at the sparks with his hands to put them out. He didn't know where he was, but whatever situation he was in, he was sure that it wouldn't be improved by being caught in a fire.

His attempts seemed to only encourage the sparks to ignite the stalks, as if they were responding to his touch with an increased pyromania.

There was more rustling behind him. Callum turned in his crouch to ward off a new wave of sparks and fell back in surprise.

A Chinese girl was standing at the rim of his burned-out circle, watching him slap at the embers. Her eyes were wide with the same shock he was feeling.

"Who are you?" she asked in an American accent. She struggled to take a breath of the thick air. "And where are we?"

Jingwei looked down at the grimy boy. He had been scrambling in the dirt, trying to contain the sparks with his bare hands, but he'd seemed to be having the opposite effect, leaving each patch with a brighter glow of flame than when he'd attacked it. He now slowly stood up in front of her, his eyes wary.

He was quite a bit taller than her; by at least eight or nine inches. His red hair was smoking slightly underneath his grey cap, which sat slightly askew on his head. Jingwei had the sudden urge to check her own hair for smoke, but resisted it. She had already made sure there was no physical damage after her... journey. And she still wasn't at all wet.

After she had found herself lying on the ground in this strange place, Jingwei had gotten up, brushed herself off, and forced her panic into the mental box she always kept ready for occasions like this.

Not that she had ever had occasions like this before. But Jingwei was nothing if not pragmatic.

She had just stepped out of her ash circle into the field of grains when she'd seen the boy's head appear out of the grass to her right. She had ducked down quickly, her heart pounding in her ears, and then watched surreptitiously as he had surveyed the area and dived back to the ground to capture some errant sparks.

Jingwei had taken the opportunity to approach him as noiselessly as possible, using the sound of the light wind for cover. Moving through the air here was an interesting sensation. It didn't block her or slow her down, but she could definitely feel it sliding around her as she moved towards the boy. Swinging her arm through the thick, glowing air, Jingwei had the sudden suspicion that you could measure light here in gallons.

As she had watched him slapping at the sparks from the edge of his circle, she had realized quickly that he had to be another unsuspecting person, like herself, who had been brought here without warning. His display of shock when he stood up and saw the plains around him were proof enough of that for her. She felt strangely comforted that she wasn't the only one around here who was having to deal with this unbelievable situation. Still, she thought she'd ask him some questions anyway. After all, he might have had an answer or two.

Standing in front of him now, it was clear that he didn't have an answer or two. He was staring at her wordlessly, his mouth dangling open. Jingwei noticed that underneath the grime and soot of the lightning strike, he seemed to be covered in grime and soot of another kind. She wrinkled her nose. Like she needed more gross boys in her life.

She banished the thought. *One thing at a time.* There were serious questions to answer here.

He hadn't responded to her first overture, so she tried again. "My name is Jingwei Li." Jingwei always introduced herself in the western style, with her given name first, and her family name last, though that wasn't the Chinese way. She had always wondered why she should be expected to honour her family by putting that name first. After all, what had her family ever done for her? "I don't know where we are, and I don't know how I got here. Do you speak English?"

The boy swallowed and replied in a British accent. "Name's Callum. Callum Swift. I don't... I dunno..."

"Right." Jingwei could see she had to take control here. "Well, Callum Swift, you're doing a pretty bad job of putting out those fires. Can I help?"

Callum's eyes narrowed with suspicion. Where he came from, no one offered help without expecting something in return. Still, he didn't want to burn down the whole... wherever they were. Jingwei looked up at him sweetly, waiting.

"Sure."

Minutes later, the sparks were extinguished. Jingwei's school jacket had made quick work of whatever additional flare-ups Callum had caused.

By unspoken mutual decision, Callum and Jingwei sat down on opposite sides of Callum's burned-out circle. Jingwei adjusted her skirt around her knees and waited for Callum to say something. Callum sat staring into the sky, wishing for lightning to come and take him home again. Both of them breathed deeply, sucking in the smoke-free air, letting it swirl around them as they became acclimatized to their new location.

Jingwei finally gave in to her impatience. "So, you got struck by lightning too? In England, according to your accent."

Callum snapped his head back down to meet her eyes, his suspicion momentarily forgotten. "Yeah! Up a tree! And now here I am! You were up a tree too?"

Jingwei scrunched up her face. "I don't climb trees. I legislate them."

Callum's nose twitched in confusion. Jingwei sighed and continued. "I was getting some..." She hesitated on the word *friends* and continued, "people to sign a petition. They were jerks, and they pushed me into a fountain. I ran away, and got hit by lighting in a parking lot. Now I'm here. What's your story?"

Callum had grown more confused with every word of Jingwei's story. "What's a parking lot?" He sent his eyes scanning up and down her dry body. She didn't look as though she'd fallen into a fountain. His eyes narrowed again and his fist curled into a ball. "You're lyin'. You're not wet. And you don't even sound Chinese." Callum had spent many nights sleeping behind one of the less-than-reputable opium dens in Limehouse listening to the heavily accented proprietors discussing business with their customers. This girl didn't have that kind of accent.

Jingwei pulled her hands into her lap defensively. "I'm American. And I don't know why I'm not wet, but I also don't know why I'm sitting here with you in a field after being struck by lightning back home. You don't seem to be questioning that! Get off your paranoia-horse! We're kind of in this together, don't you think? And what do you mean, *what's a parking lot*? It's a parking lot!"

She got no response. "A lot. For parking?"

Callum's shoulders wilted a little and his lips turned up in a grin. "You're awfully forthright, for a girl." He continued, "Sorry. Reckon we both want to find out what's going on, yeah?" He scooted forward into the circle. "So, you were in a park, same as me, when–"

"Parking lot," Jingwei corrected him.

"Right, a lot with a park in it."

"No." Jingwei was getting frustrated now, and the emotion she was trying to bottle up threatened to spill over. "A parking lot. For cars. For cars to park in. A *Parking Lot!*"

Callum struggled to understand. "What's a car?"

Jingwei was dumbfounded for a moment, and then it clicked. Suddenly Callum's clothing made sense.

"Callum. Where are you from, exactly?"

"London. The East End."

"Right." Jingwei steeled herself. "And what year is it?"

Callum sensed her hesitation. "It's 1882, last I checked. Why?"

Jingwei let out a big breath. "Callum. I'm from 2012. I live in Los Angeles, California. The United States of America. In the year 2012."

Callum burst to his feet. "What? You can't be! That's impossible!"

"No more impossible than you being from one hundred and thirty years in my past!" Jingwei stood as well, her full height woefully dwarfed by the boy in front of her. "Look, this is difficult for both of us to understand, but it looks like whatever this is, we're in it together, so you have to..." She trailed off as she noticed that Callum's eyes were fixed over her head, looking away from the mountains behind him. "Callum?"

"Look." Callum's eyes were now pinched with fear.

Jingwei turned to follow his gaze, and saw nothing but tan stalks of grain, swaying in the wind.

"I don't see anyth–"

"*Look*!" Callum interrupted her and stepped in behind her, using one arm to point over her shoulder towards the grass.

It took a moment for Jingwei to see the pattern in the ripples. Once she saw it though, the movement was unmistakable.

Something was pushing through the grass. And it was coming their way.

Callum didn't think twice. He quickly threw himself in front of Jingwei, shielding her with his body while he pushed her back to the other edge of the circle.

"Stay behind me." His voice had dropped to a whisper.

Jingwei tried to peer past his shoulder, annoyed. "Look, this is sweet and all, but you should know, women's rights have advanced a lot since your time, and–"

"*Shhhh*." Callum reached back and put his hand over her mouth. "It's here."

Callum and Jingwei both fell silent. A still moment passed, and then suddenly there was a rustle at the edge of the grass, and a tiny black nose poked out. It was followed by a short squat body, waddling on four legs. The animal was low to the ground, and snuffled warily at the two humans. It was tan in colour, and was covered with tall, vertical spines which were the same length and shade as the grass, allowing it to blend into the background perfectly when still. Its underside seemed to be shell-like, and its four legs all ended in a stump, with a single short toe protruding from each.

Jingwei stifled the urge to laugh. It looked like a giant, mutated version of Harry, a hedgehog that a girlfriend of hers had once owned.

The over-sized Harry seemed to sense her ridicule and grunted twice. Suddenly, the grass behind him gave way to seven more of the animals. They all stopped behind Harry and regarded the humans with curious, suspicious eyes.

Harry took a step forward. Its spines glinted with the motion and Jingwei realized that they were not just decorative. They looked sharp.

"Stay behind me," Callum repeated. "And don't move." He raised his hands up to show the animals his open palms. Taking a small step forward, he slowly brought himself into a crouch and looked across the circle at them, only a few metres away. "Hullo. Look. I'm not gonna hurt you. She's not gonna hurt you. No one's gonna hurt you."

"Stop saying *hurt*." Jingwei whispered from behind him. "Don't give them any ideas."

"Belt up!" Callum spoke sharply. A little too sharply for the animals. They gave a chorus of squawks and began waddling forward in a rush, ducking their heads to present the spines on their backs as weapons.

Callum stumbled to his feet and started backing up quickly, pushing Jingwei into the grass behind them. Jingwei could no longer see past him, but she could feel his shoulders tightening in panic.

The animals had made it almost halfway across the circle when a blazing wall of fire suddenly sprang up between them and the humans. Jingwei peered around Callum's protective body and gasped. The wall was over two metres high and was made from translucent purple flames that burned mere centimetres from Callum's outstretched palms. On the other side, the animals were squealing in fear, and between the tongues of flame Jingwei could see them scamper back into the grass, fleeing the fire.

"What happened?" Jingwei grabbed Callum and pulled him back as the flames faded in hue to a more normal red and started to spread quickly to the grains that surrounded the burned circle, jumping from one stalk to another with startling speed.

"I dunno!" Callum's voice shook. "It just... exploded! I put up me hands, and... I don't know where the fire came from, and I don't know where the animals went to!" He turned suddenly and looked at her, hard. "I think we're in big trouble here, Jingwei."

"Do you think so?"

The voice came from behind them, in an accent Jingwei couldn't quite place. Mounted on the back of a large silvery animal was a young man with a fierce expression on his face. Sixteen other riders were spaced out behind him, and all of them were extending their right arms out towards Callum and Jingwei, their hands flexed into fists.

The young man spoke again, grimly. "You have absolutely no idea."

Chapter Two:
The Quenchers

For a moment everyone was silent, each gaze fixed on the unknown threat before them. Callum edged towards Jingwei, reaching out his arm to protect her, which Jingwei impatiently batted aside. The young man who had spoken continued to hold out his right arm, but opened his fist, revealing a palm covered in scar tissue. He lowered it slowly and turned to a girl who had ridden up beside him.

"Watch them." He quickly dismounted and turned to the others. "Quenchers. Go."

All of the other riders jumped to the ground and rushed around Callum and Jingwei and then past them, towards the fire. The leader stayed for a moment until the mounted girl moved forward. Then he joined his people in battling the blaze.

Callum felt uncomfortable under the steady gaze of their guard. She sat on her mount imperiously, looking down on them with a watchful eye. She had very pale skin and looked about seventeen years old, but her hair was so blond it was almost pure white. She was dressed in the same uniform as the other riders; a tan-coloured cloak over a loose, light blue shirt and form-fitting brown trousers. Her boots, belt, and canister-filled bandolier were made of what seemed like some sort of greyish leather, and over her forearms she wore silvery metal greaves, the left one with a metal disk and the other with another small canister attached to it. She caught Callum looking at her and smirked, forcing him to drop his eyes.

Jingwei ignored her completely. Her attention was completely taken with the animals the strangers used as mounts. To call it a horse would've been a mistake, and to call it a fish would've been a bigger one, but those were the two animals that came to Jingwei's mind when she looked at it.

The animal was completely silver under the saddle, but had no scales or reflective covering. Its skin looked thick and leathery, and hung loosely off of its large body, which tapered back to a wide, flat, vertical fin. Its head was narrow and long, and was attached to the body by a short neck that seemed to only move up and down.

But what captured Jingwei most were the legs.

There weren't any.

The animals simply floated over the ground, their bodies twitching every so often to redirect them through the thick air. They were now milling around behind the guard, waiting for the return of their riders.

"You admire my raeas?" The girl's voice was sharp, her diction crisp and cutting like the young man who'd spoken before, and it sliced through Jingwei's wordless examination.

"Is that what you call it?" Jingwei took a tentative step forward. "How does it float?"

The guard looked startled. "It does not float. It moves through the air, as you do. You speak Brydge?"

Jingwei was not going to be distracted. "It doesn't move like I do. I have legs. And I'm speaking English." She moved forward again. "And so are you."

"You need legs, it does not. Do you ask how an Aru Elen can fly? No. It simply moves through the air as it does." The guard edged her raeas forward to match Jingwei's slow advance. She seemed surprised that the girl was not cowering before her. "And we are both speaking Brydge. Do you come from over the mountains?"

"I come from L.A." Jingwei moved forward again, looking over her shoulder at Callum, who appeared to be trying desperately to look everywhere except at their guard's legs. "How can I speak a language I've never heard of? And what's an aroo-ellen?"

The guard had had enough. "The questions will be posed *to* you, not *by* you." She roughly nudged her raeas to circle around them, carefully keeping her right arm pointed towards them at all times.

"You have no wings, or after-wings. If you are not Daevyn or Aru Elen, then what are you, and how do you come to be here?" She glanced over at the others, who had almost finished putting out the fires. "Speak quickly."

Jingwei opened her mouth to retort, but suddenly Callum was there, placing a hand on her arm. He had been listening carefully to the conversation and had caught a hesitation as the guard had looked over at the leader and the others.

Callum casually released Jingwei's arm when she turned to look at him, surprised. He spoke to the guard. "I don't reckon we'll answer any questions 'til we're talking to the bloke in charge."

His gamble paid off, and the guard turned bright red. "You will wait for the First Quencher then. It is of no matter to me." She pulled her raeas back and settled into the saddle.

"I'll bet," Jingwei muttered under her breath. "Good catch, Old-Timer. By the way, did you understand any of what she was talking about?"

"No. But I reckon we might be about to find out," Callum looked down at her. "Junior."

The corners of Jingwei's mouth twitched up at his comeback as she followed his gaze and saw the fire-fighters coming back towards them as the final wisps of smoke filtered upwards through the air. For some unknown reason, even through her fear and uncertainty, she felt safe with Callum, though she was unsure which of them was doing the most protecting. She remained close by his side as the others approached.

The fire-fighters all went to their raeas and remounted, nudging the animals until they were positioned in a loose circle around Callum and Jingwei. Only the young man who had first spoken to them remained on the ground, slowly pacing around them, unconsciously pressing his fingers into the scarred palms of his hands. He looked of an age with their female guard, and wore similar clothing, with the addition of a golden flame pin over his bandolier. Like all the other riders, his skin was light and he had long, blond hair that framed the strong features of his face.

Jingwei thought he looked like a movie star and felt strangely bashful.

Callum thought he looked like a warrior and found himself tensing in preparation for an assault.

The young man stopped in front of them and stared at each of them in turn, consideringly. His eyes passed quickly over Callum's long frame, hesitating on the boy's clenched fists. His gaze lingered again on Jingwei's short dark hair, which stood out among the crowd of fair-haired natives. Jingwei felt uncommonly vulnerable under his gaze, like an animal on display at the zoo. She glanced at the group surrounding her, the bright air reflecting off of their light hair and skin, and wondered how many visitors of Chinese descent this place had had in the last few years. She guessed not many.

The troop remained silent and still as their leader inspected the newcomers, save for the white-haired girl who had crossed her arms and was tapping her fingers against her greaves.

At last the leader spoke. "What are your names?"

Jingwei bit her lip, pushed her nerves aside, and spoke up. "First tell us yours."

Callum placed his hand on her arm again, gently. He sensed that this time, with this particular stranger, Jingwei's forthright attitude wasn't going to play very well at all.

The young man's complexion darkened. "I am Ythen Firebrand." The female guard in the background sniggered, then noisily covered it with a cough. Ythen paused for a moment and then continued, "First Quencher of the Daevyn, and representative of the Flame-Bearer of the Daevyn, Ydelle Emberhand. In her name I demand that you tell me who you are, where you have come from, and what your purpose is here."

Jingwei was impressed in spite of herself. This Ythen didn't look to be more than seventeen, but he spoke with authority. She decided to answer him honestly.

"I'm Jingwei Li. This is Callum Swift. We're from... well actually, it's kind of a long story." Jingwei saw Ythen raise an eyebrow. The riders began to shift in their saddles as they watched for a signal from their leader.

Jingwei gulped. "But, long story short, we're from Earth."

Callum jumped in. "Which this isn't, far as we can tell."

"Fact is, we're not really sure where this is," Jingwei continued.

"But we don't mean it no harm. Nor you," Callum added lamely.

Jingwei finished up. "We come in peace?"

Ythen looked at them silently for a moment, weighing their responses, and then came to some sort of decision. "Since you offer peace, I will take you to the Flame-Bearer." The riders visibly relaxed, dropping their arms. Callum let out a deep breath he hadn't realized he'd been holding.

Ythen continued, "I do not know of Earth; perhaps it is on the other side of the mountains. But in the name of the Flame-Bearer, Ruler of the Daevyn, I welcome you to Tranthaea."

Perhaps it was the way he said the name, but a small shiver ran down Callum's back upon Ythen's pronouncement. Both Callum and Jingwei acknowledged his welcome with a small bow, which seemed like the only correct response to so proper a reception. Ythen nodded in response and Jingwei and Callum both relaxed. The danger had passed, for now, although both of them had a feeling that it may only have been delayed.

Ythen stepped forward and took both of their hands, and all the other Quenchers nodded to them formally, introducing themselves with a short word and a civil smile. Even the white-haired guard was pleasant, introducing herself as Yriel Sparkcatcher. Jingwei noticed that she tended to keep a bit of distance between herself and Ythen, and, whenever her troop leader was looking, seemed to pay special attention to Callum, laughing annoyingly loudly at remarks he made, even when they weren't funny.

Jingwei took an instant dislike to her. She had known plenty of girls like this. Girls who used boys. She'd never liked them then, and didn't much like them now.

Callum was the only constant she had at the moment. She felt responsible for him, and protective.

Better step off, Blondie. Two can play at this game.

Soon enough, all the Quenchers were mounted and organized again, with Jingwei seated side-saddle behind Ythen and Callum delicately holding on to Yriel. The British boy had protested at being separated from Jingwei but had acquiesced at a quiet look from the American girl, who had wrapped her arms around the waist of the lead Quencher and was soon staring pointedly at Yriel, who was just as obviously ignoring her. Callum and Ythen watched this exchange and traded a confused glance that needed no translation.

Girls.

Yriel's raeas began to move forward, its body swishing side-to-side as it propelled itself through the grasses ahead. It took Callum a moment to get used to the strange motion of the animal. He had ridden a horse once, in a paddock on the outskirts of the city. But that had been many years ago. Since then, his own feet had been enough for him. They had carried him away from many sticky situations, and into many others. He wondered what kind of situation he was headed into now.

An abrupt flick of the raeas' tail fin jarred him, and he grabbed on to Yriel's waist more tightly. He noticed that under the tan cloak, the female Quencher's back was interrupted by two small stumps in place of the shoulder blades. Callum wondered what they were for a moment and then remembered Yriel mentioning something called *after-wings*.

Who are *these people?*

They glided at a slow pace through the plains towards what Ythen confirmed was the west, away from the mountains.

Ythen and Yriel peppered them with questions as they rode, but the inquisitorial atmosphere they'd felt at the craters was gone. Like Yriel, Ythen was also surprised that the two visitors spoke Brydge, which was the common language of Tranthaea.

"The other peoples speak other languages amongst themselves, but we all speak Brydge. It is the uniting speech of our world, passed down to the Daevyn by our ancestors."

"So, there are more people here?" Jingwei felt that the more they knew, the more they could keep their options open. They were in a tight spot right now, but that didn't mean they had to throw their lot in with the first group that came along.

Ythen answered slowly, weighing his words carefully. "Yes. The Daevyn are not the only inhabitants of Tranthaea." He swept his eyes to the sky above them and then to the south, where the plains rolled and vanished into the muted line of the horizon. "But you should be glad that we were the ones that found you. Not all peoples of Tranthaea are so... open to strangers."

"So this is a dangerous spot?" Callum's eyes were sharp as he asked.

Ythen sighed before he answered. "Tranthaea has been a peaceful world for some time." He narrowed his eyes and looked ahead again. "But all times end."

Jingwei thought back to the tense and perilous reception they had received only a short while ago and decided that if Ythen was telling the truth, then surrounded by armed guards just might be the best place for her and Callum to be. For now.

The group continued to move as the four of them traded carefully chosen bits of information, each trying to figure out what was really going on here. It took a few kilometres for Callum and Jingwei to convince the Quenchers that they weren't from the other side of the mountains. Ythen and Yriel had exchanged worried looks when Callum mentioned lightning, a subject he quieted on at a furious look from Jingwei.

Silence ensued after that, until Yriel piped up, "They have no after-wings."

Ythen almost fell off his raeas. He awkwardly swivelled his head around to look at Jingwei. "You are not descended from the Daevyn then! And not from the Aru Elen either."

"Of course not. I told you, we're from Earth. We're humans!" Jingwei watched in astonishment as the colour drained from Ythen's face.

"Humans? But..." Ythen broke off and set his mouth. "We will talk no more of this. The Flame-Bearer will hear you speak."

Yriel tried to interject, but Ythen silenced her with a look. Callum heard her mutter under her breath, "Firebrand knows best." Ythen must have heard her as well, because his face went red and his eyes narrowed. But neither of them spoke again.

The fresh silence of their passage across the plains afforded Jingwei the opportunity to think for the first time since they had arrived. It seemed as though all her senses were at war with one another. She knew that it was impossible for her to be here, and yet here she was, riding a non-existent animal across a non-existent world, her arms wrapped around one young man while another who seemed utterly dependant on her for protection rode only a few metres away. Images of Rhonda watching the clock and Hunter striding through the mall were replaced with an imagined trickling of water down her neck as she recalled the fountain. She brought her hand up to her neck, but it was dry, just as it had been when she fell in...

What is happening to me?

The silence that surrounded her tumultuous thoughts was suddenly broken by Callum, and Jingwei had to push all of her fears and uncertainties aside.

"What's that?"

Callum had noticed that they were heading towards a metallic tower that had appeared at the top of a rise amongst the sea of grain.

Yriel reached back and patted his leg. "You have good eyes, for a Human." Jingwei noticed Callum shift uncomfortably and Ythen opened his mouth to rebuke the girl's insubordination, but Yriel hurried on. "That's a Collector."

"What does it collect?" Jingwei carefully stood up in the saddle and then up onto the raeas' back, placing her hands on Ythen's shoulders and leaning up against him for balance. Out of the corner of her eye she saw Yriel's lips tighten, and she smiled to herself.

"Lightning." Ythen was leading the Quenchers towards the tower. "The Daevyn have the responsibility of the plains. We must protect them from the great harm that a fire can cause."

"And what happens if the lightning doesn't hit the tower, and strikes the plains anyway?" Jingwei carefully slid back down onto the saddle behind Ythen and adjusted her skirt.

Callum turned from her to watch the tower grow larger in the dimming air when he realized. "Of course! Quenchers. You control the fires, yeah?"

"Some of us control the fires. Some of us cannot." Yriel shot a hard look over at Ythen as she spoke. "Is that not true, Firebrand?"

Ythen clenched his fists on the reins of his raeas. "There are many things that cannot be controlled, Yriel. Your tongue is the first that leaps to my mind."

The furiously awkward silence that followed was broken only when they arrived and Jingwei jumped to the ground in front of the Collector, staring up at it in awe.

The Collector was built on a huge metal cylinder, that stood about five metres high and three in diameter. It was crowned with a metallic cross-construction that reminded Jingwei of the Eiffel Tower. The beams rose at least another twenty metres, tapering to a peak that was sure to attract any nearby lightning bolts. Running down the sides of the cylinder were thick beams of wood, with circular metal plates attached at shoulder height.

Callum had dismounted and was watching the Quenchers lining up at the beams. One by one they removed the small canister from their right-hand greave and placed its end against the plate. After a few seconds, they stepped back and reattached it to their arm. Callum turned to ask Yriel what they were doing, but she was gone, already waiting in line for her turn at the beam.

Jingwei moved up to the cylinder and knocked on it with her fist. To her surprise, a gentle echo came back to her.

"It's hollow!"

"It is filled with water; it made them much easier to build than if they were solid, but still provides weight and a sturdy setting. The First Flame-Bearer designed them and ordered they be installed. Collectors are stationed all across the prairies in protective service." Ythen was tucking a canister back onto his greave and motioned out towards the fields they had just traveled through. "We are ever conscious of our duty to the plains." The way he said it made it sound like he was repeating something that had been drilled into him over and over again.

From their position on top of the rise, Jingwei could see out over the plains they had traversed. Dozens of Collectors rose in the distance, spaced out generously across the prairies. The air was darkening swiftly now, letting Jingwei and Callum, who had joined her, see the hundreds of bolts of lightning that were lancing down from the clear sky, striking towards the towers.

Jingwei gasped at the sight.

Callum's voice echoed her thoughts. "Cor! That's a fair few! They were striking all day?"

Ythen responded, "Some. There are always more strikes when night falls. Thankfully." He continued, and answered Callum's unspoken question. "They are much harder to see when the air is bright. We only found you by the smoke."

Callum watched the continuous lightning storm blast through the sky for a few moments, with Ythen and Jingwei at his side.

"No thunder."

Ythen responded, "It can be heard if you are close to the site of a strike. From a distance, the noise is lost in the air."

Jingwei looked incredulous. "Sound-proof air? Sound-proof, glowing air?"

Callum grinned. "Brilliant."

Ythen shook his head slightly. These two strangers were odd. Each of their voices held a distinct accent that seemed harsh and foreign to his ears. Wherever they were from, he'd never met anyone else from there, he was sure. His thoughts were interrupted by a call from his second.

"We should go, First Quencher." Yriel sat mounted on her raeas, along with the rest of the Quenchers. "Or do you not want to present your prizes to the Flame-Bearer?"

Ythen grunted, but motioned for Callum and Jingwei to remount. They set off again, going down the other side of the hill. Hours passed with very little change in the scenery, save for the brilliant and silent bolts of lightning that were becoming more and more clearly etched across the sky as night fell. The raeas moved with a gentle rocking motion that soon had Jingwei's eyes heavy with exhaustion and the toll of a very long day. She fell asleep in the saddle behind Ythen, but was awoken by a hard jab in her side.

Callum was leaning out from behind Yriel. "Wake up, Jingwei. You'll wanna see this."

Jingwei blearily rubbed the sleep out of her eyes with the arm of her school jacket and peered past Ythen's shoulder.

At first, she didn't see anything but a night sky, empty of stars. The air had dulled to a pale blue glow, but the lightning was still burning away, giving a stuttering luminosity to the fields around them.

After a moment, Jingwei noticed that most of the lightning was being drawn to one large object directly in front of them. Bolts were shooting straight towards the ground, only to be pulled sharply in to strike against the sides of a tower. An *enormous* tower.

It rose at least fifty storeys above their heads. Dim lights shone from windows on every level, dulled by the bright flashes of the lightning. In the brief moments of illumination, Jingwei could see a myriad of stone buildings stacked on top of one another, tipped with metal poles and roofs. The base of the entire city was no more than five square city blocks, and it looked to be wound through with roads and passages, archways and domes. Level upon level the city rose, each stratum smaller than the one below, narrowing to a peak at the very top. Each level was crowned with multiple turrets and balconies that would provide magnificent views out over the plains. It was an architectural marvel. It was impossible.

Ythen turned to them and spoke with obvious pride in his voice.

"Welcome to Yshaar: Seat of the Flame-Bearer, Ruler of the Daevyn."

Chapter Three:
The Towering City

The party of Quenchers rode with its passengers towards the colossal structure. Callum noticed that the city had no walls, no gates, no fortifications of any kind. The only visible defense was a line of guards, spread out in uneven intervals around the base of the city. They were dressed similarly to Ythen and Yriel, but instead of wearing tan cloaks they were wrapped in royal blue capes.

The riders came to a halt at the foot of the city. Ythen called out to an approaching guard, who immediately stood aside and motioned them forward. One of the other guards turned and ran into the city, no doubt to bring word of their arrival.

They entered Yshaar and began to ride up a wide central street, which wound upwards in a tightening spiral like a circular ramp. At the base of the city Jingwei and Callum could see that the street opened up onto empty plazas and markets which were dotted by thick pillars of stone and roofed by colossal arches that supported the weight of the many higher levels.

On their left, buildings were studded with windows and balconies that hung out of the city at ever-greater heights. On their right, passages and doorways led to carefully enclosed, torch-lit chambers and buildings which made up the central column of Yshaar. But the stone city was not only made of the visually stunted grey pallet they were expecting. In the flickering light the visitors could see hints of colour that were otherwise blacked out by the heavy darkness. Many of the solid stone walls were decorated with vibrant murals and hung with tapestries. The ceilings were painted with the pale blue of a spring sky with artfully crafted wisps of cloud decorating their corners to stave off any sense of claustrophobia, and even the stones that paved the street were occasionally interrupted by a stunning mosaic.

They had only completed two rising turns about the city when the high, clear blare of a horn echoed down from the summit. It rushed past them in the ever-narrowing street, winding its way through the windows and alleys of Yshaar. Callum started at the noise, but Ythen reassured him.

"The Flame-Bearer welcomes you. She is informing the people that you are honoured guests."

Sure enough, within moments of the musical announcement the windows and doorways lining the street were crowded with the Daevyn, peering out over each other's shoulders, all trying to catch a glimpse of the strangers. Many of them were in their nightclothes, and some of the men were bare-chested, showing glints of sparse shining scales on the tops of their shoulders. Callum kept his head facing forward, doing his best to ignore the whispering and pointing. He much preferred disappearing into a crowd to being the cause of one.

Jingwei felt unsure of how to react to the attention, and chose to tentatively smile and wave. The Daevyn responded with small cheers of welcome. She turned to wave to those on the other side of the road and saw Yriel rolling her eyes. Stubbornly, Jingwei waved all the harder.

Tavern doors were thrown open as they rode past and the nocturnal life of Yshaar spilled out onto the streets to welcome them, even the smallest movement in the crowd seeming to dance and wave in the torchlight. Empty shop-fronts were collecting pools for children to gather and gawk at the strangers in the safety of numbers, equally thrilled with the opportunity to see Humans and the chance to delay their bedtimes.

As the visitors rose through the levels of the city, they began to notice a change in the architectural and decorative styles. Simple paintings were replaced by magnificent frescos and studded with glittering stones. The torches were encased in shining metal holders, and any rough stone became smooth and even. Blank walls with windows and doors were now framed with pillars and etchings. The height of the levels doubled, and some of the buildings they passed now had second storeys. Porticos and balconies encroached upon the streets from above and the Humans became conscious that they were being viewed from all angles.

Even the faces at the windows changed. Instead of a wide-eyed curiosity, they now showed an intense scrutiny; still welcoming but less unaware. They had added jewelry and decorations to what Callum and Jingwei had come to understand as the basic Daevyn costume. Just as the people in the lower levels of the city, they all had blond hair in a variety of shades, but now that hair was styled in braids, twists, and bobs, even on the men, who were mostly clean-shaven. Jingwei fingered her short black hair self-consciously while Callum jammed his cap farther down over his bright red hair.

The empty streets and vendor-less markets of the lower city faded away behind them and were replaced by squares decorated with fountains and vegetation and sculptural artistry for the more fashionable elite.

Eventually the party of riders reached the summit of the city. They entered a circular plaza that was surrounded by an open fence of columns, beyond which lay only the air and a long drop back to the plains below. A heavy metal dome arced above them. The plaza was filled with echoing vibrations, the dome acting as a giant bell that tolled almost sub-sonically with every lightning bolt that struck the city's peak and sheltered them from the soft booming of the barely-audible thunder.

The air was charged with the crackling feeling of static. Callum looked over at Jingwei and saw that her hair was standing on end. He laughed out loud, drawing frowns from Ythen and Yriel, and motioned to Jingwei. Jingwei reached her hand up to her head and, feeling the energy, began to madly press her hair down again. She scowled at Callum and his cap, which prevented his hair from doing the same as hers. The surrounding Daevyn pretended not to notice.

At a signal from Ythen, the riders dismounted. They formed themselves into a crescent, all facing inward towards what Jingwei, in her bitterly self-conscious mood, thought looked like a doorless stone outhouse in the centre of the plaza.

She edged towards Callum and was about to speak when she saw movement in the outhouse.

A figure stepped out from the darkness of the entryway. She had a tall, regal bearing, and was dressed in low-cut flowing robes of rich, chocolate brown and royal blue. Her hair was even whiter than Yriel's, and it framed a sharp and beautiful face. The only ornamentation she wore was a bright red gemstone set on a simple silver band around the crown of her head. The stone seemed to capture the light of the lightning bolts that flashed around them, making it glimmer from within with a steady burn.

The woman studied each of the Quenchers in turn, her gaze lingering on Ythen, Callum, and Jingwei. At an unspoken signal, all of the riders bowed deeply, followed hurriedly by the two visitors. Only after they had risen did the woman speak.

"I am Ydelle Emberhand, Flame-Bearer of the Daevyn. I greet you as guests."

Jingwei was impressed in spite of herself. She swallowed away the dryness in her throat and glanced at Callum. He was standing with his mouth open again, gawking openly at the Flame-Bearer. Jingwei sighed and answered for them both, "Thank you. I am Jingwei Li, and this gaping beanpole beside me is Callum Swift."

The Flame-Bearer's eyebrow twitched and her lip quirked in a subdued smile.

"You speak for him. Is he your servant?"

Callum's mouth was working furiously and silently while Jingwei responded. "Not yet, Your Highness. But we've only just met."

The Flame-Bearer laughed out loud. "You have spirit indeed, Jingwei Li. Quick and decisive, a living Firedart! Your voice will be welcome in my house."

Callum finally found his voice. "I'm not no one's servant!" Beside him, Ythen winced.

The Flame-Bearer arched her eyebrow at his unfamiliar accent. "So you have a tongue as well? A matched set then. Ythen Firebrand, you have indeed brought me a unique pair." She gestured with her hand, and from behind her stepped two small figures.

As they emerged into the light, Jingwei and Callum both gasped. The figures were not human, and didn't seem to be Daevyn either. They stood about five feet tall, and had beautiful wings folded behind them, veined and transparent, like a dragonfly's. Their bodies were humanoid, a fact Jingwei and Callum were very aware of, as the bodies were naked.

Below the necks, the creatures were painted the same royal blue that the Flame-Bearer wore, right down to the tips of their toes. The backs of their bald heads were covered in shining silver scales that extended down the rear half of their bodies to their heels. The paint and the scales were their only coverings.

The creatures, one male and one female, stepped forward and began to gather the reins of the Quenchers' raeas, preparing to lead them back down the main road to a stabling area. Callum's face was burning bright red as the female stepped up next to him and took the reins of Yriel's mount. He stared fixedly at the floor in front of him. Jingwei was having a similar experience on her side.

Yriel placed a hand on the back of Callum's neck. "Do you not find the Aru Elen beautiful?" She ran her hand down his arm and squeezed his wrist. "I myself find them attractive. You will recall, I wondered if you were one of them upon our meeting?"

Jingwei overheard her remark and shot a look at Yriel. "You might have noticed that he's wearing clothes. And doesn't have wings."

Yriel grinned wolfishly at Callum but didn't respond. Ythen had sent the last of the raeas down with the winged creatures and stepped up to the group, addressing the two Humans.

"These Aru Elen are our servants. They are gifts from the masters of the Aru Len. Aside from their developed wings, they do not look dissimilar to the Daevyn. I hope you will forgive our questioning."

Callum was grateful for the interruption. "No harm done."

Jingwei wasn't as easily placated. "Um, I'm not a tooth fairy. I don't have wings, I'm not bald, my backside isn't covered with scales, and I'm wearing clothes! I don't know about you, but that spells out H-U-M-A-N to me!"

A loud gasp came from across the courtyard. The Flame-Bearer had been forgotten, but had been gliding slowly towards her guests, listening with humour to their conversation. She stood now with her hands raised halfway to her mouth, her eyes wide.

"Flame-Bearer?" Ythen stepped forward in a quick bow. "Are you well?"

The Flame-Bearer recovered herself quickly and set her face into a mask of control. "First Quencher, take our guests into the Keep to the Hall of Record, and then come to me at once in the Throne Room."

Without another word she turned and disappeared through the empty doorway. The others could hear the sound of her footsteps fade as she hurried away into the depths of the city.

"Was it something I said?" Jingwei asked, trying to laugh off the uneasiness she felt.

"Come with me," Ythen said as he sent Yriel off to dismiss his Quenchers. He led them into the stone outbuilding, which turned out to house nothing more than a small empty room with the entrance to a spiral staircase set into the floor.

Ythen led the way down, ignoring multiple branching passageways as they descended into the core of the city. Jingwei followed him, and Callum brought up the rear. After a few minutes of silence, they were joined again by Yriel. She began to tease Callum about his response to the naked Aru Elen.

"Perhaps you do have wings after all?" She coyly slid her hands onto his shoulders, grabbing at the vest he wore. "Perhaps if I could only see—"

Ythen suddenly stopped and turned back. "Enough, Yriel! Let him be!"

Yriel stepped back as if she had been slapped. "You do not have the right to stop me from speaking to another man."

Ythen huffed, and then continued down the stairs.

Another man? Callum and Jingwei exchanged a glance. Suddenly it all made sense.

Jingwei grinned up at Yriel, and allowed Callum to squeeze past her, and then cut Yriel off by turning to follow him.

Yriel poked her in between the shoulder-blades. "It may not be wise to look so carefree when you make an enemy of such a powerful woman." She continued to follow in a silent sulk.

It took Jingwei a moment to understand who Yriel meant. Ythen confirmed her thoughts.

"The Flame-Bearer is not your enemy. She is not offended or upset by you. It is simply the fact that you are Human."

Callum spoke from behind him. "Human? What's so off about that? Seems like you've heard of us."

Ythen seemed unsure of how to respond. Callum realized that he was probably unaware of how much he was allowed to tell them.

"We have seen Humans before. But not for a long time. The only living Humans in Tranthaea now are Keepers."

Callum asked the obvious question as Ythen led them out of the stairwell and into a torch-lit hallway. "What's a Keeper?"

This time Yriel responded, "A Keeper is a guardian of Tranthaea. They have the power to harness one of the Five Elements."

"And they're human?" Jingwei was excited. If there were other humans here, maybe they could explain how she and Callum had got here, and how they can get back home.

"Three of them are Human." Ythen stopped in front of a large pair of double doors, set deep into the stone walls of the Keep. "The other two are... complicated."

"Complicated? What does that me—"

"Can we see them?" Callum interrupted excitedly. He'd also grasped the possibility of answers from these other humans.

Ythen pushed open the doors that led to the Hall of Record. He motioned for Callum and Jingwei to enter and without entering himself began to close the doors behind them.

"Your fate will soon be decided." He looked apologetic as he eased the doors closed between them with a solid *boom*.

Chapter Four:
The Obvious Solution

Ythen and Yriel hurried back down the corridor and entered the stairway, rushing silently down, side by side. Ythen kept his eyes on the stairs ahead of him, refusing to meet Yriel's glances. He knew that if they connected, she would start talking to him about the Human visitors, and their relationship was complicated enough already. He ignored her and listened to their feet thumping rhythmically against the steps as they descended. Several levels farther down, and after a few more twists and turns, they arrived in silence at the entrance to the Throne Room.

As always, the Throne Room was a hive of activity. Servants were running and flying in and out of the room by way of various entrances and exits. Members of the Daevyn High Council were standing in politically fluctuating groups, discussing policies and gossiping. Older men and women all, they wore their hair in intricately woven designs; the styles were complex and had political meanings that Ythen did not understand. One of the women wore a selection of silver ornaments in her hair that seemed impossibly entangled, yet stunningly artistic at the same time. Another man wore a currently-unfashionable goatee and had shaved his head completely, save for a flame-shaped spot over his left ear, but was otherwise satisfied with more common decorations; he wore only a simple silver ring with a reflective metal nugget on his right hand.

Ythen knew little about the High Councillors in general, and even less about those two in particular. He tried to stay out of the politics of Yshaar as much as possible. He knew that they led the two opposing factions of the High Council, and that the Flame-Bearer depended on them both for advice, but preferred the council of another.

Another, whom Ythen could see at the end of the Throne Room, standing next to the Flame-Bearer.

The room itself was long and thin, almost tunnel-like but wider, and the length of the room was divided by a long carpet, woven to look as though supplicants approaching the throne were walking on a bed of searing embers. The floor on either side was painted blue; a sky blue near the main entrance that darkened as it neared the throne until it was almost black. The high stone walls were uncommonly bare; there was a single carving above the throne which was of the same design as Ythen's flame pin.

The throne was set on a low black dais, and was made of semi-blue crystal. On the throne sat the Flame-Bearer, her robes draped dramatically around her. To her left, joining her in deep discussion was the figure of her favoured advisor, whom Ythen recognised all too well.

He gulped, and started out towards the throne, followed closely by Yriel.

As they passed by, conversations ceased, and the eyes of all those in the room became fixed on the two Quenchers. Ythen knew that he had not been a popular choice for First Quencher, especially after the incident that had given him his name, but he had endured judgement from others many times before. The Flame-Bearer still believed he was up to the job, and that was enough for him. He would not disappoint her.

He squared his shoulders and stopped in front of the throne, bowing low.

"So, Firebrand has returned to Yshaar. I hear that he brings guests of great import. Perhaps they are gift enough to atone for the scars of his failure. Perhaps not."

The speaker was the figure standing next to the throne. She was a small Aru Elen female, but one who stood and spoke with great pride and authority. Unlike the others of her kind, she had long, crimson hair and wore a fitted black cloak that faded into wisps of dark grey smoke at her feet. The cloak was decorated with red embroidery; the designs flickered like tongues of flame. Behind her were folded a pair of transparent wings; the veins in them glowed like liquid gold. Around her neck she wore a necklace of fire with rivulets of lava that poured down her shoulders and arms, collecting in molten pools on her palms. Her eyes sparked with wit and disdain.

She was Kala, the Spark Keeper of Tranthaea and special advisor to the Flame-Bearer.

"Peace, Kala." Ythen lifted his head at the sound of the Flame-Bearer's voice. "Ythen has proven his worth often enough to slow even your tongue."

Kala clicked her tongue against her teeth with a swift snap. "To slow it, but not to still it." She turned her eyes from Ythen to Yriel and then back again. "But that is not why you called me here. What is it about these guests of yours that troubles you?"

The Flame-Bearer hesitated for a brief moment and then looked down the hall and clapped her hands loudly. The sound carried easily down the long room, echoing off the stone walls, and within seconds the servants and all the Daevyn had exited, leaving their ruler alone with the two young Quenchers and the Spark Keeper.

Kala raised an eyebrow. "Is it as bad as that?"

The Flame-Bearer closed her eyes and Ythen could see a tightening at her temples. She breathed out once and looked over to Kala.

"They are Human. Both of them."

Kala sucked in a quick breath in surprise. Her face showed no emotion, but Ythen could tell she was shocked.

The Flame-Bearer continued, "The only Humans I've ever known are Keepers. That is why I called you, Spark

Keeper. Do you know why they are here? Do you know what they want?"

Kala stood in silence, her eyes playing over the empty room. Ythen stepped forward to fill the gap.

"Flame-Bearer, I do not think that the Humans themselves know why they are here. The story they told us of their arrival made them as confused as it did us."

Kala snorted. "And that is all it may have been, Firebrand. Just a story. The truth is, you have no idea how they got here."

"They told us they arrived by lightning," Yriel piped up.

That shut Kala up. She pursed her lips and looked to the Flame-Bearer in silence, and then came to a decision. "Ydelle, there is something you should know. Something about the history of the Daevyn that no Flame-Bearer since the First has ever known."

Ythen widened his eyes. He'd known that Kala was old, but hadn't suspected she'd known the First Flame-Bearer.

Apparently Ydelle hadn't known that either. She rose suddenly from her throne. "Do you think you are Flame-Bearer over me, that you withhold information about my people? Are not our histories written on the walls of our Keep?"

Kala bowed her head in submission. "Of course. The stories of the Daevyn are woven and re-woven throughout the city. But those are the stories of your descent. I speak of knowledge of your defense."

"Defense?" Ythen was quick to latch on to the word. "Defence from what?"

Kala shrugged in false indifference. "From Humans."

She continued quickly over the protestations of her audience. "The First Flame-Bearer was a Human, as you know. What is not woven into the stories is that he was brought here from a place called Earth. By lightning, just as your Humans have claimed. He created the position of Flame-Bearer and from him descended the Daevyn."

Kala's voice had a pleasant hypnotic quality to it. At a signal from her, Ythen and Yriel found themselves sitting at her feet, staring up at her with attentive faces. Ydelle had settled back onto her throne and was listening keenly, her eyes guarded.

"The First Flame-Bearer was ambitious, and jealous of his power. He knew that others like him would come, brought by the lightning to Tranthaea, and so to protect that which was his; the throne, the Daevyn, and the rule of the plains, he ordered the construction of the Collectors."

"To catch the lightning?" Yriel interrupted.

Kala smiled patiently. "Yes, but also to trap those who travel by it. The First Flame-Bearer decreed that the Collectors be built over tanks of water." Her voice dropped and the embroidery on her cloak flickered white hot. "Any Human who dared to come here and challenge his rule, and the rule of his true descendants, would appear inside the cylinders, and drown."

Kala stepped back, her story complete. Ythen rose unsteadily to his feet. "Do you mean to say that there may have been more...?"

Kala stepped in close to the throne and placed her hand on Ydelle's shoulder, her tone deadening, devoid of sympathy. "The Collectors may well be filled with the bodies of Humans who would threaten the rule of the Flame-Bearer."

"And also those who had no such ambitions." The Flame-Bearer was sitting very still, but her face had gone pale.

Ythen was stunned. To protect the Flame-Bearer was his responsibility, to protect the Daevyn an extension of that. But to unknowingly be an accomplice to multiple murders...

"Then why are they alive?" Yriel was still sitting cross-legged on the floor. She looked up at the three sets of eyes above her. "The two Humans. Why aren't they floating in a Collector?"

"That is the question, is it not?" Kala stepped forward and turned to face Ydelle, who remained silent with a look of grave concern on her face. The Spark Keeper spoke to her in a low voice. "They must be very powerful to have survived a journey that so few have."

Ythen thought then of the three Human Keepers. If they were the benchmark of Human survival, then the two strangers in the Hall of Record might be very powerful indeed. And very dangerous.

Ydelle forcibly straightened herself in her throne, once again taking on the physical weight of the position of Flame-Bearer. She coolly looked at Kala and said, "What then do you advise, Spark Keeper?"

"The way of the Flame-Bearer on this matter has been set by her predecessors. The Humans must die." Kala shook her head sadly and her wings buzzed behind her. "It is not a pleasant thought, but easy decisions are the province of the low-born."

Ydelle gave Kala a regal look that said she did not need a lecture on her responsibilities. The Spark Keeper lowered her eyes, gave the Flame-Bearer a small bow, and offered a suggestion.

"If you like, I will question them before they are executed. Perhaps we can find a way of dealing with The Human Problem once and for all."

The Flame-Bearer looked to Ythen and Yriel in turn, reading their thoughts in their eyes and on their faces. Finally, she looked back to Ythen and spoke.

"Bring the Humans to me. I will do what is right for the Daevyn."

Chapter Five:
The Tapestry & the Firedart

Jingwei stared at the door that Ythen had just closed. *Your fate will soon be decided. What does that mean?*

"I prefer to decide my own fate, thank you very much," she said to the uncaring door.

Across the room, Callum had already started exploring. The room they had been left in – the room that the Flame-Bearer had called the Hall of Record – made him uncomfortable. He figured that they were probably down near the base of the city again, having travelled up the road and down the stairs. The thought of all that city above and around him made him feel a little queasy.

The room itself was long, but the ceiling was low. Chandeliers hung down, and he had to duck to keep from hitting his head. The floor was painted blood-red and the flickering light made it look as if it were freshly shed. The walls held torches that were thrust far out from the wall by long metal bars. The reason for this precaution was readily apparent.

The walls were lined with tapestries. Exquisitely detailed portraits of people and animals, cities and battles covered the walls. It was clearly a woven history of the Daevyn. Callum went from image to image, exploring the stories of the past. Many of the images reminded him of the stained-glass windows of an abandoned chapel he had once slept in. He remembered staring up at the coloured pictures which had been illuminated only by the light of the moon. He had invented names and stories for each person depicted and watched them come alive and fade as clouds passed overhead. For that one night, he hadn't felt completely alone.

He looked at the next tapestry. It depicted a circle of five people standing around a sixth. The sixth was lying down, and Callum couldn't help but feel that they were dead. He glanced down again at the blood-red floor and moved on.

Other tapestries detailed the building of Yshaar, captured the battling of fires on the plains, and celebrated the coronation of various Flame-Bearers over the centuries.

Some of the tapestries seemed ancient, their threads hanging loosely and even drifting down to the floor as Callum passed by. Their colours had faded and required some creative interpretation by the viewer to understand. One showed two people facing each other, each surrounded by a soft glow: one in violet and the other in amber. The weaving was worn and Callum couldn't tell if the looks on their faces were those of respect or confrontation, or both. He dismissed the idea and continued on, quickly becoming indifferent to the visual history. If this is what museums in London were like, no wonder folks came out of them looking bored stiff. Callum smiled slightly.

Inattentive people were easy marks.

Callum wandered down the length of the room, dodging light fixtures as he went. Interspersed with the tapestries were more interesting exhibits, including old tools and weapons. At the end of the room Callum found a matching set of greaves. They were the same type of greaves that the Quenchers wore, one with a small canister attached and the other with a metal disk. Only this set wasn't the silvery metal that he'd seen on the plains; it was a burnished bronze. A small plaque underneath read: "Firedart and Buckler."

Callum was leaning in close to get a better look at the display and trying to puzzle out the writing when he was startled by a shout from the other end of the hall.

"Callum!" Jingwei sounded excited. "Look at this!"

Callum muttered some sort of reply and carefully lifted the canister down off the wall. He turned it over in his hands as he wandered back towards Jingwei. There was a strange symbol delicately carved into the underside of the canister; it was an odd collection of geometric shapes that he ran his fingers over as he made his way back towards the doors.

Jingwei didn't wait for him to arrive. "They're descended from *humans*, Callum! I bet that's why they get so crazy whenever we mention it! Look!"

Callum slipped the bronze canister into his pocket and stepped up beside her.

The tapestry before them was a stunning piece of art. In a rainbow of vivid colours it described the history of the Daevyn as clearly as if it had been voicing it aloud.

Jingwei was right; the First Flame-Bearer had been human. He had arrived in this world via lightning, the same as they had. The glittering white threads that made up the bolt eerily reflected the torchlight, creating the illusion of pulsing movement.

But after that man had arrived, things had changed. Callum blushed at the weaving that showed that the human had mated with the Aru Elen, the fairy-like people, to create the Daevyn. A succession of humanoid Flame-Bearers and their descendants appeared; with each generation the wings of the Daevyn receded and their hair turned whiter and whiter.

"They obviously tended towards the human side of their DNA." Jingwei was leaning so close to the tapestry that her nose was almost scraping the cloth.

"What's dee-en-ay?" Callum turned to look at Jingwei with a perplexed look on his face.

"Right, I forgot, you're from the Dark Ages. Never mind."

Callum thought he'd just been insulted, but he wasn't sure how.

Jingwei continued, "Looks like they keep those fairy people for servants and... *eww*. Mistresses."

"And misters. There were men out there too, yeah?"

"Don't remind me! There isn't enough paint in the world... I should talk to this Flame-Bearer of theirs, and tell her that where I come from, her servants would all be arrested for indecent exposure."

Callum stepped back from the tapestry. "Well, la-de-da! Is your family that powerful? I seen you wearing their coat of arms."

Jingwei saw with surprise that he was pointing to the school crest on her jacket. "No, that's for a school I go to. My parents are gone. I'm a foster kid."

"I thought your name was Li, not Foster?"

Jingwei tried to suppress a smile. "No, it is Li. A foster kid doesn't mean a kid named Foster. It means an orphan who's raised by someone else. By a whole system of someone elses, really."

Callum nodded glumly and slid down next to a torch. "My parents are dead too. But I'm not lucky enough to be a student."

"Lucky?! What're you, some English gentleman's squire? Riding horses all day and jousting all night?"

Callum grinned up at her. "You have a rubbish idea of life on the streets."

Jingwei slid down beside him, carefully hanging on to her skirt. "You live on the streets?"

"I do. Did, I reckon." Callum grinned ruefully. "Now who knows what I do?"

"You don't have a house, or a job, or anything?" Jingwei bunched up her jacket and sat on it, cushioning herself from the cold stone floor.

"Well..." Callum hesitated to tell her about this part of his life. "I kind of have a job. Of sorts." Jingwei looked at him impatiently. He sighed and confessed, "I'm a dipper." She stared at him blankly. "A finewirer?" Still nothing. "A pickpocket?"

"What!" Jingwei jumped back up to her feet. "Like in Oliver Twist? That's so cool!" A strange smile crossed her face. "Hey, give me my jacket."

Callum handed it up to her, and she threw it on. "Ok. Now, try to take the student ID that's in the inner pocket. Well, come on, stand up!"

"Don't need to." Callum's face broke into a wide grin. "There's nothing in that pocket."

"Wha–" Jingwei looked down and dug through her jacket. "Where did it..." Her voice trailed off as she looked back up and saw Callum standing before her examining her student card. He held it up in the air as if he were inspecting a diamond for flaws.

"You know, this photograph is coloured. And you've a funny look on your face."

"Give me that!" Jingwei reached out to snatch the card from his hand, but he quickly raised his arm above his head, out of her reach.

"I'll climb you if I have to, I swear I will!"

Callum laughed and dropped the card into her hands. "I believe you."

Jingwei put the ID card into her side pocket. "You've got pretty quick hands for an Old-Timer. Not bad." She looked at Callum with grudging respect.

Callum beamed under her praise. "It's how I won my surname. You wouldn't mind telling my current partner, would you?" The only things he'd ever heard from Bridget were put-downs. She was outspoken and brash, just like Jingwei, but unlike his new companion, Bridget's barbs had always felt malicious. With Jingwei, he felt that he was being teased without being mocked.

Jingwei understood completely. "He's a jerk? I know the type."

Callum wrinkled his nose. "*She. She*'s a jerk, if by jerk you mean a right git. You?"

Jingwei smiled at the translation and quickly told him about her run-in with Hunter in the mall, leaving out the part when she rose from the water completely dry. She ignored Callum's cringe when she mentioned that she had been prepared to kick Hunter between the legs, and finished the story with a sigh.

"I hate bullies."

"Not half!" Callum said in strong agreement.

Jingwei paused as if unsure how to continue, and then visibly switched topics. "Callum, what did you mean when you said you won your surname? Weren't you born with a family name?"

Callum scuffed his feet and didn't respond.

Jingwei nodded. "I get it. My name was the *only* thing they left me, and I'd rather have had an inheritance. At least you got to choose your name. I promise, you're not missing much."

Callum was taken off guard by Jingwei's sudden sensitivity. He had known strong girls in his time, but never one that was also kind. He decided to take a chance. "Jingwei? How old are you?"

She looked at him for a moment as if unsure of his motives. "I'm sixteen. Why?"

Callum hoped that the torchlight disguised the red spreading across his face. "Nothing." He sent up a silent prayer; *Please God, don't let her ask me—*

"How old are you?"

Callum searched madly for a way to distract her from making him answer the question. Her black eyes didn't leave his though, and he already knew enough about her to know that she wasn't the type to give up. He looked for help on the walls, ceiling, and floor, but none was forthcoming.

"Well, how old are you?" Suddenly Jingwei squeaked. "You're younger than me aren't you? And you called me Junior! Oh, that's *too* cute."

She reached over and lightly shoved Callum. "So, you're what... fifteen? Fourteen?" Another shove. "Thirteen."

And looking at the tapestries in front of him, which showed the great history of the Daevyn, Callum suddenly had the perfect idea. He turned to Jingwei and said, as suavely as he could, "To you, I'm one hundred and forty five years old."

Jingwei stared at him blankly for a moment, and then let out a peal of laughter that filled the hall, followed by a decidedly unladylike snort. Callum's voice joined hers in a hoot, and together they laughed, releasing the tension that had been building since they began their adventure together.

Their cackles were still echoing through the hall when the double-doors swung open, revealing Ythen standing in the corridor, looking anything but jovial.

"The Flame-Bearer wishes to see you now."

Chapter Six:
The Judgement

The Throne Room was once again filled with people and noise. The buzz of conversation and the buzz of wings overlapped and intensified as Ythen, Callum, and Jingwei approached the main entrance. Ythen made sure that a path was cleared for them down the corridor, but Callum still reflexively ducked every now and then as a low-flying Aru Elen zipped over his head on an urgent errand.

They arrived at the stone archway leading into the room and were permitted entry by the pair of Daevyn guards that stood on either side of the door. All of the conversation came to a swift and sudden halt as they entered. The rapid flapping of wings continued overhead, though the pitch changed as the servants stopped rushing about and instead hovered in place, watching the two

Humans approach the throne with the First Quencher between them.

The Daevyn retreated back towards the walls as the trio passed by, opening up a clear view of the Flame-Bearer. Jingwei saw that Yriel stood next to the throne, and with her was a small, but imposing woman draped in black.

"Who is *that*?"

Ythen kept his head forward and whispered out of the corner of his mouth, "That is Kala. She is a Keeper."

Jingwei felt a thrill of excitement. "She's a Keeper? What's her deal?"

"She is the Spark Keeper of Tranthaea, who harnesses the power of fire and flame. She is an advisor to the Flame-Bearer." Ythen seemed like he was about to say more, but stopped himself.

Before Jingwei could ask him about it, they had arrived.

They stopped just short of the dais and bowed, then Ythen stepped aside, leaving Jingwei and Callum alone in front of the throne.

The Flame-Bearer leaned forward. "Humans. I have welcomed you as guests. You have offered me peace, and for this I am grateful. But I have been advised that you are dangerous to me, to the Daevyn, and to Tranthaea. Dare you speak in your defence?"

Uncharacteristically, Callum was the first to respond. "Dangerous! Blimey! We just got here!" Jingwei looked at him in surprise. It seemed their little talk in the Hall of Record had done him a world of good.

He continued, "We get dragged to this world, without so much as a *by your leave*! You snatch us up and bring us here, surrounded by armed guards the whole way, call us guests and then lock us up while you decide what to do with us, and then you have the cheek to call *us* dangerous?"

Callum broke off and looked around. Ythen and Yriel looked petrified at his outburst. The Flame-Bearer and the Spark Keeper both had faces of stone, but Jingwei looked like she was barely containing her laughter.

After a moment of listening to Jingwei choke down giggles, the Flame-Bearer spoke again.

"While your method of defence is... unorthodox, it seems that you have cut to the heart of the matter. No matter what your race's intentions, I cannot hold you accountable for actions you have not taken." She stood up and raised her voice, sending her words down the length of the room. "I am the Flame-Bearer of the Daevyn, and my word is law. Here is my justice: that to do what is right for both of our peoples, you are declared free and safe on The Plains. I welcomed you before as guests. I welcome you now as friends."

Thunderous applause broke out in the crowd. The Daevyn court pressed in on the visitors, slapping their backs and shaking their hands.

Pushed outside of the mass, Ythen noticed that Kala was speaking sharply to the Flame-Bearer, who replied in kind. Kala slapped her hand down on the arm of the throne and turned away, opening her wings to shoot over the crowd and out of the Throne Room. The Flame-Bearer resumed her seat, her face quickly clearing of a momentary concern.

She clapped her hands and the room quickly grew silent.

"Ythen Firebrand." She calmly swept a stray lock of white hair behind her ear as he approached the throne and knelt. "You have served the Daevyn well by bringing us new friends." A rumble of surprise and disdain rose from the crowd, which the Flame-Bearer quelled with a look. "It is the unfortunate life of a warrior that good service begets greater service. I place the care and safety of our two Human guests in *your hands*."

Ythen noticed the emphasis she placed on the last two words, and winced.

"Do you accept this charge, First Quencher?"

Ythen raised his head and saw Yriel watching him from beside the throne. She looked livid.

"I do."

"Excellent." The Flame-Bearer did away with the official tenor of her voice and called out merrily, "They will be my guests at dinner! Have them dressed in our finest clothes!" She motioned for Ythen and Yriel to follow her as she swept out of the Throne Room and a host of Aru Elen shepherded Callum and Jingwei down a side passage, silently miming to one another their excitement about the prospects of a proper makeover for their sooty guests.

Not long after, Ythen stood anxiously near the entrance to the Banquet Hall. Inside, the buzzing wings of the servants as they prepared for the feast was a welcome relaxant to the turmoil in his mind.

While the Keep was busily preparing for dinner, the Flame-Bearer had taken Yriel and him aside and given him another task, one that he had hesitated to accept, especially with Yriel present. Her resentment of his leadership was becoming more obvious with each passing day, and he would soon have to do something about her blatant insubordination if he was to retain the respect of his Quenchers. But *her* position made *his* position extremely complicated...

He was interrupted by a whirlwind of activity from down the hall: the arrival of the Humans. They had been taken away by the servants to be washed and dressed in traditional Daevyn clothing.

Callum was walking haltingly down the corridor, surrounded by a flock of Aru Elen females who were fluttering over him, constantly adding finishing touches. Although Ythen had long since grown used to it, it was apparent that Callum was still uncomfortable with their nakedness, and perhaps even more uncomfortable with the tightness of his trousers around his legs, which he kept pulling at.

Callum had chosen a cloak of royal blue, the symbol of the City Sentinels, the personal guard of the Flame-Bearer. Ythen wondered if that had been a political choice, and then dismissed the thought. More likely Callum had just grabbed the nearest cloak he could cover up with.

Otherwise, he was the very picture of a Quencher, aside from his red hair which stood out prominently among the fair-headed Daevyn.

Farther behind him was Jingwei, who was also in the traditional Daevyn uniform. She had chosen a Quencher's tan cloak, and had thrown it back as she strode down the corridor towards the boys.

Ythen had to admit, she made the trousers look better than Callum did.

Callum seemed to agree. When she reached them, he gave a low whistle and murmured, "Not half bad, Junior."

Jingwei quickly leaned in and grabbed the edge of his cloak and flipped it up in the air, showing his legs off for all to see. Two female Aru Elen hovered nearby for a moment before buzzing off again, their hands over their mouths.

"Not bad yourself, Old-Timer."

Ythen frowned. These were not titles that he understood. He shook his head.

Humans.

Jingwei said goodbye to her Aru Elen dressers, who nodded politely and flew off.

"Not big talkers, are they?"

Ythen refocused his eyes on her face. "The Aru Elen have no tongues and their masters don't allow them to have any unspoken language."

"Their masters? You mean the Flame-Bearer?"

Ythen grimaced. "The Aru Elen are gifts to the Daevyn. They were given to us as a sign of peace from the Masters of the Aru Len people, the Aru Faylen."

Callum's eyebrows rose in confusion.

Ythen shrugged. "The Aru Len are a sky people. The Aru Faylen are the upper caste, and the Aru Elen are the lower. We desire peace with their race, and so the Flame-Bearer accepts their offering of servants."

Jingwei looked up at him disbelievingly. Ythen defended himself from her gaze. "They are not slaves. They volunteer to serve us in order to serve the greater peace between our peoples." Jingwei didn't look convinced, but Callum nodded. Ythen guessed that wherever he came from had provided him with an understanding of servitude and social strata that Jingwei didn't have. He continued. "It is politically complex. Please do not judge our culture too harshly. You are new here, after all."

Jingwei considered that for a moment, then nodded, a smile returning to her face.

Ythen turned and offered his arm to Jingwei just as Callum did the same on her other side. The two boys stared blankly at each other for a moment until Jingwei settled the issue by striding forward into the Banquet Hall alone.

In spite of himself, Ythen grinned. This girl was... unusual. He followed along behind her, the Human boy at his side, matching him stride for stride.

The Banquet Hall wasn't actually a hall at all. It was a large, round room. On one side were windows that looked out over the plains. The dome-like ceiling was dotted with holes that became shafts which eventually led to the outside of the city a few levels higher up. Because the Hall was so much nearer the surface than the Throne Room, the shafts allowed light from the flashes of lightning outside to permeate the smoke that filled the room.

The smoke came from dozens of cooking fires. Jingwei had expected a long hall with tables and benches leading up to a head table where the Flame-Bearer would sit. Instead, she saw that the room was a collection of fire-pits that were scooped into the floor, each encircled by a selection of stools, in front of which were various pots and kettles filled with steaming soups and gravies. Over each fire was a spit, being slowly rotated by a black-painted Aru Elen. Each spit held a perfectly roasted animal, none of which Jingwei recognised at first glance.

She heard a loud rumble and turned to see Callum standing beside her. He glanced down at his stomach and winced apologetically.

"Sorry. Haven't had nowt to eat in a while." He rubbed his stomach. Jingwei recalled that he was a street orphan and wondered how long it had been since he'd had a good meal.

Ythen stepped up on her other side. "I hope you are both hungry. There is enough here for everyone, and maybe a little bit more."

Jingwei began to walk forward, visually searching the room, her heart sinking. "Not everyone."

Ythen raised his eyebrow questioningly. She hoped this wouldn't offend him, or her other, more royal host. "I'm a vegetarian."

Ythen blinked. Callum spoke up from her right side. "She doesn't eat meat, that one."

Ythen blinked again. "Why not?"

Jingwei opened her mouth to deliver a well-practiced sermon on the morality of vegetarianism but clamped it quickly shut as they passed a spit that held a very familiar animal. An animal they had been attacked by earlier today.

An Aru Elen was carefully plucking the long spikes out of its back as it crisped over the fire. It noticed her gaze and pointed at the animal silently, its eyes questioning.

"He wants to know if you would like some croen for dinner tonight."

Callum spoke up quickly. "Croen, eh? I'll have some. Serves 'em right."

Jingwei sputtered, but couldn't find any words. Callum made a mental note to remember this moment.

The three of them continued to wander through the Hall as other Daevyn began to migrate in and settle down at the fire-pits.

Eventually an Aru Elen whose front was painted a royal blue gestured for them to follow him to a large pit in the centre of the room. They wound their way through the room, carefully sidestepping the fire-pits that pockmarked the dark stone floor in a seemingly haphazard design. Once they reached the central pit they found the Flame-Bearer waiting, along with Yriel and two Daevyn High Councillors. The Humans sat and without waiting for introductions all the other diners began to call out and point to various plates and pots, motioning for the servants to bring them forward. Soon after, the low conversational buzz was interrupted only by the crunching of bones and the smacking of lips.

Jingwei was seated in between Yriel and Callum. Yriel very clearly had nothing to say to her, so she turned to listen to the boys' conversation.

Ythen had just tossed another bone into the fire as Callum finished a story; "...then I sneaked the purse back into his pocket, without the coins! He told me he must've left 'em at home, and made his wife give me a full quid for returning the watch, never knowing that I'd nicked it from him in the first place!"

Ythen roared with laughter at the anecdote. "So that is what you do? I will have to keep a watchful eye on my valuables." He tilted his head and regarded the flame pin sitting high on his chest.

Callum blushed a little and gestured a negative with his spoon. "Keep it. Your go."

Ythen settled back onto his stool. "The First Quencher," he said in response to Callum's query, "is the head of the forces of the Daevyn. I lead and direct the patrols that scour the plains for fires, to protect our lands and people from the dangers they present. It has been a very dry year; the work has been more frequent, and more difficult."

Callum gulped down the remainders of a bowl of soup and grabbed a croen leg. "I always wanted to take the Queen's shilling and be a soldier. But I had a knack for pinching. Aren't you a little young for such a big job?"

Yriel's voice cut in over Jingwei's head. "The Daevyn do not withhold responsibility because of age. We place it upon any who merits its burden." She reached forward and plucked a croen spine out of the embers, using it to spear a charred piece of flesh that had fallen from the spit. "And sometimes we give it to those who do not." She stuffed the meat into her mouth and stood up abruptly, chewing violently as she walked away. Moments later, she was sitting at another fire-pit, eating with great gusto and glaring back at Ythen between bites.

"What's her problem?" Jingwei was fishing through a bowl of stew, looking for anything leafy or green. She set the bowl down with a sigh. "I mean, sure, I get that she's your ex, but still. She seems a bit extreme." She looked him up and down in an exaggerated critique. "You're not bad looking. You could do better."

Ythen's proper facade disappeared momentarily, and he suddenly looked less like a warrior and more like a teenage boy. He choked on a bite of what looked like beef and struggled to compose himself as Callum clapped him on the back and Jingwei peered at him innocently.

Ythen waved Callum off, swallowed, and then answered. "Yriel feels, as do many of the Daevyn, that she should be First Quencher."

"What? That stuck up little—"

"But she wasn't chosen by the Flame-Bearer. I was." Ythen looked around the circle, saw that the Flame-Bearer was busy with a High Councillor and then leaned in and whispered, "Yriel is the Flame-Bearer's daughter. She has a hereditary right to the position, and is an admirable fighter and leader."

Ythen pulled back. "She would be an excellent First Quencher."

"Wait." Callum set his plate down and bit into what looked like a piece of fruit. "But they don't have the same last name. The Flame-Bearer is Emberhand, and Yriel is Spark-something-or-other."

Ythen explained through a mouthful of ribs. "We do not get our second names from birth. They are given to us based on our achievements." He coloured again and went back to his food.

Callum nodded in appreciation. Jingwei was digging hopefully through a basket, trying to find a piece of the fruit Callum was eating. "So what does yours mean? Firebrand?"

"Mine is a spur, a reminder of past failure and a motivation for future success."

Jingwei dropped the basket, unsuccessful. "Well, that's vague," she said bluntly.

Callum elbowed her side and mumbled something she was sure was impolite.

Ythen smiled weakly. "Since you are under my protection, perhaps it is best if you know my limits." He set his plate down and wiped his mouth on his sleeve before speaking.

"When I was given the title of First Quencher, I was called Ythen Firestorm. I was given the name for leading the Quenchers against a fire that threatened to destroy not only the plains, but the city of Yshaar as well. When we successfully extinguished the blaze, it had eaten its way almost to the base of the city.

"Days later, a lightning strike out near the mountains started a small fire. I led some of my Quenchers out against it, and found that it had almost burned itself out. We moved in to clear up the remaining flames when I stupidly tripped and rolled my ankle.

"I fell into the embers of the blaze, but caught myself with my hands." Ythen held out his hands, palms up. The heavy scarring that Callum and Jingwei had seen out on the plains was highlighted by the glittering glow of the fire-pit.

"My own Quenchers had to enter the coals to pull me out. My clumsy foolishness put myself and them at risk." He shook his head. "When we returned to Yshaar, I asked that the Flame-Bearer give my title to another. She refused, and instead renamed me Firebrand, as a reminder of the scarring on my hands."

Jingwei glanced over at the Flame-Bearer. "Seems kind of harsh."

Callum, though, shook his head. "No, she was teaching him. Making him a better leader."

"That is my thought as well, Callum." Ythen smiled wearily. "Although I have not seen any positive change as of yet. The High Council fears my inadequacy, the Flame-Bearer's daughter shows insubordination at every turn, and now I have been asked to serve again, in a position I judge myself unprepared for."

The voice of the Flame-Bearer broke into their conversation. "It is well, then, that *my* judgement on the matter will prevail."

She had dismissed her advisors and was watching the trio over the dying flames of the fire.

Ythen bowed his head apologetically, but didn't back down. "Flame-Bearer, you see qualities in me that I fear are not there."

"Well, perhaps with age my vision is failing. Some youthful eyes may more readily see what can be seen. Perhaps you would be wise to take your wards with you on your task, so they can judge you for themselves?"

Callum leaned forward eagerly. "What're we doing?" Jingwei was far less sure, but before she could elbow him the Flame-Bearer spoke.

"Callum Swift. Do you wish to serve the Daevyn in this matter? To do so will earn you the everlasting gratitude of the Flame-Bearer and her people." She allowed her voice to lose its official tone, a bit of a trick with the sharp diction of her accent. "You did just say that you wanted to be a soldier, did you not?"

Jingwei quirked an eyebrow. She'd thought the Flame-Bearer hadn't been listening when he'd said that. Not willing to allow Callum to be taken advantage of, she piped up before he could agree. "A soldier? What exactly will he— *we* be doing?"

The Flame-Bearer smiled as the last flame flickered and died in the pit.

"You will lead my armies to war."

Chapter Seven:
The Trouble with Trees

Ex-excuse me?" Jingwei stumbled over the words in shock. An invitation to war was not what she had expected to hear.

The Flame-Bearer seemed confused by her surprise. "You have accepted my hospitality as friends. Do you not wish to extend our friendship by becoming allies?"

"We just got here! You want us to go to war? I'm not a soldier! And neither is Callum," she said, placing a protective hand on his knee.

Callum defensively pushed her hand away. He was starting to warm up to Jingwei, but the last thing he needed now was another Bridget in his life, telling him what he could and couldn't do. These people had treated him better than any others in his whole life. They had clothed him, fed him, surrounded him by more luxury than he'd ever dreamed of, and called him their friend. If he could repay their kindnesses, he would.

He said, "Who are you fighting? I thought this world was at peace."

The Flame-Bearer dismissed a fluttering Aru Elen with a wave and motioned to her daughter to rejoin the circle. Yriel grudgingly came back over and took her place next to Jingwei.

Once she had settled, the Flame-Bearer spoke again. "We are at peace, at the moment. Rest assured, we are not the aggressors in this conflict. We are merely reacting to a threat against our people. When we have spoken, you may decide to join us, or to remain safely behind in Yshaar."

She stood and, motioning the others to follow her, walked towards a window that looked out over the plains.

"Even now, our enemies encroach upon our lands. Soon they will be upon our very doorstep, and it will be too late to turn them back. Do you see?"

Callum looked out into the blackness over the heads of the others. For a moment he saw nothing but the endless plains of grain, illuminated by the occasional flash of lightning. He leaned forward, allowing his eyes to adjust to the darkness.

Then he saw it.

A dark mass, darker than the night air, was holding a position about a kilometre to the south of Yshaar. The assembly blotted out the prairie like a giant, malevolent stain.

Callum could hardly believe his eyes. To finally find safe harbour in this world, only to be surrounded by a giant army of–

"Trees. They're trees!" Jingwei turned on the Flame-Bearer in anger. "It's just a forest!"

Callum stepped back, confused. "How can you go to war against a forest?"

"More importantly," Jingwei snapped, "*why* would you go to war against a forest?"

Callum couldn't understand why Jingwei was so angry. She was chewing on her lip and had taken a step towards the Flame-Bearer that was mirrored defensively by Yriel and Ythen on either side of her.

Ythen tried to explain. "It is not just a forest, Jingwei. It is a strange place. A dangerous place."

"*Dangerous!* An hour ago you thought *we* were dangerous!"

Looking at her now, Ythen was inclined to believe it.

Yriel didn't look at all impressed. "Do you recall seeing the forest on your way into the city?"

Callum thought back. It had been dark, and his eyes had been on the city itself, but he thought he would remember seeing such a large forest interrupting the grasslands so close to the city.

"I don't," he said.

She smiled up at him and then shot a scowl down at the shorter girl. "That is because it was not there."

"What?" Callum moved back to the window and looked out again. The mass of trees wasn't moving, as far as he could tell. How could it have grown that fast?

The Flame-Bearer spoke from behind him. "We do not know the intentions of the forest, but we cannot allow it to run rampant over our lands, unchecked." She turned to Jingwei, who was standing with her arms crossed and her back towards the Flame-Bearer. "The plains of the Daevyn must be protected."

"And what about the trees? Who's going to protect *them*?"

Yriel stepped forward, her face darkening. "Protect *them*? We have lost Quenchers to the forest, in body and in mind. Many go in, but not all come out again. Those that do tell stories of roots and vines that ensnare more than just the physical form. There are whispers in the forest: whispers that drive men mad. We have suffered losses to the trees, greater than mere numbers and physical strength. Should I not demand justice for my people?"

Jingwei didn't answer. Yriel snorted and turned back to the window, joining all the others in looking out over the view of the encroaching forest.

Callum broke the silence. "How'd it get here? It can't have just walked... can it?"

Ythen supplied the answer. "We do not know. The Korrahl Forest has always remained in the south, growing no more than one would expect. Yet Yriel is telling the truth; some of the Daevyn who have entered it have never been seen again, and others... have not been the same."

"I have always been of the mind to leave such a place alone." The Flame-Bearer spoke out to the horizon. "The darkness and mystery of the trees are best left to the forest itself. But this year has been one of drought. The rains do not fall, and our water is limited. Even the city wells have begun to dry out." Her hands tightened on the windowsill as she looked out at her lands.

"The lightning strikes are starting fires that are harder to control. Dry grasses burn quickly, and the fires spread with great speed. What little water is in the ground is precious to us and our way of life."

Ythen picked up where she left off. "And now the forest advances on our lands and our city, pulling what little water remains from the soil." He turned to look at Callum. "The forest must be pushed back so that our people can survive."

The Flame-Bearer placed her hand on Callum's shoulder. "I am sending the Quenchers to scout the tree-line in the morning. If a sign of retreat cannot be found..."

Callum finished the thought for her, "You'll burn it down, won't you?"

Her face was strained as she turned to look up at him. "I will do what I must to protect my people."

Callum made his decision.

"Then I'd like to come along."

Ythen clapped his hand on Callum's shoulder. "Are you sure? It may not be pleasant."

Callum swallowed. "I'm sure. Jingwei, you coming?"

He turned from the window and found he was talking to the empty air. Behind him, the Flame-Bearer gave a sharp gasp before Ythen raced across the room to the doorway, weaving in and out of burned-out fire-pits. He reached the corridor, looked out and then back in. He shook his head.

Jingwei and Yriel were nowhere to be seen.

Chapter Eight:
The Well-Executed Escape

Jingwei had heard enough. By the time Yriel had turned back towards the window to talk to Callum, joining the others in looking out over the southern plains, Jingwei had already begun edging quietly towards the entrance to the Banquet Hall. By the time the Flame-Bearer was talking about the drought, she was striding down the corridor, and by the time Callum had volunteered to join the scouting party, Jingwei was racing up the stairs and exiting into the summit plaza.

She hurried down the central street, taking care to remain in the shadows as much as possible, her new light brown cloak blending into the stone walls in the darkness.

Most of the windows and doors facing onto the street were now empty, the inhabitants asleep or on their way to bed. Many of the torches had been extinguished as well, and Jingwei didn't see any guards. She assumed that most of them were down at ground level keeping a close eye on the forest, protecting their towering city from trees.

Jingwei ground her teeth in frustration. *Attacking a forest for growing too close to a city? They're crazy!*

She may not have been able to save the rainforest with her petition, but she could certainly try to save this one.

Jingwei considered her options as she crept carefully past a curtained doorway. The noise of revellers floated from within, but no one heard her passing.

Maybe if I tie myself to a tree, like those protesters do. Jingwei had seen a news story where the green activists had chained themselves up in trees so that the lumber companies couldn't chop them down.

She stepped cautiously over a tray of freshly-painted pottery someone had set out in the street to dry overnight. Come to think of it, maybe they wouldn't chop the trees down. She hadn't seen any blades since she had arrived in Yshaar, not even a knife at dinner.

So how will they do it? Jingwei danced quickly through a pool of light cast by a torch to reach the darkness on the other side. Realization suddenly hit her. *Of course. They'll burn it down.*

From behind her came a loud clattering. She spun around in a crouch. There was no one there, but one of the painted pots was noisily rolling down the ramped street towards her.

Jingwei stopped it with her foot and set it level on the ground. She peered back up the street, searching for whatever could have disturbed the pot, but seeing no movement.

Maybe she was just being paranoid. She turned and quickly continued down the spiralling road towards the base of the city.

Yriel breathed a sigh of relief from the doorway that now sheltered her. She had ducked in as soon as she'd kicked over the pot, pressing herself against the stone archway, motionless.

Stupid artisans. Almost gave me away.

She held her breath. The pot stopped clattering down the street. There was silence for a moment, and then the sound of footsteps heading quickly in the opposite direction.

Yriel had been listening to Ythen talk in the Banquet Hall when she'd turned to look at Jingwei and had noticed that the Human girl was no longer standing with the others. Quietly, she'd crept to the corridor, disguising her movement among the last few exiting diners, where she had seen the flutter of a cloak as it had disappeared into the Keep's stairwell, going up.

Yriel had hesitated for a moment, considering her options. If she informed the others immediately, Jingwei could be stopped from warning the enemy, which she was obviously going to do, although Yriel had no idea why. However, if she was caught in the forest red-handed, trying to give away the Daevyn's plans... it was the perfect trap.

Yriel had seen her opportunity to prove her worth to her mother and take up her rightful position at last. She'd quietly hurried to follow Jingwei, maintaining a safe distance so that the traitor wouldn't get suspicious. She had made it up the stairs and down the street unnoticed until she had accidentally kicked over the pot.

Huddling in the doorway, Yriel waited for another moment until Jingwei had moved on. Once she was sure that the coast was clear, she eased back out into the road and scurried down a few doorways.

It was clear to her where Jingwei was heading, but Yriel knew that the stranger would have trouble getting past the guards at the foot of the city, with them being on such high alert due to the sudden proximity of the Korrahl Forest.

She would need help to reach the tree-line. And Yriel would do all she could to get her there.

A few levels down, Yriel found the building she was looking for. Engraved into the stone above the doorway was an unusual symbol: three short lines radiating evenly from a single point. Yriel ducked in quickly and found herself in a medium-sized room with a short, thick wooden post sticking out of the centre of the floor. Extending horizontally from the top of the post were three shafts, just like on the symbol. On the far side of the room was a square hole in the floor which at the moment was filled with a wooden platform. To its right was a very fat man, dozing on a stool, his body leaning precariously to one side so that it looked as though he may fall over at any moment.

Yriel rushed over to him and shook him awake.

"Ascender Yllard, I need to use your services." The Ascender wearily rocked on the stool; his eyes remained closed. Yriel leaned in closer and spoke into his ear. "Now. Or my mother will hear about this."

Yllard cracked one eye open, saw who was speaking to him and lumbered himself quickly off the stool to stand at attention.

Yriel smiled wryly. "That is more like it." She stepped onto the wooden platform and turned back to the Ascender. "Send me to the base of the city."

The Ascender nodded and shuffled to the capstan in the middle of the room.

"Wait." Yriel considered her position for a moment and quickly adjusted her plan. "No, send me to one level above the base." That would allow her to get an excellent view of the guards' positions, and when Jingwei appeared, she would be able to do the most good.

Ascender Yllard started pushing one of the spokes, walking quickly in a circle. Yriel heard a sudden cacophony of creaking sounds as the massive pulley system began to work, and the platform she was standing on began to drop.

She would be at the base of the city long before Jingwei reached it. And from there, she could easily steer Jingwei into her trap.

Jingwei was now only a few hundred metres from the city's entrance. Most of the way had been easy going. She had hugged the walls and avoided windows and doors, but the street had widened out again eventually and she'd had to make her way through empty open-air markets and plazas. There had been some Daevyn about, but her confident walk and the Quencher's uniform she wore had kept her safe from prying eyes.

Jingwei stopped at the entrance to another city square and pulled the cloak's hood closer around her face. She moved forward, slipping past a well that was in the centre of the square and eased herself up alongside the wall, peering around a wide column that held up a looming archway. Farther down the street, just ahead of her, was a row of seven guards. They were standing with their backs towards her, presenting her with a line of royal-blue-cloaked wing stubs, but were spread along the width of the street.

Behind her, a small-but-growing noise gave her little warning before a pair of Daevyn women casually entered the square and walked towards the well. They each carried a large clay pot and began chattering loudly. Some of the soldiers turned to see what was making the commotion.

Jingwei leaned back against the wall, trying to look nonchalant. The guards were on the ball, which was too bad for her.

One of the two women drew up a bucket from the well, and then with a snort of disgust, threw it back down, complaining.

"I wonder how my husband thinks I am supposed to boil him a croen when I can get no water in this city?"

The other woman answered. "I know exactly what you mean. I keep telling my Yric that if only we got an Aru Elen or two, I could send them to all the nearby wells to find enough water for his dinner. Of course, he will not hear of it. He had the nerve to tell me I should take my clothes off and paint myself blue. He said that perhaps then I would grow wings. *And* lose the use of my tongue!"

"Men!"

The two women strutted back where they had come from and disappeared around the corner, content in their displeasure. The guards turned back to their work, looking out over the encroaching woods.

Jingwei had no idea what to do. Most of her previous attempts at activism had involved being as loud as possible. All this tip-toeing around was not what she was used to.

She peeked around the column again. She had no experience in sneaking past armed guards.

Suddenly a loud crashing sound came from an alleyway that intersected the main road just past the line of guards. Jingwei ducked behind an empty vendor stall near the archway and then peeked out to watch as one of the soldiers sent four of his comrades to investigate the disturbance.

Only three were left. Jingwei started to think in circles.

This is my only chance. What can I do? I have to do something, but what can I do? I have to do something, but what can I do? I HAVE to do SOMETHING!!

She was startled by a tingling sensation that ran down her back, starting at the base of her neck and trickling its way down as though there were a cold ribbon wrapping itself in a tightening spiral around her spine. She let out a quiet gasp, but the noise was swallowed up when behind her, the well echoed with a loud *splash*!

The three remaining guards turned around, surprised.

"I thought that well was dry."

"Does it sound dry?"

"Maybe somebody fell in trying to get some water."

"Maybe we should throw you in to check."

"I would like to see you try!"

The soldiers argued jovially amongst themselves as they rushed through the archway and to the well, cracking their heads sharply together as they all leaned in to see what had caused the splashing sound.

Jingwei moved from behind the stall and flattened herself against the wall as they passed by, and as soon as their heads were in the well she whipped around the archway's column and down the street into the darkness beyond the city's lights.

James Bond, eat your heart out.

As she left the structure of the city and her tan cloak helped her disappear into the grass, she was fully focused on what was to come, and didn't hear one of the guards exclaim, "It is not possible! The well is full again!"

Yriel watched Jingwei vanish into the fields from her viewpoint near the city gate. The guards she had distracted by pushing a loose lightning rod off the roof were still in the alley, trying to stand on one another's shoulders to see where it had come from. The other three remained at the well, laughing and dropping stones in to listen to the echo.

A nice bit of luck, the well rehydrating. Yriel didn't think Jingwei would have been able to escape without it.

Coincidence. Yriel recalled what Kala had once told her in a training session. *A good warrior takes advantage of opportunity.*

Yriel smiled to herself. She was a good warrior. The best. She deserved to lead the Daevyn. They would all see, soon enough. She would prove it.

She glanced back at the guards. They would soon return to their posts, and she estimated that she'd given Jingwei enough distance so that she could follow her, unseen.

She slipped into the darkness and began to track the Human.

The wall of trees in front of her was much more intimidating than Jingwei had expected it to be. From a distance they had seemed just like any other trees, but the closer she'd gotten, the more frightening they'd become.

Now that she had reached the tree-line, she was starting to understand what Ythen had said about the forest.

It is a strange place. A dangerous place.

The dark mass of the forest had resolved itself into individual shapes as she'd approached. The trees were tall and thin, their trunks covered in a loose, papery bark that was a dull, corpse-grey. As she watched, a patch of bark that had been flitting in the breeze tore from a tree in front of her and tumbled listlessly to the ground. It reminded Jingwei of peeling off a piece of dead skin.

She shivered.

Suddenly she wished that Callum had chosen to come with her. There was more to him than met the eye. Ythen, too. She bet that underneath that handsome warrior exterior there was a... handsome warrior. He'd know what to do.

Stop it, Jingwei, she thought. *Focus. You're here. Let's do this.*

She stood before the tree-line. The wind had fallen and the dark, night air was still, yet some of the higher branches were swaying in the thick air. She could feel something from them. An intelligence. A wariness. She knew that she was being watched.

Oh well. In for a penny...

"Um... hello? My name is Jingwei Li. I'm here to warn the forest about an attack." Her voice came out much smaller and more frightened than she had wanted it to. She wished the lightning had seen fit to send along her bullhorn.

She felt a sudden mental shift that brought her back to reality. The intelligence she'd felt was still there, but now seemed focused elsewhere.

Behind her.

Jingwei whirled around, her eyes searching the grasslands beyond. She saw nothing but the lights of the city rising high above the plain.

There was a rustling sound in the forest, and when she'd turned back to the trees a cathedral-like passageway had appeared between them, leading farther into the woods beneath the thick canopy.

Jingwei gulped. This was not the sort of environmental encounter she had expected when she'd signed up for the Greenpeace online newsletter. She looked at the passageway again and tried to imagine the trees burning, thanks to the torches of the Daevyn.

In for a pound.

She stepped past the tree-line and entered the Korrahl Forest.

The tan of Jingwei's cloak was absorbed into the blackness of the woods. Yriel sighed in relief. She didn't know what had made Jingwei turn around so suddenly, but she'd almost been caught out in the open. She had dived to the ground just in time.

Yriel stood up and brushed off her clothes. Now she could bring the Human in. She'd heard Jingwei admit to her treachery and walk into the woods. Confession and a witness. It would be more than enough evidence for the Flame-Bearer.

She snuck forward quietly and passed into the forest, moving swiftly to try to catch up to the betrayer.

It seemed to Jingwei that she had walked for hours. She continued to stumble forward, exhausted. The trees never grouped close enough together to bar her way, but were never far enough apart for her to see more than a few dozen metres in any direction. Up close, their slim, uniform trunks were speared with short, thin branches that sported two-pointed leaves of a rich, dark green.

The only means she had for determining the distance she'd travelled was the ground underfoot. The grainy stalks of the prairie had long since been replaced by earthy mulch, dotted with sprouts of weeds and undisturbed blankets of moss. Jingwei knew by this that she had passed south into the forest's original borders. The dense air of Tranthaea seemed thinner in the woods, as if there were more life using it, so there was less to go around.

Soon enough the land started to rise before her, and walking became a struggle. The hill was steep and Jingwei was forced to use the trunks of the trees to pull herself up, stepping on their roots as though they were the rungs of a ladder. She didn't know how, but for some reason she could tell that the forest was amused by this.

Jingwei wiped a bead of sweat from her forehead, unknowingly leaving behind a streak of dirt that stretched from the bridge of her nose all the way over to her left ear. She was secretly glad that the journey had become so intensely difficult. It gave her something to think about besides the fact that she was in a strange land and had just left behind the only friends she had here...

...To go talk to some trees.

Yes, Jingwei didn't want to think about that too hard. Nor the fact that she had no idea where she was going or what she was going to do once she got there. She reached her hand out and grasped another low-hanging branch and pulled herself forward and up with a grunt, banishing her doubts from her mind.

You gotta do what you gotta do.

Eventually Jingwei reached the top of the hill. She stopped for a moment to catch her breath and took in the view.

The forest stretched out for kilometres in every direction. Far in the distance behind her to the north she could see the city of Yshaar rising up into the sky, its torches burning brightly, as if in warning. The forest behind her looked exactly the same as the forest ahead of her, and Jingwei began to hope that she had not made a huge mistake.

A movement at the bottom of the hill she had just climbed caught her eye. Jingwei leaned forward, straining to see. Nothing was moving.

But I could have sworn I saw—

And there it was again. The quick swirl of the tan cloak of a Daevyn Quencher. A moment later, she saw it again, only closer. This time she saw the face of her pursuer illuminated by the pale blue light of the night air.

Yriel looked up at her and smiled a smile that didn't reach her eyes.

Jingwei was suddenly overcome by the panic that she had been containing in her mental box since she had appeared on the plains next to Callum. Her doubts overwhelmed her as her situation became clear in her mind, and she turned and started running down the south side of the hill, away from Yriel.

She dodged trees and branches, moving so quickly that it seemed as though her feet could hardly keep up with her. Her passage was noisy; the thumping of her feet and the crackling of fallen twigs left no doubt as to her position.

Jingwei was nearing the bottom of the hill when unexpectedly a flock of small animals erupted under her feet, fleeing the raucous disturbance she was causing. They were tiny, no more than four centimetres across each, and covered in a short, thick fur. With a groan-like hum dozens of them suddenly detached themselves from the trunks of trees and began rolling quickly away in a frenzy, bumping into each other and getting underfoot.

Jingwei shrieked in surprise and lost control of her momentum. She tripped over her own feet and fell hard, somersaulting down the remaining length of the hill, her world spinning in all directions. She cracked her wrist against something solid and cried out in pain, just before her head crashed into a tree trunk and everything went black.

Scratches covered Yriel's clothes and body. The forest had not been kind to her as she had tracked Jingwei. The trees were grown very close together and the branches seemed almost purposely placed to catch on her cloak and hair, tearing at her with hundreds of sharp, wooden fingers. She pushed her way through the last few thickets and reached the top of the hill where she had seen Jingwei only moments before.

She paused, gasping for breath, allowing the air to steady her body and her lungs. Below her, the Korrahl Forest grew thicker and darker. Yriel rubbed her hand nervously over her greaves, recalling the names of some of the Quenchers who had entered this forest and never come out. Her name would not be added to that list.

There.

Yriel saw the prone body of Jingwei at the bottom of the hill. She looked injured, possibly dead. It made no difference to Yriel. The Human's presence in the forest would be enough of an indictment to seal her fate.

A crunching sound from behind her made her turn around. From her vantage point, she could see that the thick, close forest she had just broken through was now even thicker. The trees seemed closer together, their branches interlocked at uneven heights, creating a series of walls. Between those walls, the forest now had clear paths running through it in every direction.

What had seemed to be a random, natural forest only moments ago was now a giant, living maze that led back to the plains. Eventually.

Possibly.

She spun around again. Right in front of her, skylined on the crest of the hill, was another fence of trees. They were tall and wedged together and impassible. She could only catch glimpses of the forest beyond, but what she saw made her blood run cold.

The trees were swaying fiercely. Jingwei's body was limp, but in motion, high up in the air. She was being lifted by the trees, passed from branch to branch, from tree to tree, slowly being pulled farther and farther south into the darkness of the forest.

Chapter Nine:
The Armoury

Callum slammed his palm against the stone wall of his room in helpless frustration. The Flame-Bearer had forbade them to go looking for the girls tonight. *Too dark, too dangerous,* she'd said.

Callum didn't know Jingwei that well, but he guessed that she wouldn't hesitate to put herself in danger.

Especially if it meant causing trouble for him.

The moment they had discovered that Jingwei had disappeared, Callum knew where she had gone. She'd made no secret of her love of trees from the very beginning, which Callum found strange, since as a vegetarian, dead plants were the staple of her diet.

He understood that she felt passionate about this, but couldn't wrap his head around the idea of betraying the only friends they had in this world! The Daevyn had given them everything, and now Callum was locked in his room, probably suspected of being a traitor himself, just by association!

Callum raised his face to the ceiling and let out a huge breath. Leave it to a girl to ruin his chance at happiness. Again.

He looked around the small room, which now seemed more like a prison cell than a living chamber.

The stone walls were painted black. There were tiny holes carved into them, thickly dispersed over the surface. At various places around the room, panels opened in the walls and candles were inserted behind the stone facade. The light from the candles glittered through the holes, giving the room the illusion of a night sky filled with stars.

Callum wondered where they had gotten the idea from, since the sky here had no stars, no sun, and no moon. Then he realized that the walls could also resemble hundreds of little fires dotting the plains.

Or a dark forest.

He dismissed the thought from his head. Turning, he once again looked over the room. Next to the door was a tall wardrobe. In it were new sets of Daevyn clothes, as well as his old rags, freshly laundered. Threadbare patches were revealed now that the protective and warming layers of dirt and soot had been washed away. He considered putting them on again, just to feel comfortable, but decided against it. His hosts had been insulted enough for one night.

The only other furniture in the room was the bed. It was a large mattress sunken into the floor. Callum stepped towards it and let himself fall forward, plunging into the soft bedding. He flipped over and stared up at the painted ceiling. Never before had he experienced such luxury. It was an uncomfortably foreign feeling.

A bulge in his pocket reminded him of the bronze canister he had lifted off the wall in the Hall of Record earlier that evening. He had palmed it when the Aru Elen servants were picking out his new clothes and had managed to slip it into an interior pocket in his Daevyn cloak. He removed it now and turned it over in his hands, letting his fingers play against the engraved shapes carved into the side of it. It felt warm in his hands. Each end of the cylinder was slightly domed; at one end the dome was flattened, and on the other he noticed a small closed hole at the peak of the curved metal. Callum tried to poke it open with his fingers but it was recessed into the end of the cylinder and he couldn't get at it.

There was a knock at the door.

"Callum? It is Ythen. May I enter?"

Callum sat up quickly as a shot of adrenaline surged through his body. This was it. Maybe he was going to be arrested as a co-conspirator. He stood up and set himself, burying the canister safely back into his pocket, and then called out to Ythen. He wasn't about to go quietly.

The door swung wide and Ythen stepped into the room, leaving it open behind him. He glanced around the room, took in Callum's defensive posture, and smiled.

"You are not in any trouble, my friend. The Flame-Bearer will not hold you accountable for the rash actions of another."

Callum sighed in relief and dropped his shoulders.

"However, I am glad that you are prepared for action. That is the reason I came to see you. The Flame-Bearer still will not let us go search for Jingwei and Yriel tonight." He ground his teeth in frustration, then sighed. "And rightly so. They will not be removed from danger simply because we embrace it. But we will leave at first light to scout near the forest. Perhaps we will find them there."

Callum nodded. Jingwei had left little doubt as to her destination.

"Good. Well, in the meantime, I am inviting you to the armoury. It would be well for you to know the use of our weapons and how to ride a raeas."

Ten minutes later Callum and Ythen were standing in the armoury. They had used something called an Ascender, which reminded Callum of a lift with no sides. He had ridden on one once, when he'd snuck into a hotel late at night and convinced the operator to take him up and down a floor in exchange for a shoe-shine. The Ascender was massive in comparison, but felt more comfortable to Callum, who hadn't enjoyed being caged up in the fenced-in lift.

Upon alighting near the base of the city, the Human boy had followed Ythen through a maze of passageways that led through well-lit tunnels coated in glossy layers of vibrant paint and out onto railed balconies that were hung with brightly coloured flags and spiralled around towers before being swallowed up by the city again. Callum had marvelled at the simple opulence that a proud people could bestow upon plain stone walls and floors. It was nothing at all like the noisy, dirty streets he had grown up in, which seemed built to hide the past. Here they gloried in it, and used it to mark their paths to the future.

After an overwhelming number of lefts and rights, they'd finally arrived. To Callum's surprise, the armoury was not a simple room, but was a collection of specially-built spaces connected to one another by a maze of corridors. Each area was dedicated to a specific function. One was a tack room, full of the saddles, reins, and other equipment needed for riding a raeas. It smelled richly of leather and oil, and sounded of clinking metal bits and the shuffling noise of saddles being polished to a sheen. Another was a smithy, where every surface was covered with leftover grime from previous generations of the thick smoke that curled through the air and sank to the floor, even now coating every surface with black tar. The smiths' thick arms were dripping sweat as they swung their enormous hammers, beating out metal, digging into the forging fires, and tapping delicate designs into greaves.

There was a full stable, with an impossibly large riding yard where the raeas could be exercised, but the final room was the one that most captured Callum's attention.

The walls of the last room were covered with arm greaves of various sizes and shapes. One wall held the right greave, with its locking space for the removable canisters. Another held the left greave with various attachable metal disks. The third was lined with banks of silver canisters.

Callum unconsciously placed his hand against the inner pocket of his cloak that held the bronze canister that he'd pinched. A lot had changed since they had been locked in that room, fearing the judgement of an unknown monarch. Callum thought that maybe he should return it. Or perhaps he could just leave the canister here, and no one would notice.

Ythen stepped up to him and grabbed Callum's forearms. He held them up in front of him, wrapping his fingers around Callum's wrists as if measuring them. After a moment, he dropped them and turned towards the wall that held the right greaves.

"Callum, are the weapons of your world similar to ours?" Ythen turned and held up his own armoured forearms. "Do you have these?"

Callum shook his head and followed Ythen over to the wall.

Ythen nodded and lifted some pieces off the wall. "Very well. They are called the Firedart and Buckler. They serve us as long-range weapons, though if practised, a warrior can use them in hand-to-hand combat. They were designed by the First Flame-Bearer, a powerful warrior. We still keep some of his original weaponry in the Hall of Record. Some say that his canisters contained the energy of unusual lightning; perhaps that which brought him here. He had two such canisters, one of which is now in the Hall of

Record. The other was lost to history. The one we know of is far too dangerous for us to use in combat, so we keep it on display to remind us of the victorious history of our people. Perhaps you viewed it, while you were there? It is a beautiful set of weapons." Callum shook his head and swallowed nervously as Ythen turned and held up some greaves.

"The one that goes on your right arm is the Firedart." He slipped it over Callum's wrist, flicking a small metal bar across the palm as he did so, and secured both the bar and the greave tightly with leather straps. "This bar is called the generator. It acts as a triggering device."

"One of these canisters," he said, grabbing a thin one from the lower left section of the back wall, "contains some of the lightning that we gather in the Collectors. You saw us recharging ours on the way back to Yshaar yesterday, do you remember?"

Callum replied in the affirmative.

Ythen continued, "This one is a training canister. It will not harm us, but will allow you to learn." He inserted the canister into the locking mechanism on Callum's arm, with the hole pointing towards his wrist. "The one that goes on your left arm is the Buckler. It is a metal disk that you can use as a shield."

Callum looked at the Buckler. It was no larger than a dinner plate, and surprisingly lightweight.

"If you catch a dart on your Buckler, remember to touch it to the ground occasionally. If you forget, the charge will build up enough to shock you quite severely. Shall we try them out?"

Callum looked back up at Ythen, hoping he was joking. He was not. Callum followed the Quencher out of the room and down another passageway, into a training area which was filled with debris that a person could stand on or hide behind. Torches lined the walls intermittently, brightening some areas of the room beyond the pale illumination of the night air, leaving shadowy corners to hide in.

Ythen stopped and waited for Callum to walk up beside him, locking a training canister into place on his own arm. "To shoot a dart, you simply have to point the canister at your target, and squeeze your fist. The generator on your palm will sense the pressure and fire a dart. Try it."

Callum nervously lifted his right arm up and pointed it towards a broken pot across the room. He braced himself and flexed his fingers a few times before crushing his hand into a fist over the metal bar.

A thin yellow bolt of light shot out of the canister and blew past the pot, splashing against a stone wall far into the corner of the room.

Ythen chuckled and stepped closer, steadying Callum's arm. "Not so hard. Just a light touch. Take your time."

Callum took in and let out a deep breath. He aimed his arm again and gently squeezed the generator.

This time the dart shattered the pot, scattering pieces of it across the floor.

"Well done, Callum! It took me three tries to hit my target when I first trained." He walked past Callum and after a few paces turned back, standing directly in Callum's line of fire. "Now, shoot me."

Callum hesitated. "Beg your pardon?"

Ythen grinned. "Or perhaps I should say, *attempt* to shoot me." He took a step to the right.

Callum quickly lifted his arm and fired off a shot.

The dart landed smack in the middle of Ythen's Buckler, which hadn't been there a moment ago. The dart's energy made the metal disk ring.

Ythen laughed lightly at Callum's shocked expression.

"How'd you stop it?" Callum asked. "It's too fast to follow with your eyes!"

"I did not have to follow the shot, I merely had to follow your arm. You told me where you were going to shoot, Callum." Ythen reached his left arm towards the wall to ground the Buckler. "Try to use your eyes and body to confuse me, so I cannot predict—"

He cut off short as a yellow bolt struck his unprotected chest, giving him a mild shock.

Ythen looked up in surprise at a grinning Callum, and promptly fired off two rounds. To his amazement, Callum was able to block the first dart before being struck by the second.

"Not bad."

They continued to practise various offensive and defensive techniques for the next hour. Callum was a quick study; the graceful movements and sharp eyes that had served him so well as a pickpocket made him a perfect match with these weapons, and although Ythen was clearly the better fighter, Callum began to land more blows towards the end of their sparring bout.

The time passed quickly, and soon both boys were breathing heavily. Callum was unused to moving through such thick air, and the effort was taxing. When they each only had one shot left in their canister, Ythen abandoned all congeniality and ducked behind a large stone block with a loud *whoop*! Callum understood immediately and dropped behind a rock of his own. It was sudden death.

Ythen could hear Callum breathing heavily on the far side of the training area. He crouched down and began a quick crawl through the shadows. He stopped behind a low pile of singed tapestries and gathered himself.

A noise came from across the room. Callum was scuffing his feet. Ythen pictured Callum rising into a crouch, preparing to pop over the top of his cover and take a quick shot at him. Ythen silently counted to three and then peered carefully over the fabric wall. There was no movement.

Suddenly, a flash of metal bolted out from behind the rock Callum was using for cover. Ythen quickly rose and lined up his arm for a shot... and then saw Callum's Buckler hit the floor and begin slowly spinning its way to stillness.

In the second that Ythen was distracted, Callum leapt out from behind the rock in the other direction, threw himself into a somersault and then pulled up in a crouch, firing off a dart that took Ythen in the shoulder before he could bring his arm to bear on the new target.

Ythen was still for a moment and then laughed out loudly. "Swift, indeed! Congratulations, Callum. You are surely worthy of wearing the blue."

Callum smiled and ducked his head. He started to untie the leather bindings of his greaves, but Ythen reached out a hand to stop him.

"Now we see if you can do that while riding a raeas."

Callum's shoulders slumped. It was going to be a long night.

Chapter Ten:
The Living Woods

A feather-light touch brushed Jingwei's cheek, bringing her slowly and gently out of unconsciousness. Her eyes fluttered open.

Trees surrounded her. She was lying on her back in the dirt, looking up along the lengths of numerous trunks that pointed towards the sky; each branch that protruded was clearly defined in the pale early morning light.

She was still in the forest. Memories came flooding back to her. The tree-line. The hill. The furry creatures. The fall.

Yriel.

Jingwei tried to sit up. A searing pain in her wrist made her crumple back down in sudden tears. She looked over at her arm and grimaced at the unusual angle at which her wrist was twisted. Her head was throbbing too, a reminder of her sudden stop at the bottom of the hill.

Cradling her broken wrist, she slowly leaned up on one elbow and surveyed her surroundings.

Yriel was nowhere to be found. For that matter, neither was the hill.

Instead, standing tall before her was a tree. It was massive; at least forty storeys high. Its trunk was not as thick as the redwoods she was familiar with back in California, but wasn't far off, and looked just as sturdy. Its branches were long and straight, jutting out perpendicular to the trunk, with round clumps of green foliage on the end of each. They grew shorter as the height of the tree increased, giving the top two thirds of it the rounded appearance of a dark green egg.

The bottom third of the tree had a very different appearance. Long branches extended from the trunk but then thinned out to become willowy and drop the remaining distance to the ground. The long, slender stalks were the same grey colour as the trunk, and created a silvery curtain that enveloped the lower third of the enormous tree.

Jingwei rose slowly to her feet in wonder. The intelligence she had felt at the tree-line was intensified here. She watched in silent awe as one of the tendrils gently lifted and floated towards her, landing effortlessly on her shoulder.

Why do you abandon your people?

Jingwei jumped back with a start, wincing at the pain in her head and wrist. The voice had come from inside her head, and it definitely hadn't been her own.

"Wh-what? Who said that?"

The tendril cautiously placed itself on her shoulder again, this time taking a firmer grip.

I am Huon Arrahl. Why do you betray your own and come to me with tidings of war?

Jingwei stared up at the tree in wonder. It was sentient. The tree was sentient! That meant that maybe all of the trees were! It was unbelievable! Her mission was suddenly forgotten.

"How did you know why I came here? Can you read my mind?"

No. I know your intentions because you told me before you came to me.

"Wait. I told you? I didn't tell you. I told the trees at the edge of the forest. Did they pass the message along?"

I am the trees at the edge of the forest. I am the trees in the centre of the forest. I am the forest. I am Huon Arrahl.

Jingwei looked around her. The forest behind her was still now, but she had faint recollections of being balanced high in the air on mobile branches as the trees travelled beneath and around her, passing her on from one to the next.

"You mean you control the trees? All of them? Are they like your servants, or your slaves?" An image of a naked Aru Elen servant sprang to her mind and she banished it quickly.

You misunderstand. I do not control the trees. I am the trees. They are all my bodies, and I am their mind. I am one. I am Huon Arrahl.

"Yes, you said that before." Jingwei still didn't understand.

The voice in her head felt impatient. *You have many trunks on your body. I see them even now working independent of one another. One is wounded, yet the others move freely. Even your branches move individually. Yet one mind directs them all. So it is with me. I have many trunks, and many branches. They are me, and I am them. Are we so different, you and I?*

Jingwei looked down at her arms and legs. Her left wrist was cupped gently in her other hand, her fingers playing nervously over her skin.

"I guess not."

Jingwei. I ask you again. Why do you abandon your people, and bring to me warning of their aggression?

"First off, they aren't my people. I'm not a Daevyn. See? No wing stubs." She turned in a circle, careful not to tangle herself up with the tendril on her shoulder.

"I'm a Human. I was brought here by lightning... look, it's a long story, and we don't have much time. Let's just say, I'm on your side here, and I don't think the Daevyn should burn you down."

The trees all around her began creaking and groaning as they shook and swayed. Jingwei glanced around nervously and took a step closer to the big tree.

"Are they angry?"

The tendrils of the tree rippled in a sigh. *There is no they. Only me. Huon Arrahl. And yes, I am displeased that the Daevyn come to destroy me. Should I not be?*

Jingwei was struggling with this conversation. She was unaccustomed to holding discussions with trees and felt like she was on the defensive, a position she liked to be in as little as possible.

"Of course you should be. That's why I'm here. Now listen…"

Huon Arrahl.

"Right, Huon Arrahl. They'll be coming in the morning." Jingwei looked around at the brightening air and realized that it was morning already. "The Daevyn are angry that you're advancing on their city. They mean to defend themselves."

Defend? How can they defend when I do not attack?

Jingwei was getting frustrated with Huon Arrahl's attitude. She had abandoned everything, risked everything to come out here to save the trees, only to find that the forest was more concerned with philosophy than survival. "Well, if you aren't attacking, then what are you doing sending your trees so far out into the plains?"

I am thirsty. The air is drying. Can you not feel it? Do your leaves not wither on their stems?

"Thirsty? You're a tree! You have roots! Dig deeper and find water!" Jingwei was now holding on to the tendril with her good hand and talking at it, as if a more direct line would better get her message across.

The body to which you speak has roots, and I have dug them deep into the ground. The water is no longer there. My other bodies have no roots. They move here and there and back again, and they drink life from the air.

The many tendrils of Huon Arrahl's central body were wiggling now, expressing some unknown emotion.

I have many bodies to feed, and so I have gone north in search of water. But the plains too, are dry. I mean no harm to any life. If the Daevyn find my presence disturbing, then I will withdraw myself, and extend to the east. Perhaps in the depths of the mountains I will find sustenance.

"So, you'll pull your trees away from the Daevyn city?"

They are already moving. I thank you, Jingwei Li. Your bravery and convictions have been of great service to Tranthaea tonight.

Jingwei felt a thrill go through her. She had just averted a war and saved a forest. Not a bad night's work for a sixteen-year-old schoolgirl from California.

Huon Arrahl's voice was growing softer and slowing down, as if it were falling asleep.

But now your virtues have brought you far from safety. I would lead you back to the Daevyn, but my strength is sapped.

"What!?" Jingwei couldn't believe what she was hearing. "I just saved you, and you're going to let me wander, *lost*, through your woods because you're *tired?*"

Forgive me. It has been many years since I have had to focus so much of my attention on one place for so long. You have exhausted me...

Huon Arrahl's voice faded into silence and the tendril on Jingwei's shoulder slipped off and rejoined the skirt of branches that hung gently around the tree's lower third.

"Well, that's just great. Jingwei Li, the great hero and peacemaker, lost in the woods that she just saved from clear-cutting. What a way to go."

She looked around. The trees were now mostly still. The entire forest was silent, save for a slight rustling as each branch swayed towards and away from the centre tree in a rhythmic pattern.

Jingwei cradled her broken wrist and started to limp in a direction she hoped was north, accompanied by nothing but the sound of the snoring forest. Soon the air began to glow brightly again; not the pale, shadowy glow of the dawn, but the warm, rich light of the morning.

The pervading nature of the light meant that Jingwei cast no shadow, nor did anything else in the forest. Her tired eyes began to play tricks on her depth perception. Branches and twigs were now closer than they seemed. Bumps and divots in the dirt were higher or deeper than they first appeared.

Jingwei stumbled into a particularly deep depression, jarring her wrist and waking her with pain. She noticed that the depression sloped into a long ditch, the far side of which was steep and rocky, and didn't look at all like something she wanted to climb in her state.

She sidestepped over to a makeshift bridge of fallen branches and other forest detritus. She stepped onto it, edging slowly across the narrow gap, hoping that Huon Arrahl wouldn't be upset that she was stepping on its toes, or something like that.

The branches creaked and groaned and then gave way with a sudden snap, and Jingwei fell heavily to the floor of the ditch. She managed to keep her wrist out from under her body, but was forced to land awkwardly on her side, bruising her right elbow and jarring her entire body with pain.

She lay on the ground for a moment, trying to master the throbbing before she would have to get up and continue on.

Then she heard a noise. The shuffling of feet echoed from farther down the ditch, where it sloped deeply and tunneled down into the ground.

Jingwei forced herself to sit up and face towards the approaching noise. She grabbed a rock in her uninjured hand and held it above her head in nervous preparation. She tried to calm herself.

I've already dealt with lightning, time travel, pyromaniacs and philosophical vegetation today. I can handle anything.

The owner of the shuffling feet came into view, carefully manoeuvring itself out of the tunnel's entrance.

Jingwei screamed.

Chapter Eleven:
The Scouting Party

The raeas' gently swaying movement was a blessing for Callum's bruised ribs and sore body. He'd awoken this morning with a fresh knowledge of the exact placement of every muscle in his body after the training session with Ythen the night before, and his midsection was still aching from the kick that the furious policeman had given him. The adrenaline that had been fueling him since he'd arrived in the crater yesterday afternoon had long since worn off, and last night's workout had sapped him of any remaining strength.

After the weapons training, Callum had been introduced to the raeas he would be riding. Ythen had explained that raeas were gentle creatures, which were of little-to-no use in battle, except that they moved the Daevyn from one place to another. He had shown Callum how to attach the saddle and reins, and then helped him mount.

Callum had been pleased with how easy they were to ride. Unlike horses, raeas didn't bump up and down as they moved, but instead swayed side to side through the air like a fish. If you maintained a low centre of gravity, it was very difficult to be thrown off, unless the raeas bolted, in which case you may find yourself on the ground with a pair of very shaky legs.

But now Callum found himself seated securely on his raeas, passing out of the city onto the plains. After a luxurious sleep that his exhausted body had accepted gratefully and a quick morning meal, they had wasted no time getting underway. The morning air was clear and bright, but the party of Quenchers that Ythen was leading remained quiet and alert, their mood suspicious and watchful.

Ythen himself was at the head of the column, riding just ahead of Callum. He and Callum had been pulling out their riding equipment when the news had come from the watchmen; *the forest has retreated.*

There had been no news of Jingwei or Yriel.

Now, riding out onto the plains with the dark mass of the Korrahl Forest nowhere in sight, Callum thought he could understand Ythen's worried expression.

He nudged his raeas to catch up with Ythen and glanced over at the blond boy's stony face.

"I'm sure they're all right, Ythen."

Ythen's mouth hardened. "I hope that they are. But Yriel has always been foolishly headstrong, charging in to danger with no thought to the consequences, and it seems that your Jingwei is the same."

Callum opened his mouth to deny that she was *his* Jingwei but Ythen didn't give him the chance.

"I have no doubt that they have found trouble. As one of my Quenchers, Yriel is my responsibility, and you and your friend have also been given over to my protection. The Flame-Bearer will be forced to remove me from my position now. That the girls are missing at all is just another proof of my incompetence."

Callum snorted. "Not hardly. I doubt that the whole Daevyn army could keep Jingwei out of trouble if she had a mind to find some. Which she does."

Ythen cracked a smile as he weaved his raeas through the gradually curving foothills that lay to the south of the city. Last night these hills had been covered with trees, and now there was no trace of them, save for the hard bed of crushed grasses. The ground looked as though it had been danced upon by giants who left no footprints, only the flattened proof of their enormous weight and power.

Callum followed closely behind. The evidence of such a large force frightened him, and he wondered where the forest had gone, and if Jingwei or Yriel had in any way influenced its movement, or had been taken with it.

They rode in silence for a few hours, each scanning the horizon for a sign of the retreating forest. Ythen sent riders out in all directions to act as scouts, but there was no movement and no sign of their quarry. The yellow plains were unbroken; the only disturbance to the horizon was the black mountain range fifty kilometres to the east and the towering city of Yshaar, shrinking behind them in the north.

Eventually Callum broke the silence.

"Do the trees move around a lot here?"

Ythen didn't turn his head as he answered, remaining focused on scouting ahead. "We don't know. The Korrahl Forest has always inhabited the south. It expands as a forest does, but never have we seen it move from one location to another as it has in the last few days. The Daevyn avoid entering it at all costs, as they have since the beginning. Something malevolent lives in the forest, and we have now lost two more to its secrets."

Callum fingered his greaves and looked nervously at the line of Quenchers riding behind him. "Ythen? Is this just a search party, or is it still a war party?"

Ythen didn't answer, so Callum pressed him. "I mean, if the trees don't threaten Yshaar no more, then are you still gonna attack them?"

Ythen stopped his raeas at the crest of a low hill. He spoke clearly and with finality, "It is the Flame-Bearer who makes those decisions, not I. What we do will be decided by what we find in the forest." He gestured ahead with a nod. Callum pulled up beside him and followed his gaze.

They had found the Korrahl Forest. The boundaries of the woods were a few kilometres distant yet, but were clearly visible from the top of the hill. The tree-line was thick and prohibiting.

Callum saw no sign of Jingwei. He didn't know what he had been expecting, maybe to see her waiting at the foot of a tree, her sarcastic smile mocking the boys who felt they had to rescue her.

They had just started down the slope towards the trees when they heard a shout from farther back down the line. Ythen immediately pulled his raeas around and looked to the sky.

A heavy slap of wind overhead was all the warning Callum got. He leaped sideways off the raeas, throwing his body flat onto the ground. The sharp pain in his ribs was quickly masked by a rush of adrenaline. Rolling over, he emptied his Firedart wildly into the sky, searching for his attacker.

He didn't have to search for long. Above him, soaring in a wide loop that would lead it back towards the search party, was an enormous flying creature.

Piercing red eyes were sunk deep into hollows on its stubbed head. Three long, curved beaks protruded from the head, which seemed lumped onto its mottled navy blue and white body as if it had been placed there by accident. The body was composed almost entirely of opposing triangular wings and ended in a short tail that was shaped like a cross, which it used as a vertical and horizontal rudder, allowing it the manoeuvrability of something half its size.

As it finished its circle and began to dive back towards the party, Callum could see that it had a wingspan of about eight metres and that it was twice that in length.

"Thranvorl!" The alerting shouts now came from many throats; all too late. The Quenchers had been focusing on the land around them and ignored the sky above. Callum realized that what would normally have alerted him to the beast's presence did not exist in this world; the lack of shadows had undone any warning that the thranvorl had been circling above them. The Quenchers were well-trained warriors though, and were already forming defensive formations as darts started to lance upward.

The massive predator slowly beat its wings, its eyes fixed on Callum's prone body. It opened two of its beaks and issued a disharmonic shriek, ignoring the weak blasts of the Firedarts. Callum abandoned all thoughts of bravery and half-crawled, half-rolled down the side of the hill, desperately searching for cover.

The thranvorl swooped towards him, its centre beak open wide, the black tongue within straining forward to catch its prey.

Callum saw a small hollow in the hillside and threw himself into it. He turned back and tried in vain to trigger his Firedart, squeezing furiously on the generator, but his canister was empty. At the last moment he raised his Buckler in defense, knowing that it was a useless gesture.

The thranvorl screeched a cry of victory just as Ythen flew down from the crest of the hill on his raeas, gripping the reins with his left hand and blazing darts towards the thranvorl with his right. A well-aimed shot found its way into the thranvorl's right eye, causing it to shriek and pull up seconds before its beak found Callum's hiding place.

Ythen pulled up beside the hollow and tore out his canister, flinging it to the ground only to replace it with a fresh one from his bandolier.

His eyes never left the thranvorl, tracking its movement as it tore up into the sky in pain.

"Stay there, Callum!" He spurred his raeas back towards the top of the hill that now separated them from the rest of the Quenchers. "Stay safe!"

Then he was gone.

Callum crouched down in the crevice. From the other side of the hill he heard the agitated screams of the thranvorl and the war cries of the Daevyn soldiers. Every now and then the thranvorl flew over Callum's hiding place as it lined itself up for another attack on the Quenchers, but it was far too busy now to pay attention to a single weaponless boy.

Callum felt ashamed, and worse than useless. Not only was he of no help to the Quencher's defence, he had cost them time with their leader at a critical moment by needing rescuing. He huddled down and wrapped his blue cloak around himself. It was stained with dirt and torn in a few places, marring the glorified royal blue symbol it had once been.

Callum impulsively grabbed some dirt and began rubbing it into the fabric. He didn't deserve to wear this colour, once exclusively reserved for the Flame-Bearer's honour guard. He reached behind him and grabbed a rock, then used its sharp edge to tear holes in the cloak. The fine cloak was soon turned into rags, the comfortable uniform of Callum's past. Warm tears of embarrassment and shame wet his cheeks, and he angrily rubbed them away with a dirty hand.

In frustration, he threw the rock out over the plains as hard as he could. The soft thump it gave as it landed was lost in the sounds of battle from over the hill. The thranvorl must have been a hardy creature as it was still holding its own against an entire company of Quenchers. Callum could only imagine what havoc it could wreak if it traveled in flocks.

A movement above the distant hills caught his eye. It seemed that the thranvorl was now coming from far to the south, making a long drive towards the battle that still raged behind him.

It took a moment for the reality to sink in.

Wait. If the battle is still going on... then that's a different thranvorl. A second thranvorl.

Callum started to panic. Another one of those monsters could completely destroy the search party, especially if it had surprise on its side. Callum knew he had to do something, to warn Ythen at least, but what? How?

He hurried to gather up the hanging tatters of his ruined cloak, preparing to make a run for the crest of the hill. As he did so, his hand bumped into a hard object in the cloak's inside pocket.

It was the bronze canister he'd pinched from the Hall of Record. The canister that Ythen had told him had once belonged to the First Flame-Bearer. The one that he'd been warned was too powerful and dangerous for anyone to use.

He pulled it out of the pocket and slapped it into the locking mechanism on his arm. There was no other choice.

The second thranvorl was now looming large over the hills. It had almost reached the ridge, its massive wings pounding as it drove itself powerfully through the dense air. There were no warning cries from the Quenchers to the north; they still had no idea that it was coming.

Callum took a deep breath and braced himself against the back of the crevice. He carefully aimed the Firedart at the head of the approaching beast and squeezed the generator.

A single, thick bolt of pure white energy burst out of the weapon, shot forward, and impacted just above the centre beak of the thranvorl. Its mouths opened in a soundless scream and it lost all control, hurtling towards the earth. As if in slow motion, the massive body grew larger and larger, its wings folding uselessly behind it, its head leading a corkscrewing path directly towards the Human boy. A fraction of a second later, it slammed into Callum's hollow, sending up clouds of dirt and stone.

When the dust settled, the broken corpse of the thranvorl covered the hillside, its wings twisted at odd angles. Callum's refuge had been buried beneath the weight of its immense body.

A short distance to the south, Yriel roughly batted away another branch that seemed to reach out and claw at her cloak. She had hoped that the going would be easier once the morning air brightened and she could see where she was going, but the trees seemed to have wakened with the dawn and simply would not let her pass unhindered.

It is not fair.

She was Yriel Sparkcatcher, daughter of the Flame-Bearer of the Daevyn, heir to the throne of The Plains, and rightful First Quencher. She'd had everything, and not that long ago. She had been trained by her mother's top councillors and advisors in affairs of state and by the best warriors in tactics and fighting. She had accepted her position and had been fully prepared to use it to advance the strength and glory of her people. She had even found love with an up-and-coming young Quencher.

She had been ready.

And then, she had been betrayed.

By her mother, who chose Ythen to lead her warriors.

By her boyfriend, who had accepted, with all the false humility he had been able to muster.

By her people, who had forgotten her.

Yriel's eyes burned with angry tears as she fought through the forest, hacking away at one branch after another, taking another turn in the maze as she stumbled north.

I do not want power, Mother. I do not want honour for myself, no matter what you say. I only want to serve our people, to make our people stronger.

I can do that. Ythen cannot. You cannot.

She remembered saying those words to the Flame-Bearer, and seeing the pain in her mother's eyes.

Yriel had swallowed her guilt and pushed aside an apology. She had stood in her mother's presence, defiant and proud, listening to the Flame-Bearer tell her that her desire for strength was her weakness, and that she could learn something from Ythen and his humility.

In hindsight, it had been a mistake. Confronting her mother, rejecting her boyfriend. But there was no way she could take it back, no way that she could undo what she had done.

But she could atone for it. That is why she had followed the Human girl, to prove her worth to her mother and to the current First Quencher, improper though his present appointment may be.

She stopped and looked down the path she was on. The forest finally ended only metres ahead; the plains spread out before her. In the distance, she could see a thranvorl swooping down low behind a hill, and bolts of light shooting up at it as it dove.

She smiled grimly and checked her Firedart.

She would show them.

She would save them.

And then, finally, they would understand how much they needed her.

The darkness surrounding Callum was absolute. He blinked his eyes a few times, unsure of whether they were open or not. All around him was blackness. He reached his hand up to a sore spot on the back of his head and pulled it away when he felt something sticky.

Blood.

Callum rubbed his eyes fiercely, producing stars that burned and faded in the darkness. His eyes were still recovering from the white blast that had erupted from his Firedart.

When he had shot the dart at the thranvorl, the accompanying kickback had thrown him through the back wall of the hollow, which had given way under the force of the blast. He'd burst into an underground cavity, landing hard on his back and striking his head against a rock. The opening he'd made had immediately been covered by the fallen body of the flying predator and an avalanche of shattered rocks had sealed him into darkness.

Callum had never been claustrophobic. In his career as a thief he had been forced to hide in tight spaces many times, but never had he been in blackness so complete. He reached his arms out and felt rough stone less than a metre above him. It was the same on both sides. He got to his knees slowly and crawled in the direction he thought was out, scuffing his legs against sharp rocks on the way. Within seconds he reached an obstacle. Fallen rocks and dirt had closed off access to the outside world, making it impassible even had the thranvorl's body not been covering the hillside.

Callum forced himself to breathe. The air underground was just as thick as above, but the floating dust from the collapse made it feel as though he was drinking dirt. He wondered for a moment why it was dark inside if there was air to breath, and the air was what gave off the light.

Now what?

The wall of dirt and rocks in front of him answered his question.

Only one way to go. Further in.

He slowly managed to twist himself around in the tight space, wriggling up against the walls that surrounded him. Once he'd completed his turn he started to inch forwards, the thin fabric of his trousers doing little to protect his knees which, along with his palms, quickly grew bloody as they scraped over the coarse tunnel floor. His ribs ached with every laboured breath and his head was pounding, although his intermittent checks seemed to suggest that the bleeding was slowing.

That's it, he thought. *If I ever get back to London, I'm going to steal me a full suit of armour.*

He continued crawling and eventually noticed that the tunnel was sloping downward and curving gently to the right. By the time he'd estimated a half-hour had passed, Callum had no idea where he was, except that he was no longer inside the hill that he had started in. He began to alternate between crawling on all fours and shuffling along on his stomach as the ceiling began to get lower and lower.

Soon he found himself in a place where the wall to his right pulled back until he couldn't feel it with his arm anymore. The ceiling above him was only centimetres from his back, but if he lay flat and still on the floor he could imagine that he was lying down in a regular-sized room.

Callum shifted to the right, reaching his arm out to feel for the wall. The quiet of the space around him was still jarring after the noise of the battle above. He thought momentarily about Ythen and the Quenchers battling the thranvorl and then of Jingwei and Yriel vanishing into the forest and hoped they were all doing better than he was.

He was distracted from his thoughts when his hand found a hole in the floor. He scooted over to it and explored it blindly. It was about the diameter of a carriage wheel and cut down deeply into the rock, opening up into what Callum assumed was a cavern below. He tossed a loose rock down into the hole and was rewarded with the clacking echo of a floor not far down.

Satisfied, he inched forward and, grasping the edge carefully, lowered himself down. His feet dangled as he reached out with his toes. He couldn't feel the floor beneath him, but remembering the sound of the rock hitting the ground, he closed his eyes and let go.

The floor was only a few centimetres away, and he landed safely, dropping into a crouch and swivelling his head about in nervous expectation.

The air in this cavern had a slight glow that allowed him to make out vague shapes at the boundary of the open space. He edged towards them cautiously and found them to be large stalactites and stalagmites, protruding heavily from the floor and ceiling of the cavern, giving a sculpted look of false life to reddish stone.

Callum weaved his way around a few of the natural pillared formations. Ahead, in the dim light, he could make out what looked like a tunnel entrance. He made a beeline for it, hoping that it would lead up to the surface.

He turned into the opening and suddenly stopped. Far ahead were two more shapes. But these ones were moving.

Callum leapt back around the corner. The two figures were large and ungainly. They looked to be about eight feet tall and were coming in his direction; the sound of their shuffling co-mingled with what he assumed was a form of speech; clicks and groans and buzzes wafted down the passageway ahead of them.

Callum began to back away from the entrance and raised his Buckler. Maybe he could hide behind a pillar and vanish into the dark until they passed, whatever they were.

Without warning, two claw-like grips grabbed his arms from behind and shoved him face-first into the wall.

A high, heavily accented voice whistled out from the darkness. "You trespass here, little Daevyn warrior. The gru'Esh do not take kindly to trespassers."

Callum struggled in vain. The iron grips on his arms did not lessen. Suddenly, a third hand grabbed his hair violently, painfully brushing against the reopened wound on his head and pushed forward, cracking his forehead against the stone wall, hard.

Callum felt a moment of sharp pain, and then what little dim light there was faded into blackness.

Chapter Twelve:
The Lost Humans

Dirt flew into Ythen's face as the thranvorl's wings pounded the air just above the ground, whipping up dust clouds that blinded the Quenchers and pelted them with flying debris.

Ythen shouted hoarsely into the dust and his warriors responded immediately; wheeling their raeas in formation and spreading out over the defended terrain. One heavy crash of a wing could kill any men it landed on, and Ythen wasn't about to lose groups of Quenchers at a time because they were huddled together in fear.

As the dust cleared, he took a rapid inventory of his troops. Less than half remained mounted, and of those on the ground only a few were left standing. The others were groaning in pain, cautiously testing wounded limbs, or simply not moving at all.

Behind him, from on the other side of the hill came a bright white flash, followed by the thundering sound of a rockslide. Ythen whirled around to make sure that no new enemy was approaching from the south but didn't have time to check on Callum.

For now, the Human boy was on his own.

Nothing came over the hilltop. Ythen brought his eyes back to the sky above. The thranvorl was curving around in a steep climb, preparing for another attack run. Its body was scored with the burn marks left behind by countless darts, but none had penetrated its thick skin. During his initial combat training years ago he had been told that the Daevyn weapons were useless against the thranvorl. The predators hunted from the skies above Tranthaea, and were therefore often struck by lightning. They had developed skin on their backs that absorbed and dispersed the power of a lightning bolt, and even their more sensitive underbellies were far too tough for a mere Firedart to do any damage.

Ythen was fighting down panic. He had never faced a thranvorl before. None of his warriors had. Whenever one had attacked him in the past he would simply order his small troupe of Quenchers to dismount and cover themselves with their tan cloaks to blend into the plains. They might lose a few raeas to the hungry beast, but they would survive.

Ythen knew that tactic would not work this time. The sheer number of warriors he had with him made them a perfect target; there was no way the creature could miss them. With a small party of Quenchers, he could use the poor eyesight of the thranvorl against it, but with so many...

That's when the idea came to him.

The thranvorl finished its turn and started its dive. Ythen desperately scrambled up onto a nearby raeas and, through the din of warriors calling out positions and pleading for aid, bellowed, "Quenchers to my right! Cover! Send the raeas to the left! Quenchers to my right! Cover!"

The well-trained Quenchers responded without hesitation, flipping their hoods up and doing their best to vanish into the grasses to Ythen's right. Those that still had a raeas under their control steered them to the left as they dismounted, yelling and smacking them to make them all bolt in the same direction. Ythen remained where he was, reloading, silently willing the thranvorl to take the bait.

The huge predator was halfway through its dive when its one remaining good eye saw a herd of raeas gliding swiftly to the west. Instinct made it bank to follow, yawing hard to the right to keep its prey visible to its left eye.

Too late, it realized its mistake as it saw Ythen standing alone in the tall grass, his right arm raised and tracking.

Ythen fired first, his dart lancing towards the thranvorl's left eye. It was followed by an upward rain of bolts from the remaining concealed Quenchers, more than one of which found its mark on the low-flying predator's head.

The thranvorl let out a deafening shriek of pain and pulled up, its wings thundering wildly out of tandem as it sought to escape from its unseen vanquishers. It flew blindly towards the south, its harsh cries echoing vaguely before being swallowed up by the thick air as it faded into the distance over the forest.

Ythen let out a breath of relief. It had been a long shot, and he hadn't really expected it to work. He lowered his hands to his sides, trying to keep them from shaking.

All around him Quenchers were standing. Some were helping others up; a few ran off to collect what raeas they could. Ythen knew he should help them regroup and check his warriors for injuries and losses, but he had a more pressing responsibility.

He ran up the hill, recalling the blast of light and the sound he'd witnessed only moments before. He hadn't had time to think about it then, and even now had no idea what had caused the commotion, but he fervently hoped that Callum was all right.

When he reached the ridge-line, he couldn't believe his eyes.

The hillside below him had vanished, hidden behind the massive body of a *second* thranvorl. Dust still swirled in the air around it, and steam rose from underneath its mottled body.

And standing near its tail, curiously examining the cross-rudder design, was Yriel.

She looked up at Ythen across the thranvorl's body while he took in the scene. When she felt he'd had enough time she spoke with a teasing lilt to her voice.

"What? No 'welcome back' for your brave warrior? I have been through a night of misery trying to save your skin; I followed the traitor, risked death in the forest, and now saved you from the thranvorl, and not even a 'thank you?'"

Ythen didn't rise to the bait. "Where is Callum?"

Yriel's sure grin faded a bit. "What do you mean? Is he not with you?"

Ythen began to half-run, half-slide down the rubble on the hill. "He was. When the thranvorl attacked us I set him to wait in a small crevice in the rock."

Yriel looked down at the body covering the hillside. Her pale face whitened a little more. "Do you mean he is underneath...?"

Ythen had reached the smoking head of the thranvorl. Its dead eyes stared blankly back at him, giving nothing away.

"Callum!" Ythen called out over the body, knowing already that it was a useless gesture. "CALLUM!"

He rounded on Yriel who had come up on the other side of the corpse. "You. You say that you brought down the thranvorl. How? Did you see Callum? Was he still on the hillside?"

Yriel raised up her hands to ward off the onslaught of questions. "Do not interrogate me as though *I* were your enemy, Ythen. I did not see the Human on the hill; my attentions were taken by the monster that needed slaying. If he has fallen in the battle the blame is yours, not mine." Her eyes grew hard as she stared up at him. "I saved the Daevyn warriors from a second attack. You lost the second of your wards. Which of those is the action of a true First Quencher?"

"Do not burden me with your jealousies now, Yriel!" Ythen slumped down beside the thranvorl's head. "Many have died today, Callum not the least among them." Ythen wanted to mourn the fallen, but knew that his responsibility was to the living. He looked up at Yriel pleadingly. "Jingwei is still missing. She was granted the protection of the Daevyn. Can we not set aside our past to save the honour of our people?"

Yriel considered him for a moment, her head tilted to one side. She appeared to be rehashing an interior conversation. "Fine." She sat down next to him. "I will help you find the Human girl. And when we return to Yshaar—"

"I will gladly resign my title in your favour. Just help me find Jingwei."

Yriel looked at him for a moment in surprise, unsure of whether or not to believe him. That had not been what she was going to suggest, but it was an offer too tempting to refuse. She nodded and proceeded to tell Ythen what had happened last night, starting in the Banquet Hall and ending in the woods, pointing out her ripped and ragged clothes to demonstrate the ferocity of the forest.

"I eventually found my way out, no thanks to the trees." She shivered. "They are a worse enemy than we have feared."

"Then she is lost in the Korrahl," Ythen said, "and I do not have with me the numbers required to search for her."

He stood and brushed the dirt off his clothes, then reached down to help her up. She took his hand after a moment's hesitation.

He looked at her and nodded decisively. "I will go to the Aru Len. Perhaps the Aru Faylen will help us search."

Yriel was surprised when Ythen did not immediately release her hand as she followed him to the top of the hill. She had assumed that he had long since abandoned any feelings he'd had for her, but it seemed like a common need may have opened him up once again. Yriel smiled to herself as they crested the hill and together they looked down at the remainders of the Daevyn search party.

The surviving Quenchers had rounded up all nearby raeas and were loading the bodies of the dead onto them, preparing to send them back to Yshaar. Lines of wounded sat or lay at the foot of the hill, surrounded by an honour guard of the luckier warriors. When they saw their leaders appear over the crest they let out a weak, but heartfelt cheer.

Ythen let go of Yriel's hand and was about to step down to see to his people when Yriel grabbed his arm, holding him back.

"The Aru Faylen will probably help us. But you may want to ask Kala for aid as well."

"The Spark Keeper?" Ythen was surprised. "She did not support the Flame-Bearer's decision to allow the Humans to live! Why do you think she will help us save one of them?"

"Kala is an advisor to the Flame-Bearer. Her wisdom is a great asset to our people. Whether she disagrees or not, she will surely not disobey the Flame-Bearer." Ythen made to interrupt her but she spoke over him. "I know you do not like her, and she has made it no secret that she does not approve of you, but I have spoken with her many times, and she is a good friend to me. If we ask her, I believe that she will aid us. More than that, she will be a powerful set of eyes to search for the Human, and you need all the help you can get."

Ythen sighed. She had a point.

"Very well. We will send back the dead and wounded to Yshaar, and continue on with the others to the foot of the mountains," Ythen said. There was usually an Aru Len representative stationed there for their dealings with the groundlings.

"And Kala's home is in the mountains as well." Yriel released his arm and then reached up to wipe a bit of dirt off his cheek. This time Ythen remained silent and did not meet her gaze. After a moment, Yriel frowned and then gathered her tattered cloak around her and marched down the hill. She looked over her shoulder at Ythen and shouted back, "If the Human can be found, they will find her, Ythen Firebrand. Have no fear."

Ythen stood on the hill for a moment, looking east towards the mountains with a sense of foreboding. They raised themselves up against the sky, dark and powerful and majestic.

Yes, thought Ythen, *they will find her. But at what cost?*

Chapter Thirteen:
The Warrens

Callum groggily opened his eyes, clamping them shut again immediately. The world around him seemed to be shifting and shaking as a whirlwind of colours and lines swirled before his eyes.

His senses soon became accustomed to his surroundings. He found that he was lying on some sort of litter. He peeled his eyes open again, slowly allowing his brain to register what it was experiencing. The blurry movement he saw was the ceiling of the passage sliding past as he was carried down a tunnel. The lines in the rock above him dropped fluidly out of his field of vision, looking like water flowing in a horizontal waterfall. He felt queasy and tried to focus on something else.

A crust had formed around Callum's eyes, which he now tried to blink away. Blood from his head wounds had dried in miniature rivers and pools on his face, but when he went to brush them away he found that his hands were tied down by his sides.

"You awaken." The voice came from his left, its peculiar whistling sound breaking through his mental haze. Callum turned his head to see the speaker, and immediately wished he hadn't.

The creature was about eight feet tall, its head almost brushing the ceiling of the tunnel through which it travelled. The smooth sphere of that head was interrupted only by a sharp protruding edge that stood in place of a nose and ran from the top of its skull to the bottom. It had four nostril slits: two on each side of this ridge, one lower down and further from the ridge than the other. The white, bulbous eyes of a cave-dweller bulged from its face above the slits and a slim toothless mouth opened below them; the only two breaks in its otherwise solid black exterior.

Callum's eyes travelled down the body of the hatchet-faced creature. Its head sat upon a long, thick torso that looked as though it were fully armoured, though whether that armour was hard plates or skeletal bones, Callum wasn't sure. Four arms extended from the body: two from the shoulders which ended in four digit hands, and two from visible joints in the chest that also looked heavily armoured and had three-piece claws at their end.

The body sat on a horizontal oblong abdomen that was supported by four legs which were armoured and hooked, just like its two chest-arms. The claws at their base gripped the dirt and stone and propelled the creature securely through the loose rocks of the tunnel floor.

Callum's mind flew back to a book of pictures that he had rescued from the ashes of a house fire in London. It was one of the few possessions he had to his name, and was the one that he was the most protective of. He wondered in the back of his mind what had happened to it. Bridget had probably taken it by now.

In it, on a page that had been charred but not destroyed, there had been a picture of a creature: half-man, half-horse. It had seemed awful and magnificent. The creature hovering over him now was only one of those things.

Callum tightened his hold on the litter.

The creature's outer nostrils flared. "You are afraid." It turned its head slightly towards Callum, its blind eyes not quite looking at him. "Many times in the past have the Daevyn sent their warriors to our dens, but seldom have we caught them so easily. And seldom have they been as frightened as you."

Callum struggled to speak. The air in the tunnel was dry and his throat was coated with dust. "I'm not Daevyn."

The creature let out a series of clicks that sounded eerily like laughter. "No? You wear their carapace and you speak their words. Do you think the gru'Esh so easily taken in?"

Callum didn't know how to explain all that had happened to him in the last two days. He merely repeated, "I'm not Daevyn. I'm Human."

To Callum's horror, the gru'Esh suddenly leaned its torso down over his body and, opening its outer nostrils, sniffed deeply. It straightened up and let out a bewildering assortment of clicks and buzzes which were answered in kind by more gru'Esh up and down the tunnel.

The creature turned back to Callum and spoke to him again in Brydge. "Your body confirms your speech. You do not lie. Why then does a Human come to the gru'Esh in the guise of the Daevyn? Who are you, and what is your business in the Warrens?"

Callum painfully moved his head. In the dim light of the underground air, he could make out a black gru'Esh shape before him, carrying one end of the litter with its shoulder-arms. There were more behind it, and the sound of movement in the other direction told Callum that he was in the centre of a long line of marching gru'Esh.

"My name's Callum Swift. I got here..." Callum stopped short for a moment, surprised at the realization that it had only been a day since the lightning had deposited him and Jingwei on the plains of Tranthaea. Looking around himself now, he decided to leave Jingwei out of the story.

"I only just got here yesterday. The Daevyn took me in. When they said they were going to attack the forest I joined up. Then there was an attack by some great flying monster and I fell into the tunnels by accident. And now I'm here."

The gru'Esh creature remained silent as the column continued moving. The crunching of rock and dirt under clawed feet echoed down the passage and was swallowed up by the distance.

Callum suddenly noticed that the air was getting brighter and thicker again. His head began to pound less violently as he breathed deeply. He saw that the gru'Esh around him were closing their bulbous eyes, sealing them with a hard, spherical lid, and were grabbing handfuls of dirt from the floor and walls and packing it into their nostrils. At first, Callum was disgusted. Even he'd never been *that* dirty. But then he remembered that these beings lived underground, in the dim, diluted air. He guessed that the dirt somehow filtered the air, making it darker or thinner or somehow more suited to gru'Esh anatomy.

Soon the walls around Callum fell away as the line of gru'Esh passed out of the tunnel onto a large stone bridge that soared over a magnificent ravine which cut deep into the ground. Its jagged walls were weathered and worn and impressed into them was the history of Tranthaea; strata of varying thicknesses and colours were packed one on top of the other. Browns, reds, and oranges climbed one another to the surface, each honouring an era long past. Callum leaned out to look below him and saw that the canyon's walls faded down into obscurity, connected by a series of massive bridges that ran across the gorge at varying angles and depths. Over a kilometre above him another bridge spanned the ravine on the surface, and above that was the sky.

It seemed very far away.

Callum watched his captor pat dirt onto its face and grew nervous as he realized that the gru'Esh were planning on crossing the bridge with their eyes closed.

The creature beside him inhaled a short *snuff* of air through its soil filter. "Do not fear our path. We are not limited in our senses, as you are, Human. We sense many things that you cannot. Our way is sure, and your journey safe."

The gru'Esh flared its outer nostrils again and adjusted its course on the bridge, centring itself. A cascade of pebbles and dust rained down from the canyon walls above and it cocked its head as if listening to their passing.

"You say the Daevyn ride for the forest?"

"That's where they were headed when I saw them last." The gru'Esh creature was silent for a moment, as if absorbing the information. Soon enough the column passed out of the ravine and back into the darkness of the tunnel system. Callum waited while his eyes readjusted.

Eventually the black gru'Esh spoke again.

"So, the Daevyn have gone to war against Huon Arrahl. The great top-dweller race has indeed fallen from its path." It extended a hand, palm up, towards Callum while its chest-arms quickly freed him from the litter, the claws snipping neatly through the bindings. "I am mi'Orha, Clan Leader of the je'Esh, third tribe of the gru'Esh. Your coming to our people may be a blessing."

Unsure of how to respond, Callum tentatively raised his hand and touched it to the palm that was extended towards him. It was apparently the right thing to do, as mi'Orha dropped its hand after they touched. Callum rested back down and wondered at his luck. Peaceful world or not, surely not everyone he met would be so eager to welcome him as a friend.

mi'Orha turned forward again as its people continued to shuffle along the corridor. "I lead my people to a Tribal Congress. The clans are faced with a terrible danger, and so the gru'Esh will decide our fate together. Your words may bring knowledge and guidance to our decisions. You will join us."

It wasn't a question. Callum scrunched his forehead and then grimaced in pain. "Do I have a choice?"

mi'Orha's mouth opened and two lines of teeth slid out of its black gums to form a gruesome smile. "Of course. If you prefer, we could leave you here."

Callum closed his eyes. The blackness behind his eyelids was only slightly darker than that of the seemingly unending tunnel.

"Let's go to a meeting."

mi'Orha's teeth *snicked* back into their sheaths. "Indeed."

Jingwei leaned her head back against the rock wall. The giant cavern echoed with the sound of hundreds of gru'Esh conversations. Whistles, clicks, and buzzes filled the cave as the members of the various clans greeted one another and began to speculate about the upcoming Congress.

She didn't know how to feel about her situation. The fear she had been hiding since she had arrived in this world was now buried behind layers of exhaustion and pain; she didn't know if she could dig it out even if she tried. Her wrist still ached, but she had torn off a long strip of her cloak to use as a tourniquet and it felt more secure, though any movement still shot jolts of pain through her arm.

Her ankle was swollen now as well, but her headache was mostly gone, except when she opened her eyes, or closed them, or breathed too deeply. The long trip from the surface in the Korrahl Forest had agitated her limp until her large, grey captor had recognized her pain and allowed her to ride side-saddle on its rigid back through the dark maze of tunnels. When the space around her had finally opened into a lit chamber, Jingwei had been treated to the sight of hundreds of gru'Esh scurrying hurriedly about.

There were more grey gru'Esh, just like her guard, but also represented were black, brown, and red. Aside from their colouring, Jingwei found that they were virtually indistinguishable from one another, save that their chests were covered in armoured plates that seemed to be arrayed in different patterns depending on the clan, but the interlocking pieces were so intricately connected that from a distance, the pattern was unreadable.

Her captor had set her down against the wall and skittered off to find its Clan Leader. In its haste it dropped its torso parallel to the ground and used its chest-arms as a third pair of legs. It drove into the crowd and was quickly lost from view.

Jingwei took the break to look around. The cavern was massive. It was hollowed out of dull red and blue stone that intermingled in swirls and layers on the walls. The dusty floor was raked downward towards a flat circular area at the base that looked almost like a stage, but instead of having seats or boxes like in a theatre or stadium, gigantic boulders and cave formations twisted around one another and rose to the ceiling, creating a naturally-divided viewing gallery carved from the rock. The entire cavern was roofed by a ceiling of stone which was peppered with holes that allowed some of the bright air of the surface to filter in, lighting the cavern from above, but dimming to a comfortable level by the time it reached the ground.

Jingwei hadn't realized that they'd ascended so close to the surface again. She gazed up at the tiny holes that opened into the bright space far above her and wished for a way out.

Out of the mass of noise and movement before her stepped a large grey gru'Esh. It approached Jingwei on four legs, followed closely by the guard that had brought her here.

"You are Jingwei Li, Human. I am br'Atakh, Clan Leader of the po'Esh, first tribe of the gru'Esh."

It paused, flaring its nostrils. It took Jingwei a second to realize it was waiting for a response.

"Sure." That seemed sufficiently polite, seeing as they had kidnapped her.

"You have news of the surface. News of the Daevyn, and of Huon Arrahl."

br'Atakh didn't seem like much of a talker to Jingwei. She decided not to answer its questions until she got a few answers of her own.

"Is that why you brought me here? Because I might have information? Well, I might *trade* some information with you. But I wouldn't expect much more than that from me. Not until you tell me why you dragged me underground, halfway across the world, against my will!"

br'Atakh held up its shoulder-arms, palms forward in a defensive position. "We are sorry for your treatment. We have need of your knowledge. Once you have spoken, you may go."

Jingwei rolled her eyes, but inside she was applying mental pressure to the box of emotions and fears that had suddenly dug itself up and now threatened to burst open with every word. "Oh, sure. Look, I've seen this movie, and it always ends with the heroine being eaten by the alien monsters," she said with strained nonchalance.

br'Atakh's emotionless face somehow managed to look shocked. "We do not eat Humans!" It backed up, its nostrils flaring in disgust. "I will speak with you no more until the Tribal Congress begins. Perhaps then you will understand our need."

It rushed off into the mob of gru'Esh, which was rapidly growing as the creatures continued to stream in from tunnel entrances all around the cavern.

Jingwei turned to the gru'Esh that had found her. "So, you're vegetarians too? Nice to finally meet somebody here that doesn't eat animals." She suddenly wondered what Huon Arrahl would say to her vegetarianism. Would the forest be offended that she didn't eat meat?

The gru'Esh spoke. "I am gru'Esh. I eat what the ground provides. Leaves in the early season, fnark in the middle season, gru'Esh in the late season, if I am lucky enough to survive to mate."

Jingwei looked up at her captor, speechless. She decided she didn't want to know.

Her gaze travelled across the cavern. Her eye was caught by another large group of gru'Esh entering from a tunnel. This group was black, and their numbers poured into the viewing area, darkening the colour palette of the room.

Suddenly, Jingwei saw a flash of blue amidst the black, and there was Callum, still wrapped in his royal blue cloak, his red hair practically glowing in the dim light.

She tried to stand, but her ankle protested, and she settled back down against the wall when she realized that Callum was being brought over to her.

Callum landed next to Jingwei with a thump and a groan. As much as she had suffered in the past day, it looked as though he had been through worse. His hair was matted with dried blood that seemed as though it had more than one source. His palms and knees were skinned and scabbed over, and his clothes had been torn to rags. He was still favouring his ribs as he tried to make himself comfortable, and she self-consciously tried to hide her broken wrist from him, feeling outclassed.

He frowned at her when he noticed her movement. "Alright, Jingwei? What happened to you?"

In spite of herself Jingwei laughed out loud. "What happened to me? What happened to you! Look at you!

You look like you died, and someone brought you back to life just to kill you again!"

Callum chuckled and winced. "Well, it's been a rough day." His eyes met hers and softened. "But really, are you alright? Lemme see your arm."

Jingwei reluctantly allowed him to examine her wrist, exclaiming whenever he reached a tender spot.

Satisfied, Callum slumped back. "Well," he said blandly, "it's not pretty, but neither of us is dead yet."

"The day isn't over." Jingwei pointed out, nodding down at the natural amphitheatre. "Do you know what's going on?"

"Only bits and bobs. mi'Orha – that's the Clan Leader of the je'Esh – told me that the gru'Esh are facing some sort of danger, and they think I... we," he amended, "might be able to help get it sorted, or tell them something new. I dunno how."

"That's about all I know too." The gru'Esh were settling into the viewing area now, whirring and clicking up a storm. Callum and Jingwei could see mi'Orha and br'Atakh down in the centre area with a bright red gru'Esh. They were standing silently next to one another, obviously waiting for another party to arrive before they began.

Callum took the opportunity to question Jingwei on what had happened to her. He listened with surprise at her story, at first disbelieving. But soon he was nodding and interjecting the events of his own day as the two of them tried to put the pieces together.

"... and that's when they brought me over to you," Callum finished.

"But that still doesn't explain why they brought us here, and why they're all gathering in the first place."

Callum shifted against the wall and grunted. "mi'Orha told me a bit about that. Why they're meeting."

Jingwei raised her eyebrow and waited for him to continue.

"There are four gru'Esh tribes. They only meet once a year, normally, to..." Callum blushed, "to mate, and to fight."

Jingwei lifted her other brow in surprise. "I hope that's not why we're here!"

"No!" Callum shifted uncomfortably again. "They gather once a year to battle, and after they battle, the survivors eat the defeated, and then only mate with members of other tribes."

"Why only the other tribes?"

"Well, from what I understand, the tribes aren't just family groups; each tribe is its own gender. Four genders and no matter who they fancy, they can't all mate with one another. The je'Esh, the black ones who caught me, can only mate with the an'Esh, those are the red ones, and the po'Esh, the grey ones that found you. The an'Esh can only mate with the black je'Esh and the grey po'Esh, and the po'Esh can mate with any other tribe. But the ka'Esh can only mate with the po'Esh. They're the most desperate at the Tribal Congress, and so they're the most warlike of the tribes." Callum looked up and saw the confusion on Jingwei's face. "Yeah, I didn't really catch on either. But mi'Orha told me that they meet, fight, eat, and mate once a year and they only ever have a Congress to talk about emergencies that endanger all the gru'Esh. mi'Orha said that they haven't had an emergency Congress since any living gru'Esh can remember."

Callum leaned his head back against the wall and closed his eyes. "And that's what this meeting is."

"So what's the emergency?" Jingwei didn't really care. She didn't like being anyone's prisoner, especially not a race that only met up to fight, eat, and mate. What about just being social? Hadn't these gru'Esh ever heard of Charades?

"mi'Orha wouldn't tell me. It said I would hear and understand at the Congress." Callum struggled to sit up. "Which looks like it's about to begin."

Jingwei looked down at the floor of the amphitheatre. The fourth Clan Leader had arrived, heading a long procession of chocolate brown gru'Esh from the largest tunnel entrance. It marched up to the other three leaders and greeted them with a cacophony of noises that carried up through the chamber.

The rest of the brown ka'Esh found places to settle amongst the crowd and soon a stillness rose from the crowd.

Callum's captor, mi'Orha, stepped forward. Its voice echoed throughout the cavern, the rock structures amplifying the sound through the thick air. "I offer welcome to the gru'Esh, and to our guests, the two Human top-dwellers. For their sake we speak this Congress in Brydge." It drummed an arrhythmic beat on its torso with its shoulder-arms. "I am mi'Orha, Clan Leader of the je'Esh, third tribe of the gru'Esh."

mi'Orha stepped back and the grey creature that had spoken to Jingwei took its place, beating a different tattoo. "I am br'Atakh, Clan Leader of the po'Esh, first tribe of the gru'Esh."

The red gru'Esh took its turn. "I am g'Nharr, Clan Leader of the an'Esh, second tribe of the gru'Esh."

Finally the brown gru'Esh stepped forward. It pounded on its chest and released a long string of clicks and buzzes, then fell silent. Jingwei's guard bent its torso down close to the Humans and translated. "He says, 'I am v'Aros, Clan Leader of the ka'Esh, fourth tribe of the gru'Esh, long may it hold the Warrens.'"

The other three Clan Leaders flared their nostrils at the ka'Esh's addition to their recitation, but otherwise their impassive faces remained unreadable.

v'Aros continued on in its own language, "We have no need of Humans here. The business of the gru'Esh is no business of the top-dwellers. Even the Human Soil Keeper, that pathetic creature, knows better than to interfere with our affairs."

mi'Orha quickly defended himself in Brydge. "The Humans have information of the world above and news of the other races of Tranthaea. They are not here to interfere, but to supplement our knowledge."

The grey po'Esh leader who had brought Jingwei interjected, "You would not hear their words? Though they may save the gru'Esh? Are you so proud, v'Aros?"

v'Aros turned towards the other Clan Leaders and spewed a clatter of noise at them, which Jingwei's guard politely declined to translate.

The crowd began to buzz and whir; many of the brown ka'Esh drummed their shoulder-arms loudly on their chest carapaces.

g'Nharr of the red an'Esh shouted over the din. "Silence!" It waited until the noise died down, then continued, "the an'Esh will hear their words. If the ka'Esh will not, let them be deaf as well as blind."

v'Aros made a grumbling noise in the back of its throat, but didn't object again.

mi'Orha looked up at the Humans. "Callum Swift and Jingwei Li. You have been brought here to speak to the gru'Esh in a time of great danger. Will you share your knowledge with us and help to save our people?"

Callum and Jingwei exchanged glances. Neither one knew what danger the gru'Esh was talking about, but they didn't seem to have many choices. After an awkward silence Callum spoke up.

"We'll tell you what we can. But first, you've got to tell us what this danger is."

v'Aros took a few quick steps away from the other Clan Leaders. It spoke a flurry of words in the gru'Esh language, which the guard translated, "And where is the knowledge that you speak of, mi'Orha? Perhaps it has drained out of his head, alongside his life-blood?"

mi'Orha ignored v'Aros. It stepped past the ka'Esh Clan Leader and spoke to the Humans and the crowd before them.

"The Warrens are our home. They are our strength. We live, breathe, mate, and die in the Warrens. They are ours to defend and to extend. And so we have done, and so the gru'Esh before us have done." The crowd interrupted to drum their chests in agreement. mi'Orha paused, then continued, "But now there is a danger to us, to our children and to our homes."

It suddenly leaned down and scooped up a rock and threw it with great strength far across the cavern. The rock hurtled through the air, struck a dirt wall, and fell to the floor, bringing with it a small avalanche of loose dust and gravel.

"The tunnels are collapsing. The dirt is drying and our fortifications are weakening. Cities and bridges that were once strong now crumble under our feet. The filters we build to darken our air fail us, and even now we sit in pain, our eyes burning in the light."

mi'Orha rolled opened its eyelids to show the white eyes underneath. Jingwei thought she could feel their blind gaze.

"All the tribes have lost warriors and children to this threat." mi'Orha closed its eyes again. "The water in the land is going. With it goes our tunnels, our cities, our lives. The Warrens are in danger. You are Human. You are not

Daevyn, nor are you Aru Len. You have met with Huon Arrahl and one of the Keepers. Can you tell us where the water has gone? Can you save the gru'Esh?"

The crowd was silent and still. All faces had turned to the Humans at the top of the amphitheatre, their blind eyes closed tightly and their sensitive nostrils open, searching for hope.

Callum swallowed. "We don't know where the water's going." The mass of gru'Esh started to grumble. v'Aros cocked his head and took a step forward. Callum hurried on, "But the Daevyn are troubled too! The plains above are dry and the lightning fires are getting harder to contain and control."

Jingwei interrupted, "I spoke to Huon Arrahl. It's worried too! There was almost a war between it and the Daevyn over water. They don't know where it's going. Just that it's gone."

v'Aros unsheathed its teeth and exploded into a diatribe of gru'Esh rhetoric. Its voice carried up and over the amphitheatre, but was soon drowned out by the thunder of noise coming from the crowd. The guard had stopped translating and instead had moved in front of Callum and Jingwei, flexing its arms and flaring its nostrils.

On the floor, g'Nharr and br'Atakh were arguing with v'Aros while mi'Orha attempted to pacify the crowd. It was clear to Jingwei, even without translation that v'Aros was attempting to stir the crowd up against them in the hopes of starting a brawl. According to Callum, the brown ka'Esh had the least chance of successfully mating. Jingwei guessed that it would take any opportunity it got to start the *fight, eat, and mate* process.

And it looked like it was going to work.

The brown ka'Esh were spread out among all the gru'Esh, and were belligerently pushing and yelling at members of the other tribes. The more peaceful po'Esh were retreating down to the stage area, most likely to protect the Clan Leaders from the coming violence.

Callum peered past the body of their po'Esh guard, who looked now as though his job had changed from watching them to protecting them.

Suddenly, as if reacting to a signal, violence erupted in the gallery. gru'Esh from all tribes began battling, swinging some sort of weapons over their heads as they strived to survive the fight and win the right to mate. It took Callum a moment to realize what the gru'Esh were using for weapons; they were the chest arms of fallen gru'Esh.

He watched in horror as a ka'Esh warrior tore the arms out of the chest-sockets of a smaller po'Esh and then use them to duel with an an'Esh while the amputated po'Esh escaped to find a set of his own weapons somewhere else. With what seemed to be an apologetic look in their direction their guard abandoned them to join in the fracas and was soon wading through the battle with weapons of its own raised over its head.

Callum started as he felt a tug on his arm.

Jingwei was beside him, whispering in his ear, "Now's our chance! Come on, let's go, while they're busy killing each other!"

Callum glanced back at the fighting mob, then at the tunnel entrance behind them, and then down at his torn and bloody clothes.

Jingwei threw his arm over her shoulder and grabbed onto his waist, careful not to touch any of his bruised ribs.

"Ok, Old-Timer. I won't bump your head if you don't jiggle my wrist."

Callum grinned through the pain and removed his arm, placing it instead around Jingwei's waist. He lifted gently and took some of the weight off her sprained ankle.

"Let's go, Junior."

Together, they hobbled unnoticed into the blackness of the tunnel, leaving the crashing sounds of claws and carapaces behind.

Chapter Fourteen:
The Search

The line of Quenchers moved slowly into the foothills of the mountains, riding parallel to the forest's boundary just to the south. Behind them stretched the wide open plains, a tan expanse fading off into the distance, illuminated by the harsh afternoon air and the almost invisible flashes of lightning. Before them rose the Mountains of Du Garrah.

The mountain range ran to the north and south as far as the eye could see. Black walls of hard rock cut the sky, rising sharply from the prairies and from the forest to form huge cliffs. Low foothills rose around the base of the cliffs but terminated at the sheer black walls. The mountains peaks disappeared into thick banks of white and grey clouds that crowned the range for its entire length.

Those clouds were the home of the Aru Len. Ythen knew that the sky people had long been allies of the Daevyn, in name if not in fact. The Aru Len ruled the skies as the Daevyn ruled the plains, and they had long ago come to a mutual respect and understanding regarding the boundaries of their worlds. The Daevyn did not push for expansion into the mountains, where gathered the clouds in which the Aru Len made their home, and the Aru Len supplied the Daevyn with servants and breeders, to help balance the strong Human element of the Daevyn heritage.

As they wound their way through the foothills, Ythen mulled over what he knew about the Aru Len; the People of the Sky.

Their society was a caste system, with two levels. The Aru Faylen ruled over the Aru Elen, whom Jingwei had called fairies. Ythen had never understood why the Aru Faylen were the ruling class, but then the Aru Faylen had always seemed more alien than the humanoid Aru Elen. Whatever it was that had given them control, it was strong. The Aru Elen were allowed no clothing, and no language of their own. They had no tongues, but Ythen had never asked if they were born without them, or had them removed. They lived in absolute servitude to their masters the Aru Faylen: the Masters of the Sky.

Yriel interrupted his thoughts. She shouted out his name as she rode back to the line from her forward position as scout.

"Ythen! We've arrived at the ravine. The Crossing still holds."

Ythen nodded curtly, inwardly breathing a sigh of relief. He had not traveled this far east since his days in training. Back then, all the future Quenchers had taken a tour of the plains' borders, from the tree-line of the Korrahl Forest in the south, to the Mountains of Du Garrah in the east, to the great northern water – the Sea of Nalani – and then around to the west where the plains bordered a strip of marshes that withered away into the dunes of the western desert.

He still remembered The Crossing from that journey. It was a large bridge that connected the two sides of a wide and deep ravine which ate its way kilometres down into the ground, its bottom swallowed up by distance and darkness. The ravine was stitched by multiple bridges near this location, each lower than the next, creating what looked like an enormous, crooked ladder that an ancient giant could use to climb out of the depths onto the surface of the world. The Daevyn called the multilayered joining The Roots of Tranthaea, and the highest bridge, The Crossing.

Yriel rode silently behind Ythen now, allowing him to take the lead as he made his way out onto The Crossing. In an unexpected return to the dynamics of their lost relationship she had been gracious and cooperative since agreeing to put aside their differences to focus on finding Jingwei. Ythen was grateful for her support and had returned the gesture in kind. They had a job to do, and would be stronger together. Losing Callum to the thranvorl had been bad enough. He would not lose Jingwei too.

For a moment his mind held an image of the short Human girl. There was something about her that had captured him; her boldness, her assurance, her good humour. She was so different from him; where he was ruled by protocol and tradition she was guided by her passions, fiery and quick to act.

So like Yriel, and yet so different.

He put Jingwei from his mind, confused and unwilling to admit that there may be more than one reason he felt compelled to find her.

The raeas glided cautiously out onto the stone bridge. They had been able to catch enough of the skittish mounts to send back the dead and wounded to the city and still have a sufficient number to push forward at a reasonable speed. The animals had still not fully recovered from the vicious attack of the thranvorl; they twisted and shivered under the Quenchers as they rode out onto the bridge. As he had the last time he'd been here, Ythen found himself wishing that The Crossing's creators had thought to build railings on the sides.

He heard a murmuring from behind him. He swiveled to see what was going on and saw a long line of green faces as the young Quenchers rode out onto The Crossing. More than one looked as if they were going to be sick as they tried not to look down over the edges into the distant blackness of the ravine below.

Ythen sighed. They would feel more comfortable walking on their own feet, leading their raeas by the reins, but he knew that none of them would ever do it while he rode. They didn't want to look weak in front of the other Quenchers.

Ythen sat up straight in his saddle and swung his right leg back over his raeas, dismounting smoothly. Without looking behind at his troops he continued forward, but smiled slightly as he heard the scuffling sounds of multiple riders landing firmly on the thick stone bridge.

Yriel let out a loud snort and stayed in her seat as they travelled the expansive bridge. Ythen's smile broadened. Maybe she hadn't changed *too* much.

The heady thudding of many pairs of feet echoed across the canyon. Dust and dirt that had collected on The Crossing over time was disturbed and now drifted down into the depths of the ravine. At one point Ythen peered over the edge and thought he saw movement on one of the bridges that spanned the gap farther down into the darkness of the gorge, but couldn't be sure. He forced himself to dismiss his curiosity. There were other, more important things to focus on.

He continued across, his eyes fixed on the encroaching tree-line of the forest that they had followed from the west: a forest so old that it was split by this ancient division in the land, and before he realized it he had reached the other side.

Once his feet were again crunching through the dirt, Ythen remounted his raeas and continued on without a word. The path before him led up through the foothills that collected at the base of the mountains, and wove in and out of the trees ahead. He hoped to find an Aru Len where the path ran into the walls, who could pass on his request to the Elders. The Elders were the governing body of the Aru Len, and their representative was known to the Daevyn as a Delevate.

Ythen hoped that the Delevate would not only speak to the Elders on his behalf, but that they would be willing to carry a message to Kala, the Spark Keeper, as well.

The trees in the forest that now spread across their path had changed as the Quenchers had ridden east, and were no longer the thin, grey saplings that lived to the south of Yshaar. These trunks were thick and wide, with gnarled brown bark and leaves that were a golden-green in colour and seemed to almost glow in the light of the air. Now that they had traversed The Crossing, the forest rose with the foothills, pressing towards the north so that the Quenchers were forced to pass under the low, heavy branches of the large, squat trees.

Ythen urged his riders to move along at a faster pace, anxious to get out from under the pressure of Korrahl. Perhaps he was imagining it, but it seemed to him that the forest had eyes, and the spot between his after-wings itched with its invisible gaze.

Do not become paranoid, Firebrand, he told himself. *The journey is nothing but steps towards the destination. Keep your mind clear for what is yet to come.*

Ahead, small breaks in the trees allowed the Quenchers an ever-more imposing view of the black walls of Du Garrah. The file of riders behind Ythen was chillingly quiet. They darted their eyes among the trees and forward towards the mountains, their fists flexing loosely over their Firedart generators in nervous anticipation. There was a brooding atmosphere of tension among them, as if too much pressure was being applied to their collective psyche, at first so slowly that it was hardly noticeable, but now threatening to overwhelm the fatigued warriors that had already been through so much in so short a time.

The Quenchers began to bunch together, abandoning their single file format. Ythen sent Yriel back to them to keep them focused. He flipped his hood up and forced his raeas to continue forward, its silver shape weaving silently through the trees. Ahead, he saw the edge of the forest slipping in and out of view.

Soon Yriel's voice startled him, coming from close behind and to his right, "We should not bring them to the representative. The Aru Len Delevate will not look kindly upon favours asked of them when the askers are backed by a war host."

Ythen grimaced. She was right, and he should have thought of it. His raeas broke through the tree-line out into the open foothills again.

"I will tell them to stop here. You and I will continue on."

Ythen watched as Yriel drooped her head in exhausted deference and he wondered when she had last slept. Certainly not during her night in the forest, if her stories of its malevolence were true. He turned his mount and surveyed his riders as they all trooped safely out of the forest. Once they were accounted for, he issued his orders and he and Yriel set out alone towards the mountain wall while the Quenchers set up a temporary camp.

Soon the camp was behind them. Here in the open foothills, the prairie grasses had turned into shrubbery and scrub brush that laid a thick carpet over the ground. Ythen glanced down as his raeas glided over the greenery. Had they not been mounted, they would have been wading through waist-deep thorn bushes. Not for the first time, Ythen was thankful that the Daevyn had domesticated the plains-dwelling beast.

They continued on in silence for a few more minutes, watching the black wall of the mountains steadily approaching. As they crested the sloping rise of the final hill Ythen came to a stop, with Yriel beside him.

There, hovering at the base of the mountains was the Delevate.

It had been years since Ythen had had any dealings directly with a representative of the Aru Len ruling class, and upon seeing one again he realized that he was still fascinated by their physiology.

The Aru Faylen had a roundish, lumpy body that was about half a metre in diameter. There were no visible sensory organs; no eyes, ears, mouth, or nose, but a thick stalk rose from the body and was connected to three large, bony, whirling blades that acted as rotors, keeping the Aru Faylen in the air. The metre-long blades were made of dull white calcium; hard, but porous and as they spun the holes in them were opened and closed with small fleshy sphincters that took in the information and nutrition the creatures needed to survive.

As Ythen and Yriel rode down the hill towards it, the Aru Faylen rose slightly in the air, its rotors changing speed and pitch to a higher hum. It opened some pores, allowing the air to pass through them, creating musical sounds that soon distinguished themselves into words.

"I greet you, Ythen, First Quencher of the Daevyn, and Yriel, Daughter of the Flame-Bearer. I am Throm, Delevate for the Aru Len. What tidings do you wish me to carry?"

Ythen dismounted and gave a small bow, making sure to stay clear of the spinning blades.

"We wish to ask for the help of the Aru Len."

The hollow sounds of Throm's voice hummed against the black rock behind him. "The Aru Len are always pleased to serve. What is your request, that I may bring it up to the Elders?"

Ythen answered, "We need to find someone. Someone we believe is lost in the Korrahl Forest. Our numbers are too few and the forest, too large. Will you ask the Elders if they will provide us with eyes in the air?"

Throm was silent except for the humming of his blades. Finally he responded.

"Is it the Humans that you have lost to the forest? The boy and girl?"

Ythen was surprised. "How do you know about them?"

Throm was quick with his answer. "We are the Masters of the Sky. We watch over all of Tranthaea. We may not have eyes, yet still we can see. Is it the Humans that you have lost?"

Ythen hated to admit his failures to the Aru Faylen. It was bad enough having to do it with Yriel. He swallowed his pride.

"One of them. The girl. The boy was killed in battle with a thranvorl."

The two Daevyn heard a noise that was the Aru Faylen equivalent of sucking in one's breath. Throm's hovering pitch suddenly became higher and whining. The Aru Len had a healthy fear of the immense sky predators.

"An unfortunate loss. There are so few Humans in Tranthaea." He lifted up higher off the ground, slowly beginning to rise above their heads. "I will take your request to the Elders."

"Wait!" Yriel stepped forward quickly. "Can you also inform Kala? Her home is at the summit of the mountains, is it not?"

Throm sank slowly back down to his original hovering position. "It is." He banked sideways to address Ythen. "First Quencher, do you wish for the eyes of the Spark Keeper to be on the forest as well?"

Ythen hesitated. Kala had not been receptive to the Humans in Yshaar, and he doubted that she would be more so now. He caught sight of Yriel beside him, her hands clenched tightly together, her eyes pleading.

He gave in. "Yes, if you can ask her."

Throm bobbed in acquiescence. "Of course. And for this favour, what shall be my reward?"

Ythen's blond hair was whipping around his head in the draft from Throm's blades. He smoothed it down in confusion. "Reward? You are the Delevate. It is your duty to bring messages to the top of the mountain."

"To the Elders, yes. But I have no duty to the Spark Keeper. A favour demands repayment in kind."

"Well, what do you want of me?" Ythen was getting frustrated. Jingwei was still missing, and this Aru Faylen was haggling over price!

"Just what I said. A favour in kind. Someday, I may have a need. A need that a person of influence, such as the First Quencher of the Daevyn, is able to satisfy. Do we have a deal?"

Ythen thought carefully for a second. The Aru Faylen would speak to Kala for a favour from the First Quencher. And once Jingwei was found, Ythen was going to give his title to Yriel. With a little luck, if he timed it right, this favour would cost him nothing, and end in the recovery of Jingwei.

Finally, something was going his way.

"I agree to your terms."

Without another word Throm took off, shooting high into the air with incredible speed. In less than thirty seconds he had vanished into the clouds that crowned the mountains.

Ythen and Yriel remounted their raeas and rode swiftly and silently back to the camp the remaining Quenchers had set up. A warm fire was burning, and they were greeted by the smell of roasting fnark. The small underground-dwelling animals lived encased within a single shell that was covered in small thick bristles. The bristles helped push it slowly through the dirt. It had a large hole at one end of its body for ingesting dirt and a collection of small ones at the other for excreting the same, minus any nutrients it needed. Ythen had never particularly enjoyed the gru'Esh delicacy, as he found it to be too spicy, but food was food and a Quencher couldn't be picky this far from Yshaar.

The air had grown considerably darker by the time their request was answered. A lookout reported seeing a red light falling from the mountaintops just as Ythen heard the droning of hundreds of wings passing far over their campsite. He woke a dozing Yriel who muttered something about an icy beach, and the two of them grabbed burning branches and rushed back to the wall. As they arrived, the red light the lookout had seen resolved itself into the shape of Kala touching down; her necklace of fire made her crimson hair shimmer brightly in the darkness. Throm descended beside her, the downdraft of his blades blowing out the torches and leaving them all standing in Kala's glow.

The Spark Keeper didn't hesitate to speak. "Firebrand. You have killed one Human, and lost another, is that correct?"

Ythen bowed his head but did not speak.

"I see." Kala turned to Yriel. "And where were you when these tragedies of leadership were taking place?"

"I was following the girl until the trees forced me out of the forest, Spark Keeper. I returned in time to defeat a thranvorl, saving the lives of the First Quencher and his troops." Yriel kept her eyes on her feet as she spoke, but Ythen could see the small smile of pride on her face.

Kala's mouth twitched. "Very good. Perhaps the Daevyn are not lost after all." She turned to Throm. "Your people will search the forest?"

Throm answered, the musical tones of his voice somehow proclaiming deference. "They will, Spark Keeper. The Aru Faylen search from above, while the Aru Elen search within the trees themselves. We will find the Human girl for the Daevyn."

Kala arched her eyebrow. The glow from her necklace cast dancing shadows across her face.

"No, Delevate. You will find her for me."

Ythen looked up, confused.

Kala continued. "When the Human is discovered, bring her to my palace. I have plans for her—"

Kala interrupted herself when she noticed that Ythen had trained his Firedart on her. She smiled, her white teeth glittering fiercely. "Kindly lower your weapon, Firebrand. You will find no allies here."

Ythen saw Throm hovering just past Kala's shoulder, silently assenting to her will. Beside him, Yriel had turned towards him, her face screwed up with indecision.

"Yriel!" Ythen didn't mean to sound like he was begging, but his voice seemed to form itself around his desperation. "She is betraying the Daevyn!"

Kala smoothly stepped forward and reached out to Yriel,

turning her cheek to look her in the eye and capture her full attention.

"Yriel Sparkcatcher," she said, "I have spoken frankly with you many times. The true potential of the Daevyn is known to you. But your mother and this... *boy*," she spat out the word, "will not allow them to reach it."

Ythen watched Yriel struggle to understand what the Spark Keeper was saying.

Kala continued, "There are plans in motion, plans that cannot be undone, and soon Tranthaea will be mine. Mine to give to whomever I feel worthy of its rule."

Yriel's face, which had seemed to be wavering between shock and awe, lit up at this. Kala smiled cruelly.

"I have watched your training since you were a little girl. I have even trained you myself. I taught you the truth of your people's past. You have the sure hand, the clear sight, and the firm mind of a ruler. I would give *you* Tranthaea. *I* find you worthy."

Kala spoke the last four words in a whisper, her lips almost brushing Yriel's ear. Ythen watched his compatriot's face as she lapped up the validation and began to show not the disgust he hoped for, but agreement instead.

Impossible, Ythen thought. Yriel had always wanted more. She had always felt as though she had missed out on her proper place. Even when they had been together she had not been shy about her feelings on the matter. But Ythen refused to believe that she would betray her own people just for the chance to rule.

Surely Yriel was not taken in by these promises. Surely she would not turn her back on her mother. Ythen flicked his eyes back over at Kala. The Aru Elen Keeper was ignoring him, her attention focused solely on the Flame-Bearer's daughter. Yriel remained silent, but her jaw was moving almost imperceptibly as she clenched her teeth in confusion and frustration.

He was sure that she would do her duty. If she was reminded of it.

"No!" Ythen gripped his Firedart, his palm squeezing gently on the generator. He was still speaking to Kala, but his eyes were now on Yriel. "Whatever use you have for the Humans, the Daevyn will see you stopped."

Yriel looked at him. In his gaze, she searched for any of the love that he used to feel for her. But instead of love she found desperation; instead of respect, hope.

Hope that she would be someone she was not.

Hope for a lie.

She felt the ties between them snap. She had been foolish to think of repentance, foolish to think that she should be the one to bend, to change. Her mind was strong, as Kala had said. She was the rightful ruler of the Daevyn, and he was a usurper. This boy had done nothing but play with her heart and steal her position. She could rescue the Daevyn from his weak leadership. She could show them all that she was able to do what was needed to keep the Daevyn strong. She turned towards Kala, who was offering her the world, and smiled through her tears.

She raised her Firedart and pointed it at Ythen's head.

Ythen's eyes widened in shock. He stuttered over the word before he spat out, "Traitor!"

"You are the traitor!" Yriel returned sharply as she stepped forward and cautiously undid the laces on Ythen's greaves, dropping his Firedart and Buckler onto the ground. "You have dishonoured the Daevyn with your weakness and failures. I will restore us to the greatness of our ancestors!"

Kala stepped forward and raised her hands towards Ythen, palms out. "Now, children. This is all very entertaining, but I have more important things to do." Yriel made as if to speak again, but Kala cut her off. "As do you."

Yriel hesitated and then nodded, her commitment complete.

Kala continued speaking as her palms began to glow. "Throm, as the Elders have decreed, you will find the Human, Jingwei Li. But once found, you will bring her to me. In response, I will not strike down your homes with fire. Bring her to me soon; I have several questions for her that cannot wait much longer."

The glow tightened into a form and the Spark Keeper's hands began to release slow-moving ropes of fire that wrapped themselves around Ythen in a large sphere.

"Yriel, you will take your rightful place as leader of the Quenchers. Return to Yshaar and tell the Flame-Bearer... well, just make up whatever story you like. I trust your judgement." She smiled again at Yriel, who glowed under her praise. "You will soon lead greater armies than those of the Daevyn, I promise you." With that cryptic statement, she turned back to Ythen.

A glowing ball of translucent fire now surrounded him. He cautiously reached out and tested it. It was warm to the touch, but did not burn. Nor did it give. He growled and threw his elbow against the bright wall of his prison, to no effect.

Kala chuckled lightly and twitched her index finger. The glowing ball expanded slightly, just out of his reach as he remained hovering in the centre.

Ythen stubbornly stretched out at the wall again, but the curved flames remained just out of his reach. He could *feel* them around him, as if they were a psychic prison as much as a physical one, but the walls in his mind were just as impenetrable as the one before his eyes.

He turned his gaze on the Spark Keeper. "Why do you do this? Kala! What has the Human girl done to you?!"

Kala lifted her hands slowly above her head. "Silly little boy. She has done nothing *to* me. It is what she can do *for* me that I am interested in."

With that, she flung her arms to the sky and the fireball prison hurtled upwards towards the clouds and the mountain summit, carrying Ythen inside.

Chapter Fifteen:
The Gully

Callum and Jingwei were hopelessly lost.

For the first few hours of their escape they had been lucky. The gru'Esh had remained in the Congress cavern; the only hints of their violent governance were the echoes of clacking and thudding that whistled down the passages behind the fleeing Humans.

The two of them had limped quietly out of the cave and into a long tunnel that darkened quickly as it descended. They were careful not to make any noise, although they both knew that if the gru'Esh came searching for them, the cave-dwellers' heightened senses would be able to detect them soon enough, regardless.

They had wandered through the Warrens aimlessly at first, hoping that whatever tunnel they were in would miraculously lead them to the surface, but after the fifth time Callum had tripped on a rock and fallen painfully to the ground, they'd adjusted their plan. They'd decided that at every point where their tunnel intersected another, they would go a few metres in every direction. The passage they would choose to follow would be whichever one seemed like it had the best chance of heading up.

They had spent hours scuffing blindly through the dirt, sometimes falling and bruising their already skinned knees and otherwise bumping their heads on the abruptly dipping ceiling.

Eventually, they'd sunk to the ground in exhaustion, numb to fear and pain. Callum had scratched a small hollow into the side of the tunnel wall with a rock and they'd pressed into it, huddling against one another for warmth in the cold dirt. They'd slept fitfully, each taking a turn on watch while the other dozed, wrapped in the tattered remains of their cloaks.

Jingwei woke up with a sharp rock sticking into her back. She grunted and reached around behind her, grabbing the rock and throwing it grumpily down the tunnel. It clattered to the ground, the noise of its passage reverberating into the darkness.

She frowned as reality began to creep into her senses. She had been having a very strange dream. In it, Jingwei had been standing on a beach. Before her, the water was deep and dark, and large waves were crashing soundlessly around her. Out on the water there had been an ice floe. Without a sound, it cracked in two, and as the two drifted apart from one another, she could see that standing on one was Callum, and on the other, Ythen. Both of them had been dressed in some kind of armour, and each had looked less like the boy she knew and more like a fierce warrior.

Then each of them began to glow. Ythen shone a bright yellow light, as bright as the sun this world didn't have, and Callum shone a vivid red that flickered like long-dead embers that have been reawoken by a slow breath, and the light caused the ice beneath their feet to begin melting, slowly at first, and then faster and faster, and soon pieces of ice were breaking off and falling into the sea around them with tremendous splashes. Jingwei had thrown out her hands to stop it. And it had worked, somehow. For a moment.

But then the ice had resumed melting and the floes beneath their feet began to gradually be swallowed up into the watery abyss beneath them, and as each boy began to plead with her she had realized that she could only choose to save one.

She'd heard a snort coming from behind her and had whipped around just in time to see the derisive face of Yriel Sparkcatcher standing there before the dream faded away...

Beside her, Callum was snoring gently. Jingwei frowned again. *Some guard.* She carefully reached over and flicked his ear.

He awoke with a start, sitting up suddenly and then groaning and wrapping his arms around his sore ribs.

"Wazzit? Are they coming?" His thick London accent was made all the more incomprehensible by the exhausted slur of waking.

Jingwei could just make out his haggard face in the dim air. "You tell me. You were sleeping!"

Callum gave her a wry look. "I was knackered! And it was my turn. You were on watch, remember?"

Jingwei cut off a retort. She considered for a moment, and then shrugged. "Oh well, they didn't find us yet, so no harm, no foul. What are you smirking at?" she demanded, seeing Callum struggling to keep a straight face.

"You could see that?" Callum looked around. "You could see me smiling!"

"Of course I could! And don't you think for a second that you can get away with laughing at me. For all you know, I was sleeping because I took extra shifts on watch so that you could rest—"

Callum interrupted her. "Pipe down! Think about it! You could see me smiling!"

Jingwei bit off another sassy remark. He was right. The tunnel was being slowly illuminated as the air in the tunnel got brighter.

"It must be morning! And we must be near the surface!" Callum uncurled himself, ignoring a loud rumbling in his stomach as he stood up excitedly. "Come on!"

Jingwei allowed him to help her up and together they slowly tramped down the passage, looking for a way out.

Soon the air was bright enough to see detail in the walls of the tunnel. Hard-packed clay and stone had given way to looser dirt and they could see roots dangling from the ceiling, some thick enough to belong to trees, others delicate enough for flowers.

"There." Jingwei pointed ahead. Just a little farther down was a hole in the roof of the passageway. A steep dirt embankment led up to it and it was criss-crossed with thick roots, but brightly lit air poured through into the tunnel.

They limped to it and Callum inspected the twist of roots that formed a sort of natural grating over the hole.

"I should be able to break enough of them, and then bob's-your-uncle." He reached up and took hold of one of the thinner roots and started to twist it.

A noise echoed towards them from down the tunnel. Jingwei was the first to turn and see the tall brown shape of a ka'Esh approaching. The panic of yesterday's escape from the violent Congress returned in full force as she grabbed hard onto Callum's arm and shrieked, her nails digging into his bicep.

v'Aros unsheathed its teeth as it approached. "Quiet, Human. Congress goes below. Law says v'Aros can eat bodies of enemies." Its Brydge was broken, but it got its point across. At this moment, thanks to the battle the Humans' presence had caused, none of the gru'Esh were vegetarian.

Callum had dropped his arms from the opening and now stepped in front of Jingwei, protecting her with his body. He had made the same move two days ago on the prairies and Jingwei had felt insulted. She had no such compunctions now.

"Help!" Jingwei didn't really believe that anyone would hear her, and even if they did, they might be just as likely to eat her as v'Aros was. But standing with her back to the wall, literally, she knew that she was out of options.

v'Aros stopped a few metres short of Callum's reach. It cocked its head to the side and its mouth turned down into a frown. It flared its outer nostrils. "You not afraid?" Its sightless eyes were turned towards Callum. "Blood pumps, body tightens. But in courage, not fear."

Callum set his jaw and pushed Jingwei farther up the slope towards the opening. mi'Orha had removed the First Flame-Bearer's canister from his Firedart when he had been captured and had never gotten around to giving it back. He was unarmed, but that wasn't going to stop him from doing what he could.

v'Aros continued, "We fight. Winner eats all." It took a step forward, lowering its torso to the ground in preparation for a lunge. Jingwei felt Callum take a deep breath and set himself.

v'Aros charged. Jingwei didn't scream this time, but braced herself against Callum's back. v'Aros' battle cry filled the tunnel.

The shout was joined, and then overwhelmed by a sudden new noise. Without warning, the passage around the charging gru'Esh crashed down around it, flooding the tunnel with dirt and dust.

Callum watched as rocks and stones poured down onto the gru'Esh Clan Leader, at first only slowing its rush, but soon halting it entirely, and finally burying it. One final boulder crashed down and entombed it completely.

Jingwei and Callum stood in amazement, unsure of what had just happened. Callum waved his hands in front of them, trying in vain to clear away the dust cloud while Jingwei stooped over in a fit of coughing. The collapsed section of the tunnel ended less than a metre from where the Humans stood and seemed localized over the gru'Esh's body.

They were not given much time to wonder. Seconds after v'Aros' body had been crushed, the roots that had covered the opening to the surface untwined themselves over the Humans' heads and, reaching down, twisted around the bodies of Callum and Jingwei and quickly raised them through the hole and out onto the surface.

The shining intensity of the air blinded them momentarily. After spending a full day and night in the near-blackness of the Warrens, the light seared into their eyes, making them pause their struggling as their vision slowly became accustomed to the brightness.

They were in a small clearing in the forest. The roots gently placed Callum and Jingwei down and released them, withdrawing to the hole in the ground and becoming still, once again barring the opening. Jingwei visually followed the line of the roots to the large brown tree trunks surrounding the clearing.

"Huon Arrahl?"

"Sorry, no." The deep voice came from behind them. Jingwei and Callum whirled around and saw that they were not alone.

Standing on the other side of the clearing were four people. Two were Aru Elen. Each of them was painted a creamy, butter yellow down the front that matched their glistening rear scales. Their mouths were hanging open in astonishment at the sudden and dramatic appearance of the two young Humans.

The two Aru Elen gave each other a quick look and suddenly spread their wings, shooting into the air, but before they could get more than a few metres off the ground the other two figures burst into action.

There was a flurry of activity. The ground beside the two figures erupted and rocks and dirt tumbled upwards, collapsing and reforming as they flowed into the air. Loose vines that were hanging from the tree branches suddenly gained life and shot out towards the fleeing Aru Elen in a cloud of whirling leaves, wrapping themselves around the flying creatures' legs and pulling them quickly back down to the ground.

The Aru Elen struggled, but the vines were too thick and too strong. Before they knew it, they had been bound firmly and deposited into a large cage that had been drawn up out of the ground. They peered through stone bars, their eyes wide with fright, their mouths gaping noiselessly.

Across the clearing, Callum and Jingwei sat motionless, watching the two free figures dust themselves off and walk over.

"Well, that was interesting." The speaker was a short, fat woman. She wasn't ugly, but Callum certainly wouldn't call her beautiful. Her skin had once been the rich olive colour of a denizen of the Mediterranean, and was now darkened and creased under the heavy tan of a lover of the outdoors. She wore a simple brown skirt and loose grey shirt which, like every surface of her body, including her bare feet, were covered in dirt. Her short, curly chestnut hair was accentuated by a long thin braid which held colourful stones and trailed down behind her left shoulder. Her hazel eyes twinkled as she stooped down before them, leaning heavily on a metre-long stone rod that she seemed to use as a walking stick.

"Have no fear, children. You're safe now. We won't hurt you. Isn't that right, Rata?" She turned to look over her shoulder at the other figure, who nodded.

He was a tall, thin, imposing black man. Jingwei looked him over and the first word that came to her mind was *manicured*. He was wearing what looked like a perfectly tailored suit, but when viewed closely was in fact a collection of plants. The pants and jacket were composed of a thick, velvety moss, while the vest was made of large, dark green leaves, precisely folded to create the desired effect. He wore no shirt, allowing his dark, sculpted chest to be seen under the vest. His head was shaved, save for a carefully cultivated top-knot and a finely groomed goatee.

He spoke in the deep voice they'd heard earlier. "Indeed. After all, it's not every day we get to entertain some fellow Humans."

Jingwei found her voice first. "You're both Human too?" She took the man's extended hand and allowed him to help her up. "From Earth?"

Callum got to his feet with the woman's assistance as she answered Jingwei's question.

"We are. And it's very nice to speak to someone who has been there recently."

"But how recently?" The man stepped back and looked at them. "What year are you from?"

Callum pursed his lips. He wasn't about to answer any questions until he knew who he could trust. Jingwei seemed to feel the same way. "Look, we're very pleased that you pulled us up from the tunnel, and I'm sure you had a good reason for kidnapping those fairy-things, but I don't think we should have to tell you anything until you've told us a few things."

The man stared at her for a moment, then looked to Callum.

Callum shrugged.

The tall man blinked once and then burst out laughing. "Well, you're obviously from sometime after the 1970s! That's a liberated woman if ever I saw one!"

The fat woman smacked his leg with her stone rod. "Not necessarily. I'm from well before then, and I don't have any difficulty speaking my mind, do I?" She smiled up at him sweetly.

The man bent down and frowned seriously in her face while he rubbed his leg. "Ow."

The woman grinned triumphantly and turned back to Callum and Jingwei.

"My name is Ila. I am the Soil Keeper of Tranthaea, and this is Rata, the Seed Keeper. We welcome you, and invite you into our home."

Jingwei felt her face flush with embarrassment. *Of course.* These were two of the Human Keepers that Ythen and Yriel had told them about. She mentally kicked herself and shook her head. *Wake up, Jingwei.*

Callum simply nodded. Knowing who they were didn't mean he had to trust them. He looked around the clearing, but didn't see anything to indicate a house nearby. "Your home?"

Rata smiled down at him. The Seed Keeper was only a few inches taller than the boy, but when Callum looked up at his face he felt as though he were a little boy again. There was a gravitas in Rata's visage, even when it was broken by a grin.

The tall black man gestured towards the trees behind him. The branches parted with a rustle and the trunks groaned as they leaned back, revealing a path. Ila didn't wait for the others, but started down it alone, not leaning on her walking stick, but not ignoring it either, and Jingwei followed after a moment's hesitation. Callum moved in behind her protectively, and Rata brought up the rear, the trees behind him resealing the forest after they passed by.

The path led down into a small, narrow gully. On either side of them the land rose up, eventually finding its way into some low foothills. High up in front of them, only a few kilometres away rose the sheer black walls of the mountains. Callum hadn't realized how close they were until now, nor how far to the east they had traveled from Yshaar while underground.

Just ahead, in the centre of the gully, there was a small hut. Its walls were built of mud and stone, but looked as though they were supported by the surrounding foliage. A thatched roof of living branches and leaves covered the structure. At first Jingwei thought the hut would look more at home on the African Serengeti than in a forest, but after seeing it for a moment she realized that it fit here perfectly, making use of the environment without disrupting it in any way. Sitting in front of the house in a small, natural clearing was a large stump that was apparently used as a table, with smaller stumps in a circle around it.

Ila set her staff down beside the door and motioned for Callum and Jingwei to take a seat on two of the small stumps. She joined them and Rata followed her.

"Now then," she said, leaning forward and placing her hands on the table. "Who wants to start?"

Her eyes played back and forth between Jingwei and Callum. Neither one spoke. "All right then. I suppose we should prove ourselves. I don't remember being that trusting when I first got here either." She glanced at Rata. "Here's something you two may want to know. Those two Aru Elen were looking for a young Human girl, who apparently got lost in the woods while visiting a city. Curious, that."

Jingwei blushed but didn't speak.

Rata took over the tale. "The truly strange thing is, they weren't searching on behalf of the Daevyn." He was carefully watching Jingwei for any reaction. "They were searching on behalf of the Spark Keeper."

Jingwei finally spoke up. "Only me? Why weren't they looking for Callum too?"

"It was my understanding that the Human boy was dead." Rata looked over at Callum for an explanation.

"Surprise." Callum didn't even bother to look up.

Jingwei ignored him. "And doesn't the Spark Keeper work for the Daevyn?"

Ila placed her hand on Jingwei's arm, but the girl shook it off. "The Keepers are not bound to any people. The Spark Keeper works for no one but herself. I don't know why she's looking for you, but you can bet it has nothing to do with the Daevyn."

"So, why'd you save us? You're Keepers too." Callum's voice had a challenging ring to it.

Rata responded openly, without getting defensive. "Not all Keepers are the same. Kala has ambitions beyond her calling that drive her to places we would never go. Ila and I are content with our positions."

"And what positions are those? Are you Earthlings or Tranthaeans? How do we know we can trust you, if we can't trust her?"

"We are both." Rata was unfazed by Callum's onslaught of questions. His deep voice sounded strong and sure of itself as he answered, "We were brought here from Earth, as you were. We were chosen to become Keepers, the guardians of Tranthaea. I am the Seed Keeper. I can harness the power of the living flora just as Kala harnesses the power of fire. The trees, plants, and all vegetation are under my protection. Ila is the Soil Keeper. She controls the power of the ground itself. Rock and stone, the foundations of Tranthaea, they are her province."

Ila scuffed her feet on the ground. "But once, many years ago, we were children like you. Called from another world to serve this one."

"We're not children." Jingwei scowled. "And called by who?"

Ila just shrugged. "Called by Tranthaea. We don't know why it calls who it calls, just that it does."

Jingwei sat back on her stump, deep in thought and Callum piped up. "Where... when are you from?"

Rata answered for them both, "Ila is from ancient Greece, about 435 BCE, as close as we can figure. I'm from the nation of Earth, in the year 3207 CE, but we both arrived here at the same time." He looked affectionately over at Ila. "I still remember how ridiculous you looked in your toga."

Ila raised her hand to smack him but he ducked back, smiling. She looked questioningly over at the two young people.

Jingwei exchanged glances with Callum. He sighed and nodded.

"I'm Jingwei Li, and this is Callum Swift. I'm from LA, in the United States. 2012. Callum's English. From 1882."

She stopped and looked at both Ila and Rata in turn. "And thanks for saving us."

"Right." Ila steepled her fingers and peered over them at her guests. "Now to business. Why does Kala want you, Jingwei?"

"Search me."

"I beg your pardon?"

"It means she don't know, I think." Callum was getting used to interpreting Jingwei's unique version of the English language. He shifted in his seat to keep from becoming too uncomfortable. "You've got to see, we've not been here that long. This is all still pretty new to us. And I for one won't be too gutted to put it all behind me when we leave."

Ila and Rata looked quickly at one another and glanced away again. Ila said, "Well, until you know what she wants, it'll be best if you stay away from her."

"What's her problem with us, anyway?" Jingwei demanded. "She didn't seem too happy when the Flame-Bearer welcomed us."

"Kala has a long and complicated history." As he spoke, Rata's stump grew an intricate web of curved branches that allowed him to lie back and put his feet up as if in a cozy recliner. "She and her sister were born to the first Human to arrive in Tranthaea."

Callum volunteered, "The First Flame-Bearer?"

"Exactly."

Jingwei was shocked. "Kala is that old? Then isn't she the heir to the Daevyn throne?"

Rata waved her question aside and continued his story. "The First Flame-Bearer was a powerful man. It was he who brokered the alliance between his descendants, the Daevyn, and the Aru Len. To consummate the deal, the Aru Faylen gave him many Aru Elen, including their most beautiful female. She became the mother of Kala and Alkira, Kala's sister."

"The sisters both took after their mother, growing fully functional wings when they were young, where most Daevyn only have stubs, or after-wings, but they retained enough humanity that they still grew hair instead of scales. It made them more beautiful and sought after than any other young women."

"When Kala came of age, she showed great proficiency in fire-handling. Eventually she was given the position of Spark Keeper, the first Spark Keeper of Tranthaea. It was only after she accepted the role that she discovered her father wouldn't allow her to be both the Spark Keeper *and* the Flame-Bearer."

Ila interrupted with a chuckle, "I bet she wasn't too pleased to hear that from daddy dearest!"

Rata continued. "Because of the Daevyn's obsession with fire and lightning, she was well-positioned to advise the Flame-Bearer, but it is no secret that she has higher ambitions."

"Unfortunately, we just don't know what they are. We've always assumed that she felt the rule of the Daevyn was hers by right, as the daughter of the First Flame-Bearer, but that doesn't explain why she wants you."

Rata dropped his feet and sat forward. "You must have something she wants, and badly, if she's willing to threaten the Aru Len to get to you."

"Threaten them?" Callum had been paying close attention to Rata's story and leaned in close.

"Yes. The ones we kept from leaving had just come to ask us to bring you, Jingwei, to Kala if we saw you. They said if they didn't find you, Kala would start blasting them out of the sky with her lightning."

Ila pounded her fist suddenly against the stump and a small avalanche of rocks tumbled down the side of the gully. "I swear, if she starts attacking those flyers, I'll..." Her voice trailed off.

Jingwei looked at her encouragingly. "You'll what?"

Ila muttered, "I'll make her palace floor uneven. Let's see how she likes a few stubbed toes."

Jingwei frowned in disappointment, and recalled that v'Aros had called the Soil Keeper 'pathetic' during the debate in the Warrens. Ila saw Jingwei's dubious glance and responded defensively, "We've been here a long time, and for a long time this world has been at peace. We aren't violent warriors, we're guardians. We don't attack, we protect."

Callum remained focused on the Aru Len. "So, what are you gonna do with the two Aru Elen you've captured?"

Rata looked across the stump at Callum with penetrating eyes. "What do you think we should do with them?"

Callum frowned a little and raised his shoulders. Jingwei watched him visibly struggle with the problem. She guessed that no one had ever asked him his opinion before, especially when it was a matter of life and death. She wondered if he could handle the responsibility.

Callum came to a decision. "I reckon we should let them go." He stopped Jingwei's interruption with a wave of his hand. "No, it's not fair to keep them prisoner; they were only doing what they had to do to survive." He shifted on his stump and grimaced. "Besides, maybe if we explain that we don't know anything, they won't tell her they saw us."

Jingwei was prepared to argue but saw that both Rata and Ila were nodding in approval. Rata stood up and took Ila's hand.

"It is a merciful decision, Callum Swift, to grant life. It seems only fair that we do the same for you."

With that, they each placed a hand on Callum's chest. He stood for a second with a puzzled look on his face. It was soon replaced by astonishment. He began slapping his torso and head so hard that Jingwei thought he might have gone crazy. It took her a moment to register that the bleeding head wounds he had suffered had vanished, and by that time Rata and Ila had hold of her shoulders and had already cured her headache and rolled ankle, and her wrist was no longer broken.

"You can do that?" Jingwei stood up and gingerly tested her ankle. "I thought you were just the trees and dirt people."

Ila laughed out loud. "Oh, we are! But when you become a Keeper, there are a few perks too!" Her face was a mess of dirty laugh lines, but she looked tired too. Jingwei wondered how much it had taken out of her and Rata to heal them.

She was given no time to find out. Rata set off towards the clearing to release the captive Aru Elen, hoping that he would be able to convince them not to give away the Humans' location. Ila hurried into the hut and came out moments later with a hearty soup that she'd been preparing for breakfast.

She sat and watched Callum and Jingwei wolf down their first meal in what seemed like ages and listened to them explain all they had been through in the last few days. Rata came back halfway through and so of course they had to start at the beginning again. When Jingwei started to talk about Huon Arrahl, Rata assured her that these woods were not its body, but a separate, non-sentient forest.

"You are privileged to have met Huon Arrahl, Jingwei. It is one of the oldest and wisest beings in Tranthaea, and it mostly keeps to itself. So much so that some of the other peoples do not even know of, or believe in its existence."

Jingwei recalled the fear and ignorance that the Daevyn had felt about the forest, and nodded, digging back into her breakfast.

By the time they reached the bottom of their soup bowls, Callum and Jingwei were feeling happy and healthy again. Rata cleared the dishes away while the other three reclined in hammocks that he had called up.

Jingwei spoke while they were swinging in relaxation. "It's the water, isn't it? What all this is about."

Callum hummed in agreement from his hammock across the gully. "Has to be. Everybody's seeing it. The Daevyn have dry fields, with fires that are harder to control. Huon Arrahl has to move about to find water to drink, and the gru'Esh tunnels are collapsing because the dirt is so dry."

Jingwei leaned out over the edge of her hammock. "Ila, do you think that has something to do with what Kala is up to? Is it something to do with water?" She sounded nervous, and Callum noticed.

"Why? Do you know anything about the water?"

Jingwei hesitated, but gave in. After all they'd been through together, he had earned the right to know.

"When I was back on Earth, just before the lightning brought me here, I fell into a fountain."

Callum chuckled. "I remember you saying that. Thought you were winding me up."

Jingwei picked up a pebble and threw it at him. "Do you remember what you said to me then, Old-Timer?"

Callum watched the rock sail lazily over his head. "Nope."

"You wondered why I wasn't wet. Well, I wasn't wet because when I stood up in the middle of the fountain, I wasn't wet. Everything around me was, but not me." Jingwei's voice quavered a bit, as if she were holding back tears. "I don't know what happened, but what if that's why Kala wants me?"

Callum rolled over onto his side to face her across the gully. "Dunno. But just before I got here, I think I might have accidentally blown out some lamps. With my mind."

Jingwei sat up in interest. "How many lamps?"

"Dunno," he said again. "All the lamps in the park, I reckon."

"Cool!"

Ila interrupted from her hammock across the way. "So, you each have a strange ability. Well of course you do, otherwise you wouldn't have been brought here. I remember I caused a small earthquake in my village when some raiders came to steal our sheep. That was just before I was brought here; in fact, I fell into a crack the quake caused, and when I climbed out, here I was. Rata almost caused an inter-stellar incident when a seedling that was meant to be presented to some planetary lord suddenly took root in the man's hands and grew into a two hundred foot oak."

"That was an occasion to remember." Rata had rejoined them from the hut. "The food was terrible, and his palace had needed a skylight anyway."

All four of them laughed, the joke temporarily chasing away the seriousness of their situation.

Callum brought them back after a moment, his voice sounding trepidatious. "So, does that mean we're meant to be Keepers? Is that why we were brought over?"

"Maybe. Maybe not." Rata sat down on his stump again, this time growing it into a rocking chair that creaked back and forth with the sound of thick branches moving in the wind. "We became Keepers, but the First Flame-Bearer didn't. And others in the past haven't either. Not all Humans become Keepers, and not all powers in this world rest in a Keeper's hands. It seems that Tranthaea brings over who it needs, no more, no less."

"Goodo." Callum was mollified. Maybe he wouldn't be expected to become a guardian of a whole world, after all.

"In any case, what should we do about Kala?" Jingwei rolled out of her hammock and set her feet on the ground. "We can't hide from her forever, can we?"

"I doubt it." Ila got up and walked over to the hut. "But if you think she's causing the water to disappear, maybe you should find out why that's happening. Maybe then you'll be able to protect yourself, or at least have a bargaining chip to work with."

She picked up her staff and walked back over to them. "You should find Jera, the Sea Keeper. He should know what's happening to the water, and even if he doesn't, he'll be able to help you find out."

"Great." Callum swung off the hammock, eagerly testing the limits of his newly healthy body. "It'll be a nice change to have something to do, and not just be wandering about, scarpering from this thing and that. Where do we find him?"

Rata rose from the rocking chair, which had slowly uncurled into a low bench, and pointed a long finger along the length of the mountains. "He can usually be found near the Northern Sea. Nalani is the greatest collection of water on Tranthaea, and he always has been a bit of a homebody."

Jingwei got up from her hammock, which rewrapped itself around a tree. "Hold on. Why are you sending us alone? We have no idea what we're doing. Why don't you come with us?"

Rata grabbed a bag that looked like it had been woven out of some sort of grass and swung it over his shoulder, draping the strap across his chest. He hooked his thumbs into the vine he wore as a belt. "We are going to find Alkira."

"That's Kala's sister, right?"

"She is. She is also the Sky Keeper. If anyone might know what Kala is up to, she will."

Ila walked back over to the two young Humans and smiled. "Ah, to be young and go on an adventure." Rata rolled his eyes behind her. She reached back and smacked his chest. "I saw that, Rata."

She gave Callum and Jingwei the once-over and clicked her lips together at the tattered rags that were all that was left of the once-grand clothing they had been given to them by the Flame-Bearer. "Those are hardly good clothes for travelling around in. Maybe these will serve you better."

Jingwei looked down when Ila tapped her gently on the chest with the stone staff. She gasped.

Her clothes had been replaced. She now wore leather walking boots and loose black pants. Her pale blue shirt was mostly hidden behind a beautiful aquamarine cloak. She looked over at Callum and saw that he had been clothed anew as well. He was draped in a mottled cloak of browns and reds and oranges. His shirt was russet, and he was wearing the same boots as she under brown pants, much looser than the ones the Daevyn had given him. He looked strong and handsome, just like Ythen.

Jingwei frowned. Where had *that* thought come from? She glanced back at Callum, and then at Ila. The Soil Keeper could have made the pants a *little* tighter. With legs like that...

Ila smiled at Jingwei knowingly and then turned towards Rata.

"Well," she said. "Shall we?"

He stepped up beside her and she put her arms around his waist. They looked over at the two young Humans.

Ila's eyes twinkled. "Good luck."

With that, the ground beneath them fell away and the two Keepers disappeared in a cloud of dirt and dust. When the dust settled the ground was smoothed over again and there was a small growth of moss in the shape of an arrow pointing north, in the direction of the Sea of Nalani.

Callum stepped up beside Jingwei and put his hand on her shoulder. She didn't shake it off.

"Let's go." His voice sounded very close. She felt his hand brushing off her shoulder, and turned towards him quickly, but he had already stepped away and was walking past the hut towards the north.

Jingwei bit her cheek and followed him back into the forest. She hurried to catch up with him, but once she did she remained silent, letting him do all the talking as he marvelled at his new clothes and the polished greaves of his Firedart and Buckler, and the vigour he felt now that his body was back to full strength.

They moved quickly through the woods, driven by healed bodies and a sure objective. After about an hour of walking Jingwei noticed a dry creek bed that ran north-south, and they began to follow it, using its path to avoid most of the underbrush that threatened to slow their passage.

Callum led the way. His eyes kept moving as he took in the view in front of him and his left hand kept straying to the empty space where his Firedart's canister was meant to be. He felt strangely defenceless without it, even though he'd only just learned how to use it.

Behind him, Jingwei was silent. Only days ago he had thought he would enjoy any moment he could get without a dry, scolding lecture from the Chinese-American girl, but he was now realizing that she was more to him than an annoyance, or even just a travel companion.

I wish I knew how to flirt.

Callum was just about to turn back and say something when he noticed that the path ended in a sudden drop-off ahead.

The dry creek bed must have held a small waterfall when it was running, and Callum peered over the edge and saw that the drop was small; it was only about a metre and a half down. He carefully lowered himself over the side and dropped to the ground below, then looked up at Jingwei's face that peeked past the rocks above him.

"Jump. I'll catch you."

Jingwei looked down at him in disbelief. She had never been good with heights. She was a firm believer that if she had been meant to like heights, she would have been born taller. She opened her mouth to berate him, but then saw the look on his face and hesitated.

He looked hopeful. He looked like he wanted her to trust him, wanted her to believe that he would catch her.

And suddenly, she did.

Jingwei's feet had left the rocky edge before she knew it, and she didn't even have the chance to scream before she was safely gathered into Callum's arms and then placed delicately on the ground.

She straightened her cloak around her shoulders and didn't look at him while she waited for a flush to fade from her cheeks.

"Thanks."

Callum didn't respond, so she looked up at his face and saw him looking curiously over her head.

Jingwei turned around and saw the dark entrance to a cave that would normally have been hidden behind a wall of plummeting water.

Without hesitation Jingwei shook her head.

"No." She had had enough underground experiences to last her for a while, thank you very much.

Callum ignored her and stepped up to the mouth of the cave. "Wait. There's something in there."

Jingwei nervously peered past his shoulder. "What is it? Another monster? Another hunter, looking for us? Another surprise attack? Another reason to *not go into the cave?*" With each utterance she smacked her palm harder against Callum's back.

Callum twitched away from her in surprise. "Leave it out, Jingwei, you nutter! You're not batting a full wicket!"

Jingwei looked up at him silently for a moment, confused. "You know, sometimes I wonder if you're even speaking English."

Callum grinned. "I know the feeling." He turned back towards the cave and his eyes crinkled in concentration. "No, it's not danger. It's something else. I don't really... I can't explain it. I can just feel it. I know there's something there."

He turned to look at her. "It feels like it did when I blew up the lamps back home."

Jingwei looked at him for a moment and then gave in. "Fine. But we move fast. In, out, and on our way."

"Agreed."

And without another word Callum ducked his head and stepped into the cave.

Jingwei shook her head as she followed him in.

Boys.

The cave wasn't large; it only took a minute to traverse its length, so the bright air from outside kept it dimly lit even as it twisted and turned deeper into the rock.

Callum trailed his hands along the walls as they passed by. At the opening, the stone was rough and natural, but the further they went in, the smoother the stone became, the more pronounced the edges and lines seemed, and the more obviously sculpted and chiseled the whole cave was.

But Callum's focus was on whatever he could feel at the end of the tunnel.

Jingwei was less single-minded. She noticed as they went that the walls had been carved with drawings at one point. Etchings that had once been artistically placed were now faded and water-worn. Most were hardly visible, and the ones she could see were confusing. Drawings of faces rising up from the ground, body-less, with large, toothy grins. A large valley, filled with lakes and rivers. A single sapling standing on a hilltop. None of the places or peoples looked familiar.

Strange. It surprised Jingwei to realize that she was starting to think of Tranthaean landscapes and inhabitants as familiar.

That single tree. What if that's supposed to be...

"Jingwei." Callum's excited voice interrupted her thoughts. "You have to see this."

She hurried to catch up with him and found herself entering a small room carved out of the stone. It had no wall carvings and was empty, save for a small stone box that sat in the middle of the floor.

The box was wrapped in chains of glowing coals. The black metal of the links had broken away in some spots, showing the white and orange embers burning inside them. Jingwei could feel the heat from where she stood, but Callum was crouched beside the box, his hands hovering over the hot coals. He seemed unaffected by the heat, but the light of the fire was reflected in his eyes.

He looked up at her excitedly, and they both spoke at the same time.

"Bang-up."

"Cool."

Callum turned back towards the box. He could feel the heat, but it didn't bother him. He moved his hands slowly over the chains, feeling them burning at his fingers. In the back of his mind he could hear Jingwei yelling at him to *Stop!*, but he kept going.

Each link felt raw and powerful and old, as if they had been burning here for a long, long time.

Except that one. That one felt... false.

Callum looked down at the unique coal-link, narrowed his eyes for a second, and then crushed it between his fingers.

All of the other links went dark and rattled loosely to the floor of the cave.

Jingwei felt a cool rush of air surge past her out of the cave. She rushed to Callum and checked his hands quickly.

No burns. They weren't even red.

She growled and smacked his shoulder.

"*Don't* do that again."

Callum gave her a boyish grin that promised nothing and she sighed. They both turned to look at the stone box before them, and Callum reached forward to open it.

The lid came off smoothly and Callum set it aside. The interior of the box was filled with a dark red moss that had three hollows set into it. Two of the hollows were empty; one had the shape of a perfect circle, the other was made up of two overlapping triangles, like a child's drawing of a Christmas tree. But the centre inset was still full, and contained...

"The First Flame-Bearer's missing canister!" Callum scooped the bronze antique out of the box and turned it over in his hands. It was identical to the one he'd stolen from the Hall of Record, from the size and shape to the colour and engraving. He quickly snapped it into his Firedart. "I wonder how it got here?"

"Who cares?" Jingwei was inspecting the other two hollows. "*I* wonder what else used to be in the box?"

"Who cares?" Callum rejoined. He stood and held his arm out, checking the weight, more confident now that he was armed again. He turned to the exit as Jingwei placed the surprisingly cool cover back onto the stone chest and watched the coal-links reignite and crawl back up the sides of the box to lock it down. She stood up and followed him out as he walked purposefully down the tunnel towards the bright outside air and tossed over his shoulder, "Let's go find the Sea Keeper."

It took another few hours before they reached the northern edge of the Korrahl Forest where it met at cross-corners with the black cliffs to the east. They stopped and waited, making sure that there were no sentries visible before they broke the tree-line.

Callum had been cheery the whole way there, much to Jingwei's amusement. He had changed so much from the scared boy she had first seen on the plains a few days ago.

She was contemplating this when he turned back to her.

"You know, you look right smart in blue."

Jingwei dropped her head and busied herself with the buttons on her shirt, muttering a nonsensical reply. *Don't be silly! He's just a kid, even younger than me! Not like Ythen... What is wrong with me? Seriously, take me out of immediate, life-threatening danger for a few minutes and I turn into a silly, boy-crazy...*

She looked up, preparing to shoot off a clever zinger to put him in his place when she heard a quiet thump on the ground behind her and saw Callum's eyes open wide in surprise. She spun around and squeaked when she saw one of the yellow-painted Aru Elen they had set free earlier that day. It looked at her with sadness in its eyes, and then stepped forward and took hold of her arms, spinning her around. Before she knew what had happened, she was soaring up into the air; the ground dropped away beneath her and the black walls of the mountains flashed past her eyes as they rocketed up. The humming of her captor's wings was reinforced as the other Aru Elen joined them, holding a furious Callum in its grasp, carefully pointing his Firedart out at the ground.

Callum wasn't sure which he was angrier about, that they'd been caught so easily, or that the Aru Elen holding him was naked underneath that paint.

For that matter, he wasn't sure whether his captor was male or female. He closed his eyes against the blurring face of the cliffs. He didn't want to know.

After a few minutes of climbing, the sound of the Aru Elen's wings faded. Callum wrenched his eyes open, suddenly afraid that he had been dropped and was now plummeting to the ground below, but they had only arrived at the summit of the mountains, and the echo of the Aru Elen's wings was no longer being bounced back at them.

The mountaintop ended in a flat plateau, studded with craggy black rock formations and dangerous fissures. The Aru Elen flew them silently over the lifeless waste, weaving gently to avoid the tallest pillars.

Soon, the hum of the wings changed to a lower pitch. The Aru Elen were slowing down and lowering their altitude. Callum knew that they must be nearing the end of the line. Their Aru Elen captors were obviously bringing them to Kala, in spite of Callum's hopes to the contrary. They banked sharply around a giant lump of melted rock and there before them was their destination.

Rising up from the barren mountaintop was a magnificent palace. Its glossy black walls were almost perfectly reflective, broken only by rivulets of glowing, molten lava running in narrow streams down its length. The high walls were lined with crenellations. Sharp towers rose far above the flat stone plain of the summit. The highest of these stabbed harshly into the pure white of the clouds that massed above the mountaintop.

It was the palace of Kala, the Spark Keeper of Tranthaea.

And suddenly Callum knew that this had been a one-way trip.

Chapter Sixteen:
The Audience

Callum and Jingwei were marched through the front gates, prodded along by their Aru Elen guards, who were unarmed save for Callum's confiscated Firedart. Jingwei had considered running for it when they landed, but Callum had caught her eye and shaken his head. There was nowhere to run up here.

The sleek black palace rose up from the plateau as if it were just another natural rock formation. Its obsidian features looked sharp enough to slice a wayward hand, so the Humans were careful to keep their arms by their sides as their guards manoeuvred them through the long passages.

There were no staircases in the palace. Callum and Jingwei were pushed up and down levels through polished, round-bottomed channels that looked as though they had been worn into the stone by centuries of lava flows. The black hallways were lit only by thin rivers of molten rock that drained slowly downwards.

Eventually they reached their destination, what Jingwei figured was the centre of the palace. They stepped through an archway that was decorated with large red stones that seemed to glimmer from within, and entered a grand throne room.

The room was easily double the size of the Flame-Bearer's. Unlike the Daevyn chamber, Kala's throne room was empty of people, and was instead surrounded by a ring of columns that rose from the floor in twisted and curved shapes, as if they had been melted by a freak accident halfway through the construction process. The solid black walls were fashioned from the same glossy rock as the rest of the palace, and they seemed to both absorb and reflect the light, giving the room an air of claustrophobic expanse. The smoothness of the walls and floor and ceiling was unbroken except by the large bonfire that had been built at the end of the room.

Seated on the fire was Kala.

The tongues of flame curled and nipped around her cloak, bending themselves into the shape of a magnificent throne with a tall, flickering back. A light smoke rose from the fire and filled the space behind the throne; the glow from the flames trapped within it created an aura of barely-contained power that seemed to emanate from the Spark Keeper.

Kala's eyes burned as they approached. Her wings buzzed restlessly behind her, creating vague shapes in the smoke and stirring up the flames of her chair. The Humans were brought before her, and with a sudden burst of energy the throne exploded into a wild conflagration which she gently swooped out of, unharmed.

She landed next to Callum and looked up at him.

"So, the Humans have survived after all, only to abandon the safety of the towering city? Do you value your lives so little that you would throw them away on a world you do not understand?"

Jingwei was in no mood for games. "The only thing I don't understand is why you brought us here. Does it have something to do with the water disappearing?"

Kala looked over at Jingwei and smirked at her straightforward approach. "The poor little Human. Such a soft heart for living things, but such a hard head when it comes to her own well-being."

Callum shifted his weight but didn't speak. Kala noticed.

"Ready to rush to her defence? Go on then, boy. Tell me how it wasn't stubborn and foolish to rush off into the forest at night, alone. No? Nothing to say? Good. You're such a pretty boy, it would be a shame to ruin the illusion by speaking."

Callum opened his mouth but nothing came out. Jingwei didn't have that problem. "You kidnapped us. Why? What do you want us for?"

The chamber echoed with Kala's laughter. "Kidnapped you? My silly girl, I've rescued you!" She lifted her hands and three small flaming chairs burned into existence.

"Please, sit." She delicately lowered herself onto a chair.

Callum looked at Jingwei, who wouldn't take her eyes off of Kala. He reached out his hand but felt no heat rising from the chair, and sat down carefully.

The seat supported his weight and quickly adjusted itself to his body.

Jingwei glanced over and saw that she was the only person left standing. She narrowed her eyes at Kala and moved to sit quickly on her chair.

The moment she touched the fire it vanished and she fell to the floor, hard.

Jingwei scrambled to her feet, glaring at the Spark Keeper. "Very funny!"

Kala didn't respond. Her brow twitched in what Jingwei almost thought was uncertainty. The Spark Keeper's eyes traveled to Jingwei and back to where the chair had been burning only seconds before. She reached up and clapped her hands, and a red-painted Aru Elen flew into the room, carrying a wooden chair. He set it down and flew off. Jingwei carefully tested it before putting her full weight on it. Once she was seated, Kala began.

"Let us not waste one another's time. I can see that you do not trust me. And rightly so. You are visitors to a strange world; you should not easily trust anyone." She switched her gaze from one to the other. "I do not trust you either. Yet I find that we are in the unique position of being able to help one another."

"Here it comes," Jingwei snorted. Kala ignored her and continued.

"I am not Human, but I have Human blood in me. My ancestors were brought over to this world and trapped here, just as you have been." She looked over at Callum and noticed his reaction. "So you *do* want to go home?"

Callum was surprised. What with all the activity and busyness of the last few days he hadn't given much thought to whether or not he wanted to go home, or even whether or not he'd be able to if he wanted to. He looked over at Jingwei and saw by her expression that she was thinking the same thing.

"I guess so," he said, finally. "This isn't where we belong, is it?"

"Precisely." Kala raised her hand and a tongue of flame detached itself from her chair and combed her crimson hair back over her ear. "And I find myself in a position that may be of some use to you."

"What does this have to do with the water? What are you up to?" Jingwei shifted uncomfortably on the hard wooden chair, but remained focused on the Spark Keeper.

"You do go on about water, don't you? What makes you think I have the slightest interest in water? I'm the Spark Keeper, not the Sea Keeper."

Jingwei stood up and walked behind her chair, placing her hands on the back and leaning forward. "Ila and Rata told us you were up to something. Now, what do you want us for? You won't get it, not from me!" In spite of the defiance in her voice, Callum noticed that her hands were gripping hard on the chair back, and her knuckles were turning white with the strain.

Kala's face had darkened at the mention of the two Human Keepers and the embroidery on her cloaks flickered a deeper red. "Those two have always been jealous of my position as Spark Keeper. They came over here and got stuck with ferns and dirt, and are always trying to cause trouble for me. I think that they want to replace me one day." She let out a harsh laugh. "What fun it would be to watch those two untrained peace-lovers fight over who gets the Spark once I'm gone!" She leaned in towards Callum conspiratorially. "Best not to trust a word they say. Everyone has an ulterior motive."

Callum didn't move. "And what's yours?"

Kala pulled back. She considered them for a moment, and then nodded to herself.

"Very well." She rose gracefully to her feet as the chair burned itself out beneath her.

Kala turned her back to the two Humans and began to pace. "It has always been known that Human visitors are often brought to Tranthaea via lightning. But none, not even the Daevyn, have been able to understand how." She turned to face them. "It has been many ages since a Human survived the journey to Tranthaea. You two may be the secret to discovering how to use lightning as transportation."

Jingwei looked sceptical. Kala noticed and moved towards her. "Do you not understand? You have traveled by lightning, I can create it. If we worked together, I could transport you back home. Back to where you belong!"

Callum could see Jingwei preparing a verbal attack. He didn't trust Kala, but he wasn't willing to lose a chance at returning home just because Jingwei had a sharp tongue.

"But what's in it for you?" He leaned forward in his chair, his red hair glowing in the flickering firelight.

Kala drummed her fingernails against her palms before answering. "You aren't the only ones who want to leave Tranthaea."

In spite of herself, Jingwei was intrigued. "You? Why do you want to leave? You're from this world. And you seem pretty powerful."

Kala's eyes sharpened as she forced the words out from between her clenched teeth. "There are five Keepers in Tranthaea. Five powers in the world, each with its own agenda, each with its own reasons and goals. I am tired of the constant struggle for balance." She raised her arms and the throne once again burst into existence behind her, larger, brighter, and more magnificent than ever. Her voice now carried through the throne room. "Give me a world with no other powers and I will give you a world free of conflict, a world of peace and obedience." Her eyes shone with a wild passion.

Jingwei's voice was flat. "So you want to rule... Earth?"

Kala waved away her accusation. "Only to free it. The other Humans who have come here in the past, including my father, have told stories about your world. It was born and is constantly being remade through the forge of war. How many have died? How many more will die? One powerful ruler could erase all of that. Peace and order.

These are the gifts I offer your world, if only you help me find a way to get there." Kala had made her way back to her throne and now sat on it imperiously. "This is my pledge. If you help me, it will not be forgotten." Her eyes darkened and the throne burned white-hot. "If you do not, my memory will hold that also."

Callum was aghast. She wanted them to get her to Earth so that she could *take over*? It was unbelievable.

Kala anticipated his response. "Was your world so kind to you that you feel you owe it a debt, Callum Swift? Or you, Jingwei Li? At my side you could rule, if not there, then here." Her voice quieted and was almost lost in the snap and hiss of the throne. "Name your price, Humans. I offer you a choice of worlds. You have only to accept."

"Here? We could rule here, too? But you'd have to..." Suddenly it clicked for Jingwei. "Is that what you're up to with the water?"

Kala's sharp eyes shot over to the Chinese-American girl.

"Somehow, you're making the water vanish to create conflict here. If there's war, there's a chance for you to take over, is that it? You're looking to capitalize on the conflict!" Kala didn't respond, so Jingwei pressed on. "And after all your talk about wanting peace! But then we arrived. Two Humans, who might just take up positions of power like others before us. Did we spoil your plans?"

Kala answered, all friendliness gone from her face. "You are a clever girl. Perhaps too clever for your own good. You should have died in the Collectors. I tried to have you executed in Yshaar. But since you persist in surviving, I will be honest with you. Yes, you constitute a threat. So now I am giving you a choice. You may join me, and we can rule together in this world and your own. Or, you can die. Either way, I assure you, you will tell me what I need to know about lightning travel."

Callum rose from his seat and stepped forward. Jingwei joined him and spoke for the both of them. "Maybe so. But not willingly."

Kala sighed. She clapped her hands again and three red-painted Aru Elen flew into the room.

"Secure them, and take them to the dungeon." She shook her head in mock sadness as the guards clamped coal-black irons on the Human's wrists. They locked the cuffs using a small metal mechanism, not unlike a lighter, which sprayed a miniature bouquet of sparks over the surface of the clamps, sealing them in place. Kala turned and stalked away towards the entrance to a passage that seemed to lead even further into the mountain palace. She stopped and looked over her shoulder at Jingwei. "Perhaps I will keep you alive, little girl." The Spark Keeper's wings began to buzz and her body lifted slowly off the ground, turning to bring itself back in line with her head. "I will keep you alive just long enough for you to witness the destruction of your world. The destruction that you could have prevented."

Her sharp eyes flashed with finality. "Take them away."

Chapter Seventeen:
The Vault

Yriel's head began to nod as the swaying motion of the raeas seduced her fatigued body into sleep. Aside from a quick nap at the Quencher's campsite, she'd had no real rest since she'd snuck out of Yshaar, hot on the heels of the Human girl. That had been two nights ago.

Much had happened since then.

The ride back towards the Daevyn city was long and slow. A raeas was not a speedy animal, and the fifty kilometres between the mountains and the city seemed today like an insurmountable obstacle to the exhausted Daevyn girl. Nor was the destination any draw. Yriel would have to meet her mother and deceive her in order to convince her to bring the armies out of the city and onto the plains.

She was sure that she could do it. Only once her mother was removed from power would Yriel be able to lead her warriors to a great and glorious victory. Only then would she lead her people to greatness.

Only then would they all truly understand what she was capable of.

The late afternoon air was cooling around Yriel as the raeas continued moving forward. When riding west, nothing was required of the rider save for sturdy balance; the raeas knew which way was home.

Yriel was able to play through her final confrontation with Ythen over and over again. Kala's promises echoed in her thoughts as she saw the Daevyn boy's disappointed and angry face sneering at her in her mind's eye.

Now he would know what it felt like to be betrayed. He had taken what she loved from her, now she would return the favour.

As the raeas slipped slowly through the tall grasses, its sides making *swishing* sounds as it brushed up against the grains, Yriel's thoughts became muddled by fatigue, and she began to drift into sleep.

And into dreams.

Yriel had been having strange dreams lately. Vivid dreams. Dreams that blurred the line between fantasy and reality.

This dream was no different. At first, all she saw was blackness, a blackness thicker than the night air and twice as dark. But soon enough thin glowing veins began to appear in the void, the light pulsing painfully but noiselessly against her eyes.

The black resolved itself into stone walls. She recognized this place. A room she'd visited secretly before. A room she'd been forbidden to visit again.

In the dream, Yriel stepped forward. The web of dim orange light that surrounded her began to fade and was overpowered by a soft purple glow that emanated from the top of a plinth in the centre of the room.

What is that?

Her waking mind struggled against the thick, fluid quality of the dream, desperately trying to place the glowing object. Something about it looked familiar. An image of woven threads flashed through her thoughts and then vanished. A tapestry: seen frequently, ignored just as often. The thought flickered in time with the pulsing veins in the walls and was extinguished.

All of the light suddenly went out, save for the violet glow coming from the middle of the room. And then, from behind her came a brilliant red light that cast Yriel's shadow down the centre of the room, over the plinth and up the wall on the other side.

Yriel began to quaver in fear. She had been told never to come here again...

A voice from behind her bellowed, and Yriel watched her shadow flinching on the wall before her.

"How do you come to be here? Speak!"

Yriel closed her eyes and willed herself away. The inky blackness of the unknown returned to her, drowning out the violent red light of the dream. She felt a firm pressure on her shoulder, as if someone had grasped onto it, hard, but then it eased and she woke, lifting her head in a sudden snap.

Her heart was pounding in her chest as her thoughts caught up with reality.

Of course!

She remembered the tapestry, and the stories she'd been told as a child. That violet light was a sign. It had to be.

Yriel knew that she needed to possess the item in that vault. It would be hers, just as the Daevyn would be.

A motion ahead of her drew her attention. Less than a kilometre away, much closer than she had been expecting, the flapping colours of the Daevyn flags were being carried across the plains.

Excellent.

She would not have to convince her mother to leave Yshaar. The Flame-Bearer had already brought her armies onto the field.

Yriel spurred her raeas forward, ignoring the pain in her already bruising shoulder. It was time to claim what was rightfully hers.

Chapter Eighteen:
The Prison

The guards had whisked Jingwei and Callum out of Kala's throne room and through a dizzying maze of corridors, each one as black and glossy as the last. They flew past walls that were so smooth and reflective they seemed to be mirrors that led down dark cross-corridors, magnifying the size of the palace. The air seemed to be sapped of strength and light in the oppressive decor, and most of the illumination came from the rivulets of lava that flowed along the walls, defying gravity as they snaked up and down in designs meant to astonish and terrify.

They did both, and very well.

Finally, they arrived at the dungeon. Jingwei had long ago lost track of the path that had lead them there, but she sensed that they had sunk far into the depths of the mountains. Whatever ideas she'd had of musty, smoke-filled passages lined with rusty cell bars were immediately squashed as they entered the room.

The dungeon was a vast cavernous space, roughly carved out of the sharp, black rock. The lava on the walls abruptly stopped flowing at the entrance, instead pouring upwards into pools that, against all odds, seemed to sink into the ceiling, pumping the liquid light back up to the higher levels. The black walls of the room beyond ate up what little light filtered into the cavern, making the size of the space almost impossible to guess. A globe of light glowed in the blackness, thought whether it was a small light nearby or a large light far away, Jingwei had no idea. From the way that the room swallowed up the buzzing sound of the Aru Elen's wings, she guessed that it was large, far larger than the amphitheatre they had seen in the Warrens.

The blackness felt different here. In the Warrens, among the gru'Esh, the darkness had felt like the *lack* of light. Here, in a dungeon in the depths of the mountains, the darkness seemed to have substance in the same way the air outside carried light with it. The darkness seemed... unyielding.

It made Jingwei shiver.

The guards flew them a fair way into the room and set them down. As soon as they had released their prisoners, they stepped back and watched as a cage of fire slowly built around the Humans, eventually forming into what looked like a ball of melting flames. The curved wall of the cell sunk into the floor beneath their feet, vanishing into the black stone.

Satisfied, the two Aru Elen left, backing out the door and then, a moment later, flying down the passage the way they had come and quickly disappearing around a bend in the tunnel.

Left alone in the inky blackness, Callum and Jingwei remained silent. The only light in the room came from the walls of their cell and from the globe of light in the distance.

Callum's eyebrows were knitted and crumpled on his forehead. The burning cell around them felt strangely oppressive to him, as if it were more than just a physical prison. He tried to push the feeling aside, but the force of it gave him an instant headache. He shook his head and looked around them at the blackness. Callum had never been afraid of the dark. He'd spent most of his life in dark places, hiding from people much more frightening than imaginary monsters could ever be.

Still, the solid *realness* of this darkness made him uncomfortable, and he could see by the glow of their prison that Jingwei had started shivering.

She was always sure to come off as strong, but he'd never met anyone who cared more about others' opinions of her. He knew that sensitivity was exactly what she was always trying to hide.

He suppressed a smile. It wouldn't do to let her know he'd noticed her shaking. She would hate his efforts to help her even more than she would hate the fact that she needed help to begin with.

Callum stepped closer to Jingwei, ready to say something that would allow her to comfortably retort, hoping that would restore her to her blustery norm.

He didn't have the chance to say anything. Instead, Jingwei squealed loudly and began to run around in circles, practically dancing as she hopped back and forth. The blackness around them advanced and retreated with her movement, and pushed out from around them and then back in as he rushed to her side with concern.

He needn't have worried. As soon as she noticed he was there, she gripped his arm with both hands.

"Look! It moves with us!" She danced away from him again, and this time he watched the sphere of fire around them stretch to accommodate their new positions, growing several times in size.

Callum groaned in frustration and Jingwei ran back over to him.

"What? It's good news! It means we can move around! This is the worst prison ever!"

Callum winced at her enthusiasm. He hated to be the one to have to point it out, but...

"It means we'll not get near the walls of the cell. It means we can't get out."

Jingwei became still for a moment, realization sinking in. "Oh. Right." She stepped away from him again, watching the sphere expand as she did so. The wall of the cell was now about three metres away from her. She took a step or two back towards Callum. The cell shrunk so that the wall was only two metres away. She feebly stretched out her arms, coming up laughably short.

"Well, it's not like we know how to break out anyway."

Callum didn't answer; his face was screwed up in thought.

"Right? Callum?"

Without a word he reached awkwardly into his cloak and tossed an item over to her. She fumbled the catch and watched it clatter to the floor in front of her.

It was the device the Aru Elen had used to lock them up.

Jingwei reached down and scooped it up. It was long and thin, about the length of a ball-point pen, but it seemed to work like a cigarette lighter. She flicked the cap experimentally and gasped as a shower of sparks shot out and burst against her wrist restraints.

The restraints unsnapped and fell to the ground with a heavy *clank*. Jingwei stared at them for a moment, wide-eyed, and then looked up to Callum.

Callum shrugged. "S'what I do."

"You have *got* to teach me how to do that!" Jingwei rushed over to him and flicked the mechanism again, unlocking his bonds. "It's so *cool!*"

Callum took the mechanism back and didn't answer, but stood looking over her head, a curious expression on his face. He was rubbing his wrists and suddenly his eyes lit up, and then he blushed a deep red.

"What?" Jingwei didn't know what he'd been thinking, but facial expressions like that always made her curiosity too strong to ignore. "What is it?"

Callum scuffed his feet and fumbled about in his mouth for an answer. Jingwei stood looking up at him and marvelled that this boy could be so quick-witted and clever and at the same time be so dense and tongue-tied.

She reached up and grabbed his face with both hands, pressing on his smooth cheeks, forcing him to meet her eyes.

"Callum. What?"

If it had been possible, she would have sworn he turned a brighter red.

"Well... that is... um... I noticed the cell gets smaller when we're closer. Together."

Jingwei released his face and took a step back. The fire cell expanded to mirror her movement, adding centimetres to the distance between her body and the cell wall. She stepped back in and watched as the cell retracted, its walls now only just out of reach.

She looked back up at Callum, who was desperately trying to look at anything but her, and finally understood.

"You dog, you planned this whole thing didn't you?" He opened his mouth to protest but she silenced him by wrapping her arms around his torso and pulling him close.

Callum stood frozen in embarrassment. Jingwei had buried her head into his chest and her fingers were intertwined across his back. He could feel her body pressed against his, and knew that she could hear the quickening of his heartbeat as they remained locked together.

Slowly, feeling more unsure of himself than he ever had before, he wrapped both of his arms around her and pulled her in even closer, savouring the smell of her hair and the warmth of her body.

She wriggled her neck until her face was looking up towards him and then smiled sweetly.

"Shouldn't one of those arms be trying to reach the wall?"

Callum opened his mouth and then clamped it shut again, grinning wryly. He stretched out his right arm, carefully extending the sparking mechanism. It ended about a centimetre from the wall.

He triggered the cap and sparks burst out to trickle down the wall. The glow of the fireball dimmed, but didn't go out.

"Just another centimetre."

"Sure." Jingwei snuggled deeper into his chest, her voice muffled through the thick layers of his cloak. "I bet you say that to all the girls."

This time the shower of sparks burst directly onto the wall, and then danced all along the sphere, dimming it with each fiery touch. By the time the sparks reached the other side of the ball, the cell had dissipated, leaving only a rain of glittering sparks to cascade down over the Humans' embracing forms.

Callum watched in silence as the glowing trails drifted down to the floor and were extinguished. Finally, Jingwei pulled away from his arms. She smiled up at him and then impulsively jumped up and kissed him on the cheek.

"That was for being brilliant, stealing the key, and breaking us out."

She leaned forward again and slammed her foot down on his, causing him to leap back in surprise and pain.

"And that was for enjoying it."

She sent him another smile and then turned away, scanning the darkness, searching for the way out.

"I don't suppose you remember which way the door was?"

Callum came back to himself and limped over to Jingwei. She was right, in all the excitement they had lost track of the direction of the entrance and were now adrift in the vast blackness of the prison.

The only visible thing in the sea of darkness was the small globe, glowing faintly at the other end of the cavern.

Callum stepped forward and took Jingwei's hand. "Any port in a storm," he said, and together they walked towards the light, each of them grinning secretly in the dark.

The globe grew slowly in their vision as they carefully crossed the wide, open floor of the cavern. Every few metres Callum would use the mechanism he had liberated from the guard to send a scattering of sparks into the air to make sure that they weren't about to walk into a hole in the floor or trip over an unseen raised platform.

Soon they were standing next to the fireball. Jingwei gasped as soon as the light was strong enough to see what was inside.

"Ythen!" She dropped Callum's hand instantly and rushed over to the pale fire cell.

Ythen was sitting on the floor, his blond hair hanging scraggily down around his shoulders. His clothes were worn and filthy from his battle with the thranvorl, and his scarred hands were bloody. He had been beating them in frustration and dismay against the hard floor of his prison since the night before when he had been caged.

He slowly looked up at the sound of Jingwei's voice, unable to believe that he was anything but alone in the oppressive blackness. It wasn't until Callum had dispersed his cell with the sparks and Jingwei was kneeling next to him, wrapping her arms around him that he fully realized what was happening was real.

"Jingwei? What are you doing here? How did you get in?" He looked up at Callum. "I thought you were dead!"

Callum tucked the sparking device into a pocket. "Been hearing that loads, lately."

"We were captured." Jingwei lifted the corner of her cloak to wipe his dirty, tear-stained face. "Kala tried to get us to tell her how to travel to Earth. She wants to invade, the nasty —"

"But when Jingwei got shirty with her, she sent us down here." Callum stayed standing back, feeling jealous about the tenderness with which Jingwei was applying her touch.

"Callum stole the fiery key thing—"

"Lifted." Callum interrupted. "I lifted the fiery key thing."

"Right. And so here we are." She drew up Ythen's chin and searched his face. "We're leaving now. Are you coming with us?"

In spite of himself Ythen smiled. "I have endured quite enough of the Spark Keeper's 'hospitality.' I will join you most gladly." He stood slowly, supported by the unassuming figure of Jingwei. He looked at the two Humans before him and marvelled. Each had been alone in their own time, as he was so often here. Yet they possessed a strength that he envied. To be able to stand toe to toe with the Spark Keeper and hold your own, and failing victory, to steal the keys off your guards as they transport you to the cell, break through the unreachable cell wall, and then rescue the one person who had been meant to protect them... Ythen only wished that he could possess such strength of will as they.

"You stole the sparker? They will soon notice its absence. We should hurry if we are to escape before they do."

"Do you know the way out?" Callum pursed his lips. "We lost track of directions."

"I never took my eyes off the way out. It is there." Ythen pointed between them and started walking, his limbs aching from the day and night spent on the hard, cold floor.

On the way across the cavern he shared with them the story of the battle with the thranvorl, and of Yriel's return and treachery. Callum was especially upset that she had claimed the kill of the second thranvorl that he had brought down. Ythen clapped him on the shoulder and promised that all of Tranthaea would know the truth soon enough. He then asked them for their stories, and the short version of each of their journeys quickly brought them to the prison entrance, which when close enough was dully illuminated by the glow of flowing lava from the corridor beyond.

Sitting outside the entryway on a stand of stone so flat that the edges were sharp were two Firedart and Buckler sets: Ythen's and Callum's, along with their bandoliers, still stocked with extra canisters. Kala obviously thought her ingenious cages so fool-proof that she felt no guards or other precautions were necessary.

"Overconfidence. That'll get her." Jingwei waited impatiently for the two boys to strap on their weapons, wondering at the curious looks that Ythen kept darting at Callum's bronze canister, and then led the way down the passage, leaving them both struggling to catch up in the dark.

They made their way down the black corridors, stopping at every crossing to check for guards, and always choosing the path that led down. Ythen was confident that eventually the palace hallways would open up from the walls of Du Garrah onto the foothills below, as Kala could hardly expect any non-flying supplicants to climb the cliff faces every time they came to see her.

The corridors became steeper and were soon graded so badly that the three of them had to hunch over and sidestep down the sleek slopes. These halls were lit by columns of glowing stalactites and stalagmites, whose brittle, translucent surface only thinly covered the burning rock buried beneath.

Callum had just begun thinking that they had to reach the bottom soon, or else they would run out of mountain, when he heard a faint noise echoing up from below.

"Shhh." He motioned wildly with his arms at Jingwei and at Ythen, who was being supported by the Human girl a few metres away.

They quieted immediately and all three strained their ears, hoping not to hear a sound.

They heard a sound. The frantic buzzing of wings rose quickly from the depths of the corridor; the sound enveloped them and grew until it seemed to be coming from inside their heads. Soon it was a deafening roar, the long smooth sides of the passage thrusting multiple echoes at them. It was difficult to think in the closed-in space with the terrific noise coming from everywhere and nowhere all at once.

Callum threw his hands up over his ears. A strange reflection on his Buckler caught his eye. The flowing light of the columns had revealed a small fissure in the otherwise unbroken wall to his right. He scuttled over and peeked inside.

It was a steep ramp that wound upwards in a tight spiral, much tighter than that of the stairway in the Keep in Yshaar.

It was the opposite direction from where they wanted to go, but Callum had lots of experience with running and hiding, and knew that they couldn't just wait for the guards to pass. If the Aru Elen checked the dungeon, down was the first place they would start looking for the escaped prisoners, and Callum couldn't count on finding more places to hide in the lower passages. The first priority was to stay out of sight.

Callum motioned for Jingwei and Ythen to follow him and the three of them ducked into the crack, rushing up the slope as quickly as possible.

The harsh buzzing sound of the oncoming swarm of Aru Elen faded behind them as the trio mounted the ramp, quickly losing themselves in the immensity of the Spark Keeper's palace.

Chapter Nineteen:
The Spire

Up, up, up. The ramp seemed to have no end, and the three escaping prisoners soon tired of the climb, their weary legs already sore from the difficult, stuttering descent down the steep corridors. Ythen was especially hurting. His legs were still stiff from the day and night he'd spent on the hard surface of the prison floor.

Kala's citadel was spread out beneath them; views of the great black fortress and its surroundings flashed in and out of existence as they laboured past tall, thin windows that broke up the otherwise unending blackness of the spire. With intermediate glances they could see that the distance to the palace below increased, and as the rock waste around it became enshrouded by a thick mist Jingwei realized that they must be in the soaring tower she and Callum had seen earlier, the one that had reached into the clouds.

It had been about twenty minutes before Callum came to a standstill. He turned around and leaned down, resting his hands on his knees and breathing heavily. The ramp's grade had decreased over the last few rounds and was now flat enough to allow for a stop. He motioned for the others to take a break, and then rose and crept forward to scout a bit farther up the circular passage.

Jingwei sat down hard on the stone floor and winced as her legs began to cramp. She reached out to rub her calves but Ythen beat her to it.

She looked at him, speechless for a moment, and a bit offended. He smiled up at her with a tired grin. "Do not worry. I have had to do this for many exhausted Quenchers after a long day's journey."

Like Yriel?, Jingwei thought. But she didn't say anything, grateful for the relief. The blond Daevyn let go of her legs and leaned back against the wall of the ramp. Jingwei shivered as she tried to relax.

Callum had returned and stood looking over them with a frown on his face. "Alright, Jingwei?"

Ythen answered him. "Her legs are fine." He seemed to realize what he'd said and his face went red. He spluttered for a moment while Callum glowered at him.

Jingwei took it all in from her seat between them, secretly delighted. She'd never been really chased by a boy, let alone been fought over by two!

Her thoughts were interrupted by Callum reaching down and placing his hand on her shoulder in a gesture she thought was more than a little possessive.

"There's a door up ahead, just round the bend. I'm gonna try it and see what's there." He lifted his hand and brought his Firedart to bear in front of him, quickly striding up the ramp.

"Then I'm coming with you." Jingwei got slowly to her feet, aided by Ythen. They hurried up behind Callum and reached him just as he got to the door.

He looked at them over his shoulder and grunted, then reached forward and grabbed the latch, jerking it sharply and quickly to avoid any unwanted noise.

He gave it a slight push, and the door swung open.

Callum peered into the room, his eyes peeking carefully over his Buckler. The small space was round, about three metres across. It was carved from the same slick black stone as the rest of the palace, but was lit by brilliantly clear air instead of foreboding rivers of lava and so the glossy stone took on a light sheen, looking far less ominous.

The walls of the room were little more than thick pillars separated by large archways that opened onto a wide balcony which ringed the room. One of the archways housed a thick wooden door that seemed to lead to nowhere but a long drop, while the rest were empty and provided a spectacular view. From the top of the tower at the top of the palace at the top of the mountains Callum could see across all of Tranthaea. The lofty city of Yshaar was dwarfed in comparison to their new location and looked like a needle in the distance, framed against an endless desert behind it to the west. In the south, the Korrahl Forest stretched for kilometres over hilly country, its borders lost to the horizon. In the east, Callum could see very little due to a heavy gathering of storm clouds, but the snow-capped peak of a tall mountain jumped out at him through the mist. To the north, the shining Sea of Nalani seemed to gather the air's light and reflect it back off of its ever-changing surface.

Callum took in all of this in a flash and then focused his attention on the spectacle in the middle of the room.

There was an old man.

He was floating in a globe of clear fire, much like the cells in which they'd been held in the dungeon, except this one was criss-crossed with ropes of flame that shifted, connecting and reconnecting with one another in an unbreakable pattern of confinement. The bonds were thick and glowed a deep, almost purple, red that Callum had never seen in a fire before.

Jingwei and Ythen pushed in behind Callum. Callum heard Ythen suck in some air when he saw the man floating in front of them.

"Jera!"

The Sea Keeper did not move, or even acknowledge Ythen's cry. Jingwei squeezed past Callum and stepped closer to the cage.

The man seemed ancient. His wrinkled face looked like her fingers after she'd spent too long in the shower. It was surrounded by a thick mane of white hair and a long beard, both of which floated slowly in the air around his head as if he were submerged underwater. His robes were many-layered and multi-hued, with each layer expressing a different shade of blue, from an almost-black tunic to a rich sapphire surcoat to a nearly white outer robe.

His bare feet dangled above the floor. He remained still, his eyes closed, his arms limp by his sides.

Ythen rushed over to him. He placed his hands on the surface of the cage and pushed. There was no effect. He turned to Callum.

"The sparker, quickly. We must free him!"

Callum stepped forward and released a shower of sparks onto the gilded cell. The fire didn't dim at all; it didn't even flicker.

Jingwei snatched the sparker out of Callum's hand.

"Let me try." She flicked the mechanism multiple times in quick succession, pouring sparks onto the surface of the sphere.

If anything, the ropes grew brighter, as if strengthened by the added flames.

Jingwei tossed the sparker back to Callum and sighed. She leaned in close to the globe, pressing her hands against it, pushing her face right up to the surface.

The old man's eyes flew open.

Jingwei stumbled back in surprise, letting out a small shriek before she caught herself. Callum and Ythen, who had been circling the cell looking for a weak point rushed back over to her. She pointed wordlessly at the floating man, who was now carefully rearranging some of his robes which had floated up around his knees.

Ythen left Jingwei to Callum and stepped forward. "Jera? Are you all right?"

"Yes indeed, quite all right my boy, thank you. Of course," he gestured at the ball of fire around him, "things could be better. Nice to have visitors though. Can you stay long?"

Jingwei's mouth dropped open. Callum's hand, which had been on her arm, supporting her, slipped free.

Ythen bowed slightly to the man. "I think it would be best if we left quickly, Sea Keeper. May we offer you any assistance?"

Jera grinned, and a mouthful of gleaming white teeth were revealed. "I thought you'd never ask. Which one of you has water as their Talent?"

Slowly Callum and Ythen turned their eyes to Jingwei, who looked as though she was considering bolting for the door and taking her chances with the guards.

Her voice slipped out quietly. "How did you know?"

"No idea!" His cheerful voice seemed distant, as if the sound was having trouble escaping from the cage. "But I felt it from one of you. About time you showed up, too. It's been a long three hundred years, and I'm tired."

Jingwei goggled. "Three hundred years?"

Jera winked at her. "But I don't look a day over two ninety-five, right?" He looked over at Callum. "Water sports. That's what keeps me young. Can you swim?"

Callum shook his head.

"Shame. But from the look of you, I'd guess Fire. Yes? Thought so. It's the hair. Spark Keepers so often seem to have red hair. Don't know why."

Callum held his hand up to stop the monologue. "Spark Keepers? I think you've made a mistake. I'm just a boy. Kala is the Spark Keeper."

"Oh, I see. And you think she should stay in that position, do you?"

Jingwei snorted. Jera's grin widened. "I think you and I are going to get along just fine, Ms..."

"Jingwei Li. And this is Callum Swift. And Ythen Firebrand."

"Yes, yes, hello Ythen." He nodded to the Daevyn and then turned back to the Humans with a wink. "Ythen and I go way back." The old man's eyes crinkled in good humour as Ythen's eyebrow's lifted. "Not three hundred years, of course, but still. When was it now? The day you were named First Quencher? Or before that, back when you were still chasing that girl all over the plains...?" Jera saw Ythen's expression morph into anger and diplomatically abandoned that line of conversation. "Well, we've met, anyway. So... Callum and Jingwei. Fire and Water. An interesting balance, that. Not bad. Not bad at all. All right. Go on then." Jera leaned back and crossed his ankles, his floating body reclining slowly as his robes drifted up around him. He casually reached down and covered himself up again. "I'm waiting. Show me what you've got."

Jingwei and Callum exchanged glances. She could see in his eyes that he was near panic; the idea of becoming a guardian of an entire world was overwhelming for her as well, but if what Jera said was true then Callum would have to challenge Kala for her position. Suddenly she saw in him the young boy that had been slapping at fires on the plains, afraid and unsure of himself. She had needed to support him then, just as they had supported one another since. In spite of how much they had grown in the past few days, events seemed to be outpacing them, pushing them past boundaries they hadn't known existed. Jingwei swallowed her own nerves, reached out her hand, and placed it on Callum's chest, feeling the quick pumping of his heartbeat.

Ythen scowled and stepped back. Jingwei ignored him for the moment, looked into Callum's eyes, and said, "One step at a time. Let's get him free and get out of here. We can deal with everything else later."

Callum bit his cheek and nodded slowly. Together they turned towards the cell containing the expectant Sea Keeper and raised their hands.

Jingwei closed her eyes. She didn't feel anything different or special. The thick air surrounded her and she breathed deeply, trying to search for the moisture in the air. She tasted its coolness on her tongue.

"Concentrate." Jera's voice filtered out to them from inside his cell.

Callum frowned. He glanced over at Jingwei and saw that she had closed her eyes. Ythen had stepped back to close the door to the room and appeared to be standing guard. Jera still floated in the cell. He raised his eyebrow to Callum, who rolled his eyes and then shut them.

Callum furrowed his brow. Behind his eyelids, all he saw was blackness. He felt like a fool, half expecting the others in the room to burst out laughing at his gullibility.

Jera's spoke again. "You feel nothing because you don't know what to look for. Let's call this your first lesson. Callum, find what is there and weaken it. Jingwei, find what is not there, and strengthen it."

Callum squeezed his eyes tighter until stars and white flecks began to float in his vision. He tried to imagine where he was in the room, and where the cell was. The stars in his eyes shifted, adjusting themselves into a shape that he vaguely recognised.

Callum realized that the circle of white that he could see wasn't an afterburn on his eyes, but was instead the fire globe. He loosened his eyelids slightly in realization and suddenly a full image of the cage solidified in the blackness before him, each rope singly defined, each layer of the cell wall bared to him. More than that, he could *feel* them. Not just like an annoyance in the back of his mind, like before in the prison, but physically. The placement of the moving bars was as if they were crawling over his palm; he could follow each one and anticipate its movement.

He took a breath, and thought. In his mind, the ropes became still. He heard a rustle of fabric from behind him as Ythen shifted. Callum ignored the sound and remembered what Jera had said. *Find what is there and weaken it.* In his mind's eye the globe dimmed, the fire ropes vanishing.

Callum opened his eyes. Jera stood in front of him now, his feet planted firmly on the ground. The globe was still visible, but much less so.

"Not bad for a first try. Not bad at all. All right Jingwei, your turn."

Jingwei was still standing quietly, her face scrunched up. She'd stepped forward and placed her hand on the rounded wall of the cell. Jera had told her to find what *wasn't* there, and she still hadn't found anything, which may have been the point, she wasn't sure. She was tempted to open her eyes and sarcastically pronounce the operation a success when she noticed something.

The air that played over her arms and face was dry, but not entirely so. The coolness she'd felt on her tongue was the result of a tiny bit of moisture. As she concentrated, Jingwei noticed that she could feel the water in the air throughout the entire room, and could almost see the thick, wet clouds that surrounded the tower.

But in front of her there was nothing. An empty sphere, void of moisture. Jingwei drummed her fingers against the cell wall. For a reason she did not understand, the void bothered her. She opened her eyes, pressed her palms hard against the fireball, and imagined all the water in the room dousing the flame and rushing into the space, filling it with cool, life-giving liquid.

The fireball exploded.

Jingwei was knocked to the floor where she desperately clung onto the nearest thing she could find, which happened to be Callum's foot. A wave of fire washed overhead, surrounding Callum and then moving past him towards the door. She heard a cry as she raised her head to a bewildering tableau.

Jera was standing unharmed in the middle of the room, his prison destroyed. Callum was hovering over her, seemingly untouched by the flames that had engulfed him only seconds before. And Ythen was still near the door, fighting to hold on to what looked like an uncooperative ball of fire that was palpitating between his palms.

The struggle on his face was evident, but he kept his hands pressed together and stumbled through one of the archways onto the balcony, stopping just in time to keep from falling off the edge. He thrust his hands forward, releasing the small fireball which quickly grew back to its original size and soared away in a vast arc, burning a tunnel through the clouds, over the mountains, and into the land beyond.

Callum helped Jingwei to her feet and they quickly padded over to the ledge where Ythen was standing. He was staring down at his hands, playing a finger over the scars on his palm.

"It didn't burn me. I..." He turned to look at them. "I don't know what happened."

"I'll tell you what happened!" Jera hollered from inside and clapped his hands as they turned back into the room. "You freed me!" He glanced at Ythen and placed his finger on the side of his nose conspiratorially. "All three of you." Ythen looked confused, but Jera brushed the moment aside with a wink. "Now, Kala hasn't come to see me much since she brought me here, so we should be safe for the moment. Why don't you tell me what you all are doing here?"

The young Humans had long since gotten into the habit of explaining themselves, and it didn't take long to furnish Jera with short versions of their stories, interspersed with Ythen's own tale.

When they were finished, Jera looked up at them from his place on the floor where he sat cross-legged with his robes artfully arranged around him.

"Fascinating." He chewed his lip thoughtfully. "So she's taking the water away. I wondered what she was using me for." At a look from the kids he nodded. "Oh yes, she was using my power. I'm not sure how, but that cell she built was constantly taking it out of me." He buried his hand in his beard and scratched. "Exhausting work. But why? And where's she putting it all? Fascinating," he said again, before falling silent.

Callum broke the silence. "But, please sir; will you help us stop her? She's barmy! She wants to invade Earth!" He added in a helpful addendum, "That's where we came from."

Jera looked up sharply. "I know all about Earth, thank you very much. It'll take more than three hundred years to make me forget home!"

Callum blushed. Of course, Jera was the third Human Keeper.

"I'm from Canada. Year: 1984." Jera rose slowly to his feet. "Good times."

"That's not that far off from 2012, when I'm from! LA!" Jingwei laughed. She looked at the old man in his robes and felt a strange sense of familiarity. It was nice to feel a connection to home after so many days in such a strange place.

"That's all well and good, but what do we do now?" Callum asked.

Jera gave Callum a wry smile and brushed some dirt off of his robes. "I don't know about you, but I'm going to follow the water. I never told Kala, but I've recently noticed that although the water's still moving, my strength was being used less and less."

Ythen asked, "What does that mean?"

Jingwei answered him. "It means that if she didn't need his power to draw the water away anymore, then something else is doing the work."

"Exactly right." Jera stepped over to the edge of the balcony and looked down through the darkening evening air at the clouds below. "And that means that Kala may have started something that she can't control. I have to find out what's going on."

"But can't we just stop her? Catch her now, unawares?"

Jera laughed out loud and turned back. "Callum, I love your enthusiasm, but this is Kala's home ground. She's a powerful Keeper and has more guards than I've had birthdays, and we have Ythen, a very tired old man, and you two." He cocked his head. "Still want to storm the gates?"

Callum shook his head and looked to the ground. Jingwei opened her mouth to reassure him but stopped when Ythen stepped forward and put his hand on Callum's shoulder encouragingly. She smiled up at the Daevyn boy.

He smiled back.

"Right. Time to go!" Jera rounded them up and had them stand on the ledge beside him. "Jingwei, pay attention. You'll enjoy this. Callum, not so much. Ythen... well, you're a bit of a puzzle, aren't you? So we'll just wait and see, yes? Hold your breath."

He raised his arms up above them. They heard a loud sucking noise, as if someone were trying to reach the last few drops of water with a straw, and then they were falling off the balcony, down the full length of the spire, each encased in enormous drops of water!

Jingwei recovered first. After gasping in shock, she found that she could breathe easily in the water. It was thicker than the air, but not by much. She looked around her, watching the tower stones and clouds flash by, their lines broken and refracted by the water. She could see Jera, calmly surveying the fall in his drop, and Callum and Ythen, struggling madly together, clutching each other's cloaks and gaping like goldfish.

Their descent slowed and then stopped as their momentum shifted forwards. The drops raced each other along the palace walls for a second, hiding their passage behind thick, black crenellations before they sailed out past the walls and over a sudden rise in the cliff tops that looked like a broken spine.

Then the ground was drawing up quickly beneath them. In a moment they struck, the water drops bursting and splattering like a series of broken water balloons, darkening the already black stone of the plateau as the passengers alit.

Jingwei stumbled a bit as her drop burst, but managed to maintain her footing. Jera landed dignified and composed, as if he has just stepped off a short flight of stairs, but Callum and Ythen both ended up on the ground in a heap, a gasping pile of tangled limbs and clothes.

"Hallelujah, it's raining men." Jingwei made herself sound calm and collected.

Jera roared with laughter, his beard floating expansively around his head. He smoothed it away with his hands. "Sorry about that. Travelling by rain can be a bit of a shock the first time."

Callum looked up at him. "Less of a shock than travelling by lightning, sir."

Jera laughed again and clapped an arm around Callum's shoulder. "Oh, I like you too. You all will do just fine." He stepped back and his drop of water reformed around him, lifting him up in the dusky air.

"Wait, Sea Keeper, where are you going? You cannot leave us here!" Ythen had pulled himself out of the tangle with Callum and stepped in behind Jingwei's left shoulder.

"You'll be fine!" Jera's water-drop drifted toward the cliff's edge. "I have great faith in you."

"But what should we do now?" Callum placed himself on Jingwei's other side.

Jera's voice was muffled by the water. "Tranthaea must know of the Spark Keeper's treachery." His expression darkened. "Inform the Daevyn, the gru'Esh, the Aru Len. Kala has been drying this world. It now only needs a spark to explode into destruction. Stop her. I will help you if I can."

And before the three could say anything else, his water-drop plummeted over the side of the cliff, and he was gone.

Ythen didn't waste any time. "The Sea Keeper is correct. We must get to the Daevyn and report to the Flame-Bearer. Kala has betrayed us all."

Jingwei nodded. Callum had walked over to the edge of the cliff and was looking down at the distant foothills below. "But first we have to get down."

"Not 'til tomorrow." Jingwei was looking up at the sky. The lightning over the plains was visible now. Night was falling quickly, and the air was turning dark and chilly. "We need to find a place to camp for the night."

They searched for about fifteen minutes in the spine-like rock formation until Callum found a crack in the stone that would do them nicely. It was wide enough to fit two bodies and a small fire, with enough of an overhang that the light shouldn't be visible from the fortress. Ythen used some scrub brush and his Firedart to start a blaze small enough to be invisible to distant eyes but large enough to keep them warm, and scrounged up some stalks of a few thick, meaty, cactus-like plants that they roasted over the fire, sucking at the warm juice until they felt full and drowsy. When they were finished, Callum volunteered to take the first watch.

They settled in for the night.

Jingwei found herself cuddled into a ball, her cloak wrapped tightly around her. Across the fire from her, beneath a thick overhang of stone was Ythen, who was already snoring softly. A short distance away, just outside the fire's glow she could see Callum's back as he sat hunched against the cold.

Two such very different boys. One was a Human like her. Callum was sweet and kind, and cute. And he was so protective. But he was younger than her. And still so unsure of himself. Maybe she only felt close to him because they were sharing this experience.

And then there was Ythen. Responsible, respectful, not to mention easy on the eyes. A true leader. She hadn't spent much time with him, but sometimes that wasn't necessary, right? And she could see from the way he looked at her that he felt the same way.

Both of them were a better bet than Hunter Wells.

Jingwei tried to banish the thoughts that swirled around in her head. She had always prided herself on being focused and intelligent, and not flighty and flirty like so many of the other girls her age.

Time to concentrate. She had more important things to think about. Jera had hinted, and not very subtly, that she was here to replace him as Sea Keeper. She was still dazed when she considered the idea.

Scared, too. Not that it would be a problem leaving Earth behind. She didn't have any real friends, or any real family. But what did she know about this world? For all her bravado, Jingwei had never enjoyed being a risk-taker.

But sometimes you have to take a risk if you want to get the reward. Jingwei's gaze strayed back over to Ythen's sleeping form, and then to Callum's still silhouette. Her eyes stayed mobile, drifting back and forth between them as the Sea Keeper's prediction faded from her mind, only just settling on one figure before they closed in exhaustion and she fell asleep.

Callum sat a few metres out with his back to the fire to retain his night vision. He'd thought he'd heard the buzzing of wings once or twice, but both times it had been a false alarm. The wind whistling through the pointy ridges of the rocks created a humming sound that would've been soothing had he not been so on edge.

And it wasn't just the possibility of recapture that had him squirming. His thoughts were a jumbled mess; they seemed to be flickering in front of him, dancing around his shadow, cast by the firelight's glow. Too much had happened, too much to think about. *Callum Swift, Spark Keeper.* It sounded impossible. Just as impossible as flying creatures, blind cave-dwellers, talking trees, and lightning travel.

And then there was Jingwei. She seemed to fill the space between his restless thoughts, refusing to allow them purchase in his mind, keeping them swirling around in a losing battle for focus. As frustrating as she was, the only sense he could make of his whole situation was that Jingwei had come to mean more to him in the last few days than he would have thought possible. When he had first met the small Chinese-American he'd found her obnoxious and annoyingly forthright. She'd spurned his help, teased him continuously, and now, for some reason, he didn't want it to end.

But he expected it would. Ythen was a good chap, and Callum had noticed how Jingwei's eyes lit up whenever he talked to her or took her hand.

And if he was being honest, why would he even expect her to choose him over Ythen? Ythen was a trained warrior, a leader, and an all-around-good guy. Callum was a street rat, poor, uneducated, and young.

Callum sighed.

There was a slight rustle behind him, and he whirled around, his Firedart tracking.

Ythen's clipped voice issued from the darkness. "Hold. Callum, it is only me. I have come to relieve you." He sidled up and sat on a rock beside Callum.

Callum stood and stretched his legs, then turned to head in to the fire. He could feel the embers from here, and he knew now that if he wanted to, he could have it blazing like a bonfire in no time.

Ythen hesitated. He wasn't sure if he wanted to have this conversation, but knew if he didn't he might soon regret it. He heard Callum move to go back to the fire and spoke.

"Callum, wait. I wish to ask you something." Ythen swallowed. "I have no desire to interfere. If you and Jingwei are... together, then I will respect that. I consider you a friend."

Callum nodded gratefully, and silently. Ythen continued. "But if you are not, then I would ask your permission to pursue her." Ythen looked past Callum at Jingwei's sleeping form. "She is... something else."

Just past the fire-pit, Jingwei's chest rose and fell in the slow, rhythmic pattern of sleep. Her face was exquisitely defined by the hot, red glow of the embers and, lacking the sarcastic twist it normally held, her mouth was curled up into a sweet smile that made Ythen forget their situation, if only just for a moment.

When he'd first seen her, her short, black hair, her dark eyes, her light-tan skin tone; all of these things had seemed unusual to his eyes, so used to seeing yellow hair and pale, white skin. But now, they seemed to him to be the epitome of beauty. Once, he'd thought her too similar to Yriel for his tastes; too strong, too independent, too wild. But now... he had come to not only appreciate her strength, but to rely on it. Where his relationship with Yriel had been competitive, with Jingwei it was complementary.

"Well, we can agree on that, right enough." Callum stepped back towards the First Quencher, his face hidden in shadow. "But blimey, Ythen, I just don't know what we are, or what she wants us to be. I hardly know what I want us to be."

It was Ythen's turn to nod silently. Callum continued, "I think, in her time, it is more customary for women *and* men to... pursue *each other*. I say we let her decide, and stay mates regardless of her decision." Callum put out his hand.

Ythen reached out and shook it, firmly.

"You are a good man, Callum Swift. Wise beyond your years. And you will make an excellent Spark Keeper. Now, go and get some sleep. I will keep watch until morning." He turned and faced out over the plateau, closing his eyes tight to let them adjust to the darkness.

Chapter Twenty:
The Muster

Callum shook Jingwei's shoulder gently. She groaned and rolled over, pulling her aquamarine cloak up around her chin.

"Just five more minutes..."

She'd been having such a nice dream, but as her eyes fluttered open, shielding themselves in shifts against the bright morning air, the dream started to fade.

It had been about Ythen. Or Callum. Or had it been Hunter? She remembered that there had been a bridge. Yes, definitely a bridge. Or maybe a tunnel...

Callum shook her again. "Jingwei. It's morning. We've gotta scarper before Kala's scouts find us. Ythen's gone to look for a way down."

Jingwei rolled over and grunted. She slowly let her eyes adjust to the light while Callum busied himself kicking the remains of the fire-pit apart so that the Aru Len wouldn't find it.

When she finally got up, she found Callum sitting on a rock. She wasn't surprise to see him practising creating flames on the palms of his hands. Her own sensitivity had increased after yesterday's lesson from the Sea Keeper. It was as if a dam had broken, and their abilities were now nearer to the surface than they had ever been before.

Callum lit a few more flames. They *cracked* into existence and then *puffed* out, creating a flickering light show in front of him. His skills certainly seemed to be developing quickly.

Jingwei moved a bit away from him and then closed her eyes. She found what little water was in the air, but decided to leave it there, and turned her mind instead to the clouds above her. She focused, and then opened her eyes to find a ball of water floating in the air in front of her.

It seemed that this really was her Talent. Now that Jera had helped her break that barrier, she found it easy to manipulate water. She broke the water into several balls and juggled them through the air, only dropping one to splash on her feet, which, against all odds, remained perfectly dry.

Impressed with herself, she splashed some of the water onto her face. She had to focus to allow herself to get wet, but once she did her face, hands, and hair all got a thorough cleansing.

She finished up and made the water-ball follow her over to Callum, who was now moving a series of flames in a complicated pattern through the air in front of him. He looked up at her approach and grinned, but his smile faded suddenly when she shot two small balls of water out that splashed into his dancing flames, extinguishing them.

He responded by opening his palm with a quick, forceful motion, sending the tongues of flame in all directions, making them hover at different heights all around the camp.

Jingwei understood immediately and concentrated, sending water-balls to snuff out each flame, one at a time.

She only missed twice, and was forced to bring the ball back around in a sharp curve to hit the flame dead on.

On her final shot, she noticed that the flame was burning brighter than the others; it was almost white. She sent her last ball of water at it and it struck dead centre, sizzling and evaporating on impact.

The flame flickered on in the air.

Jingwei looked at Callum, who was looking to the sky and whistling nonchalantly.

She quickly called another shot of water into existence and threw it at him. He responded just as quickly, summoning a flame and intercepting her shot.

There was a quick sizzle and both the flame and the water-ball vanished in a puff of steam.

Callum laughed.

Jingwei narrowed her eyes.

When Ythen returned, his hands full, he found the two Humans battling one another fiercely; the plateau was ringing with the sound of their laughter. Whoops of victory and defeat carried over the black stone and he sighed.

They might be powerful, but they had forgotten very quickly the danger they were in here.

He entered the camp, ducking quickly to avoid a stray shot of water.

"I see that you two have embraced your Tranthaean destinies." He stepped up to Jingwei. "I also hear it. As Kala may have. Perhaps silence would be a better watchword for this moment?"

Jingwei giggled and hung her head in mock shame. When she looked back up again she found herself staring at a bouquet of freshly picked wildflowers in Ythen's hand. They were orange and red and yellow, and as the petals flitted in the breeze they looked like they were ablaze in his hand.

"These are for you, Jingwei Li. They are called Forgeflowers, and are a traditional Daevyn gift of courtship. With them I wish to declare my intentions towards you. Do you accept them?"

Jingwei froze with her hands half extended. She glanced at Callum out of the corner of her eye and saw that he was scratching a rock against the ground with his toe, very industriously not watching them. She looked back up at Ythen's nervous face and took a deep breath, remembering the dream she had in the Warrens and the look of hope on Callum's face at the waterfall.

Jingwei felt the bittersweet pang of regret, knowing that whatever action she took, one of the boys would be hurt.

But she had made her decision last night, and now, in the clear light of the morning, she knew that it was the right one.

"I do." She reached the rest of the way and took the flowers from him. "And thank you, Ythen."

Callum suddenly laughed out loud. Jingwei turned on him furiously and saw that he was looking down at her hands. She looked down as well.

The Forgeflowers that Ythen had given her had wilted at her touch, and were now lying dead in her hand. She'd been so flustered at Ythen's advance that she hadn't felt the rush of water that had defended her sensitive Talent against the fiery nature of the flowers, drowning them.

She looked up at Ythen, whose face was red with embarrassment.

"I'm sorry, Ythen. I didn't mean to. They're very..." She looked back down at the flowers. A greying petal fell to the ground between them. "Nice flowers," she finished.

Callum was still chortling in the background, and so was too busy to stop the ball of water that smacked into his face.

He spluttered and cleared his eyes as Jingwei proudly stalked back to the crack in the rock to lay her flowers down in peace.

Ythen stepped up next to him and looked at him questioningly. "No hard feelings then?"

Callum returned his gaze with a grin. "It's not over yet." He slapped Ythen on the back and looked down at the Quencher's other hand. "What are those?"

Ythen held up his makeshift cage. In it were three creatures he had caught this morning in their nests among the rocks of Du Garrah.

"These are stimae. They will be our way down off the mountain."

The creatures were each about the size and shape of a thin log of firewood. They were covered in a short, thick brown fur with a hole at each end that made them look almost like hollow tubes. Bulbous black eyes sat on top of their bodies, marking their front end, and six stubby legs protruded from the bottom, but their bodies were stiff. Their feet scrabbled for purchase but the thin cage didn't allow for any movement. Two long bumps ran parallel down their backs. They shuffled and hissed, but did nothing that gave Callum any clue as to how they were going to help the trio down off the mountain.

Ythen saw his confusion and smiled. "Do not worry, Callum Swift, future Spark Keeper of Tranthaea. You will see."

Callum rolled his eyes.

Ythen took the cage over to the cliff's edge. Callum followed behind and soon Jingwei joined them from the rocks. They looked out over the foothills and plains far below.

The heat and light in the morning air had banished all low-lying clouds, affording them a full view of the plains.

What they saw surprised them all.

The plains below the mountains were crowded with life. Out to the west Ythen could see the blue banners of the entire Daevyn army camped on the plains. Below them, near the base of Du Garrah, the foothills housed a collection of holes that were disgorging swarms of gru'Esh. Callum could make out the black of the je'Esh and the red of the an'Esh, and was willing to bet that the other two tribes were present as well.

To the south Jingwei noticed that the forest was slowly advancing, with two small figures at its head, but it seemed that Ila and Rata's search for Alkira had failed; no Aru Elen Keeper was with them. Farther to the north, another small figure, who looked to be surrounded by a globe of blue, was almost lost in the shimmering reflection of the border of the shining sea. As they watched, the figure slowly detached itself from the watery horizon and began to move to the south, but Jingwei knew that it would not arrive at the meeting ground any time soon.

Still, the three Human Keepers were on their way.

As they watched the races draw nearer to one another, Ythen noticed a slight buzzing noise that slowly grew louder and louder. Suddenly he swung around in realization and grabbed Callum and Jingwei and threw them to the ground beside a boulder, motioning at them to stay hidden behind the rocks.

Seconds later, a massive flock of Aru Len droned overhead, led by the black-clad Spark Keeper. Both Aru Elen and Aru Faylen soared out over the plains, swiftly descending into the mass of creatures below.

As the last of them dropped below the plateau's surface, Jingwei rose slowly to her feet.

"Jera was right. *We* were right." She turned to the boys. "Don't you see? She's caused it all to come to a head. All the conflict of the water disappearing, the Forest's advance, the gru'Esh Congress, the fires on the plains, it's all come together. Now she's going down to finish the job."

Jingwei turned back out to the plains. Her voice was low and angry. "We have to stop her."

Callum turned to Ythen. "So, how do these things get us down?"

Ythen grinned a smile that didn't reach his eyes. He wasn't pleased to see his armies being manipulated into a conflict. He reached into the cage and grasped one of the stimae. He held it above his head, his hands firmly cupping around the circular body, carefully avoiding the ridges on its back, and then he stepped forward into the air over the cliff's edge, plunging to the ground.

Jingwei and Callum gasped and rushed forward to the edge, afraid to watch Ythen's body tumble to the ground.

What they saw instead was nothing short of astonishing.

Below them was Ythen, still gripping firmly onto the body of his stimae. The creature was slowly circling as it descended; the two bumps on its back had extended out into long, hard glider wings. It lazily drifted downwards, with Ythen correcting its course every so often by swinging one way or the other.

"Come on!" Ythen's voice drifted up from below them. "We have to hurry!" If he said anything else, his voice was lost in the distance and the dense, bright morning air.

Callum stepped back from the edge and looked down at the cage. The remaining two stimae were scuttling around now, unable to escape without being able to extend their wings.

Jingwei was still looking out at the long drop to the foothills. Callum picked up the two gliding creatures and pushed one into her hands.

"If we want to stop her—"

"I know." Jingwei fumbled with the stimae for a moment, trying to find the best grip. She found it, took a deep breath, and then hesitated, looking back over her shoulder and opening her mouth.

Callum rolled his eyes and gently pushed her from behind, sending her off the cliff, and then jumped after her.

He was unprepared for the sudden jerk that he felt when the stimae extended its wings, but managed to hold on.

Jingwei wasn't as lucky. The jerk dislodged her grip and she fell from the stimae with a scream.

Callum looked down in horror, unable to take his eyes off of her as she plummeted to the ground.

He leaned forward and his glider picked up speed, chasing her falling form through the air, which seemed to pull at his cloak as if trying desperately to slow him down. The stimae seemed to understand his need and began to suck air in through its front vent and expel it through the rear, creating a jetting effect that sped its progress along.

Jingwei's body had already caught up with Ythen, who looked shocked to see her whip past him towards the ground, which was coming up fast.

Callum arrived next to Ythen and the two of them watched together as Jingwei righted herself and stretched out her arms. Quickly, a ball of water formed around her, thin at first but then thick and full like Jera's had been the evening before.

The teardrop shape slowed her fall and she allowed the boys to catch up with her, carefully moving her hand to fix her hair when they did, as if to show them she had everything under control.

Which, Callum supposed, she did.

Only a few seconds later they reached the ground. Ythen landed gracefully, releasing his stimae to glide back up, sending out bursts of air as it went. Callum landed in a heap and had to throw his stimae up into the air where it puffed away indignantly. Jingwei landed carefully as well, then allowed her bubble to burst expansively, drenching the two frantic boys.

Callum rushed through the shower to her.

"Jingwei! I'm so sorry! I didn't think you would—"

Jingwei laughed, her calm attitude not quite covering the tightness around her eyes. "Don't worry about it. I had a foster dad that did that once." She placed her hand on his chest and pushed him lightly to show she had no hard feelings. "Of course, he only pushed me into a swimming pool... Still, I managed to get out of it. We'll call it a learning experience."

Callum sighed in relief. His hands were shaking. Jingwei noticed and placed her hands on his. "I'll just have to provide you with a learning experience someday myself."

She grinned and flicked a drop of water off his nose. It whirled three times around his head, collecting friends, and then splashed down onto his hair, soaking him again.

"And you seriously have to stop asking me to jump off cliffs."

Ythen stepped up. "As long as you are all right, we should keep moving. There is no knowing what Kala might accomplish if we do not stop her."

Callum looked up from wringing out his clothes. "He's right. We should go."

The three of them looked down the hill from where they stood at the base of the mountain.

There, in the middle of the masses, was a collection of ambassadors. They looked to be arguing.

Kala was among them.

Chapter Twenty-One:
The Parlay

Jingwei pushed her way through the mob of gru'Esh, led by mi'Orha, the je'Esh leader. Callum and Ythen followed behind her as a sort of self-appointed honour guard. It was tough going, as most of the gru'Esh had covered their sensitive nostrils with dirt, filtering the bright, thick air, but also dampening their senses. Everywhere they turned there was a minor collision as the blind gru'Esh bumped senselessly around.

Ahead, through the shifting mass of creatures Jingwei could see a circular clearing. She followed mi'Orha past the last wall of gru'Esh and stepped into it. The tan grasses of the plains had been trampled flat by the leaders of the peoples of Tranthaea, who were gathered within.

As Callum and Ythen entered behind her, Jingwei took stock of the wide circle of people. Sitting well across from her on a portable throne was the Daevyn Flame-Bearer. Her white hair was wrapped ornately around her simple crown, securing it firmly to her head. Instead of her usual rich brown and blue robes, Ydelle Emberhand was clothed in close-fitting tights, over which she wore a suit of light silver armour. Her tall, slender figure that had been so regally cloaked when they'd first met her was now shown to be a lean, tightly muscled figure that belied her age. Her sharp face had shed all traces of the friendliness with which she had greeted them in Yshaar only four days ago.

The Flame-Bearer seemed to be deep in thought. She was staring intently at the ground in front of her, drumming her fingers on her throne. Directly to her right was Rata, the Seed Keeper, who appeared to be arguing with the three other Clan Leaders of the gru'Esh with a dazed look in his eyes. Behind him was a tall, grey tree that Jingwei recognized as being one of the many bodies of Huon Arrahl. The tree looked much like all the others in the Korrahl Forest, save for a single loose tendril that hung down from its uppermost branches and was draped delicately over Rata's shoulder. Apparently, Huon Arrahl was using the Seed Keeper as a translator.

The three gru'Esh Clan Leaders were standing with their backs to Jingwei, not yet aware of her presence, spitting forth rhetoric in their harsh language at anyone who would listen, which seemed to be no one. The Soil Keeper, Ila, was beside them, turning her head back and forth, conversing with a dinged-up v'Aros of the ka'Esh gru'Esh on her left and two Aru Faylen on her right, one who was markedly bigger than the other.

Ythen stepped forward beside Jingwei and whispered into her ear, "That is Throm. He is the Aru Faylen who brought Kala to me two nights ago. He is not to be trusted."

Jingwei nodded. Her attention was focused on the remaining two members of the circle.

Standing between the Aru Faylen and the Flame-Bearer were two figures with whom Jingwei, Callum, and Ythen had personal scores to settle: Kala and Yriel.

Kala was standing silently, her face a mask of benevolent concern that every so often slipped to show the pride beneath. She was surveying the chaos that she had orchestrated. The noise of arguments filled the clearing, voices layering one over the other in repeated bids for supremacy.

Across the circle v'Aros reached an arm up threateningly toward the smaller of the two Aru Faylen, who backed away in the air quickly, its thrumming propellers pitching in protest.

Jingwei clenched her fists when she saw Kala's lips twitch in a quickly subdued smile. The Human girl raised her hands and formed a small ball of water from the moisture in the air. Ythen and Callum saw and opened their mouths to dissuade her but before they could say a word the water-ball was flying through the air, aimed directly at Kala's face.

The water-ball burst into flames before it reached its target. When the steam cleared, Kala's burning eyes were fixed on Jingwei, who, along with Callum and Ythen, was now stepping between v'Aros and Ila into the circle.

Yriel's mouth dropped open when she saw them and she let out a cry of surprise. The rest of the circle was hushed as they watched the three youths come to a halt in the centre.

Jingwei didn't stand on ceremony. Before anyone else could open their mouths she pointed straight at Kala and pronounced, "This is all her doing!"

For once Callum wasn't embarrassed by her forthright approach, and he elbowed Ythen when he saw the Quencher wince. Callum had a personal score to settle with Kala, who was so misusing her powers and position.

Jera was right. She could not remain in her position. *But am I ready...?*

He caught the eye of Yriel, who was still standing beside Kala. Her already white complexion had gone even paler at the sight of the Humans and her First Quencher. She blinked once, slowly, and then with obvious effort, asserted control over her features.

Yriel coolly looked away from Callum, her eyes skimming past Ythen without a trace of guilt or regret to land on Jingwei, who was still speaking.

"—and then we escaped, and now here we are. And just in time to warn you all!" Jingwei surveyed the crowd with a victorious gaze. "So, you can go ahead and arrest her, or whatever it is that you do here."

Silence met her words. She tried again.

"Go on, arrest her." No one moved. "Seize her!" Still no response. "Off with her head?"

Kala smoothly stepped forward into the centre of the circle, carefully arranging her black robes and turned slowly, addressing her words to the entire ring.

"Ridiculous. The child must be ill." She raised her voice to be heard over Jingwei's squawks of denial. "I am Kala, the Spark Keeper of Tranthaea. What use have I for water?" She stopped her turn and leaned in so that her face was level with Jingwei's. "Human. This is not your home. These are not your people. Our world has trouble enough without you bringing false accusations to set us at one another's throats."

Ila spoke from her place in the circle. "You were looking for the young Humans, Kala. Your tame Aru Elen were searching the forest."

"And who asked me to look for them? The once-First Quencher, Ythen Firebrand, on behalf of the Flame-Bearer. I have only ever served the throne of the Daevyn."

Kala abruptly whipped around, her cloak swirling round her feet in a black and red whirlwind, a cloud of grey smoke billowing out to dissipate over the ground. She faced Ydelle, the Flame-Bearer of the Daevyn, but her voice soared past her to the crowds beyond.

"I warned you once, Ydelle Emberhand, that the arrival of these Humans would bring pain and torment to your people, and to the peoples of Tranthaea. You did not heed my advice, and now our world is straining at the peace that has reigned it for so many years. Will you heed me even now, when armies face each other over battle lines drawn by this little girl and her pets?"

Kala looked back over her shoulder at the three and her gaze struck at both Callum and Ythen. They focused on the Daevyn warrior with the white-hot heat of a smith's forge.

"Or will you be blinded to the truth and lost to her cunning as your First Quencher has been?"

Ythen opened his mouth to object, but closed it again at a motion from the Flame-Bearer.

Ydelle drummed her long, thin fingers on the arm of her throne. Her eyes flitted sharply from Kala to Jingwei and Callum, and then to her daughter and Ythen.

The rest of the circle was silent, save for the restless motion of anticipation. The stillness had even spread to the warriors that were standing in waves behind their leaders, ready to fight and die or to leave a bloodless field, depending on the words of those in the circle.

The thick air seemed especially pressing now; Callum could feel it slowly swirling around him, tickling the hairs on his neck and slipping steadily through his fingers. The intensity of the moment left his senses heightened, and he imagined that this was only a fraction of what the hypersensitive gru'Esh must feel all the time.

No wonder they were all on edge.

The Flame-Bearer slapped her hand down on the armrest.

"Jingwei Li. Callum Swift." She hesitated, and then continued, "Ythen Firebrand. Have any proof that these accusations are true? Or do you intend to malign our oldest and most trusted advisor only with hearsay while you lead us around by the nose?"

Jingwei's mouth dropped open. She couldn't believe it! Out of the corner of her eye she imagined she saw Kala and Yriel exchanging a glance, but before she could say anything, a strange, musical voice sounded, a voice rhythmically created from opened pores in whirring propellers.

Throm, the Aru Faylen Delevate, was hovering beside Yriel and slowly bobbed up and down as his propellers shifted their speeds to create the sounds necessary for speech.

"The Aru Len have a theory of our own," he said. "It is the water that has brought conflict to our land, after so many years of peace. And so the Elders have asked themselves, *who does the water serve?*"

Jingwei interrupted him. "Jera? You're accusing Jera of stealing the water?"

The smaller Aru Faylen answered her, its sing-song voice pitched higher than Throm's, "I do not see him here. The Sea Keeper must indeed be ashamed of his actions to hide from all of Tranthaea's leaders."

Throm continued, "Wrem is correct. If the Sea Keeper were not guilty, he would show himself. It is because of him that our cloud cities shrink daily."

"You're wrong!" Callum took a step towards the hovering creatures, who responded by drifting forward to meet him. "Jera was imprisoned by Kala as well. She's controlling all of this!"

"You say *was*." Yriel walked out from Kala's side and circled around behind Callum, tearing his attention away from the Aru Len representatives. "If your story is true, then where is he now?"

Jingwei answered for him. "He's on his way here. He's gone to search for answers."

Yriel snorted lightly. "They should be easy to find, as he causes all the questions."

"Don't get smart with me!"

"Why not? Are you unfamiliar with the condition?"

Kala stepped between them and placed a hand on Yriel's shoulder. Yriel flinched from her touch as if the Spark Keeper had hit a tender spot. Kala frowned down at her with a glance that Jingwei could have sworn was suspicious, but the moment passed, and the Spark Keeper spoke. "That is enough." She raised her voice and spoke to the entire circle. "I shall search for the traitorous Sea Keeper and when I find him I will make him return the water to the clouds."

This announcement was met with loud thrumming of approval from the floating sea of Aru Faylen that hovered over the plains, but a disapproving cracking from the mass of gru'Esh that swarmed between the circle and the mountain.

v'Aros showed its teeth as it lifted its shoulder-arms and began to buzz and whir in its own language. mi'Orha scuttled up next to it and translated into Brydge, "You speak too hastily, Spark Keeper. The Sea Keeper would not betray Tranthaea any more then you yourself would."

Jingwei let out a loud squawk as Ythen grabbed her arm in warning. She clamped her mouth shut and grimaced.

mi'Orha slapped more dirt over its nostrils and continued translating for v'Aros, who had not stopped speaking.

"We believe– that is to say, v'Aros and the ka'Esh believe that it is the Aru Len who are hoarding the water."

Throm and Wrem both rose slightly higher in the air at the accusation, their propellers spinning at a faster rate.

"Rain has not fallen," mi'Orha explained, "and the ground is dry. Our homes are collapsing and our people are dying. The rain comes from the clouds, but the clouds are refusing to release it."

v'Aros grew silent, but its chest-arms began beating a slow, rhythmic tattoo on its carapace. The drumming passed quickly throughout the ranks of the gru'Esh, and the pounding began to echo out over the assembly, reflected by the sheer black walls of the mountains, before being lost to the dense emptiness of the sky beyond.

Multiple voices rose in the crowds around them now as the Daevyn armies began to shuffle into formations, fearing a charge by the restless gru'Esh hoards. The oppressive thumping of the battle-drumming had joined the loud droning of the Aru Faylen fleet overhead. The Aru Elen remained on the ground to the north, but Callum was tall enough to see over much of the crowd and noticed that many of them were sporadically flaring their wings in preparation for a quick take-off.

v'Aros, br'Atakh, and g'Nharr had all raised themselves to their full height and were arguing expressively with Ila. The diminutive Soil Keeper was holding her own, her small voice somehow battling back the noisy sea of buzzes, clicks, and whirrs. Jingwei was impressed in spite of herself, until her attention was caught by something else.

Yriel was leaving.

At a subtle signal from her mother, the Quencher quickly smiled and bowed, and gathered up her cloak, melting into the crowd of Daevyn warriors. Jingwei followed her with her eyes until Yriel vanished into the sea of tan-coloured fabric and then turned her gaze to the Flame-Bearer, who throughout all the noise had remained silent.

Ydelle Emberhand was staring at Ythen with a look of intense sadness and disappointment. The First Quencher was staring at the ground in front of him, his face flushed. Jingwei wanted to grab his arms and shake him and shout at him, *don't be ashamed! You ARE doing your duty! We're trying to save them!*

Instead, she just placed her hand on his arm.

Ythen reached over and covered her hand with his, but shook his head sadly. He refused solace. Jingwei couldn't understand, nor would he let her share his pain. This was his responsibility. He was the First Quencher of the Daevyn. His role was to protect the plains and its peoples, and he had been given the job in a time of peace.

He raised his head and looked around him. How had he let it come to this?

Rata's clear, deep voice broke through the cacophony. His eyes were glazed over, and it was clear that he was speaking for Huon Arrahl.

"The ground is dry, this the gru'Esh know. The air is dry, this the Aru Len know. But their eyes are blinded by their solitary environments; one in the dirt, one in the sky. I am Huon Arrahl. I live in both worlds. My roots dig deep and my branches reach high. I search for water everywhere and I do not find it. Tranthaea withers and dies. Shall we destroy it faster with our pride and foolishness?"

The circle grew silent at Huon Arrahl's words. Even v'Aros stopped beating on its chest.

Jingwei saw Kala purse her lips just as mi'Orha stepped forward to speak, its nostrils flaring.

"Be swayed by the forest's council, I beg of you. It is older and wiser than all others here, and it speaks the truth. We feel the hearts of the peoples of Tranthaea, and they beat quickly. I sense the vibrations of anger and mistrust, like the rattling of pebbles that signal an avalanche."

v'Aros let out a clacking raspberry and then spoke in broken Brydge, "If tunnel collapses, I save gru'Esh. Others save themselves."

br'Atakh, the grey po'Esh leader whistled in agreement and the others began to argue back and forth as Jingwei watched Kala lean in to whisper into the Flame-Bearer's ear.

Ydelle nodded slowly as she listened to the Spark Keeper, and her eyes flashed away from the gru'Esh to Rata, who was still standing as if in a trance. She raised her hand and waited until the din of argument faded, though the pounding and buzzing and thrumming of the armies around them continued unabated.

"Huon Arrahl. You claim that you are the soul of the Korrahl Forest. You claim that you wish to live in peace and safety." Her eyes narrowed. "And yet, until mere hours ago, you had not made yourself known to the Daevyn, except to march your army up to the walls of our great city."

In a gracefully powerful movement, the Flame-Bearer rose from her throne, her regal armour shining in an unspoken threat. "Deception and aggression; that is your history with my people. Is this the peace that you would impose on all the peoples of Tranthaea?"

The leaves on the tree rustled as Rata turned his head towards Ydelle.

"Do not overestimate your importance, Flame-Bearer. You are but a seedling to this world, still straining to reach the sky. I am Huon Arrahl. My roots were planted long before you were born, and my branches have stretched across the plains and over the mountains when I saw fit to extend them. I desire nothing but peace and the shade of my own leaves, but if you, in your desire for power, bring war to the forest, I will defend myself."

Jingwei stepped back in shock. Kala's poisonous words had infected them all, even the peace-loving Huon Arrahl. The Spark Keeper's face was hovering over the Flame-Bearer's shoulder, her malicious grin invisible to all eyes but Jingwei's.

Ydelle's eyes were burning with fury. She turned to her armies behind her and yelled out, "First Quencher!"

Ythen gave a start and momentarily snapped to attention as his title rang out across the field.

It wasn't until he heard Jingwei let out a breath of disbelief that he realized that the Flame-Bearer was not speaking to him.

Yriel stepped forward out of the mass of Daevyn warriors and made eye contact with Ythen, waiting until he had noticed the golden flame pin on her cloak before turning her attention to her mother.

"Yes, Flame-Bearer?"

"Prepare the Quenchers."

Kala stepped forward, positioning her body between the Flame-Bearer and the rest of the circle. "A wise decision. There are too many fools here to end things peaceably."

Ydelle nodded and repeated herself, "Yes, prepare the Quenchers and pull back. We move to defend Yshaar."

Kala looked dumbstruck.

"But..."

The Flame-Bearer looked her in the eye as she continued. "I have no desire to expand my protectorate through war, and I will not bring my people to harm with unnecessary aggression. If the peoples of Tranthaea wish to end the Daevyn, they will know where to find us." She turned authoritatively and signalled to Yriel. "We ride for Yshaar."

Kala's mouth worked furiously for a moment before her eyes fell onto Callum and his companions, still standing in the centre of the circle. Her face lit up as she called out, "Ydelle! Wait!"

The drumming from the gru'Esh camp had grown louder as they had seen the Daevyn Flame-Bearer signalling to the leader of her armies, and Callum could now feel the beat as it rushed through the air and surrounded them, the physical pulse of the rhythm pushing against his back.

Ydelle stopped and turned halfway back, her face registering impatience. Kala gestured towards the three youth.

"What about them? They have defied your rule, abandoned your service, and accused your advisor of treason. Will you let these crimes go unpunished?"

Before the Flame-Bearer could answer, Ythen stepped forward. His face had cleared of all embarrassment and shame, and his voice was hard and honest as he spoke in his peoples' clear, clipped tones.

"Flame-Bearer, I have not abandoned you, nor our people. What I have said, I have said in truth, relying on your judgement and wisdom. I will not be scorned for protecting my land, and I will not be judged by a traitor. The Spark Keeper is an enemy of the Daevyn, as sure as fire burns brightly, and whether you allow me to serve you as First Quencher or not, I will see her answer for her offences."

As his final words rang out a quiet fell over the assembly. The drumming stopped and the Aru Faylen's propellers dropped to a low hum. Whispers were passed back in a variety of languages as the armies of Tranthaea absorbed the harsh indictment in Ythen's words.

Kala's smile had disappeared. The designs in her cloak pulsed with deep red glimmers and the chain of fire that she wore round her neck began to glow white-hot.

"You dare to make these accusations against me, boy?" Her voice came out as a hiss, her sharp tongue cracking against her teeth with loud snaps. "You place yourself in an arena with an enemy you cannot defeat. You have no proof—"

"Well, that's not entirely true."

The whole assembly lost itself in an uproar as Jera, the Sea Keeper of Tranthaea, stepped into the circle, his robes, beard, and hair still flowing around him as though he were floating in a personal, portable swimming pool.

He didn't wait for the noise to subside, but continued speaking to Kala. "Perhaps the word of a Keeper would do? After all, I was your prisoner too."

Kala's reply was lost in the noise that followed his statement. The peoples of Tranthaea were confused, their nerves hung on a thread that was being pulled by all of their leaders in all different directions.

Eventually Kala made herself heard above the crowd.

"You accuse me? You, who are yourself accused of stealing the water and bringing our once peaceful land to the brink of war?"

Jera sighed ruefully and smiled crookedly. "I ask you, why would I steal the water? I can pull it out of the air at whim." To prove his point, three balls of water spun into the air beside him, resolving themselves into liquid sculptures of a tree, a stone, and a flame. "I hardly need to stockpile it."

Kala lifted her hands and three small balls of flame appeared in front of her, forming themselves into an axe, a hammer, and a bucket of liquid fire. "Who said anything about stockpiling it? You seem to have an intimate knowledge of this attack on our world, for someone who claims to be uninvolved."

"As well I should," said Jera, as the three water sculptures melded into one ball. "I *am* the Sea Keeper, after all. And that's where the water is going, incidentally."

He turned towards Jingwei, Callum, and Ythen. "I tracked it. It's all withdrawing to the north, to the Sea of Nalani. Of course, I have no idea why it's still moving." He winked at Jingwei. "I might just have an over-inflated sense of self-importance, but I like to think that I'm the only Sea Keeper around right now, and I'm not doing it."

Kala's trio of flames had joined as well, creating one large burning sphere.

"So you say, Sea Keeper. And yet who else has such control of water as you?" She hesitated for a moment, unsure of what to make of the look in his eye. "You say you are not moving the water. Perhaps you would like to explain to us why you're not stopping it from moving?"

Jera had stopped smiling. "Because something else is pulling it. Something stronger than me." He dropped his voice to a whisper. "Whatever you started, Kala, something else is planning on finishing it."

Kala's eyes widened. She looked around the circle and saw the confusion on the faces of those present. Some were for her and some against, but all were puzzled, and it wasn't only the gru'Esh who could feel the charged atmosphere now.

Her eyes hardened.

Jingwei felt Ythen tense suddenly, just as Callum yelled out, "No!"

Kala thrust her hands forward and the ball of flame shot at Jera, who quickly moved the water to intercept, causing an explosion of steam and heat.

Without thinking, Jingwei summoned a hail of water bullets that burst into existence and pelted towards Kala.

None of them hit their mark; each was snuffed out by an angry tongue of fire.

The crowds around the circle roared in anger as they saw the attack unfold. The sudden flare of violence was like a trigger for the surrounding masses, and the noise level increased to an explosive cacophony of released tension as the armies rushed to join in battle.

Chapter Twenty-Two:
The Battle

Through the layers of crumbling dirt and the milky-white haze of its eyes, v'Aros could see very little of what was happening, save for a sudden flash of fire that burnt brightly into its retinas. Flaring its nostrils and breathing deeply of the thick air for more information, it quickly registered the heightened heartbeats and the sour smell of perspiration that rolled in waves off many members of the assembly.

It was the perfect moment to strike.

v'Aros had long felt that it was its destiny to rule a united gru'Esh. The possible perks of such a position were not lost on the ka'Esh Clan Leader; mating without having to kill for it every time, delicious fnark continuously on hand, the deepest and darkest burrows in the Warrens, exclusively for its use.

Worth fighting for. And now the water situation and the arrival of the two young Humans had provided the perfect opportunity.

Clacking in false outrage at the attack on the Spark Keeper, v'Aros took advantage of the confusion and quickly turned to grasp the shoulder-arms of the gru'Esh leader who most often stood in its way. mi'Orha barely registered the attack and struggled for a moment, but it was too late, and v'Aros wrenched the je'Esh's chest-arms from their sockets.

mi'Orha issued a cry of pain that was lost in the din of the armies roars, and before anyone could stop it, before mi'Orha could even defend itself, v'Aros had bludgeoned the je'Esh leader with its own arms, felling it where it stood.

v'Aros did not waste time savouring its small victory, but instead scuttled over to Kala in obeisance, raised its new weapons over its head, and issued a call in the gru'Esh tongue.

The call was answered with a feverish buzzing and clicking as the brown ka'Esh turned to destroy mi'Orha's black je'Esh. g'Nharr of the red an'Esh joined v'Aros, clutching the chest-arms of br'Atakh, once Clan Leader of the peaceful grey po'Esh.

The gru'Esh armies that were swarming between the circle and the mountains descended into the madness of civil war as v'Aros and g'Nharr advanced towards the two hovering Aru Faylen leaders, holding their weapons at the ready.

Ila had allowed the ground to open up beneath her and swallow her up as soon as she'd realized what v'Aros was up to. Holding tightly to her stone staff, she parted the dirt in front of her, tunneling underneath the violence on the surface, hearing the muffled sounds of screaming and fighting above her as she went.

She stopped at a distance she estimated was correct and then slowly rose back out of the ground, allowing the stones and dirt to crumble off her head and holding her staff awkwardly in front of her in case of a surprise attack.

No one was looking her way. All eyes were on the two surviving gru'Esh Clan Leaders who were advancing menacingly across the circle towards Throm and Wrem, the Aru Len Delevates.

Ila turned to her left and found who she was looking for.

Rata was standing stock-still, his eyes still glazed over as Huon Arrahl attempted to speak through him to the crazed armies of Tranthaea.

She rushed forward and grabbed her partner, knocking the tendril that connected him to the forest off his shoulder and pulling him south, away from the violence. The tree that had been speaking through him shuffled its roots and hurried along behind them, moving like a spider over the ground.

Rata came back to himself and quickly took in the situation.

"We have to protect the forest." He reached into the woven bag that was hanging over his shoulder and pulled out a fistful of seeds. "Defend, but not attack."

Ila couldn't agree more. Keepers were guardians, not generals. She had never been a fighter, and had hoped she'd never have to be. She followed the Seed Keeper and the lone tree south to the forest, keeping her eyes on the armies the whole time.

Throm knew that he needed to move. He closed all of his pores, save one through which he sent a one-note warning to his fellow Aru Len, and then quickened his rotation speed, rising up and out of the reach of the angry under-dwellers.

His second, Wrem, was following close behind. Wrem had left some of his pores open and was issuing a frightened-sounding squeal as he ascended. Throm made a note to speak to him about that later. A leader always needed to *seem* confident and in control; fear was a sign of weakness their enemies would perceive and exploit.

Below them, Throm could sense the Daevyn mobilizing their forces in preparation for a defense of the People of the Sky. The Spark Keeper had been correct. The confusion caused by the many accusations of treachery and aggression had indeed destabilized the Flame-Bearer, who in the absence of absolutes had decided to honour her alliances and was preparing to protect the Aru Len from the gru'Esh hoards.

The two Aru Faylen reached their brothers in the sky and Throm sent Wrem to pass on the word.

Prepare the attacks.

Everything was going according to plan.

Kala soared up into the air, her golden-veined wings a blur behind her, her black robes forced close to her body with the speed.

She had not expected the Humans to appear, or for them to have escaped her clutches with the Quencher, and for them to have also released the Sea Keeper was a triple insult.

Still, she had been able to make it all work to her advantage in the end. Kala allowed herself a small smile.

So easy, to play them all, one against the other. Kala's grin widened. The only thing peace was good for was the time it gave you to make enemies.

She came to a hover above the battlefield, about even with the tops of the mountains. Far below her she could make out the movements of her puppets as they ran along the tracks she had set out for them.

To the south, the forest had retreated a short distance. Huon Arrahl was creating a thick wall of trees on its northern border, hoping to repel any attack. He was being assisted by Ila and Rata.

Those two Keepers had no idea. They had no training in combat and were woefully unprepared for what lay ahead.

To the east, in the shadow of the mountains, the gru'Esh were a confused mass of movement. Half fighting each other, half being goaded by v'Aros and g'Nharr to attack the Daevyn, Kala was sure that given enough time the tunnel-dwellers would destroy themselves.

The Daevyn to the west were much better prepared. They were already lined up in ranks, ready to follow their leader into battle and death, if necessary.

But which leader to follow? Kala mused. Two First Quenchers would split the loyalties of the Daevyn forces, making them weaker. This was exactly the kind of divisive chaos she would banish under her rule.

A costly object lesson for the world to learn, but a necessary one.

She turned her attention to the north. Her Aru Len were already in motion, carrying out her plans step by step. Ranks of propeller-driven Aru Faylen were swarming to the plateaus of Du Garrah and then returning with their new cargo to hover above the grounded armies. A fleet of winged Aru Elen buzzed noisily beneath her to the west, passing unnoticed behind the preoccupied Daevyn lines.

The sounds of battle cries rose from the field below. The ground was brown and flat where the grasses of the plains had been trampled by the armies, creating a gigantic arena for Kala to play in.

And right in the centre she saw her most valuable targets.

The two young Humans had been separated by the suddenness of the attack. They were now standing in a no-man's land between the gru'Esh and Daevyn forces; the boy remained with Firebrand while the girl had been whisked away to the north by Jera, the Sea Keeper.

Kala frowned. She knew now why Jera had such an interest in the Human girl. *A possible trainee.* It would not do for the Sea Keeper to pass on his strength and wisdom to the interfering girl. Perhaps Kala would ensure he fell during the battle... herself.

A concentrated surge in the gru'Esh line brought her attention back to the battlefield.

v'Aros had finally managed to corral its people. Though some pockets of in-fighting still existed, the surviving remainders of the gru'Esh army began to push towards the Daevyn en masse.

It had begun.

Ythen had grabbed for Callum and Jingwei when v'Aros had advanced across the circle, brandishing its dead opponent's arms, but Jingwei was already gone. He only just caught a glimpse of her and Jera vanishing past the crowd of Daevyn warriors.

Good. He breathed a sigh of relief. *At least she'll be safe with him.*

A choking noise from behind him brought his focus back. He turned and saw Callum, his face white and his eyes wide. Ythen followed his gaze and saw what the Human was looking at.

Across the clearing, the entire mass of the gru'Esh army was slowly advancing towards them, each warrior waving the armoured, clawed arms of a fallen comrade above their heads.

Ythen turned back to Callum, who had regained control of himself and was warily checking the straps on his Firedart while keeping one eye on the advancing hoard.

"Callum." The Human's head jerked up at the sound of his name. "You are not trained for this. Go to the Daevyn. Be safe."

He saw the stubborn look he had come to associate with Jingwei enter Callum's eyes and sighed inwardly.

It must be a Human thing.

He tried a different tack. "The Flame-Bearer has no protection but the traitor, Yriel. I cannot leave her so vulnerable, but my place is here, leading the Daevyn army in our defence." Callum nodded in understanding. "Will you take my place and protect her?"

A voice from beside him chimed in. "Yes, Callum. Especially since I am not with her, as *my* place is here, leading the Daevyn army in our defence."

Yriel stepped around into Ythen's field of vision and gave him a look that dared him to argue with her right now. The gru'Esh army was less than fifty metres away, and advancing quickly.

Ythen burned to exact vengeance on the traitor who would lead her own army into a war of her mistress Kala's creation, but knew that she was right.

First things first. Yriel could wait.

Ythen turned back to Callum. "Callum, go. Protect the Flame-Bearer, and remain safe." His face screwed up at the irony. "Yriel and I will handle things here."

Callum glanced back and forth between them and the approaching army, whose roar was now almost deafening, and without a word ran into the midst of the Daevyn army, searching for the white-haired Flame-Bearer.

Ythen set himself beside his one-time partner and brought his Firedart to bear on one of the leading gru'Esh. Out of the corner of his eye he saw Yriel do the same.

He opened his mouth to issue the order just as her voice rang out over the battlefield, "Daevyn! Protect the Flame-Bearer, defend the Plains! Fire!"

A hail of miniature lightning bolts flickered past Ythen's shoulder, joining his own shots as they blazed into the gru'Esh lines.

Many gru'Esh were hit by multiple darts, felling them instantly, some were hit by one or two, stunning them, but not disabling them.

Most continued on, protected by the thick armour of their carapace, but the advance was slowed.

"Fire at will!" Ythen shouted. More darts lanced past them, slowing the gru'Esh further, but the line of fallen bodies was soon swallowed up by the opposing force's steady advance.

Throm's fleets were ready. The Aru Faylen flocks had returned from the peaks of Du Garrah, their round, hard bodies having secreted the sticky plasma that was now firmly grasping the large rocks they carried beneath them.

The air below them was becoming electrically charged as the Daevyn defended themselves with the bolts of energy they fired at the heavily armoured gru'Esh. Darts ricocheted up and down the battle lines and the thumping blades of the Aru Faylen propellers stirred the flickering sparks about in flowing currents as they flowered and burst, creating a deadly, yet beautiful fireworks show that blanketed the field.

At Throm's signal, Wrem led the charge, diving abruptly over the two ground forces whose lines had almost met. The thundering thrumming of the propellers created a downdraft that whipped the thick tan grasses of the plains into a dancing frenzy on their approach, but the armies below were too busy to notice the encroaching air force. Wrem and the following Aru Faylen waited until they were directly over various groups of the battling groundlings and then sucked the plasma back into their bodies, releasing their hold on the boulders they carried.

The large stones plummeted unchecked towards the ground.

Rata was weaving tall blades of grass into a thick fence around the tightly bunched Korrahl Forest about one hundred metres to the south of the battlefield when he heard the deep humming of the propellers.

He looked up and saw the flocks of Aru Faylen in their dive and with shock noticed the rocks they were preparing to drop on the battling forces below.

The fleet leveled off too far out of reach of his vines, but as the Aru Faylen released the stones Rata had time to shout a warning.

The noise of the battle kept anyone from hearing it, except Ila.

The short, dumpy Human Keeper felt boulders dropping towards the armies on the ground before she saw them and, without hesitation, raised her stone staff.

Immediately the rocks began to take sharp turns, some of them veering off to the north and landing heavily on the empty hills, some of them only rolling slightly off their courses, narrowly missing their intended targets.

But there were so many of them. Too many. Even a Keeper like Ila couldn't stop them all, and more than a few boulders slammed into the armies of the Daevyn and the gru'Esh, crushing dozens of warriors before the onslaught was finished.

Ila stood and surveyed the damage, stunned at the extent of the Aru Faylen's violence, and horrified at her failure to protect her wards. All the years she had chosen to hope for a world at peace, all those times she had elected not to train in combat, all those moments she had preferred rest to action suddenly stood out in her mind as wasted opportunities.

The blood of Daevyn and gru'Esh warriors alike seeped out from under the boulders and intermingled on the field, its liquid accusation unheeded by the surviving armies.

Ila's fingers loosened and her stone staff slipped out of her grasp and clattered onto the ground at her feet.

Rata rushed over to the Soil Keeper and saw the slack expression on her face, the faraway look in her eyes, and recognized that she had gone into shock. He cradled her head in his arms as he looked around, helpless.

Kala watched in frustration as the first aerial assault was completed with far fewer casualties than she had hoped for.

Although some minutes had passed, the Daevyn army was still keeping the gru'Esh hoards at bay; their lines had not yet met in full battle. Huon Arrahl had been sequestered to the south, well out of the line of fire, and the battle was not falling into the mass chaos that she had hoped for.

The Spark Keeper allowed herself to descend closer to the battlefield.

If you want something done right...

She stretched out her arms and felt the liquid fire that flowed around her neck and down her arms grow hot in anticipation.

She smiled. It was time to announce her intentions.

Jingwei followed Jera through the northern flank of the Daevyn army, carefully weaving around the mounted warriors who ignored the two Humans and busied themselves with checking their greaves and saddles before riding up to the front lines.

Behind them the two Humans heard the last of the thuds as the final few boulders crashed to the ground, eliciting and then quickly silencing cries of surprise and pain.

Jingwei turned to see what the damage had been, but Jera grabbed her arm and pulled her forward and out of the mass of people rushing to avenge the dead.

Angrily, Jingwei shook off his grasp and stopped running. Jera turned around with an exasperated look on his face.

"We have to keep moving, Jingwei."

Jingwei stood her ground. "Why? You're a Keeper! Your place is in the fight!"

Jera took a step towards her. Looking her squarely in the eye, he said, "You're right. And, you're wrong. My job is to defend Tranthaea. Even from itself, if need be. Kala is orchestrating all of this mayhem; it's her that we have to stop. No one is served if we fall in battle."

He stepped back again resolutely and brushed his long, waving hair out of his face. "A Keeper is meant to provide balance. It's up to us, Jingwei. After all, who better to extinguish the wild destruction of a fire than a couple of wet blankets?" His face was both strong and sad as he looked down at her, and then broke suddenly as he gave her a wink.

Suddenly and without warning, huge bolts of lightning burst down from the sky, carving massive craters into the ground behind the gru'Esh and Daevyn forces.

The blasts struck simultaneously, encircling the armies and knocking Jingwei and the Sea Keeper off their feet. The two armies reacted instinctively, stampeding forward, away from the fiery bolts of destruction.

Amidst the chaos, Jingwei and Jera got shakily to their feet and looked skyward in time to witness Kala release a second wave of bolts, sending down brilliant lines of fire that arced from her hands out over the field and down to the ground, creating a golden cage. This time she placed the bolts in a slightly smaller circle, forcing the opposing armies nearer to one another in confusion.

Ydelle Emberhand, Flame-Bearer of the Daevyn, was desperately trying to maintain control of her troops. She sat astride her raeas at the head of the mounted forces on the southern flank of her army and watched as her formerly trusted advisor rained fire down behind her people, driving them towards destruction.

The hair on her arms prickled as the lightning bolts that struck the ground behind her charged the air with their energy. Waves of thunder crashed over them, spooking the raeas and whipping the Quencher's cloaks over their shoulders with the force of the blasts.

The Human boy, Callum, sat on another raeas next to her, adjusting the new bandolier of Firedart canisters on his shoulder. He had placed a new canister into his weapon only moments before, removing a bronzed one that looked strangely familiar to the Flame-Bearer. His eyes flitted over the battlefield and the sky above, and every so often he turned in his saddle to look around behind him at the forest to the south. It seemed he had appointed himself as her personal bodyguard.

Well, she could do worse.

Above them, flocks of Aru Faylen swooped back to the north, having completed their first bombing run. Ydelle mentally tore up their alliance even as she wondered why there were no Aru Elen among them...

On the battlefield, the two armies' lines finally met with a roar. The tide began to turn swiftly against the Daevyn army, who were no longer protected from the gru'Esh ferocity and weaponry by distance. Their Firedarts were long-distance weapons and were much less effective at close range, but the hard bodies and limbs of the gru'Esh were devastating. The Flame-Bearer knew that the only way to beat them now was to crush them with numbers.

But the Daevyn army was being pushed back. The battle-line, which had started at the parley circle, was moving towards her. She watched as her ornate throne was trampled under the weight of the advancing gru'Esh.

It was time to act.

At a signal from the Flame-Bearer's hand, the charge was sounded and the entire Daevyn mounted division, including Callum, surged forward, their raeas' slithering quickly through the heavily charged air that was becoming even thicker with dust, smoke, and shrapnel from shattered rock.

The lightning that had been advancing behind the Daevyn and gru'Esh armies was starting to impact the ground disturbingly close to the forest.

Rata threw a few more seeds on the ground to his left, willing them to grow quickly into a net of tall weeds that could absorb a stray blast and burn out quickly, hopefully keeping Huon Arrahl safe from the fire. The weeds burst out of the seeds and shot upwards, stretching into the sky, entwining themselves around one another as they wove into a living shield.

A long, low sound echoed from the battlefield, still about one hundred metres to the north. Rata looked over and saw the Daevyn warriors on their raeas riding into the fray, hoping that their mounted attack would slow the gru'Esh advancement.

It would be a slaughter. Rata knew that the raeas were trained to fight fires, not armies. When they hit the gru'Esh lines...

Without a thought for his own safety, Rata abandoned Ila, who had somewhat come back to herself and was keeping busy silently moving rocks from the battlefield and using them to create a small wall in front of the forest, like a child with building blocks. He raced towards the line where the two armies had now met, hoping that he could reach it before the Daevyn cavalry charge.

He ran wildly, tossing out handfuls of seeds to his left and right as he went, growing them behind him as he moved forward, creating a thick line of unfurling vegetation that expanded rapidly as he passed, and arriving at the point of collision mere seconds ahead of the Daevyn raeas riders.

Callum's knees clenched the raeas as it propelled itself forward under him. He kept his arms up as Ythen had taught him, aiming carefully with the Firedart on his right and trying to use the small Buckler to shield as much of his lanky body as he could as he hunched over his mount's back.

The gru'Esh lines were only fifty metres away now, and then thirty, and then twenty-five...

Only an instant before the Daevyn cavalry would have crashed into the gru'Esh vanguard, their way was blocked by a gigantic hedge that seemingly sprang out of nowhere with the deafening sound of creaking and tearing wood, like a row of trees all crashing to the ground together.

The green line started as low shrubbery. It tore through the ground at a frenetic pace, sending small bits of dirt and grains flying as it expanded and lengthened, its branches growing inward and outward to create a solid wall of greenery.

The hedge quickly grew thick and full of brambles. In less than a second it was at least three metres tall and impenetrable, the spidery shoots swelling into thick, knotty branches that wove around one another, creating a solid wall that may as well have been built of stone.

Callum's raeas frantically swerved to avoid collision, but the Daevyn were packed too close and the front lines of the charge were forced to crash into the thick vegetation, piling one on top of the other.

The Daevyn farther back were able to slow the charge to a stop, confused. The Flame-Bearer picked herself up off the ground where her raeas had thrown her and pushed her way forward through the mob to Callum, who was painfully extricating himself from the hedge.

On the other side, some of the gru'Esh had been caught in the hedge as it grew, and only had the chance to scream before they were swallowed up by the enormous wall as it continued to expand. Other gru'Esh were being slowed down by a sea of thick nettles that rose from the dirt and quickly spread along the ground throughout their midst, tying itself around their legs and hampering their movement.

Callum made sure that the Flame-Bearer was safe and then turned to the hedge, where he saw Rata, ascending from the centre of the greenery with his arms raised, standing with each foot on one of two large branches that supported him and lifted him high into the air before the gathered troops.

All eyes were on Rata as his deep voice shouted out over the din of the armies, "Stop it! Stop fighting! We are not each other's enemy! It is the Spar—"

His words were interrupted by a tremendous flash as a huge bolt of lightning crashed into the hedge right beside him, exploding into a ball of flame as it hit, flinging him off his pedestal and down to the ground among the Daevyn army, leaving a trail of smoke in the air behind him.

Kala hovered overhead, a wild look in her eyes. She didn't say anything, but instead raised her arms again.

This time, instead of bolts, the air was filled with lightning balls that flew in intricate patterns, swirling around in tight loops and spirals before suddenly straightening their paths and crashing into the ground among the armies. Jets of fire exploded out of the ground to the west, east, and north of the opposing forces, driving them south towards the tree line in a mad rush for safety.

The Flame-Bearer forgotten, Callum quickly reloaded his Firedart with the First Flame-Bearer's bronze canister, then raised his right arm and took careful aim at the deranged Spark Keeper, slowly exhaling as he squeezed his hand.

The ancient canister's white-hot dart shot out with perfect accuracy... and missed completely.

Kala had dodged to the left with flawless timing, not meaning to escape from Callum's shot, but instead narrowly avoiding a net of vines that a wounded Rata had sprouted from the burning hedge.

She was stunned by the blast as it shot past her, the shock wave sending her tumbling end over end through the sky before she was finally able to right herself with a furious buzzing of wings.

Callum grinned quickly as he watched her gather her tattered robes around her, forgetting momentarily to continue the rain of fire down onto the armies below, and then he joined the Daevyn army as it hastened south, mirroring the crazed retreat of the gru'Esh on the eastern side of the hedge.

Yriel and Ythen had held off the gru'Esh attack as long as they could, but had been overwhelmed by the final advance. Ythen was bleeding from a head wound he had sustained when a ka'Esh warrior had found him and knocked his Buckler aside with one arm while crashing the armoured plates of his weapon down onto the Quencher's head with the other. A lucky shot to the space between the creature's torso and abdomen had felled it, and Ythen had retreated with what remained of his troops.

Now that the hedge lay between the two armies, they had their first chance to breathe since the battle had begun.

The break did not last long, however. Within moments, the protective hedge was ablaze, lit by multiple bolts from above, and Yriel was marshalling her troops to move south to avoid the lightning storm all around them.

In the midst of the battle, Yriel had been too busy to think about anything other than survival, but now, as her troops fled before her, she had a moment to consider.

She was in the front lines. Since the battle began, she had been under threat from gru'Esh, falling boulders, and lightning. She had almost been trampled by her own people, and then there was Ythen, who was still watching her every move in case she betrayed him again.

And now she felt the sting of betrayal herself. It was suddenly clear to her that Kala had no particular interest in her safety.

Ythen was watching her now, warily keeping his eyes on her as she urged her Quenchers to move south with the rest of the army. She could see that he was not happy that they had been forced together again, even in a situation like this. Maybe there was still a way for her to make it right...

Just as she took a step towards him, Ythen was consumed by a glorious blaze of fire. The lightning bolt that struck him blasted her off her feet, as well as a few of the Daevyn around her.

Yriel blinked her eyes to clear them of the afterimage, and the blurry shape in front of her resolved into that of Kala, hovering a few metres above the burning hedge.

Kala bared her teeth at the Daevyn girl and spoke above the noise, "Good, you are still alive." She casually waved her hand to her left and another section of the hedge burst into flames, broiling a battalion of gru'Esh who had been trying to climb over it in a bid for freedom.

"Take your troops south, and destroy the forest." Her gaze hardened when Yriel did not immediately obey. "Do not fail me, Sparkcatcher. This world will soon be yours to rule, as Earth will be mine. Let us finish what we've started."

Yriel glanced at Ythen while Kala waited impatiently, balancing the promise of immense power against the chances of survival if they failed.

Ythen groaned on the ground beside her. He was lying hunched over on his side, with his knees up against his chest. He seemed to be shaking, probably an after-effect of being struck by such a powerful bolt of lightning.

Powerful. That was the key. Yriel thought back to the dream she'd had last night. Or had it been a dream? Her shoulder throbbed beneath her cloak where a set of finger-sized bruises had blossomed.

Powerful. Powerful enough to rule.

She looked back up at Kala and nodded.

"Burn the forest," she repeated in affirmation. "And then—"

A ball of white-hot fire shot up from the ground beside her, striking Kala in the chest and shooting her backwards through the air until she was hidden from sight by the smoke.

Ythen had lain on the ground, huddled over in considerable pain while Kala and Yriel spoke over his body. His cloak had been ripped to charred tatters around him and his Buckler now carried a large dent in the centre that he hoped wouldn't affect its ability to stop darts from hitting him.

The bolt of lightning had taken him by surprise, but he had been even more surprised that it hadn't killed him. Instead, just like it had happened at the top of the spire in Kala's palace, the energy that hit him had been caught between his hands in a pulsating ball. He had struggled to keep it contained, fearing for the lives of the retreating Daevyn that rushed past his body, and then, once he had it under control, had turned to release it on its creator, blasting the Spark Keeper with a taste of her own medicine.

How was it that he could control the fire that Kala sent? Twice now he had been surprised by his ability to withstand the flames that had once burned him so badly and given him the moniker he wore in shame.

He gingerly got to his feet and looked around. Most of the Daevyn had passed him now in their effort to run to the safety of the forest even though the lightning strikes had stopped herding them.

He attempted climbing the hedge to see if he could find the Spark Keeper and end this battle once and for all, but the thick smoke and flames that still raged would not allow it. He could feel the fire in a way he hadn't before, as if it were burning in his brain. It wasn't causing him pain, but he was very aware of it. The sensation was frightening and confusing, but he turned from the hedge and instead focused his attention south, where he caught a fleeting glimpse of a shock of white hair moving along with the flow of blond warriors.

Yriel.

All questions of his sensitivity to flame were forgotten.

His one-time partner had been given a chance to recant, and refused it. Now she would be forced to accept the consequences of her actions.

Jingwei scowled as she flipped her wrist and extinguished another blaze. Kala's rampant use of the ball lightning had created dozens, if not hundreds of tiny flare-ups that threatened to turn rapidly into a series of wildfires which could easily consume the plains.

She and Jera had been hurriedly tracking Kala's circular path of destruction from the north, hastening to put out the small fires that threatened to become bigger issues if left untended.

She found it to be particularly unsatisfying work.

Not that she wanted to be in the battle. A few good looks at the front line had convinced her that that style of bloody combat was not for her.

Still, it would be nice to use her newfound powers for something more important.

From where she was standing she could see the whole battlefield to the south and she watched both armies hurrying along the hedge-line away from her, towards the trees. Overhead, the Aru Faylen bombing fleet had dissipated, although where they had gone was anybody's guess.

Through the smoke and the debris left behind on the field, Jingwei was able to make out a single, solitary figure hobbling around the remains of the gru'Esh bodies and the boulders that had been dropped by the Aru Faylen.

Kala's black cloak was tattered and smoking as her eyes met Jingwei's. Her burning gaze cut through the smoke and she took off, soaring high into the air before turning south, following the retreat of the armies.

Jingwei shot a water-ball after her that evaporated long before it reached its target. She called another one into the air in front of her, but before she threw it Jera's voice interrupted her from behind.

"It's laughable, you know." Jingwei whirled around to face him as he chuckled tiredly. His already lined face was worn with the effort he had expended putting out countless fires.

"Water-balls. Not exactly the kind of weaponry that a Spark Keeper need be afraid of." He reached out his hand and took the sphere of liquid from in front of her. As she watched, the ball split into hundreds of small drops, each a different shape. Animals, people, and buildings appeared in front of her eyes, each created from a single drop of clear, blue water. An entire circus was performing under a crystal clear big top. A tiny, liquid trapeze artist pulled off a daring triple somersault and landed safely with a bounce in a finely woven net. The audience erupted in thunderous applause, splashing Jingwei in their fervour.

Jera clapped his hands on Jingwei's shoulders and gave her a look that was startlingly serious on his comical face.

"This is your power. What it can be. The power to bring life, and joy, and peace, and balance to the world. You know now why you have been called here. You *must*."

The water between them transformed again. This time a liquid garden grew before her eyes; families walked carefree across the plains and children romped among the flowers. A soldier, old and bowed with age stood beneath a tree. As Jera formed a mist of rain that sprinkled over the soldier's head, the fluid creation stood up straighter and threw down his weapons, his body growing stronger and more youthful. He stretched out his arms and embraced the children, and then they were running and playing, their mouths open in silent laughter.

Jera let the watery image dissolve. "We are guardians. We choose to serve peace and life. Once, a long time ago, I had to make that choice. Now it's your turn."

Jingwei hesitated. Jera had been clear when he told Callum that he thought the boy was meant to take over the position of Spark Keeper from Kala. Jingwei had watched Callum struggle with that calling, unable to accept his obligation, but at the same time unwilling to leave Kala in power. But she had watched him grow into a new man over the last few days, and had no doubt that he would be able to handle the responsibility.

But as for her... She didn't know if she could do it.

Jera sensed her reserve. "I have held the post of Sea Keeper for three hundred years, Jingwei. I have had my time. You were brought here to replace me, I am sure." He took his hands off her shoulders. "So, let's get started. Yes?"

Jingwei didn't answer. Her thoughts shifted to her foster family back in L.A. Rhonda would miss her for a few weeks, and then chalk her up as another runaway before filling her bed with a new child in need of a home. Hunter Wells had probably already forgotten her, or found a new girl to infuriate. And Tranthaea... Tranthaea was starting, however strangely and unexpectedly, to feel like home.

Jingwei swallowed hard and looked Jera in the eye.

"Yes."

Huon Arrahl had never felt so disconnected. Its bodies were spread across the south of Tranthaea, from its home far below the Daevyn city of Yshaar, eastward to the great ravine, not far from the foothills of Du Garrah, and north into the plains, where many of its bodies were now in danger of being destroyed.

War had never come to the forest before. Tranthaea had been a peaceful world for many years, and even before that, when the Humans first arrived, Huon Arrahl had remained hidden among the trees, safe in invisibility. It had seen violence done, but never had violence done to it.

Now its existence was exposed to the Daevyn, and battles were being fought on its doorstep. Fear flooded through its branches and trunks, each drop of it finding its way to Huon Arrahl's heart in the tendril tree far to the southwest.

Though Rata the Seed Keeper and Ila the Soil Keeper had done their best to shield Tranthaea's oldest living inhabitant from danger, the battle was now approaching its border.

The time for self-defence was drawing near.

V'Aros withdrew the clawed end of mi'Orha's stolen arm from the body of a fallen Daevyn Quencher. It had killed almost as many Daevyn as it had gru'Esh today; its bloodlust was more than satisfied.

It surveyed the battlefield, breathing deeply in the dusty air. Some gru'Esh were still battling one another, though it seemed that the brown and red ka'Esh and an'Esh had triumphed in that civil dispute. In the sky, the Aru Faylen had vanished, and the Aru Elen still hadn't reappeared since they'd fled when the fighting broke out.

Even the cowardly Daevyn were content to hide behind the Seed Keeper's hedge for now, although the view through the burnt-out vegetation proved that they were not retreating to their city in the east.

Instead, they appeared to be moving down along the hedge, towards the forest.

v'Aros snarled. They meant to flank it.

It raised its voice in a piercing clicking sound, and the remainder of the gru'Esh army turned south.

The Daevyn army came staggering to a halt. Their numbers had dwindled, and the survivors were dirty, tired, and confused. The living wall of the Korrahl Forest rose before them, blocking their escape from the Spark Keeper and her savage fire bolts which still pounded the ground to the north and west, assaulting their eyes with bright flashes and their ears with pounding thunderclaps.

Memories of the forest waiting outside the city walls plagued the minds of the Quenchers. Ideas of vast numbers of trees drinking the water from the ground and the air, depriving the world of life, consumed them. Most of them no longer knew which First Quencher was in command or who their true enemy was.

Confusion and uncertainty reigned.

And as they gathered in front of the forbidding walls of the forest, their confusion turned to anger.

Reluctantly at first, and then with greater haste and force, the Quenchers penetrated the boundaries of the woods. Tall Daevyn warriors on raeas slid in and out of the trees, unsure and afraid in their newfound knowledge that the forest was alive. Straps were tightened, Bucklers were adjusted, Firedarts were reloaded.

The forest seemed to sense their anger, and the trees began to shuffle, creating gaps in some places and walls in others. Loud cracking sounds echoed around the army, coming from the canopy above, the imagined footsteps of an unknown enemy.

Callum forced his way through the pack. He had heard about Huon Arrahl from Jingwei, but it was different being in the forest itself, and feeling the presence of the creature that was embodied by it.

Ydelle followed along behind him, her face turned up towards the high branches and leaves that blocked the sky. If she turned in the saddle she could still see the tree-line behind her, and the open fields beyond where much of her army was still gathered, desperately trying to regroup amidst the continued blazing attacks from above.

She signalled Callum to stop among her warriors and stood up in her saddle. Callum dutifully took the reins of her raeas. She waited until she had the attention of all who could see her.

"Peace, Daevyn!" she called out. "Who do you attack? Who is your enemy?"

There was a murmuring response that never quite coalesced into an answer.

She continued, "The Spark Keeper has betrayed us all–"

That got a reaction. Howls and battle-cries rose from the Daevyn warriors as they shook their arms in the air. Some loosed their Firedarts into the canopy in violent agreement.

The forest around them responded to the unintended assault, its leaves shaking, its trunks creaking and groaning. Many trees shifted, encircling the Daevyn that had entered the forest's boundaries, pressing in on them.

The uneasy Daevyn huddled together, half energized and half afraid. The adrenaline of war was still pumping through their veins. Shouts of "The trees are attacking!" and "Defend the Flame-Bearer" began to gain popularity.

The Flame-Bearer tried to regain control of her troops, but they were lost to her. Fear and insecurity had corrupted their discernment and they saw enemies wherever they looked. Her regal voice became strained and was consumed by the noise of the panicking mob as they began to form up against the encircling forest.

Rata burst through the angry mob of Quenchers and found the Flame-Bearer and Callum ineffectually trying to calm them down.

"Huon Arrahl will not hurt them if they do not attack!" He could barely hear his own voice over the shouting crowd.

Rata could not believe this. He had only just stopped the battle from continuing, and already the peoples of Tranthaea were searching for another excuse to make war. He abandoned the Daevyn and rushed deeper into the forest, searching for the tendril tree that would allow him to speak to Huon Arrahl.

Perhaps he could manage a peace yet.

Ila sat slumped over with her back to the trees on the eastern side of the hedge, which by now was no more that a crumbling line of ash that stretched off into the north.

Strewn across the battlefield before her was an avalanche of boulders that had fallen from the sky. Boulders that she had attempted to guide away from their targets.

Beneath the boulders was evidence of her failure. Crushed, and dead.

But that was no excuse for freezing up.

In all her years as Soil Keeper, Ila had never had to fight a war. Her gift had been used to build and create, to mold the world of Tranthaea. Small scuffles here and there were no preparation for the large-scale destruction that she had seen when the stones hit the ground.

Ila wiped her face with her sleeve, smearing dirt across her features. Her eyes narrowed. Failing to protect the living was no way to atone for failing to protect those who had already died.

She stood up. In the distance, Jera's blue-clad form was working its way towards her, with the Human girl in tow.

And right before her, picking their way carefully but confidently over the fallen bodies of their tribe-mates as they advanced on the forest to the south and the Daevyn army to the west, was the gru'Esh army.

Ila lifted her stone staff. She was the Soil Keeper of Tranthaea.

Let them come.

Huon Arrahl heard the mindless violence of the Daevyn building to a fever pitch. It saw the gru'Esh army advancing from the northeast with malevolent intent. It felt the panic of the Seed Keeper as he searched for connection.

And it acted.

Yriel stood just outside the forest to the west. In front of her, interspersed among the trees was about a third of the Daevyn army, clamouring in panic and anger. The rest were organised in ranks behind her, crushing forward as they attempted to avoid being struck by the ball lightning and jets of flame that still ringed the armies, sending up clouds of dirt with each explosive strike.

She looked over her shoulder. At the rearguard of her Quenchers she could see a disturbance as Ythen shouldered his way forward, no doubt intent on stopping her.

She glanced up just in time to see Kala whirring overhead from the west. For a split second a tongue of flame danced in her vision and then puffed out.

Yriel nodded; message received.

Just then, a shockingly loud crackling was heard from the forest canopy. To Yriel's surprise, the trees in front of her began snapping off their own branches, grasping them in the crooks of other boughs and shaking the leaves off, leaving only...

The perfect excuse.

"Spears!" Yriel shouted. "The forest is armed! Protect the Flame-Bearer!" Yriel had no idea if her mother was in danger, or even if she was in the forest at all, but her accusation did the trick, and the Daevyn opened fire on Huon Arrahl.

The forest burst into flames in front of them as Jingwei and Jera approached. Scores of bolts from Firedarts shot into the wood and leaves, scorching the bark and leaving smoking holes in the trunks. Slow-moving flames started to lick up the bodies of the trees and as they reached the canopy, explosions of fire began to eat at the leaves, consuming them hungrily and then dropping the blackened remains to the ground in a shower of sparks and ash.

In fury, Huon Arrahl launched the spears it had meant to use to defend its bodies against the advancing gru'Esh hoard. The flight of sharpened branches soared into the midst of the Daevyn mob. Dozens of Quenchers fell, galvanizing their attack on the tree-line.

Within the woods, panic-stricken Daevyn were retreating from the angry forest into a wall of friendly fire, falling to their comrades' blind rage.

Callum and Ydelle moved to take cover in the east, working their way through the underbrush towards the mountains, frantically dodging the pounding movements of gigantic trees that were rushing towards the new front on the forest's northwestern border.

Rata burst out of the tree-line just in time to see the entire gru'Esh army about to reach his partner, Ila who stood alone against the hoard, calmly swinging her stone rod in expectation.

Kala swooped over the forest and the battlefield, joyously watching the fruits of her manipulations, shooting red, orange, and white balls of fire down indiscriminately that burned her enemies and her allies alike with equally unforgiving heat.

Ythen shouldered his way to the vanguard of the Daevyn army and peered over the heads of those in the front line just in time to see his one-time partner viciously lead the attack on the forest, cutting down her own people as collateral damage.

Jingwei and Jera burst through the crowd only a few metres down from Ythen at the same time and quickly took in the scene. Without hesitation, Jingwei ran down the line of Daevyn, her arm raised towards them to extinguish any Firedart bolts that came too near her. A line of darts puffed steamily out of existence as she ran, like smoke signals tracking her progress down the line. She reached Yriel quickly and before the blond girl could stop her, she clamped her hand on the female Quencher's Firedart.

Within seconds the entire apparatus had rusted over.

Yriel stared at her arm for a moment, squeezing her hand a few times to try to shoot a dart, without success. A reddened metal flake peeled off the cylinder and wafted down to the ground.

She slowly turned to look at the short Chinese-American girl in front of her, her face contorting into a furious mask.

Without warning, Yriel backhanded Jingwei across the face with her Buckler, sending her crashing to the ground, writing with the shock of the Buckler's discharge. Jingwei raised her hands to protect herself against a second attack, but looked up to find that Yriel was already being held from behind by a furious Ythen.

"Jingwei!"

The cry came from behind her, in the direction of the mountains. Jingwei rolled over in the dirt and ash, blood pouring from her broken nose onto the ground beneath her, trying desperately to ignore the burning forest on one side and the speared bodies of the Daevyn on the other.

A few dozen metres down the tree-line was Callum, supporting the weary body of the Flame-Bearer. Beside him were Rata and Ila, and before them, no more than a few metres away, was the advancing gru'Esh army.

Jingwei screamed out through tears of frustration. "Callum! We have to stop it!" but her voice was lost as a low rumbling drowned out the wild shouts of the battle around her and the thumping march of the gru'Esh.

The rumbling sound seemed to be coming from deep beneath them. The ground began to shake; the pebbles in front of Jingwei's face bounced up and down in warning, what grasses had remained un-trampled swayed fiercely as the ground began to heave beneath them.

Ythen was forced to release Yriel as he fell to his knees. The shaking became so violent that both Huon Arrahl and the Daevyn stopped fighting and clung to whatever was nearest; for the Daevyn that meant dropping where they stood and grabbing hold of one another and for Huon Arrahl it meant grasping firmly to the ground itself.

Many of the forest's trees could not withstand the force of the earthquake, and fell, crashing heavily upon one another in a massive pile, while others rode the buckling ground in waves that rippled through the forest with brutal energy.

The gru'Esh army came to a surprised halt in front of Ila, who alone remained standing with her eyes closed, her staff raised in the air, and a stony look on her face. The gru'Esh's sensitive nostrils detected the upward movement of the rocks and dirt seconds before the ground erupted beneath the Soil Keeper's feet.

An enormous wall of rock burst out of the ground, soaring high into the air, carrying Ila, Rata, Ydelle, and Callum with it. The gru'Esh scattered; some retreated in panic from the growing landmass, clambering over their neighbours while others were crushed in avalanches of loose rock.

The Daevyn had mere seconds to retreat before the wall of stone reached them, tearing through the ground, bursting upwards through the smooth fields and cutting their troops off from the forest to the south.

The thunderous roar of rock upon rock clamoured across the battlefield and echoed back off the walls of Du Garrah, un-muffled even by the thick, smoky air, filling the plains with the painful cries of destruction as Ila strove to build a violent peace.

Then, it was over. When the dust settled, a long ridge of dusty red rock rose above the plains, its newly-formed sides still quivering with falling stones and clumps of dirt and grains. It extended from the mountains in the east out past the edges of Huon Arrahl's northern spur, completely cutting the forest off from the two attacking armies.

As silence settled over the stunned observers, Jingwei clambered to her feet. She, along with Ythen and Yriel had somehow managed to stay atop the western leg of the ridge as it rose and they now had a bird's-eye view of the battlefield and the armies below.

Ythen checked to make sure that Yriel had survived and then abandoned her still-breathing body and rushed to Jingwei. The two of them limped quickly over to the others, who were huddling nervously over Ila. She was lying quietly on the ground, her head cradled comfortably in Rata's lap.

The Seed Keeper was crying, but Ila had a magnificent glow about her that almost made her dirty face seem beautiful.

"I hope," she whispered in an exhausted voice, "that this barricade protects your forest."

Tears rolled down Rata's cheeks and one of them landed on Ila's face, splashing a single clean spot in the midst of all the dirt.

"Thank you, my love," he said.

Yriel slid down the last few metres of the ridge and rose shakily to her feet on the plains. Her feigned unconsciousness had allowed her to escape from Ythen, this time. She looked out at her troops, but the Daevyn Quenchers were all staring past her at the massive barricade that the Soil Keeper had called out of the ground. To her right was the gru'Esh army, still out for blood. And in the western sky, what looked like strange wisps of dark clouds were moving in.

The warm afternoon light revealed that the burned-up remains of the hedge had crumbled to dust in the earthquake, and now there was nothing between the Daevyn army and the gru'Esh hoard.

Yriel knelt next to the dead body of one of her warriors and tore off her Firedart, replacing it with theirs. She stood and signalled to her officers, who took only a few moments to sort the Daevyn army into usable battalions.

She had come too far now. If she didn't finish this, she'd be labeled a traitor forever. It was time to prove that she could lead. After all, you can't conquer a world without fighting a few battles.

She just wished she didn't have to fight any more today.

Across the field, v'Aros was dusting itself off. All around it the gru'Esh army was regrouping and preparing for the final assault. A low drumming began as the army finally reunited and looked to the ka'Esh Clan Leader for instruction.

v'Aros yanked two fresh arms off the dead body of a fallen an'Esh, and kicked a pile of rubble off of its hind leg.

That was the second time that the Soil Keeper had buried it.

Now it was going to bury her.

Chapter Twenty-Three:
The Melee

High in the air above the newly formed barricade, Kala looked down in shock. The ridge of coppery stone split the landscape of Tranthaea like an ugly scab, protectively dividing the Korrahl Forest from the Daevyn and the gru'Esh.

This was not in the plan.

She estimated that about a half of the original gru'Esh army still remained, and about one-third of the Daevyn; her objective of total destruction was still a long way off.

Her fellow Keepers had acted as expected; strong on defence, but not much in the way of attack. Them, she could deal with.

But the young Humans had proved more capable than she had thought. Jera, it appeared, had taken the girl under his wing. Not a problem, the air was drying even as they battled, sapping the power of the Sea Keeper and his ward.

The boy, Callum, had proved himself a surprisingly innovative fighter, but hadn't yet shown any talents that she need worry about. Still, his Firedart had only missed her by *that much*, and the thick white dart had seemed strangely familiar. Her father had used one just like it...

But it was the Firebrand that really concerned her. He should not have survived that blast, and he certainly should not have been able to return it.

How the two Humans had been smuggled to Tranthaea without being caught in the Collectors she may never know, and they would be dealt with. But not since her and her sister and the other three original Keepers had a potential Keeper been found among the peoples of this world.

Kala consciously moved Ythen to the top of her hit list.

The boy would have to die, and soon. She would not be replaced, not when she was this close to victory.

Her thoughts were interrupted by the thrumming sound of some Aru Faylen approaching from the north. She looked over and saw that they had been successful in their search. To the south, a mass of Aru Elen were holding their position behind the forest. They had completed the wide arc that had taken them from the west, down and around to where they now hovered, unseen by the forces below.

Kala cracked her knuckles and prepared her final assault. Tranthaea would be hers, or it would burn.

A pillar of fire, at least four metres high, burst into existence in the north just beyond the last warrior in the rearguard of the gru'Esh army. It spread quickly to the east and the west, creating a menacingly flickering wall of flame that surrounded both the Daevyn and the gru'Esh armies, stopping only when it struck the Barricade.

The wall of fire hemmed the two armies in, sending out waves of heat and sparks that drove them towards the ridge and each other as it slowly crept forward, becoming tighter and tighter with each passing second.

Yriel had pushed aside her shock at the transformed landscape around her. She knew what she was meant to do and so she spurred her army forward. The northern flank of the Daevyn rushed inward as it advanced, forcing the southern flank to march on an angle, climbing the steep sides of the ridge as they went.

v'Aros and the gru'Esh mirrored their movement in the east, clambering up the rocky slopes of the Barricade and sending loose stones and dirt tumbling onto the troops below.

On the ridge, above the battlefield, Callum was loading his Firedart with a new canister from his bandolier, to replace the expended one that he had fired at the Spark Keeper. He slipped the old one into his pocket, grateful, and not for the first time, that Ythen had trained him in its use. He had used both of the First Flame-Bearer's powerful canisters, and did not regret stealing the first one from the Hall of Record on the day he had arrived in Tranthaea.

Callum had never felt so tired in his life. The adrenaline that was pumping through his system felt like it was pushing his body past its level of endurance. His knees were still shaking from the earthquake, and vertigo hadn't released him since he was shot up into the air on the rising ridge of rock.

All his life he had wished he'd been braver. Brave enough to stand up for himself against the corrupt policemen who had collected his earnings and kept it for themselves, or against Bridget, who had always put him down when he'd made a good pull, even when she'd been unsuccessful.

And now that'd he'd finally found his courage, he didn't want it. He wanted to run away and hide in a hollow. He wanted to huddle in the corner of a tunnel and wait for death. He didn't want to fight anymore.

Callum looked below him at the armies of the once-peaceful world of Tranthaea.

I don't know if I can do this.

It was one thing to be told that you were destined to be a powerful protector of a world and its peoples, it was another to be forced to destroy them in order to save them.

He cast his gaze skyward in indecision. His eyes widened in fear as he screamed a warning to the armies below.

"Thranvorl!"

V'Aros heard the cry from the ridge just as the thudding of the thranvorl's wings beat the dust into a frenzy around it. The gru'Esh lines had just engaged the Daevyn army, crashing through the un-armoured top-dwellers and melding their forces.

All around it were the fierce sounds of battle; the thudding and clanking of stolen arms as they crashed down on Bucklers, the crackling discharge of waves of Firedarts that splashed harmlessly off of gru'Esh carapaces, the crunching sound of bodies falling underfoot while the surviving warriors moved on to their next fight.

v'Aros ducked as the thranvorl made its first pass, scooping up beakfuls of gru'Esh with its three mouths and beating dozens of others into the ground with its powerful wings. Behind the monstrous sky predator, a flock of Aru Faylen poured forward, dropping more boulders and screaming through their pores as they drove the thranvorl to attack.

The Daevyn army cheered when they saw the gru'Esh advance halted by the attack, but their joy was short-lived. From the north came the dissonant cries of a second and third thranvorl. They were still a fair distance away, but the Aru Faylen who drove them were clearly aiming them at the Daevyn Quenchers.

Yriel scrambled to redeploy her forces in preparation for an aerial assault. She fumed as she saw Kala buzzing to and fro over the battlefield, safe and secure, far away from the dirt and smoke and blood of war.

The Spark Keeper, who had once seemed so idyllically powerful was being transformed in Yriel's eyes into a short-sighted tyrant, more concerned with chaos and destruction than with the safety of her own followers.

Yriel knew that Kala wanted Earth for her own, and the Spark Keeper had promised her Tranthaea.

But at this rate, there would be precious little left to rule.

Ythen and Callum were running through canisters too quickly, taking shots at the Aru Faylen that were carrying more stones from the mountains to the battlefield. Many of the flying creatures fell to their Firedarts, most of those not making it to their drop zones.

But even more of them were leaving the field, heading back to the mountains to bond themselves to more boulders after abandoning the thranvorl to wreak as much havoc as it could in the centre of the gru'Esh forces. They soon passed out of range of the sharpshooters on the Barricade.

Ythen and Callum scrambled down the slopes of the ridge in chase; a useless effort to prevent the flyers from returning with more boulders. Jingwei followed closely behind them, intent on making it back to Jera who was positioned on a small rise in the middle of the battlefield, surrounded by dueling parties.

The Sea Keeper was standing calmly, his body surrounded by a blue sphere that absorbed flying detritus, enveloping it and slowing it down so that it never quite reached his body, but instead hovered harmlessly in the blue liquid ball around him.

Jera's arms were stretched out in front of him, his hands flat, palms down. Out of his palms poured two great streams of water that pounded into the ground like miniature waterfalls, stirring up the dirt around his feet and creating a thick sea of mud that was expanding out past his bubble and through the battlefield around him.

The Daevyn and gru'Esh warriors that were fighting nearby soon found their movements hampered by the thick sludge. Already blinded by the afternoon air, lightning flashes, and Firedart bolts, the gru'Esh began to lose focus in the slippery mud and some began to call for a retreat. They stumbled about, often in the wrong direction, miring themselves even deeper into the mud and the Daevyn lines.

Jingwei joined the Sea Keeper, sloshing through the muck to his side and copying his movements. She was soon enveloped in her own water-ball, doing her best to slow down the attacks. It was more difficult now than it had been earlier. There was far less water in the air and ground, and Jingwei was forced to dig deeper in herself to find the energy to continue the flow. She hardly noticed when a thranvorl crashed to the ground in a cloud of dust and smoke to the east.

Exhausted, v'Aros fell to the ground beside the thranvorl's dead body. The gru'Esh had never fought one of the sky predators before, and it was only by ordering its troops to swarm the monster when it neared the ground that it had been able to reach the vulnerable head and bring it down.

The day had been long, and the battle not as easily won as it had hoped it would be. Every time the gru'Esh seemed to get an advantage in the field, something happened that would turn the tide, allowing the Daevyn, the Aru Len, or Huon Arrahl to beat it back.

v'Aros looked through its milky eyes towards the top of the ridge. The tall, Human Seed Keeper was standing there with his mate, upon whom v'Aros had vowed vengeance. Their attentions were not currently on the battle, but on each other, giving the ka'Esh leader the perfect opportunity to take its revenge.

Rippling waves of air tickled v'Aros' nostrils from the south, distracting it momentarily as the hidden fleet of Aru Elen finally swooped in on Huon Arrahl from behind.

Ila stood shakily next to Rata on the crest of the Barricade, her arms wrapped around his waist as she attempted to regain her feet.

The act of pulling such an enormous sum of stone out of the ground had sapped her strength, and she could do little now but watch as the battle that she and Rata had tried to end so many times continued to rage on, fueled by the confusion and madness the treacherous Spark Keeper had designed.

The Daevyn and gru'Esh armies were completely intermingled now, and the combat had gone from methodical and organized to brutal and chaotic. In the centre of the battleground were two blue spheres, seemingly untouched by the torment of the battle and strangely at odds with the sea of violence around them.

The usually composed Daevyn Flame-Bearer stood beside Ila, her once-shining silver armour now marred with dents, scorch marks, ash, and blood. She looked over the Plains of Tranthaea, her kingdom, in disbelief.

Smoke rose from the plains; the ashy wisps were all that remained of the tall, tan grasses that once grew there. What hadn't been burned by lightning or Firedart bolts was now being trampled into the mud underneath the warring armies, and dyed red with the blood of fallen warriors.

How could she have been so blind? To not have seen Kala's traitorous intent, to not have figured out that the Spark Keeper was vying not only for her throne, but also for the rule of the rest of the world.

It was too late to stop now. She had tried, but her people no longer listened to her. They were lost to the battle, their senses overwhelmed with the clanging of weaponry and the smell of ozone, the flash of lightning and the gut-churning shaking of the ground. They would finish the fight now, to the death.

Perhaps Yriel had been right.

Perhaps greater strength had been required.

A familiar buzzing reached Ydelle's ears. She spun around in alarm to behold the sight of an entire army of Aru Elen swooping down out of the southern sky into the Korrahl Forest.

Nyx followed her Aru Elen unit into the forest. She had known that this day was coming, and had painted her front a dark green in preparation. It was an exciting occasion.

The Spark Keeper herself had promised the Aru Elen freedom from their Aru Faylen overlords if they were successful in defeating the upstart armies of the groundlings.

Nyx had been there when the promise had been made. Seven Aru Elen had been chosen by the Spark Keeper to hear her words, and to agree to the pact. This they had done with a simple nod, as it was forbidden for Aru Elen to know any language, written or verbal, though even within these bounds the Aru Elen had found ways around the law.

And of course, it had never mattered before, since all Aru Elen had their tongues removed at birth. But now...

It had always been known to the People of the Sky that the Spark Keeper was descended from the Human First Flame-Bearer and his Aru Elen lover. Kala's right to the throne of Tranthaea was beyond question, and Nyx was honoured that the Spark Keeper had chosen this moment, the moment of her ascension, to join with the Aru Elen and free her people.

Nyx grabbed at a spear that was propped high in a treetop, but her hand was slapped away by a swift-moving branch. She swerved around a few more trunks, arcing her body in and out of the canopy, her orange and purple scales shimmering on her back, reflecting the deep green of the leaves.

Her wings buzzed with fierce determination. Her Aru Faylen masters did not allow her kind to pick up weapons. Kala had given a special permission for today, a small taste of the freedom that they would earn if they pledged to her.

Nyx was not about to let a *tree* stop her from fulfilling her vow.

There. Another spear, this one deeper into the forest. Its tree seemed less wary, as if it were looking in the other direction, if that were possible for a tree.

Nyx dipped to her left and closed in. Out of the corner of her eye she saw another Aru Elen approaching the spear. He was painted white, with red and gold scales. He buzzed up alongside Nyx and winked, diving suddenly towards the tree, jinking left and right to keep it confused before making a break for the spear, his hand outstretched to grab it...

The trap sprung. A branch shot out of nowhere, driving into and through the male, pinning him harshly to the trunk of another tree.

Nyx couldn't stop her forward momentum. She slammed into the trunk, grabbed wildly at the spear and took off again, the branches of the tree creaking and lashing out at her as she burst from the canopy and joined her people who were now soaring over the battlefield, awaiting the Spark Keeper's order to attack.

Huon Arrahl had been taken by surprise. All its attention was focused in the north, where the Keepers were defending it, even by changing the landscape of the world.

Its borders had been attacked and burnt by the Daevyn, and it had lost many good bodies in that fight.

And so, each tree had been made to fashion a spear, pulled from its own trunk in preparation for an attack Huon Arrahl had thought would never come.

It had been a lesson learned well, if the hard way.

But now the voiceless Aru Elen swooped into the forest, silently and quickly grabbing those spears from the trees and flying back out to hover menacingly over the forest, over the ridge, and over the plains on the other side.

The trees raged beneath them. To hope for peace was one thing, to defend oneself another, but to provide the enemy with weapons, however unintentionally...

Far to the southeast, many kilometres away from the battlefield, a giant tree flailed its tendrils in the air in grief.

Wrem loosened a few pores to allow a low keening sound to whistle through his blades and out into the atmosphere around him. The thranvorl in front of him dove steeply to escape from the noise, its giant wings thumping the air, scattering its Aru Faylen shepherds as it approached the ground. Its red eyes caught sight of the bedraggled Daevyn force in front of it and it opened its middle beak and screeched in aggressive warning before plowing into the front lines, haughtily ignoring the darts that scored its underbelly.

Wrem banked steeply, curving around to watch the third and final thranvorl make its attack run. Only six Aru

Faylen remained behind it, singing harshly to keep it moving. The rest had dropped back as they neared the Daevyn army, wary of stray darts being shot at the sky monster.

Only six.

Too few.

Wrem leaned forward, pouring speed into his movement, hoping that his voice would be enough to keep the thranvorl moving forward...

It was too late.

The diminished noise level seemed to act as a trigger for the thranvorl to go from spooked to angry, and with a surprisingly agile twist the predator opened its left beak and snapped up one of the Aru Faylen herders, leaving behind nothing but a sickening crunch and a plummeting propeller blade.

The other five flyers scattered, but not quickly enough. The thranvorl had been born to prey on smaller, more agile species, and with a few quick flicks of its cross-tail it had snagged two more mouthfuls, and beaten two more with its massive wings, sending their bodies tumbling to the ground.

Wrem knew that they were dead. Whether they survived the fall or not, Aru Faylen breathed the same way they moved and spoke; through the pores of their propellers, which needed to remain in constant motion for the transfer of air to occur. Looking at the still propellers on the bodies of the fallen, it was clear they would not be rising again.

The fifth herder was Throm. The senior Delevate sank low to hover over the ground, moving slowly, doing all he could to avoid the notice of the sky predator.

Coward.

Wrem pulled up short as the thranvorl soared into the air, escaping the noise, smoke, and chaos of the battlefield with its stomach full, flying eastward over the mountains with powerful, determined wing strokes.

Wrem released a single note through his blade valves and called the rest of the Aru Faylen.

Watch and wait. That was the way of the Aru Faylen. When the smoke cleared, a new peace would have to be negotiated with the Spark Keeper, and Wrem knew that they had done enough to be remembered as allies. The Elders would be satisfied. Now it was his duty as a Delevate to secure the future of his people.

He signalled the retreat.

Watch and wait.

Yriel had her work cut out for her holding the line as the thranvorl swooped and attacked, then circled round and attacked again. The field around her was thick with mud and blood, and even among her tight-knit defensive formation the odd gru'Esh could be seen, fiercely battling any opponent it could find.

She called out for her troops to close in tighter, hoping that the larger number would keep the sky predator from attacking. She would rather sacrifice a lone Quencher staggering out among the dead than what little remained of her army.

It didn't work.

The thranvorl screeched menacingly, its red eyes fixed on the Daevyn formation. It dove and then leveled out, storming towards them only metres off the ground, its wingtips smashing into the dirt, raising clouds of dust and debris.

Yriel shouted the order and the Daevyn formation began lancing out darts by the dozen, aiming for the head and eyes of the flying beast, but to no avail. The nerves of the Daevyn were shot and their bolts went wild.

Yriel closed her eyes and waited for the inevitable.

Ythen had seen the thranvorl sweeping in a deadly line towards Yriel's troops and, leaving Callum to pick off the Aru Faylen bombardiers, he'd leapt onto a nearby raeas and spurred it on to an intercept course with the monster.

He leaned forward intently, focusing all his energy and attention as he eased himself up in the saddle until he was standing astride the mount, his knees bent to correct for its slithering pattern of motion.

They entered the dust storm that had been raised by the thranvorl's wings. Ythen closed his eyes against the grains and counted slowly in his head:

Three...

Two...

One.

He leaped out of the saddle, blindly stretched out with his arms and legs, and landed heavily on all fours on the thranvorl's back.

The beast reacted immediately to his weight, curving its body as it pulled into a steep climb.

Ythen opened his eyes a crack as they rose and saw Yriel and the Daevyn defensive formation pass quickly behind the body of the ascending thranvorl. He wasted no time, knowing that in mere seconds the predator would have gained enough altitude to roll over and throw him to his death below.

Ythen rose unsteadily to his knees, his entire body rising and falling with the wings of the thranvorl, and aimed his Firedart at the animals head, hoping beyond hope that from this distance the dart would penetrate the thick skin and bring the monster down.

He squeezed the firing mechanism.

Nothing.

No flash of light, no dart. The canister was empty.

Ythen grabbed at his bandolier, searching for a spare.

There were none left. He had used his last shots to slow down the Aru Faylen attacks on the mass of warriors fighting below.

Now what?

The wind whipped through his hair as the thranvorl leveled off, preparing to ditch his passenger. Ythen suddenly thought back to the lightning bolt he had thrown at Kala, and the ball of fire he had released from the spire on top of the mountains.

Is it possible...?

He looked down at the battlefield below and focused on the fires that were still flaring up around the field. Some of them were quickly being extinguished by Jingwei and Jera while others were being left to burn out, as they were no longer any danger to the plains or the people on them. The wall of fire seemed relentless, rebuffing any attempt to weaken it as it squeezed in closer around the armies, forcing them to intermingle in a vicious medley of pain and anger.

Ythen closed his eyes. He could *feel* the fires burning below. The different sizes, heats, levels of intensity. He remembered what it felt like to control the fires between his hands those previous two times, and tried to feel the same way again.

A triple screech of pain from the thranvorl's beaks brought him back to himself. He opened his eyes and was not surprised to see a white hot ball of flame scarcely contained between his hands.

Another cry of pain issued from the thranvorl as the fireball scorched its back, and then Ythen was pushing the ball forward and releasing it, shooting it directly at the thranvorl's head.

There was no noise, no explosion. The flames were simply absorbed into the beast; a few that played lightly over its skin dissipated quickly and quietly, and the thranvorl ceased to live; its wings grew slack, and its body plummeted to the ground.

Ythen was thrown from it as it twisted through the air, but was caught by a tall column of water that appeared beneath him just before he hit the ground, soaking him completely, but slowing his descent and landing him softly on the muddy soil.

He looked up and saw Jingwei holding her arm out towards him in concentration. He smiled a thank you at her, but her face just screwed up even further, focused on something happening over his shoulder.

He turned to see just as the thranvorl's body crashed into the ground behind him, sending a wall of dirt, stones, and bodies flying towards him. Ythen ducked down, hoping to present a smaller target, and was doused with water again as Jingwei sent the pillar he had landed in to meet the debris as a liquid wall, stopping the flying detritus midair, and splashing to the ground in a muddy mess.

She sent him a quick wave, along with a look that said, *why am I always the one doing the rescuing?*, before turning back to assist the Sea Keeper on the battlefield.

Ythen grinned.

Middle of a war. Still sarcastic.

Some things never change.

A low thrumming behind him startled Ythen out of his reverie. He turned to the north and saw a lone Aru Faylen hovering beside the thranvorl carcass.

It was Throm.

The Aru Faylen looked tired, if it were possible for a creature without a face to look tired. His propellers moved slowly, only barely keeping his body from touching the ground.

Ythen cautiously leaned down and pulled a full bandolier off the body of a fallen Quencher, draping it over his shoulder. He loaded a new canister into his Firedart and pointed it straight at the Delevate.

"You have betrayed us. You delivered the Humans to Kala, you handed me over as well, and you broke the peace of Tranthaea. Why?"

Throm opened a valve and his musical voice hummed out in a low pitch that matched the slow movement of his blades.

"We were given no choice." He sank lower to the ground, his bulbous body now mere centimetres away from the dirt. "The Spark Keeper warned us that if we did not cooperate, our cities would burn, and lightning would strike down our Elders. We chose the only future we were offered."

Ythen didn't lower his weapon, but he did loosen his grip on the triggering mechanism.

Threats and intimidation did sound like Kala's style.

"Look around you." Ythen's voice was low and hard. "All the bodies. All the death. Without you, it would have been different. Without you, Tranthaea could still be at peace."

Throm let some air stutter through his pores in what sounded like a sad chuckle. "There will be no peace in Tranthaea while Kala lives. My participation changes nothing."

Ythen tightened his grip again. "Would you like to test that theory?"

Throm pulled himself up a little higher and emitted a small trill. "You owe me a favour, Firebrand. I choose to collect it now."

Ythen couldn't believe his ears. The Delevate was calling in his favour? The favour he was promised in return for a service which had ended in Ythen's capture and imprisonment by the very person who had started this war?

How could he possibly expect—

Throm interrupted his thoughts by creeping closer to the thranvorl's body, which was lying half-buried in the ground to its right.

"Are you an honourable man?"

Ythen hated himself at that moment. Indecision raged inside him. This creature was the cause of much of the destruction that had taken place on the battlefield today. Ythen had lost many friends to the war Throm had created.

However, conscience dictated that a debt, whomever it was held by, had to be repaid.

Ythen lowered his arm.

Throm whistled a sigh of relief and started to drift slowly back up into the air.

"You are indeed an honourable man, Ythen Fire—"

The thin red bolt from a Firedart sizzled over Ythen's shoulder and slammed into the stalk that connected Throm's body to his blades. The Aru Faylen Delevate was thrown backwards and landed heavily on the ground, unmoving.

A voice Ythen recognized spoke from behind him. "Luckily, *I* am not an honourable man."

Yriel waited calmly as Ythen spun around to face her. Behind him, the wall of fire was tightening quickly, and the northern section of the battle was closing in on the clearing surrounding the fallen thranvorl's body.

Ythen's voice was black with rage. "You did this. All of this! Our people are decimated, and for what? All so that you could be First Quencher of the Daevyn?"

He raised his arms into fighting position.

Yriel followed suit. "That is your weakness, Ythen. One of many. You have always thought too small." She took a step to the side that Ythen mirrored across from her. "Tranthaea is a world divided. So many peoples. So many differences."

Yriel stopped moving and brought her weapon to bear. "Kala is going to give me Tranthaea to unify. One world, one leader. And I have the strength to rule. I've always had it!"

Ythen couldn't believe how easily Yriel had fallen for the Spark Keeper's lies. How far she had fallen.

He shook his head slightly. He could not let himself see her as the victim. Not if he was to do what was necessary...

"And now," he asked, carefully tightening his grip on the generator. "Where is your leader? Safe and sound, while you fight her war?"

A flicker of annoyance ran across Yriel's face and was gone. "I am not fighting Kala's war any longer. If she will not give me Tranthaea, then I will take it."

That was enough for Ythen, who squeezed his fist and fired a single shot at his traitorous ex-partner and then dove to his right in a shoulder-roll, scrambling for cover behind the short tail of the fallen thranvorl.

Yriel blocked his dart almost lazily with her Buckler and fired twice at his fleeing form before she saw him disappear behind the gigantic blue-skinned body that was half-buried in the dirt.

She didn't give him time to set himself in a firing position behind the tail, but instead raced up the wing of the lifeless creature and leaped over its back, barely maintaining her footing as she slid down the wing on the other side, Firedart raised and ready for anything.

Ythen wasn't there.

Too late, she realized her mistake and swivelled around, her weapon tracking.

Ythen's form, which had been pressed up underneath the body of the thranvorl as she slid past him, lunged forward and tackled her, bringing them both to the ground.

Yriel's training took over as she quickly rolled away from his grasp, looking back long enough to place a well-aimed kick onto the side of his head. Ythen let her go with a howl of pain, but reached out again and snagged her foot as she struggled to crawl away, dropping her to her stomach and pulling her back towards him.

She flipped over onto her back and aimed her Firedart down the length of her body, squeezing off a shot that Ythen narrowly blocked by releasing her ankle and throwing his left arm above his head. The dart splashed against his dented Buckler, whose misshapen surface did not absorb the blow dealt to it but instead sent it rebounding outwards.

The ricochet lanced back and caught Yriel just below her right knee, burning a sizable hole in her skin and forcing her to cry out in pain.

She threw her arms out blindly above her head as the searing sensation burned through her body, causing her muscles to spasm in shock. Her right hand found a rock, most likely a piece of stone that had broken off an Aru Faylen boulder.

She grasped it firmly, letting the cool, hard sensation of the rock against her hand drag her mind back to reality.

Ythen tugged on her wounded leg, testing her coherence. She responded with a wild scream, and twisted to fling the rock down at his head. The rock glanced off his shoulder, tearing through what little remained of his tan cloak and breaking the skin before bouncing off into the mud.

Ythen let her go and scrambled to his feet. All around them, dueling parties from the north raced by, locked in combat even as they rushed to escape from the ever-shrinking wall of fire.

He aimed his Firedart at Yriel's chest as she struggled to her knees, her breath coming in ragged, shocky gasps. She looked up at him; pain and hatred were the only emotions he could read in her face.

He swallowed hard and squeezed his fist.

Yriel's eyes widened as her gaze flitted over his shoulder.

After years of training together, Ythen instinctively ducked in response to her warning, throwing his body down and to the left.

A massive crack sounded in the space where his head had been only a second earlier as a gru'Esh warrior smashed its hard-won weapons together and bellowed in rage as it missed its target.

Ythen used his momentum and rolled to his feet, jumping onto and then sliding over the gru'Esh's back and landing uncomfortably hard on the other side. He jammed his Buckler against the gru'Esh's hide as he rolled, letting any electrical buildup discharge into the creature's body. Behind him, he felt the gru'Esh body jolt a number of times as Yriel took advantage of the distraction and fired multiple shots at her enemies.

Ythen had more immediate things to worry about. The battle had found them again, and the gru'Esh, Daevyn, and Aru Elen forces were surrounding them, blind with rage and bloodlust. Ythen reached down to grab a spear that was sticking out of the mud but didn't have time to orient himself properly and instead used it as a club, swinging wildly at a second gru'Esh warrior, knocking the arms out of its clawed hands and forcing it to veer off in another direction, in search of easier prey.

Behind him, Yriel had fired six more darts at the gru'Esh who had attacked Ythen, stopping its advance just before it reached her as one of her darts found a chink in its otherwise impenetrable carapace.

The gru'Esh body slumped to the ground in front of her, revealing the figure of Ythen just as he reared back and let fly with a wooden spear, aimed perfectly at her.

The spear arced swiftly through the space that separated them, but was grabbed out of the air by a passing Aru Elen who buzzed off with it towards the forest to the south.

Yriel breathed a silent thank you to the flying creature just as another Aru Elen grabbed her from behind and lifted her into the air, holding her only by her right arm and her long, white hair. She closed her eyes tightly and screamed in pain. Immediately, the hands holding her released her and she fell a few metres to the ground, her wounded leg protesting violently as it crumpled beneath her.

The body of her flying attacker splashed into the mud next to her, the hole from Ythen's Firedart oozing smoke out of its forehead.

She was given no time to rest. Suddenly Ythen was next to her, pulling her roughly to her feet. He stepped behind her, his back pressed tightly against hers as he propped her up.

Dropping a canister from his Firedart, he swiftly replaced it with another from his bandolier and fired a volley into the sky, dropping two more Aru Elen before lowering his aim as he attempted to discourage any gru'Esh looking for an easy target.

"For now," he growled over his shoulder.

Yriel slumped against him in relief and reloaded her own weapon, and the two of them worked to protect each other one more time as they limped away from the thranvorl's body and nearer to the north-western base of the Barricade.

The wall of fire was growing smaller and smaller, forcing the few remaining members of the Daevyn and gru'Esh armies into closer combat. The battlefield was utter chaos now. Kala had sent a battalion of Aru Elen with their spears to attack from the skies while the Aru Faylen continued to drop boulders on any and all moving targets, though there seemed to be less of the lumpy flying creatures than there should have been. The three Human Keepers and Jingwei were madly using their powers to try to undo the damage being done by Kala, who was still hovering out of their reach and randomly firing lightning into the crowd, causing flare-ups of the fires that had once been extinguished.

The Sea Keeper and his new apprentice had been forced back towards the foot of the Barricade by the tightening noose of flames. Though enemy weapons were unable to penetrate the sphere of water encircling them, they were still being pushed as the now fully entwined armies were crushed into a chaotic blender of Kala's creation.

Callum was withdrawing as well. He had almost reached the top of the ridge now, tossing aside empty canisters as he went, using his quick eye to knock Aru Len enemies out of the sky and into the mash of chaos below.

The Aru Elen that were positioned over the vast body of Huon Arrahl had not moved. Rata and Ila were watching them closely, hoping beyond hope that the winged people would see the destruction that the Spark Keeper had brought to their world and abandon her.

Ydelle had sunk to her knees beside them, her face clutched in her hands as she was forced to watch helplessly as her people were led into destruction by her sometime adviser and her only child.

The armies had brought the battle halfway up the slopes of the Barricade.

One way or another, it was almost over.

Unlike their brothers and sisters in the northern part of the battlefield, the Aru Elen fleet that was hovering over the forest to the south had not yet engaged their enemy. They had carefully stayed out of range of the Daevyn weaponry, and had not attacked since diving into the forest to steal their spears.

Now, as they watched the final remnants of the broken armies begin to swarm the ridge, once again endangering the living forest on the other side, they acted.

The Aru Elen dove as one, their grey wooden spears jutting out in front of them as they rushed the ridge, ready to destroy all who were left to defend it.

But the defenders were not taken unawares. The three remaining Human Keepers had gathered now on a small rise in the centre of the Barricade's length. Jingwei and Callum were with them, much the worse for wear, but still alive and standing. All eyes had been fixed on the hovering fleet, anxiously waiting for them to make their move.

Kala's concentration had been absorbed maintaining the wall of fire, so Jera and Jingwei had finally been able to extinguish all the small conflagrations that had popped up over the battlefield and they'd since joined the others on the ridge to prepare for their last stand.

As the mass of Aru Elen moved into their dive, the remaining defenders sprung into action.

Rata thrust his long arms out in front of him and a cloud of pollen erupted from the plains around the western edge of the Korrahl Forest, expanding upward until it enveloped the attacking fleet, effectively blinding it.

Ila, still severely weakened from the raising of the Barricade, shot a small but extremely accurate selection of stones at those Aru Elen she judged to be leading the assault. Behind her, Jera had focused all of his power onto weakening the wall of fire that Kala was pushing forward, hoping to keep her occupied while the others dealt with the aerial threat.

Callum was tired. He was tired of fighting, tired of watching people die, tired of being used by others to fight their battle for them.

Angrily, the Human boy tore the greaves off his arms, dropping the Firedart and Buckler to the ground beside him. He stepped forward and opened his arms, palms up. The air above him began to glow a burning violet, and he suddenly brought his hands together with a loud clap, his gaze fixed narrowly on the sky above.

Simultaneously, more than half of the spears held by the Aru Elen burst into flame, scorching their wielders, many of whom dropped them quickly in pain. Others were not so lucky, and were consumed in fiery bursts that filled the sky, casting a purple glow over the battlefield; their bodies simply disappeared in clouds of ash and smoke.

The burning spears tumbled into the forest below, where Huon Arrahl began to writhe in pain.

Within seconds, the forest was ablaze.

Jingwei started in shock as the spears ignited. She looked over at Callum in awe, surprised by the look of intensity she saw on his face. Apparently, she wasn't the only one learning new uses for her power.

But her amazement quickly changed to despair when the spears hit the treetops and the forest started to burn.

A deafening groaning rolled up the ridge from the forest below as Huon Arrahl thrashed about, desperately trying to smother the flames. The trees were beating one another in agony, their leaves withering and falling with each blow, the movement having no effect except to add more fuel to an already raging fire.

"Callum!" Jingwei watched as he pointed his finger at the sky, alternating between shooting multi-coloured jets of flame out of his hands and causing long-distance individual explosions by lighting more spears ablaze as the Aru Elen threw down their weapons in terror.

"Callum! Stop it! You're burning down the forest!"

Callum continued to destroy the spears of the Aru Elen, his face grimly set. He gave no indication as to whether or not he heard Jingwei's plea.

Jingwei resisted the urge to shove him down the slope of the ridge, and instead calmed herself, searching the nearby air and ground for enough water to extinguish the blaze below them.

There wasn't much left.

She turned her palms down, as Jera had shown her, and focused.

Nothing happened. There simply wasn't enough water. She closed her eyes and searched again. The world felt dry and brittle, except for a hint of liquid behind her that tickled her mind like a glimmering reflection on the surface of a pond.

She spun around. Jera was sitting there, cross-legged, in a standoff with Kala high above.

The wall of fire had stopped advancing, and so the remaining warriors had stopped climbing the sides of the Barricade. The ring was steaming now, as the water Jera was using to hold it back evaporated under the intense heat Kala was pouring into it.

Jingwei sent a small drop of water, all she could find, to strike at the Sea Keeper's cheek. It never made it, sucked into Jera's own private war, but he noticed and glanced back towards her, startled.

"Jera!" Jingwei screamed over the noise of the battle before her, the explosions above her, and the fire behind her. "I need the water!"

The Sea Keeper shook his head quickly and turned back to what he was doing, unaware the Huon Arrahl was burning to the south.

Jingwei ran over to him and stepped in front of him. She knelt, placed her hand on his shoulder and looked him in the eye, much as he had done to her not so long ago, that very afternoon.

"Sea Keeper. You have to let me do this." Jingwei reached her other hand up in an offering. "It's my turn. I'm ready."

Jera met her eyes searchingly. They darted back and forth, and then filled with sadness for a moment, before they wrinkled with the Sea Keeper's smile. He placed his hand in hers, and suddenly an awareness of all the water that he had been using was flooding through her mind.

The complexity of his control astounded her, but Jingwei kept her composure and channeled all the water into a single flowing river, aiming at the forest on the south side of the ridge before hurling it forward.

It poured over the heads of the defenders standing on the Barricade and plunged deep into the forest. Instantly the trees were shrouded in a ball of smoke as all the fires were extinguished.

Jingwei didn't wait. Puddles of water were being sucked into the dry dirt, but she scooped them up and began intercepting more of the falling spears that Callum had ignited.

The battle below came to a momentary standstill as the wearied warriors looked up to watch a rain of burning streaks hurtling towards the trees, only to be caught by a liquid forest of individual fountains that extinguished the flames, releasing clouds of steam that quickly evaporated into the dry air.

The two young Humans continued to work together, and within moments the Aru Elen fleet was weaponless, and the forest was safe again.

Far above the plains, the Spark Keeper was outraged as she watched Callum throw down his weapons and destroy her army with pinpoint accuracy.

Not the Firebrand, then. It was the Human boy whom the others would send to take her place.

She released the wall of fire. It had been rapidly advancing, a fact she had thought was proof of her victory over the weakened Sea Keeper, but she now saw that he and the little girl had played her, drawing her attention to one front while attacking from another.

Fine then, child. You wish to test your newfound skills against mine?

She would be happy to oblige.

Below her, Jingwei had released the water as the last spear fell from the Aru Elen fleet, blackened and dripping wet.

The fighting was still continuing on the plains, but it was beginning to peter out as exhaustion set in and adrenaline faded.

All eyes were turned to the sky, where the traitorous Spark Keeper hovered, her golden wings scalded, her robes torn and fluttering.

She looked down on them with a burning hatred and summoned a carefully crafted bolt of lightning, more powerful than any she had ever created, and sent it crashing down at the Barricade.

J era felt the bolt being formed as a massive void took shape in his mind, so finely attuned to the placement of water. He quickly opened his arms, summoning any and all nearby water, pulling the seeping puddles out of the forest, the tiny drops buried deep underground, even the sweat off of the dead bodies in the field.

He pulled them all together and fired them at the lightning bolt just as Kala released it.

Y then's world suddenly seemed to move in slow motion as he and Yriel watched the thin bolt of energy lance down from the sky above.

He had felt its creation as he was battling on the field, and looked up just in time to see it coalesce and strike downward, almost invisible in the late afternoon air.

Halfway down, the bolt seemed to slow, its crackling energy becoming less erratic as it crystallized from the bottom up. Jera's liquid missile enfolded the bolt as it fell, wrapping it in a thick sheet of ice, making it solid in form and substance, but still radiating with power from behind the protective frozen shield.

An enormously strong wind blew in from the east at that moment, knocking the bolt just a hair off its course, and the massive icicle slammed into the ground right next to Callum and Jingwei, burying itself deeply into the Barricade.

K ala watched as the frozen pillar crashed into the ridge, knocking many off their feet but leaving her targets unharmed. Robbed of her kill, she looked to the east, searching furiously for the source of the wind.

Her face paled as she saw a figure soaring over the mountaintops towards her.

The figure was an Aru Elen, who, like most others of her kind, was naked. She had painted herself sky-blue in the front, with sinuous black lines tattooed all around her, moving with her body in a fluid, muscular representation of the wind. Her back was covered in scales that ranged from blue to silver to black, and glistened brightly in the dull, smoky air.

Her long hair was transparent, and created the effect of a veil of crystals surrounding her head, refracting the light so that her figure was constantly surrounded by an aura of colours that shifted with her movement, like a living rainbow. On her head she wore a tiara fashioned from clouds that Kala knew to change colour with her mood. It was currently storm-black. The figure's wings were identical to her sister's, with golden veins running through them.

Alkira, the Sky Keeper of Tranthaea, had finally arrived.

Kala looked at the ruins of the battlefield below her. Her Aru Faylen had fled, her Aru Elen were impotent against the Keepers, and the other armies were giving up as they finally realized that their true enemies were not on the field with them, but instead in the sky above.

Kala met her sibling's eyes. This was not going to be a pleasant reunion.

She turned swiftly in the air and sped off to the north as fast as her wings could carry her.

Callum's mouth gaped open as the Sky Keeper set herself down on the crest of the Barricade, right next to the towering icicle that now protruded from its peak. He was used to seeing naked Aru Elen by now; her lack of clothing didn't disturb him.

But there was something about her, a wildness and a commanding authority that demanded a certain respect and awe. For some reason Callum felt for the first time that the Keepers had a leader, and that he was in her presence right now.

Alkira glanced at him and Jingwei appraisingly and Callum felt as though his entire existence had been judged. Years of thievery and dishonesty, scrabbling around in the gutter, and cowardice as he allowed himself to be bullied by so many others flashed through his mind. But then he saw bravery. Courage, and the lives he'd saved. He saw hope for the future, and the warm smile of a girl who cared for him. In that moment he found himself hoping that he had been deemed worthy of the mantle that had been thrust upon him.

The Sky Keeper quickly made eye contact with Rata, Ila, and Jera, nodded with polite deference to the Flame-Bearer, and then turned north towards the battlefield, her stance indicating that business was to come before pleasantries.

She raised her arms over the plains and the wind rose to her call. Focused gusts of air snuffed out the remaining fires that burned low in a semi-circle around the battlefield. Jera sat beside her feet, encased in his blue bubble, and Jingwei could feel moisture from the pillar of ice trickle out into the field at his command; not enough to release the energy that was trapped inside it, but enough to create a thick layer of fog over the plains immediately surrounding the Barricade.

The Daevyn remnant reluctantly lowered their weapons. They could not shoot an enemy they could not see.

Ila also stepped forward, her short, thick stature a strange complement to Alkira's harsh beauty. She braced herself and then raised her staff. There was a crackling sound as the thick mud of the battlefield solidified around the legs of the remaining gru'Esh warriors that waded through it, immobilizing them.

A hard-won silence finally settled over the enshrouded plains.

The battle was over.

Chapter Twenty-Four:
The Investigation

Jingwei shifted uncomfortably in her saddle. The raeas let out a hiss beneath her as it course-corrected, doing its best to help its unsteady rider keep her seat.

The plains stretched out before her, the tan blanket of grain dipping and swelling as far as the eye could see. If she swiveled in the saddle and looked behind her, she could see a vast pillar of smoke rising from the prairies, painting grey and intangible swirls against the solid black walls of the mountains that stretched parallel to her path, cutting off sharply in a seaside cliff in the north and fading into the distance to the south.

The raeas floated fluidly over the grass, rocking Jingwei's body with gentle tugs as it swayed from side to side, its hindquarters flicking as it propelled itself towards the north. Beside her on her left was Callum, his head bowed forward as if he were lost in thought. On her other side was Ythen. He was gazing steadily forward, focused solely on their destination and what they might find there.

Jingwei's mind drifted back to the Barricade. Once Kala had fled, the battle had ended swiftly. Exhausted from combat and confusion, unable to advance or retreat thanks to the Keepers' interference, the two remaining ground forces had given up and collapsed wearily, the haggard and worn bodies of the surviving warriors lying almost indistinguishable among the dead.

The Sky Keeper and her three counterparts had made a few quick visits to each of the four armies that were left on the field, partly to check on the well-being of the peoples and partly to ensure that tensions would not flare up. They needn't have worried. From what Jingwei had seen, no one was in the mood to fight again.

The Flame-Bearer had gathered what was left of her troops and set up a camp and hospital to the west and sent riders to Yshaar to call for medicine and food. The gru'Esh had fallen back into their holes in the shadow of the mountains. Jingwei had watched with a sense of ironic justice as the struggling body of v'Aros had been taken underground under the watchful eyes of the Keepers to face the justice of four new gru'Esh Clan Leaders.

The Aru Faylen, under the guidance of Delevate Wrem, had fled to their homes in the clouds over the eastern mountains and the skies remained clear of their forms. They had abandoned the field and did not seem to have any interest in returning.

The Aru Elen had landed and made camp to the north. They had elected a leader of sorts to represent their position to the other leaders of Tranthaea; a green-painted female with orange and purple scales named Nyx, who was only able to communicate with Alkira through a complicated series of wing-flutterings that seemed to be the secret language of the voiceless Aru Elen.

Huon Arrahl had remained behind the Barricade, sending only a single tendriled tree over the ridge to communicate with the Keepers who had finished their tour and set up a meeting hall in what had once been the centre of the battlefield, now cleared of bodies by way of a mass burial performed quickly and quietly by the Soil Keeper.

The hall consisted of a natural tent, the high sides of which were made of newly-grown vines, with large, wide leaves acting as a ceiling. Inside was a raised, square slab of rock around which Rata had grown a selection of seats for those who chose to use them. Ila, Rata, and Ydelle were seated along one side, each still looking weary with battle fatigue now that hostilities had ceased. Beside them was Jera, slumped over in exhaustion after battling Kala's fires. Alkira and Nyx hovered lightly above the ground on another side, while Huon Arrahl draped his tendril over Rata's shoulder opposite them. The final side was occupied by Jingwei, Callum, and q'Orha; mi'Orha's young offspring and the gru'Esh Ambassador chosen to represent all four gru'Esh Tribes on this newly formed Tranthaean Council.

Conspicuously absent in the silence was the thrumming wash of the Aru Faylen.

Ythen had stood quietly off to the side, standing unnecessary guard over the prisoner: his former partner, the Flame-Bearer's daughter.

Yriel was seated in the corner of the tent, her legs pulled up to her chest. She said nothing, but stared at the ground in front of her, her eyes glued to the dark brown mixture of stone chips, mud, and blood. She had stayed silent since the battle ended, speaking to no one, not even her mother. They had shared a look of disappointment, one with the other, and then Yriel had pointedly turned away. All other attempts by the Flame-Bearer to talk to her daughter, to understand why she had betrayed her people went unanswered, and the Flame-Bearer was left with nothing but questions and the palpable hatred of a child for her mother.

Surrounding the prisoner were vertical jets of air, invisible but audible as they whispered downwards. They'd been planted in a circle by Alkira to create a cell that would powerfully slam Yriel into the ground were she to attempt any escape.

"If the Sea Keeper is correct," Alkira had said, drawing everyone's attention back to the matter at hand, "then we must act."

"I am correct." Jera had lifted his chin slowly; his hair and beard continued to drift upwards after his head had stopped moving. "The water is still being pulled to the north, to the Sea of Nalani. While I was imprisoned, Kala was drawing my power out of me, and she used it to bring a dry Tranthaea to the brink of war. Now that I have been freed," he had paused to nod thanks to Jingwei, Callum, and Ythen and then continued, "I still feel the water being pulled, as if it were moving of its own accord."

Ila had spoken. "Then we need to find out why. Why is it still moving?"

Rata had been of the same opinion. "If Tranthaea dries further, the clouds will vanish, the Warrens will crumble to dust, the forests will die, and the plains will burn."

The Council had agreed. This new threat was an imminent danger to them all, which meant that for the moment, Kala would have to wait.

Though Jera would have been the best choice to lead the investigation, it was decided that he needed to recover his strength before venturing out again, and so Alkira and the rest of the Council had looked to the nearest thing they had to a Sea Keeper.

A Sea Keeper's apprentice.

As she rode across the plains, driving her raeas to the north, Jingwei wondered if she should have refused their trust.

The plains ahead of them were full and lush and a welcome change from the trampled mud of the battlefield. The air glowed around them, and ahead of them the blanket of grains lit up, each blade seeming distinct from the others as the bright air reflected off the surface of the sea in the middle distance, creating a glowing backlighting that marked their destination.

Jingwei realized as they rode that they were not far from where she and Callum had first entered this world, not so very long ago.

So much had changed since then.

"Did you see that?"

Callum's voice broke her out of her reverie.

"Yes." Ythen was staring hard off to their right, his eyes narrowly peering into the grass. Callum tugged hard on his reins and brought his raeas around in front of Jingwei's, effectively creating a wall between her and the unknown threat.

The Daevyn slid off his mount, his Firedart raised. Callum remained on his raeas, but brought his weapon to bear as well, steadying himself with his knees as he lifted his Buckler in front of him. Jingwei was taken aback, overcome with the sudden memory of the first time she'd seen him among the grasses of the plains; timid and afraid, unable to match her confronting brashness. That Callum was nothing at all like the one seated in front of her now. This Callum was brave and confident, sure of his ability to handle whatever came.

She wondered if she looked as different to him.

There was a ripple in the grass a few metres away. Ythen leveled his arm and began to tighten his grip.

"Wait!" Jingwei called out softly. "Don't set the grass on fire. There isn't enough water in the air for me to put out a fire!"

Another ripple appeared a few metres away from the first. And then another, behind the first two.

Ythen backed up slowly. "Callum, can you see anything?"

Callum was standing in his saddle now, furiously staring into the plains from his higher vantage point but the thick grass obscured whatever was out there.

"No. But there are at least three of them, maybe more."

Jingwei nudged her raeas closer to the other two. "Could they be those porcupiney things we saw when we first arrived?"

Ythen risked a glance over his shoulder at her, his blue eyes full of confusion. "What?"

Callum kept his eyes on the field. "She means croen."

"Oh." Ythen turned back to the field. "No. It isn't croen."

A sudden flash of grey burst from the grass and streaked underneath Jingwei. Her raeas shot forward in panic, jolting Jingwei from her perch in the saddle and throwing her to the ground amongst the grains.

Jingwei rolled as she landed, her broken nose throbbing with the impact. She ended up on her knees, watching her raeas swishing quickly to the east, its body gliding in a serpentine fashion over the grasses.

Behind it, a similar but smaller pattern had carved a circle through the grass and come up behind the runaway raeas. It was following her mount closely; she could see it weaving through the grains, and whatever it was, it was catching up.

A second later the same grey shape that Jingwei had seen flash underneath her suddenly shot out of the tall grass behind the raeas, aimed directly at its prey.

The animal was about one quarter the size of a raeas, and was of a similar colouring, but had jagged black and orange stripes encircling its legs. It had two long horns on the front of its head – half again the length of its body – which ended in sharp hooks meant to hold whatever they speared. Underneath its body were two pairs of legs that were stretched out behind it as it surged forward, jamming its long horns into the fleeing raeas and carrying it to the ground.

"Gravog." Ythen tossed his reins to Callum who caught them without taking his eyes off the fields around them.

The Daevyn reached out and helped Jingwei to her feet. She accepted his hand mutely, her attention still focused on the spot where her mount had vanished into the grass. Snapping and snarling sounds reached her ears and she turned away.

There were still at least two more out there.

"Gravog?" She didn't see any more movement to the east. "What are they?"

"They are a pack predator. They move like raeas, through the air, but can pounce with the help of their legs if they are close enough." Ythen motioned for Jingwei to get on his mount and she clambered up. "They are very fast. You seldom see them coming—"

Without warning Callum fired a shot from his Firedart. It lanced through the grass and pounded into a second gravog, immediately igniting the surrounding vegetation and starting a quick burn. Ythen yelped and rushed forward, tearing off his cloak. He pounded it on the ground, trying to smother the flames before they could spread.

"Ythen!" Callum's voice brought the blond boy's head jerking around. Callum raised his hand and his eyebrow.

Ythen understood. He turned back to the fire, which was now a few metres square in size and expanding rapidly, and spread his hands over the blaze, palms down. He closed his eyes for a moment, feeling a burning heat on his hands and when he opened his eyes again, the fire was gone.

Jingwei twitched her lip from atop the raeas. "Holding out on us, were you? I thought Callum was the fireman."

Ythen swallowed hard at this use of his newfound abilities, but grinned at her tone as he nudged the dead gravog's burned body with his toe. "You should know by now, Jingwei, Tranthaea is full of surprises."

Jingwei smiled wryly as she heard a rustling noise to her right and she turned her head just in time to catch sight of the third gravog leaping out of the grass beside her, its wide mouth little more than teeth.

Without thinking, she let herself fall sideways off the raeas, feeling the rush of air as it passed over her, its hind legs brushing her right arm.

She landed flat on her back, knocking the wind out of her lungs, but still managed to reach her right hand out over her head, pointing towards the gravog's landing zone.

The predator had already started rotating in the air in preparation for a second pass when it landed with a sickening slashing sound on the bed of frozen grass that Jingwei had prepared for it, and its grey body sprouted dozens of red-stained icy blades.

Jingwei rose unsteadily to her feet, gasping as breath flooded back into her body. Ythen appeared beside her and lifted her easily into the saddle of his raeas.

"Full of surprises," he repeated, climbing up behind her as Callum frowned slightly, his eyes flickering between the two of them in the saddle and the still grasses around them.

"We should keep moving."

The two remaining raeas moved quickly with their passengers, leaving behind a collection of corpses as they edged ever closer to the shining northern sea.

The white sand of the beach was moister than Callum had expected it to be. Even high above the water line, far from the seemingly infinite blue of the sea, the grit under his feet squished as though a wave had just drawn over it.

There was moisture everywhere. The air, the sea, the land; all were thick with it. Callum had been to Brighton once during the holiday season. Easy pickings from unwary tourists had drawn him but what he remembered most was the salty tang of the air, the glorious unendingness of the ocean, the possibilities of the distant horizon and the lands beyond.

Only now that he had finally crossed that horizon line, he didn't recognise the sea air around him. This wetness had more motion, it seemed more complete than the ocean back home.

And for the first time since he'd truly accepted his ability, back at the top of the spire in Kala's palace, Callum felt it wane. In the presence of all this water, his fire-power felt weak. He doubted if he'd be able to summon more than a spark if he had to, and so physically prepared himself to fight with more conventional means should the need arise.

Jingwei and Ythen jumped down off their raeas and joined him on the beach. The sea stretched out in front of them, its furthest boundaries hidden by a thick mist that had settled over the water. The beach, which ran cleanly down the waterline as far as the eye could see in both directions, was unbroken by vegetation or rock formation. Its pristine white sand created a pure divide between the tan grasses of the plains and the rich blue waves of the sea, save for small streams of water that trickled up from the south, drawn by a mysterious force to the open sea.

It was Jingwei who noticed it first, although whether it was because of her water sensitivity or because she was more interested in the natural world than Callum, she wasn't sure.

The sea had waves. They weren't enormous ones, the kind Jingwei used to watch Hunter surf on, but they weren't mere ripples either. They moved in all directions, bashing against one another in multiple collisions that tore them apart and sent them hurtling off again. The waves washed noisily up onto the shore, pounding the sand at their feet, grasping hungrily for their toes.

But there was no wind. The air hung perfectly still around them, its unceasing brightness inviting calm and suggesting security. Yet beneath it, the water seethed.

"Jera was right. Someone, or something, is doing this." Jingwei stooped down and dipped her finger in the water as it rushed up to her, withdrawing just before it caught her feet. "The water feels wild. Uncontrollable." She stood up again and turned to face the boys. "I've never felt it like this before. It's not just a tool here. It feels... alive."

Callum nodded.

Ythen shifted uncomfortably next to Jingwei. The Humans had come a long way from being the two frightened children he had found beating uselessly at the flames of a wildfire five days ago. Standing next to them now, he felt strangely surpassed.

It had always been easy to understand why the three Human Keepers had been chosen. Their intelligence and wisdom had seen Tranthaea through difficult times before, and Ythen had always thought highly of them, but it was another thing entirely to watch two new ones be created.

Five days ago, he had not truly believed Kala when she had claimed these two visitors could be dangerous. Watching them now, these two proven warriors, strangely confident in their abilities, facing an unknown threat without hesitation, he not only believed it, but had witnessed it with his own eyes.

Jingwei reached out and took Callum's and Ythen's hands into her own. The two boys each reached into a pocket and pulled out what looked like perfectly clear marbles that Alkira and Ila had given them. The Keepers had told them that once placed in their mouths the stones would allow them to breath anywhere, even underwater, which is where Jera had been convinced they would find the answers to their questions.

They popped the marbles into their mouths and followed Jingwei as she waded into the sea.

The cold darkness of the water surrounded them quickly, and if they hadn't been holding onto one another as they entered, they surely would have been separated and lost within moments.

Jingwei couldn't see far in the dark, but was able to feel voids or expanses in the water in front of her, and so could guide Callum and Ythen around obstacles and help them float over sudden drop-offs.

She also found that she was able to breathe naturally underwater now, a gift she wished she'd had when one of her foster dads had given her that impromptu swimming lesson when she was a child.

She had been afraid to go in the water for years after that. How things had changed.

She could feel the cold of the dark water as a distant chill, like a breeze that is held off by a warm coat, rippling against the layers of protection, but unable to penetrate.

Jingwei felt Callum squeeze her hand. She was oddly comfortable between the two boys. During the battle and the journey to the sea her mind had been far too distracted to focus on the problem of being sought after by two young men, and she had to remind herself that now was no different.

They had a job to do. Anything else had to wait until later.

Callum squeezed her hand again. She turned her head towards him, her mouth turned down in a comically disapproving frown that he would never see.

He was staring away from her. She followed his gaze and saw a glimmer of light far below them in the distance.

Jingwei squeezed Callum's hand back to let him know she had seen it, and tugged on Ythen's as they turned towards it.

The gentle downward slope that they had been following soon became a steep decline. Jingwei had to lead the two boys around large rock formations that rose from the sea bed, and more than once they almost got tangled in aggressively swaying patches of kelp.

The glimmer ahead increased as they approached, eventually resolving into a glowing patch of water about thirty metres squared. As they neared it, Jingwei had the strange feeling that they were the only audience members about to witness an extraordinary production on this well-lit, underwater stage.

The pressure of the water was much greater this deep down, and Jingwei knew that if she could feel it, it must be much worse for the boys. As they stepped into the lit area, she saw the boy's faces in her peripheral vision. They were twisted with controlled pain, looking like they would if someone were applying pressure to a day-old bruise.

The water in front of them was empty, save for a large stand of seaweed that drifted lazily about, pulling lightly at its roots before bobbing back down only to drift upward again. Aside from the weeds, there were no animals, no corals, no sign of life.

And yet Jingwei felt that this place was *alive*. Something about it promised a power that she hadn't yet experienced in this world. For the first time since entering the cold water she shivered.

The trio took another cautious step into the light, their feet kicking up small clouds of silt that slowly settled back down to the seabed. The water itself glowed around them in varying levels of brightness, its movement visible in layers of illumination that drifted and swirled in complex patterns that Jingwei could feel as well as see.

Her eyes followed one of the designs as a mass of illuminated water swirled into a miniature vortex in front of her and then drove into the sand, scattering shades of light everywhere in an underwater show unlike anything Jingwei had ever seen.

Callum suddenly gasped beside her, sucking water into his mouth and lungs as he forgot to breathe through the marble. Jingwei quickly placed her hands on his chest and drove the water back out, then turned to see what had caused his surprise.

The clump of seaweed in front of her had formed itself into a face: Callum's face, only twice as tall as Callum. The face shifted with the seaweed, constantly correcting itself as a strand or two disengaged and drifted away.

Callum squeezed Jingwei's hand desperately. She gave him a placating squeeze back, hoping that he wouldn't be able to feel her pulse pounding at a ferocious tempo.

The face hung in the water in front of them, its massive brow furrowed as it gazed on them. It opened its mouth and spoke, the sound waves blasting through the water and nearly taking Jingwei off her feet.

"You are not Kala."

Jingwei was not pleased to hear the Spark Keeper's name. "No, I'm not." She released the boys' hands and stepped forward, her aquamarine cloak expanding behind her. "My name is Jingwei. These are my friends, Callum and Ythen. We are here on behalf of the Tranthaean Council. Who are you? How do you know Kala? And why do you have Callum's face?"

The information and questions seemed to overwhelm the face in the weeds. He bucked and jerked, his features rearranging themselves violently before being released altogether in an explosion of bubbles that blew from the seaweed and came to a hover above the dark green growth. The bubbles bumped against one another, absorbing each other and splitting until they once again coalesced into the form of a face. This time, the face was Jingwei's. The voice boomed out at them again.

"I know nothing of these things. Councils. Tranthaea. Friends." The bubbles that represented the eyes flashed and popped and were replaced by others. "I know only me. Kano Aradat."

Jingwei was unsettled, seeing her own face in the water before her, but she pushed her alarm aside, undeterred.

"And Kala." Jingwei wasn't about to be put off by a little ignorance and self-importance. She'd been on the receiving end of those all her life. Not today. "You said you knew Kala."

The expression on the face wavered between surprise and anger, as if the wearer couldn't choose, or didn't know which emotion to display.

"Kala. Yes. Kala created me. As I created myself."

Jingwei opened her mouth to question him, but his voice rolled on, booming out into the darkness behind them.

"Kala used the Old One to pull the water. All of the water. She used him and used us." The face began to dissolve, the bubbles popping one by one. "But she did not know how to draw us away, we were not her province. So she convinced us. Convinced us to go from where we were and to come here, and when enough of us were drawn, when enough of us were convinced that we were, I *became*."

It suddenly slammed home for Jingwei. That explained the bizarre feeling of life in the sea around her and the air above. Kala hadn't known how to control the water. She had used Jera's power blindly, and in her folly, hadn't used the water as an element, but tried to persuade it to move, as if it were a sentient being.

Which, as a result of her treatment, it had become. A being called Kano Aradat.

The last bubble popped and the face vanished, but was created again by the play of light in the water. This time the face was Ythen's; the changes in brightness in the water became the dark circles under his exhausted eyes and the worried lines in his forehead.

"And now I feel the pull. Above wants me back, spread thin and unknowing. Un*being*." The image of the Quencher's face hardened somehow, the light in the water fleeing as it darkened.

"I will protect Kano Aradat. The water is me, and I will defend my self."

"But you don't understand!" Jingwei was appalled. This was not what she had expected, but now that she knew the water was sentient, she'd hoped that it would take the other peoples of Tranthaea into account.

"All the peoples of the world above need water to survive. If you withdraw it– I mean, you, then they'll all die! You'll destroy an entire world!"

The face burst, scattering shards of light into the deepest reaches of the sea. The illuminated area was thrown into darkness, and Jingwei thrust her hands out to find her boys. They must have been thinking the same thoughts; they grabbed at her hands right away, holding tightly for fear of losing her.

The voice of Kano Aradat boomed from all around them. "I would destroy them, to save me. Just as you would destroy me, to save them."

And in that moment, Jingwei knew that he was right. Tranthaea was her home, and she had accepted that. She would do what she had to do to protect it.

All around them the darkness was complete. Jingwei could feel the water pressure rising on her body, and knew that both boys were feeling it too as their hands tightened on hers. She closed her eyes against the blackness and concentrated on easing the pressure around them. She felt a slight slackening of pressure before it slammed back down onto her, harder than before, accompanied by a roar as Kano Aradat discovered that she meant to physically manipulate him.

Jingwei mentally pushed back even as she bent her knees and jumped, forcing her way towards the surface, driving through the thick, heavy water that now aimed to crush her and her companions. Below her on her right she saw a flare of light. Ythen was doing something with his ability, and a moment later Callum began to copy him.

As Jingwei pushed her way to the shallows, fighting for every centimetre against the mighty power of the sea, she began to feel heat emanating from below. She looked down and saw a sea of bubbles rising swiftly beside her.

They were boiling the water.

The pressure on her body eased somewhat as Kano Aradat howled in pain and released them. They shot to the surface and exploded out of it, landing heavily on the white sands of the beach.

The boys were dripping wet as the three of them stumbled up the rise to the plains beyond, wild waves lashing at their heels, but they dried quickly as the drops of water seemed to leap off of them, rolling, trickling, pouring back into the sea. They mounted their raeas quickly and turned south, eager to leave the angry sea behind them.

Jingwei held tightly onto Callum and turned to look back at the Sea of Nalani once more as they fled south, back towards the Barricade. She saw a maelstrom whirling darkly in the centre of the sea, drawing the last drops of Tranthaean water into its hungry maw.

Chapter Twenty-Five:
The Alliance

The race back to the battlefield left both the raeas and their riders panting, their parched mouths cracking and bleeding, gasping for moisture in the dry air. By the time they arrived at the makeshift Council Hall, Jingwei was white-faced and shaking, her newfound dependence on the power of water ironically beginning to rob her of health and life.

They were eased down off their raeas by helpful Daevyn grooms and taken into the tent. Jingwei was exhausted but shooed away the Keepers' efforts to help her, turning them instead towards Callum and Ythen, who were suffering the debilitating effects of the bends thanks to their quick ascent from the depths of the sea. The rest of the Council members stood hovering anxiously over Jera, who was just as pale and shaky as Jingwei. Once the boys' pain had been alleviated, Ythen called the Councillors to attention and explained what they had experienced in the northern sea.

There was a general reaction of shock and disbelief among the Keepers and Ambassadors that quickly settled into a seething fury.

Alkira spoke first. "So, in her foolish ambition Kala has created a monster that will destroy all of Tranthaea unless we act."

"And act quickly," Ila chimed in. "Even now I can feel the Warrens crumbling beneath us, and it's getting harder to breathe, even for us people of the dirt."

Huon Arrahl wasn't able to speak through Rata, who was standing across the room from its body, but the tree leaned over the table and shook itself gently, dropping three dried brown leaves onto the surface.

Above the tree, Nyx buzzed her wings fiercely in a complicated rhythm, which Alkira declined to translate but responded to by nodding her head and saying, "I agree. Tomorrow morning at the latest. Jera will need time to recover before facing such an enemy."

Jera weakly waved her concern away, his limp hands only giving strength to her argument. Jingwei lifted her head and croaked out, "He'll be more powerful near the water. At least, I was. But Kano Aradat is powerful too..." Her voice trailed away but her eyes remained open and alert.

Alkira nodded briskly. "I see. Well then, does anyone have a plan?"

Silence reigned around the table. In the corner of the room, Yriel sat quietly, unable to hear the words of the Council over the humming bars of air that surrounded her cell.

No one spoke. The great unknown of their new enemy had bound the peoples of Tranthaea together, unleashing a might unheard of since the beginning of their history, yet now, even in their union, they found that their enemy could still be more powerful than their combined strengths.

Fear lay thick in the room like a heavy cloud, unseen but overpowering. Intangible, yet paralyzing.

Finally Ythen stepped forward. "Kano Aradat reacted to us." He placed his hand on Callum's shoulder. "Fire. It is the natural enemy of water. Perhaps we can shock the sentience out of the sea, using the Spark Keeper's own weapon against the monster she created."

Callum agreed, "Shock it out, or burn it out." He turned to look at Ydelle. "Flame-Bearer. How many Firedarts do you have in your camp?"

The Daevyn leader let her face drop. "Almost three for every Quencher, now that so many of my warriors are fallen."

Callum gave her a look of sympathy but continued in his train of thought, "If we give the extras to the Aru Elen and the gru'Esh and surround the sea from above and below, and all fire at the same time—"

Ythen finished his thought excitedly. "Then we might create a shock wave strong enough to destroy him."

Ydelle frowned slightly at the idea of arming those who had so recently opposed her forces, but quickly softened as she thought it through.

q'Orha, the young gru'Esh Councillor, clicked noisily in the corner and then switched to Brydge, saying, "The gru'Esh have failed Tranthaea greatly. But we will atone. We will tunnel under the sea. If we have the fire-weapons of the Daevyn, we can attack our common enemy from below."

Nyx buzzed around the hall three times, clearly offering to do the same from above.

A strong chorus of agreement filled the room as the Councillors latched onto the only idea they had with the fervour of desperation.

The plan went into effect right away. Nyx left the hall with Ydelle, heading west to the Daevyn encampment and the armoury therein. q'Orha rushed east to the gru'Esh with great zeal to begin tunneling north with its people, as anxious to earn back the trust of the Tranthaean peoples as it was to save them.

Rata and Ila began to speak with Huon Arrahl as it wandered out of the hall, the walls opening and closing around them with the crackling sound of dried leaves crunching underfoot.

Alkira knelt beside the Sea Keeper and helped him to his feet. She whispered in his ear, whatever she said causing a smile to break across his wrinkled face.

Ythen had been reassigned to the post of First Quencher and was called into action, sent to organize the movement of weapons from the Daevyn camp to the gru'Esh tunnel system, and for the first time since they had dueled on the plateau of Du Garrah, Callum and Jingwei were alone.

Callum sat silently in a vine chair next to Jingwei, who was resting on top of what looked like a lilac toadstool. They both remained quiet; the only sounds in the room were the humming of the air that kept Yriel trapped in her cell across the tent and Jingwei's laboured breathing.

Callum saw that Yriel had turned her back on the room and was facing into the corner, her back curled as she hunched over on the cold dirt floor.

He would never have a better chance. He screwed up his courage and spoke. "Jingwei? Do you miss home?"

Jingwei's face wrinkled in surprise at the question. "I don't know. Not really, I guess. Do you?"

"A little." Callum pictured the dirty streets of London, the masses of people, the shrill whistle of a policeman on the hunt. "It's all I'd ever known, 'til now."

"Yeah." Jingwei closed her eyes. "But back home, I was never really..." She struggled with the next word. "Wanted. You know? I mean, I was just there, and people dealt with me. But here..." Her voice trailed off again.

"You're needed," Callum finished for her. She nodded slowly, as if she had only realized it when he'd said it aloud. Jera had been clear. Three hundred years was long enough. He needed her. Tranthaea needed her.

"So you're going to do it then? Take Jera's place? Become the Sea Keeper, and never go back home again?"

Jingwei's eyes sharpened a bit through the hazy exhaustion on her face. "Yes," she said, almost defiantly. "Everything I want is here. Back home I have nothing. Here I can have..."

"Me. You can have me." Callum almost couldn't believe he'd said it aloud. Now it was out there; the confession hung between them.

Jingwei was silent for a moment and then turned towards him, her eyes sad. Callum read her answer in those eyes before she spoke, and hated it.

I waited too long.

"Oh, Callum. We've been through so much together, but–"

"You fancy Ythen." Callum's throat felt strangely tight. "Yeah?"

Jingwei nodded. "There's something about him... our connection... I don't really understand it. But you'll always be a great friend. Like family, really. The only family I have." She leaned forward and looked up at him. "I'm so sorry."

Callum stood up abruptly. "No. Don't be sorry. Ythen's tops. I'm happy for you both, really." He walked over to the door, passing Yriel on the way. She was still turned into the corner, her face hidden by her long, white hair.

He turned back to Jingwei and spoke once more before ducking out the exit.

"Really."

Callum found himself wandering through the Daevyn encampment. His mind was full of swirling thoughts. Disappointment and betrayal warred with friendship and acceptance; his emotions peaked and looped as he blindly set one foot in front of the other, lost in thought.

He walked unseeing through the lines of tents that had been set up by the surviving warriors. As if in a stupor, he weaved around hospital cots and weapons caches, stopping to allow a raeas to be led across his path or to watch with uncomprehending eyes as a pot of soup was slowly brought to a boil by a group of exhausted and wounded fighters.

Flags fluttered in the air nearby, sigils that represented families of the Daevyn, images that gave people something to fight for, to live for.

The babble of the camp flowed around him like a soothing panacea. At first, only Brydge, the common tongue, broke into his thoughts, but soon Callum became more aware of his surroundings. He noticed fires and cook-pots that were encircled by mixed groups of warriors. gru'Esh and Aru Elen sat with the Daevyn and ate, tending each other's wounds between mouthfuls. The chatter and buzz of dozens of dialects began to wake him to his situation.

All around him were the peoples of Tranthaea, gathered together for the first time in years as friends.

Brought together by fear, and by need. Just as he and Jingwei had been, only a few short days ago.

They'd had so many things in common, their species not the least among them! Callum remembered back to when they'd first met on the plains. He'd seen her standing behind him as he slapped furiously at the small flames around him. The wry look on her face that he had come to associate with her sarcastic good humour had imprinted itself on his mind in that moment, and now he'd become accustomed to it.

He'd never met a girl who was so infuriatingly forthright. Even Bridget, back in London hadn't been nearly so bold when faced with actual authority. Jingwei's foolhardy bravery was one of the things that attracted him to her the most, and was something Callum wanted to emulate as much as possible.

That was why he really wanted her. She'd changed him. Not by trying to, not by forcing him to be someone he wasn't, like so many others had in his life, but instead by allowing him to be who he was meant to be. She'd freed him to be him, independent and strong, like her.

With that realization Callum stopped walking.

He didn't *need* her. Not anymore. Not the way he'd thought he did. He was strong enough, now, to survive. And he didn't need this new world. He could have a new life in his old world instead.

His thoughts flashed back to Yriel as he'd passed her on the way out of the tent, her face hidden behind a veil of dirty hair. She had been betrayed, too. Abandoned by the ones she'd loved, or so she would say. And look what she had done. Look at the damage she had caused.

Not me. I choose a different path.

He'd stay and fight, for now. They needed his power if they wanted to defeat Kano Aradat. But then, when the battle was won, he would find a way to go home.

Back to London, but not back to the life he'd led there. He didn't need to be that boy anymore. He was a new man. Jingwei, and Tranthaea, had given him that gift.

"Callum." Alkira was standing in front of him, staring up at him. She was smiling and her clear hair was sending a rainbow of light across her features. "You have served Tranthaea well. We thank you for that. And for the service you will perform tomorrow, we thank you again. But now it is time to prepare yourself for what is coming." She stepped aside and offered him her arm, waiting until he took it before she spoke again.

"Come with me. We will teach you how to armour yourself."

The Daevyn armoury tent was full of smoke and sparks as a battalion of smiths pounded out repairs on the Firedarts. Through the haze, Callum could make out an open space in the back of the tent where Jingwei and Ythen waited for him with Ila, Rata, and Jera.

He followed Alkira, who wove her way through the hammers and bellows, nodding graciously at the gestures of respect she received on the way, and together they joined the group. Callum walked straight up to Ythen with his hand outstretched. Confused, Ythen shook it.

Jingwei caught Callum's eye as he stepped back and they nodded awkwardly at one another.

Alkira watched the exchange, expressionless, and then spoke.

"The Council wants to thank you for all that you have done for Tranthaea. When we were needed most, the Keepers were divided, imprisoned, and... unavailable," she finished enigmatically as all eyes settled on her. Callum wondered, not for the first time, where she had been and what she had been doing on the other side of the mountains before arriving on the battlefield at the eleventh hour. Even Rata and Ila had been unable to find her.

Alkira continued, "You three have served as we should have served. Your dedication and courage are commendable. But this fight is not yet over." She frowned. "Kano Aradat is powerful and we do not yet know the limits of his strength. You cannot go into battle unprotected."

She gestured to her body and a glimmering refractory film instantly appeared, wrapping itself around her form. It shaped itself to her curves and split into pieces that overlapped like translucent scales before hardening into a clear, thick armour that covered most of her body, protecting her while still allowing her freedom of movement.

All around the circle the Keepers armoured themselves. Ila was soon covered in a layer of what looked like heavy stone plates, but didn't seem to hamper her movement in any way. Rata draped himself in leathery leaves and petrified bark, creating an organic suit of armour that would hold off almost any attack. Only Jera remained unarmoured. Callum assumed that since he was preparing to battle his own element, armour created from it would likely prove less than useful.

The Keepers approached the three youths and began showing them how to create armour of their own. Jingwei was provided with a protective garment created by Ila, Rata, and Alkira, and though her patchwork defense looked ridiculous, the thudding sound it made when she struck her chest with her fist left no doubt that it would hold up.

Ythen struggled at first to follow their directions, but eventually succeeded in summoning up a few pieces that fit snuggly under his cloak. They gleamed as if they were freshly burnished and eager for battle. Ila tapped his chest with her stone rod and the single flame sigil of the Daevyn chiseled itself into the metal. Ythen nodded his thanks and began tapping the plates, checking for weaknesses.

Callum listened carefully to the Keepers' instructions and had no difficulty creating a suit of armour for himself. It was black as coal with blazing red and white-hot designs etched into the breastplate. It was light and thin and without flaw, and the Keepers seemed surprised to see it.

They crowded around him, full of congratulatory phrases. Callum accepted their praise humbly and mutely, knowing that they were congratulating him as if he were the Spark Keeper he had so recently decided not to be.

When the Keepers left the tent Ythen secreted himself away with the smiths, trying to find a way to remove the vambraces from his new armour and replace them with his usual greaves.

Jingwei took the opportunity to approach Callum, who beat her to the punch.

"It's fine, Jingwei. You're right. You've a place here. With Ythen, with the Keepers. It's where you're meant to be. And I'm meant to be somewhere else."

Jingwei looked confused, which was an expression that Callum was not used to seeing on her face.

"What do you mean? I thought—"

"That I was going to stay? Take over from Kala?" Jingwei nodded mutely at his words. "So did I. But I don't think I can." Callum offered no more explanation, but Jingwei didn't seem to need it. She nodded again, sadly this time, and suddenly stepped up and pulled him into a hug.

Their breastplates clanked together noisily but the sound was lost in the smiths' pounding. They held each other tightly for a moment, the thin walls of armour keeping them separated even in their embrace.

Callum let go first and smiled down at her, his red hair blazing in the flickering light of the forges.

"Come on, Junior." He stepped towards the tent flaps, beckoning for her to come along. "Let's finish this."

Jingwei lay awake in her tent that night. Sleep eluded her. Her mind swirled with the events of the last few days. Arriving in Tranthaea. Meeting Callum. Meeting the First Quencher. Running away from Yshaar, being captured by Kala, learning of Yriel's betrayal.

Becoming a Keeper's apprentice.

Choosing Ythen.

She was sure that her decision had been the right one, but that hadn't made it any easier. Jingwei had been pleased that Callum had taken it so well; she had been unsure of how to break it to him, not being used to dealing with attention from boys.

But then he had told her that he wasn't going to be staying, and she had been surprised. She felt suddenly unbalanced, as if one of her legs had been cut out from under her.

What would Tranthaea be like without Callum? She had experienced most of it with him. She would miss making him laugh, and, even more, miss making his face burn bright red with embarrassment.

But that bashful boy was gone. Somewhere in the last few days he had vanished, and been replaced by a sure, steady young man who no longer needed her to lend him courage, or what she was sure he would call foolhardiness.

Even as she knew that she would miss him, she realized that she was proud of him.

Jingwei finally fell asleep with a smile on her face, her dreams ushered in by the whispering sounds of the trees rushing north to prepare for battle.

Chapter Twenty-Six:
The War

Ythen pushed aside his tent flaps and stepped out into the softly lit morning air. In the distance he could make out the random flashes of lightning that peppered the plains of Tranthaea. Last night he had sent out a few small parties of Quenchers to battle the flare-ups as best they could. He hoped it would be enough to keep the prairies from being consumed before the attack was over.

The field in front of him was a mass of organized chaos as final preparations were made throughout the newly-allied armies. A flock of Aru Elen drew his eyes to the sky with a jarring, vertical dance as they yo-yoed up and down among the tents, shooting to the ground to deliver messages and then rebounding into the air with replies. To Ythen's right was the Barricade, marked for kilometres around by the gigantic, pulsing light of the electric icicle that protruded from its ridge.

In the camp proper, refitted Firedarts were being attached to the shoulder-arms of gru'Esh soldiers who then vanished from sight into freshly dug tunnels, moving north. The cave-dwellers had spent the night digging, creating a maze of passages that led to the vast body of water, some ending less than a metre away from the cold blackness of the sea.

Some Daevyn were holding impromptu instruction sessions and training darts were being shot and absorbed by representatives of all the peoples of Tranthaea.

Small squadrons of Aru Elen buzzed overhead, testing their speed and balance with the Daevyn firepower on their arms. Nyx was hovering nearby with Alkira, their wings humming in alternating rhythms as they discussed last minute plans of attack.

Ythen yawned widely. The air was very dry, and tasted coppery in his mouth. He pursed his lips and spit to one side in disgust. The glob of saliva didn't even make it to the ground before it evaporated into the air.

Across the compound Ythen saw Jingwei step out of her tent, fully clad in her armour. The stone breastplate was a gift from Ila, while the green arm and leg protectors were from Rata. Alkira's contribution, a translucent helmet, was tucked under the girl's arm.

She saw him looking at her and rolled her eyes, gesturing to the mismatched armour as her source of wry amusement.

A rustle from the tent next to him made him turn. Callum was standing there in his black armour, his eyes bright. He saw Ythen look over and gave him a thumbs-up and then strode over to Rata, who was organizing the gru'Esh deployment with q'Orha.

Whatever had happened between Callum and Jingwei, it seemed to be over now. Ythen's eyes traveled back over to Jingwei who was now sitting in the dust with Jera, each of them saving their strength in preparation for what was to come. The girl's short, dark hair and small stature made her look like a child playing soldier next to the powerful old man.

Ythen pitied any enemy who ever made the mistake of underestimating Jingwei.

Ythen felt something draped over his shoulder. He looked up and saw that Huon Arrahl's tendriled body was there. The tree-being spoke.

I wish you good morning, Ythen Firestorm.

Ythen shook his head and opened his mouth to correct it, but was cut off.

Yes, Firestorm. You once wore your name as a reminder of failure, did you not? The name Firebrand?

Ythen nodded.

A strange custom of the Daevyn, name-shaming. Like wearing dead leaves on your branches to remind you of a hard winter. You cannot erase history, Firestorm. Your trunk will ever bear the scars of your past. But those scars are soon covered by a fresh coating of bark, one that is stronger for the layers beneath it. The oldest creature in Tranthaea shivered slightly, its upper leaves crinkling in the dry air. *There is no growth without pain. Only a fool withers and dies in the winter and refuses to live again in the spring.*

Ythen reached up and placed his hand on the tendril.

"Thank you, Huon Arrahl."

The tree shook its branches and a handful of leaves fell over Ythen's head.

You have grown strong, Firestorm. Reclaim your name. Lead your people.

With that, the tree began to crawl out of the camp and toward the tree-line that was only just visible on the northern horizon.

Ythen squared his shoulders. Huon Arrahl was right. He had served his penance long enough. It was time to be the leader that Tranthaea needed him to be.

He joined the mass of warriors that were beginning to funnel towards the north.

Far overhead, high above the manoeuvring Aru Elen forces, Kala looked down upon the unified army as it began to move north, some under the ground, some on it, and some above it.

She had flown to the Sea of Nalani after her sister had arrived from over the mountains and the battle had been lost. She had landed on the beach and cried out in anger over the water.

Those kids! They had ruined everything! Now, instead of being divided, the peoples of Tranthaea were more united than they had ever been. *Against* her!

Half of her army had fled, and half seemed to have defected to her enemies. Jera had escaped from her clutches and claimed that something more powerful than himself was controlling the flow of water now.

It sounded like a trick to the Spark Keeper. Who could have more control over the sea than the Sea Keeper?

Kala had stood on the beach and watched the waves whipping the shoreline, drawing more water after them as they retreated. It was then that she'd felt a presence that she did not recognise. A powerful presence.

She'd flown away towards her palace immediately. There was a vault there that contained an item which had the power to save her... or destroy her. An item that, until now, she had feared to use. In the end, though, standing in the vault, she had decided to try one last gamble before resorting to that.

Her options were limited. Whatever was in the sea, the rest of Tranthaea wanted to obliterate it. Which meant that she and it had something in common.

The enemy of my enemy is my friend.

Kala flew high over the plains, moving away from the encampment, over the marching warriors and past the trees of the southern forest that now surrounded the northern sea, dipping their roots in the shallows of the water and digging deep for purchase.

The sea was dark and vast beneath her. From this height the wild waves with their white caps were dots and lines that travelled over the surface of the water like distant static.

Kala began to lower herself towards the surface.

How had it come to this? Since the days of her father, Kala had been planning to rule this world. Over four centuries of careful preparation had gone into her scheme; she'd had to wait for the right moment, the right personalities, even had to capture and hold a Keeper as powerful as Jera.

And all for nothing. She had once again been denied her rightful place, even by her own sister!

If only those kids had told her how to use the lightning to travel. She could be gone already, making her war on another world; a world that would... appreciate her powers.

She approached the surface of the water. From here, the true size of the waves was apparent. Kala buzzed down into the troughs and whipped up over the peaks in an acrobatic ballet as she searched without hope for an ally among the whitecaps.

She was certain that Huon Arrahl would have seen her diving and bobbing among the waves and would relay that information on to the Keepers. She didn't have much time.

In that instant a giant wave suddenly appeared out of the water, thrusting upwards beside her, over her, and around her, pulling her with a tremendous crash beneath the surface.

The united army of Tranthaea had arrived at the edge of the Northern Sea. The surface of the water was perfectly calm, but had been wild only moments ago, according to Huon Arrahl. It had calmed the moment that the Spark Keeper had disappeared below the waves.

The Keepers and Councillors, as well as Jingwei, Ythen, and Callum all stood in a forward position along the southern beach. From their vantage point, they could see the long, thin line of trees that bordered the sea. Above, the Aru Elen hovered, their painted toes out of reach of all but the tallest waves they'd seen, and Ila pronounced that the gru'Esh tunnels were all in place below them.

They were ready to begin.

Alkira raised herself slightly off the ground and flew forward to hover just over the water. Her wispy tiara was no longer black in anger, but instead was a undefined grey, looking as though there was an equal chance of it clearing completely or darkening into a furious storm. Her voice was amplified by the wind that carried it across the surface of the sea in the hopes that the water would hear her.

"Kano Aradat. I am here representing the peoples of Tranthaea. They are suffering from thirst, their homes are collapsing, their people are dying. Release the water back into the world we share, and we will speak to you as friends. Contain it, and you will feel our anger as your enemies."

There was no response. The sea stayed quiet and still; not even a ripple marred its surface.

Alkira drifted back to the others and landed. "Well, let's hope it's considering our offer."

Jera was seated behind her, his legs crossed on the ground in front of him. "It heard. But its focus is elsewhere. It is choosing not to respond."

"Then we must proceed."

Kala shook violently against her restraints, releasing a soundless scream and a line of bubbles from her mouth as her lungs emptied. Her powers were all but useless here, as Kano Aradat had already shown her. The thick cords of kelp that held her in place tugged back at her wrists while in front of her a school of creatures floated, each one long and thin, with two extended fins pulling from their sides, each flick of a fin portraying some part of a giant face.

Her face.

"You created me. An accident, but your greatest gift to this world." The face spoke slowly, its mouth a collection of tail fins flipping up and down. "I thank you for that."

Kala breathed in shaking gasps. Somehow the water was filtering air into her lungs, but she knew that with one wrong word, she would die.

"Yes." She sucked in another mouthful of breathable water. "You and I could be powerful allies. I rule the sky, and you the sea. Together, we can defeat the others and rule the world!"

Kano Aradat's version of her face wrinkled for a moment before his voice boomed out through the deep.

"Rule? I do not wish to rule. I wish simply to be. I do not care for lands or skies." The face broke up and the school of creatures darted towards Kala, swimming around her in a great ball of silvery flesh.

"For my existence, I thank you, Kala. You have made me aware. And now, I must request of you one thing more."

The creatures had started to bump into Kala's body as their sphere became tighter and more aggressive. She struggled to scream out through the mass of creatures, "Anything!"

"I ask for your protection."

"Yes!" The tiny bodies were pelting her now, jerking her body back and forth against the restraints. "I will protect you!"

"With your life, should I have need?"

In desperation, Kala screamed, "Yes, with my life!"

The swarm suddenly became a swirling knot of teeth and tongues that tore into Kala, shredding her cloak, her wings, and her flesh. The air left her lungs in a final agonizing shriek and within moments the flurry was expended, and the kelp waved freely in the loose wash of the water as a single lock of crimson hair settled slowly to the sandy seabed below.

F ire," said Alkira resolutely, her eyes fixed on a sudden burst of bubbles that had erupted from the sea before them.

At her signal, Rata sent shoots of vines running up the legs of the Daevyn that surrounded the sea, binding them to the trunks of Huon Arrahl's many bodies in preparation for a counterattack from the waves. They raised their right arms and fired their darts into the surface of the shallows.

At the same moment, Nyx buzzed noisily above and a storm of darts lanced down from the sky to penetrate the middle of the vast body of water.

Underground, many small groupings of stones were shifted by Ila to form the word, "NOW." The gru'Esh responded, firing their darts at the walls that blocked their tunnels, sending shocks of electricity into the water beyond from below.

Ythen and Callum released their powers simultaneously. Callum loosed a single, continuous streak of fire that blasted down from the sky and crashed into the surface of the water, pouring energy into the sea and sending a boiling cloud of steam vaulting into the air that was quickly sucked back down by the tyrannical power of Kano Aradat. Ythen eschewed firing his own bolt and focused instead on the thousands of other darts being shot from around the border of Nalani, intent on magnifying their power and amplifying their effect.

The hair on Jingwei's arms stood up straight. The air and ground were buzzing with the charges that Callum and Ythen were funneling into the water. Above, below, and all around her the Tranthaeans were discharging weapons, firing bolts of light into the water, creating a mist of steam that now hung eerily over the water's surface like a cloudy shield.

Within seconds the army had finished its volley. The air around the sea crackled and hummed and the dirt below their feet quivered as the last of the energy found its way into the water.

All was quiet.

Callum and Ythen were leaning on one another, exhausted from controlling the flow of fire-power.

"Did it work?" Callum asked between gasps for breath. "Is he gone?"

Jera and Jingwei both shook their heads, their eyes closed in concentration.

"No." Jingwei spoke first. "He didn't even feel it." She finished her sentence with a tone of disbelief.

Jera interjected. "He absorbed Kala." He looked up at Alkira apologetically. "She's gone. He absorbed her. She's a part of him now, which means—"

"Fire can't hurt him anymore," Callum finished for him.

There was a stunned silence. Their one and only hope of defeating Kano Aradat and saving Tranthaea had just been extinguished.

In that moment, the sea came to life. Gigantic waves crashed against the shoreline, uprooting trees and dragging them and the Daevyn warriors tied to them into the depths of the sea. Others hung on and withstood the force of the waves, exchanging canisters and firing at will into the water, unaware that their actions were having no effect at all.

Beneath the ground, columns of water burst through the walls, flooding the tunnels. Some gru'Esh were lucky enough to make it to vertical shafts that they could use to escape the rushing water. Many were not.

In the sky, whirlpools and maelstroms reached up out of the sea, forming a forest of miniature hurricanes that scattered the Aru Elen, knocking some violently out of the sky and dragging them unforgivingly under the surface.

Jera was on his feet instantly, his arms spread out in front of him, doing his best to contain the sea. Alkira was beside him, weaving the wind in an attempt to force down the waterspouts, tears streaming down her cheeks as she worked to both avenge and battle her sister's memory. Ila was kneeling on the ground in concentration, blocking up the holes that Kano Aradat was flooding and Rata, Ydelle, and Huon Arrahl were orchestrating a massive retreat from the water's edge, intent on saving as many lives as they could. Jera started forward and within moments the old man had vanished into the waves.

"Come on." Jingwei didn't even look at Ythen or Callum when she spoke, but instead started down the beach, dropping pieces of her mismatched armour as she went. She was already up to her knees in the water by the time they caught up to her.

Chapter Twenty-Seven:
The Confrontation

Jingwei sank down behind Jera, following his example and creating for herself what was basically a sloped void in the water that acted like a tunnel-slide. The boys slid down above her like two guardian angels watching over her every move.

But Jingwei knew the unsettling truth: in this watery environment, she had to watch over them, not they over her.

They reached the sea floor. Jingwei released the tunnel and the water rushed to fill the space above and around them, cutting off their access to the surface world. Ythen and Callum had each taken a huge breath before the water flooded in around them, and they waited uncomfortably while Jingwei formed air bubbles out of the water and dropped them neatly over their heads. Jera had explained how to create them earlier that morning. The bubbles would not only protect the boys from the pressing sea that threatened to fill their lungs, but also filtered fresh oxygen out of the water around them, replenishing their air even as they sucked in great gasps. Satisfied with her work, Jingwei turned her back on the boys. Ahead, Jera had already stepped into the square patch of light that Kano Aradat used to entertain his guests.

They hurried to catch up.

As soon as they entered the light, Jingwei felt again that intelligent presence they'd seen the last time they were here. The four of them settled in, waiting for Kano Aradat to make himself known.

Jera lifted his hand and swirled the water in front of him, creating a gentle current that flowed forward and disturbed the seaweed, gesturing as if he were politely ringing a doorbell. If he was hoping for a response, he was not disappointed. A powerful submerged wave slammed into the group, sending Jingwei, Callum, and Ythen tumbling over the sand, stirring up clouds of murky dust as they rolled.

A thundering sound echoed through the water, seeming to bounce off of invisible walls all around them and reverberate back, rattling through their bones.

Jingwei pulled herself to her feet and consciously floated upwards, rising above the cloud of silt. She saw the boys below her, their forms struggling to regain footing in the murky, dirty water, their panicked faces warped through the undulating surface of the bubbles around their heads. Ahead of her, in the middle of the light was Jera, standing in the centre of a gigantic whirlpool that stretched around him and shot up clear to the surface, leaving him standing in the open air, encircled by walls of swirling water.

Jera's usually-flowing hair and beard were whipping wildly in the wind that the whirlpool created, making him look frantic. His eyes were wide as he stood on the dry spot of ground at the base of the waterspout, unable to touch the water around him, unable to control it. Above him, the air was dry and cold and pummeled him as it blew down the long tunnel from the surface.

Jingwei tried to move towards him, but could not. The water pressure around her was too great. Kano Aradat had them all exactly where he wanted them.

Jera shouted above the noise of the whirlpool. "Very clever, making yourself immune to fire. Water's greatest rival, now water's greatest strength."

A voice boomed through the water, coming from everywhere and nowhere, "Flattery? Is this the Keeper's way? Kala also tried to show me the meaning of friendship. I showed her the meaning of sacrifice."

"A lesson well-learned." Jera met Jingwei's gaze through the tumultuous wall of water. "It is always useful to remember a lesson, even if the style of teaching is a little backwards."

Jingwei's eyes narrowed in confusion and then widened in sudden understanding.

Backwards? He couldn't mean...

"And now I have you here." Kano Aradat's voice seemed to swirl around Jingwei now, its volume lifting and dropping as if it were carried by an underwater wind. "The Sea Keeper. The one who tries to control me, to make me give up myself."

"Not to give yourself up, but to share yourself with others." The rushing water began to close in on the Sea Keeper, the circle of dry sand beneath his feet shrinking with each passing moment. "You are powerful, Kano Aradat. More powerful than Kala, and more powerful than me. More powerful than each Keeper, individually. And with your knowledge of yourself comes the choice, to use that power to defend or destroy."

The water's voice was silent for a moment, as if considering. Jingwei struggled to move forward, trying to break free of the sea's hold on her as the cone of the waterspout closed in on Jera's body. Behind her, Callum and Ythen had struggled to their feet and joined her, unable to move further due to the pressure, their faces screwed up in pain.

They could only watch.

The voice thundered through the sea again. "I will defend. I will defend Kano Aradat."

Jera smiled at Jingwei, and she nodded back sadly.

The whirlpool crashed in on itself, pouring tonnes of cold, dark water into the open void and crushing the Sea Keeper with the weight of his own element.

An explosion of bubbles and pounding waves beat at the three youths. Jingwei reached out and focused her energy on holding the spheres of air around the boy's heads, allowing them to breathe.

When the commotion subsided, there was no trace of Jera, just a deep impression in the sandy seabed where he had been standing.

Jingwei shook with anger and sorrow and allowed a flow of tears to leak from her eyes and join the vast saltiness of the sea.

Kano Aradat spoke to her. "You offer me a gift in your grief, increasing me. For that, I thank you."

"Don't thank me yet." Jingwei knew now why the Sea Keeper had ventured into the lair of Kano Aradat, why he had allowed himself to be captured and absorbed by the sea, and what he had wanted her to do now. She didn't waste any time.

"Ythen, send a message to the surface, to Alkira. Tell them to attack again, with everything they've got." Ythen didn't hesitate, but simply closed his eyes in intense concentration.

"Callum. Did you hear what Jera said about remembering our lessons?"

Callum nodded. Jingwei continued, "Remember how we freed him?" This time she didn't wait for a response. "We have to do that again, only backwards."

A bolt of lightning lanced down from the sky, slamming into the beach near Alkira and the other Keepers. They had been overwhelmed by Kano Aradat's counter-offensive, and all their energies had gone into organizing a retreat that would save as many lives as possible.

The impact blew Alkira off her feet and threw her down onto the sand. Stunned, she buzzed her wings and lifted herself up in the air, scanning the sky for danger before she looked down onto the beach and saw what Ythen had done.

Below her, the sand had been melted into hot glass by the intense heat of the lightning bolt. The clear, hardening liquid spelled out a single word in large, translucent letters.

Attack.

Alkira gave the signal, and bolts of energy once again poured into the sea.

B eneath the surface, Kano Aradat raged. Each bolt of lightning, each dart fired from a Tranthaean arm seared him, burning new currents into the flowing depth of his being.

Jingwei smiled grimly as the howls of pain echoed around her. Jera was a clever old man. He'd known that by absorbing Kala, Kano Aradat had absorbed her power, making himself immune to fire. And the Keeper must have figured that if the sea-being absorbed the opposing power, it would balance that immunity, once again making Kano Aradat susceptible to destruction by fire.

A big risk, but one he had obviously felt was worth taking. And now Jingwei had to finish what he'd started, and destroy the Sea Keeper's killer.

She closed her eyes. Beside her, she could feel Callum, his breathing ragged and choppy under the intense buffeting of the waves. She pushed those thoughts out of her head and began to concentrate.

Just like on the spire, she could feel the water around her. It was wild and raging, so very unlike the water on top of the tower, so very uncontrollable.

Backwards.

To free Jera, she'd had to work with Callum; he had weakened the fire and she had strengthened the water. They needed to work together again, but this time they would have to do it the other way around.

She stretched out her senses. The power of the water was vast and unconcentrated; she tried to find it all, but it spread her out thinly. She felt fragile and weak, like a piece of paper trying to hold back the tide.

Beside her, Callum was struggling to find light in the darkness. There was no fire in the sea, but he could feel the bolts that struck Kano Aradat from all sides, above, and below. And then there was the light itself, the beams that the water had somehow trapped beneath the surface to bring illumination and warmth to the empty space Kano Aradat used as an audience chamber.

Callum gripped the light, and harnessed the energy, expanding it and strengthening it, and spreading it throughout the sea to the furthest reaches of the water.

Jingwei slowly reached out her hands. Her palms were open; one hand was pushing away from herself, holding the pressure of the water at bay as Kano Aradat bucked and reared in pain, squeezing them with an otherwise crushing force. The other was held high above her head, out of the reach of her robes that flailed in the currents around her as if she were in the middle of a windstorm.

Callum looked over. He was as ready as he was ever going to be.

Jingwei frowned, her brow furrowed in concentration. It wasn't enough. The attack from above was helping, but Kano Aradat was still too strong, too focused. He would not be defeated. She looked over her shoulder at the boys, dismay written clearly on her face.

Ythen understood immediately. He quickly reached his hands up and tore apart the bubble that was providing him with air, then pulled her body around to face him. She floated up, her face pulling level with his. Neither of them spoke as they moved together; Ythen simply reached out and brushed a lock of hair out of Jingwei's face before he leaned in and kissed her, lightly, on the mouth.

Jingwei struggled to maintain concentration. Half of her wanted to let go of her power and return the kiss, the other half wanted to scream at him, *"Really? Now? I'm a little busy here!"*

Kano Aradat's voice echoed around them, its sound high and wild in desperation.

"Little Keepers! I accept you into myself! Protect me!"

Without a word, Ythen released Jingwei, and with a final look of regret and duty, turned to face the lit patch of sea-bed, clasped his scarred hands together over his chest, closed his eyes, and then violently threw his arms forward.

Ythen's body seemed to fracture as every blood vessel in it suddenly glowed white-hot. Light ruptured out from him in sweeping, burning blades of fire that sliced through the water around him in a twisting pattern which evolved as he bucked and contorted in pain. The beams began to move faster and faster, surrounding the Quencher and closing in on him until he looked as if he were ablaze. Ythen's skin started to blister and smoke, causing the water around him to become even darker and murkier. He screamed in pain, fury, and determination.

The fire coalesced in front of him, a gigantic burning orb too bright to look at. With his eyes still closed, Ythen slowly reached out to it with both hands and began to mold it, gathering and concentrating the pure power into a tiny ball that he then compressed between his palms. All was quiet for a moment, and then Ythen opened his eyes.

An enormous beam of light burst out of his hands and shot forward. The white bolt shimmered as it exploded through the darkness, boiling the sea as it went, leaving behind a trail of super-heated water and frantically ascending bubbles. Ythen's body went limp.

Jingwei's eyes blurred. Freedom exploded in her mind, giving her access to the water as never before.

Each drop was suddenly clear to her, individual and unique. The currents and waves, the light and the dark; all were lines that she could draw, rhythms that she could play, movements that she could control.

Just for a moment, while Kano Aradat's attention was fixed on Ythen, Jingwei could do what needed to be done.

She concentrated on her hand, raised high above her head, whispered Jera's name in tribute, and closed her fist.

At the same time, Callum released his hold on the light, pushing it with his mind. The square pool of brightness dimmed and expanded, its energy rushing through the water, dampening Kano Aradat's power. Callum weaved the darts striking the sea from above and electrifying the ground from below into a complex net of fire that swept through the water, enclosing Kano Aradat's consciousness into a smaller and smaller ball as he abandoned the outer rims of the sea in an attempt to escape the flaming web.

Jingwei had claimed the power of the sea. Kano Aradat had been taken by surprise, his attention torn between Ythen and the fire-net. Suddenly his power was his no longer, and in the split-second before he reclaimed himself, Jingwei opened her hand.

A massive explosion of energy erupted from her, pushing the water back in a series of concentric rings that plowed through the sea, releasing more ferocious detonations as they went. Riptides and violent surges rammed through the water, battering the sea floor and the beaches, exploding to the air above in waterspouts and raining down again upon the surface of the sea.

Heavy mists formed in the air as the sea evaporated, creating clouds that rocketed out over the plains and instantly started pouring water down through the dry air onto the parched landscape.

What had once been the conscious being of the sea was scattered, blasted to all corners of Tranthaea, leaving behind only a dying scream that finally faded away into silence in the cavernous trenches of the deep.

Chapter Twenty-Eight:
The Replacements

Callum staggered forward out of the shallows, struggling under the burden of Ythen's weight. The older boy was shorter than the Human, but was a good deal thicker than Callum's thin frame, and it was all Callum could do to carry him to the beach and lay him out on the sand.

Ythen's body was scorched and scarred. It had been burned by his power and beaten by the sea, pounded with heavy fists of water and battered along the sea floor. As soon as Jingwei had been sure of victory, she had grabbed it and pushed it towards shore, dragging herself and Callum along behind. Once they'd arrived in the shallows, Callum had stepped up and lifted the body, bringing it to its resting place on the beach where it now lay, surrounded by the three remaining Keepers and the Council members.

Alkira settled onto the beach, her wings fluttering up behind her. She kneeled beside Ythen's still body, her hand on his chest, searching for signs of life.

All were silent on the beach. The waves had ceased and the only sound was the slow shuffle of the survivors as they began the trek back south to the Barricade.

Ydelle Emberhand stood back, supported by q'Orha, Nyx, and Huon Arrahl. The Flame-Bearer's face looked old for the first time Callum could recall. What had once held regal dignity was now laid bare by worry and exhaustion. Her eyes never left Ythen's form; she had already lost her daughter to this war, and was now looking down on the body of her most loyal and steadfast champion.

Callum had collapsed onto the sand and was lying back, gasping for breath and supporting himself on his elbows as he watched the Keepers inspect the Daevyn warrior. With hardly a thought he motioned down the front of his body, and the growing ache caused by rising to the surface so quickly was extinguished.

If only all pain were so easily dealt with. In front of him, Jingwei was cradling Ythen's head in her lap and gently smoothing back the boy's blond hair from his ashen face.

Alkira stood up next to the body and shook her head slowly. Rata and Ila rose as well, and Jingwei started to sob, rough hiccups that racked her body, shaking her as she clutched Ythen's head to her chest in grief.

"I'm sorry, Jingwei." Alkira kept her wings folded and her feet on the ground, a sign of her solemnity.

Through her tears, Jingwei shouted up at the Keepers, "Heal him! Why don't you heal him!?" She looked up at Rata and Ila. "You healed us, before!"

Ila stuck her stone rod in the sand and kneeled down beside the weeping Human. "Broken bones and bruises are one thing. Death is another." She put her arm around Jingwei, who shook it off. "Life is not my province."

"Then who's is it?" Jingwei looked up at her angrily, challenging. "Rocks, trees, puddles of water! All of them have a Keeper, but what about us? What about the people?"

"They have me," Alkira said simply. She knelt eye to eye with Jingwei, meeting her stare and not backing down.

"The air in this world is not just for holding the clouds or lighting the sky, Jingwei. It is Life itself. It supports and sustains all the peoples of Tranthaea. To be the Sky Keeper is to be the guardian of the air, the light, and the peoples of this world."

"Not very good at your job, are you?" Jingwei ignored the gasps from the others on the beach and dropped her head to look down at Ythen's body. "First you're *unavailable* when your sister tries to destroy the world, and now you can't even save—" Her voice broke.

Alkira's eyes sharpened in automatic defense, and then she let her shoulders slump. "What you say is fair. I have been absent, searching for something I thought could protect our world, only to return in failure to find it on the brink of destruction." She leaned over and lifted Jingwei's chin, looking her in the eye. "You must know, I would heal him if I could. But my powers are limited, just as yours are. I was forced to use all I had to contain Kano Aradat, and I must rest or I will be Consumed."

"So none of you can do anything then?" Jingwei still spoke defiantly, but her words rang with a sorrowful desperation.

Alkira didn't answer.

From behind her came Rata's voice, deep and rich. "Perhaps, if we pool our resources."

Jingwei's head popped up again.

From beside her, Ila responded, "That hasn't been done in hundreds of years, and even then it Consumed one of the healers."

"And it took all five Keepers to try. We are only three."

Jingwei gently laid Ythen's head down on the sand and stood up next to him. "Four." She met each of their gazes in turn. "Jera told me that I was to replace him. And I will." She turned to look at Callum, who was still lying on the beach, his arms now crossed over his face.

Callum had seen this coming. The moment Rata spoke he had remembered seeing a tapestry in the Hall of Record: five people standing over a dead body. Five Keepers. It was a cruel trick of fate that would make him bind himself to this world by bringing back the man Jingwei loved. He had been so ready to leave, so ready to begin again back home. To leave Jingwei and Ythen to one another.

But even as the silence fell, even as they all looked to him, he knew that there was only one possible answer.

Callum dropped his arms to his sides, smacking them deeply into the sand. He opened his eyes and took a deep breath.

"Five."

Without another word the three Keepers walked over to him. They joined hands, Rata on his right, Ila on his left, and Alkira across from him.

Ila spoke first, followed by Rata and then Alkira.

"Brought forth by fire, here to reveal the truth."

"Crowned with fire, here to protect the people."

"Keeper of fire, here to serve Tranthaea."

Callum felt a warm rush spread through his body, from the bottom of his feet to the tips of his hair. An awareness flooded into him. He could feel every bolt of lightning that crashed into the plains. The torches that lit the dark passages of Yshaar were burned into his brain. And the light in the air felt malleable to his touch.

The others released his hands with murmured congratulations and turned toward Jingwei, who was already standing by. They left a space open in the circle, and Ila cocked an eyebrow at Callum.

"It takes all living Keepers to raise a Keeper. Come on, Sparky."

Callum joined the circle, wrapping his hand around Jingwei's. She was still shaking, but determinedly looked into his eyes as Ila started to speak.

"Trained through water, here to quench the danger."

"Threatened with water, here to bring strength."

"Victorious over water, here to protect the people."

"Keeper of water, here to serve Tranthaea," Callum finished, his mouth dry.

Jingwei's eyes opened wide as she felt the new horizons of her power, but she quickly pushed those feelings aside and turned back towards Ythen.

"Now what?"

"Now we try." Alkira knelt at Ythen's side, followed by the four other Keepers. Each of them placed their hands on the body and closed their eyes.

Jingwei could feel the expansive nature of her power as she focused it. All around her, the air seemed to energize as each Keeper drew on their strengths, funneling them into a common purpose. Jingwei didn't really understand what was happening; it seemed to her that the Keepers were mixing their powers together, as if pouring them into a communal pot or entwining them into a single rope.

Behind her eyelids, Jingwei could see a light. An intense ball of light that was alternately streaked with blue, red, green, brown, and white. She opened her eyes in surprise, but there was nothing there. The air over Ythen's body was empty.

"Concentrate." Alkira didn't open her eyes when she spoke. Her brow was furrowed with deep lines and a bead of sweat rolled down her face, tracing a line in the ornamental paint she wore. She waited until Jingwei had refocused and they were set and then reached into the air in front of them and grasped the ball gently.

With a sudden burst, she thrust the ball down, slamming her hands into Ythen's chest. Jingwei heard the cracking sound of a rib breaking, and then a rush of air as Ythen gasped, pulling life back into his body.

The three older Keepers collapsed backwards onto the sand, each of them spent. Callum fell to the side, retching into the sand. Jingwei pushed her exhaustion aside and grabbed onto Ythen, wrapping her arms around him tightly.

He lay on his back, unmoving, taking large, ragged breaths as he took in the scene around him. Finally, slowly, he raised his hand and placed it on Jingwei's cheek, lifting her head from his chest.

He wiped away a tear with his thumb and gave her a weak smile.

"How did we do?"

"We won. Thanks to you." Jingwei leaned forward and kissed him. He groaned as she leaned on his rib cage, but when she tried to pull away with an apology, he held on.

The others left them alone on the beach and began to make their way back south, to the Barricade. Jingwei and Ythen stayed behind, content for now to simply be alive and be together, warmed by the bright, moist afternoon air.

Chapter Twenty-Nine:
The Right Man for the Job

In the morning, the camp was a bustle of activity as the various peoples prepared to return to their homes and rebuild their cities, their societies, and their lives.

In the Council Hall, the leaders of Tranthaea were settling up their business. What was meant to have a celebratory tone was marred by the empty space in the corner of the room that had once been the prison cell of Yriel Sparkcatcher, traitor to the Daevyn. The victors had returned to their camp to find that she had escaped from her prison of air, no doubt when Alkira's attention was on containing the sea and reviving Ythen. No one had seen her leave and there had been no sign of where she'd gone.

Though her escape cast a pall over the celebrations, there seemed to be an unspoken agreement not to discuss it. It was a problem for another time.

Instead, there were handshakes and hugs as congratulations were shared across the room. Callum accepted them graciously, but distantly. His future was now tied to this world, a world that he had only yesterday been keen to leave behind. In what he recognized was a childish sense of stubborn defiance, he was once again wearing the ragged clothes that he had been wearing when he'd first arrived in Tranthaea, six days ago. The trousers, shirt, and vest felt uncomfortable on his skin now, as if they no longer belonged there. His red hair, the hair that Jera had once told him had marked him as a Spark Keeper was now hiding underneath his old grey cap.

Callum had even declined a new name. Upon arriving back at camp, Alkira, Ila, and Rata had informed Jingwei and him that it was customary for Keepers to take on new names with their positions, as a way of dedicating themselves fully to their new position.

Jingwei had adopted the name Kaia this morning.

She was standing across the room, holding a translated conversation with Nyx, the Aru Elen Ambassador, regarding Alkira's mysterious search in the days before the battle. Callum could hear the Human girl relating to the flying creatures an abridged version of the story of the stone box they'd found in the waterfall cave. Nyx nodded and buzzed in puzzlement while Alkira patiently interpreted, her toes dangling loosely above the ground. In between them, the new Sea Keeper looked comfortable. At home.

Jingwei... *Kaia* would be happy here. But then, she'd chosen it.

Callum felt something fall on his shoulder and looked up to see Huon Arrahl behind him, its tendril draped delicately over his vest.

Callum Swift. You are unhappy.

"Is it that obvious?" Callum had never spoken to the tree-being before, and found the voice in his head unnerving.

You look like a young sapling that is host to parasites, full of life in appearance, but rotting within. You do not wish to serve as Spark Keeper?

Callum found himself wanting to explain all the reasons that he felt he should leave, and all the reasons he felt he had to stay, but instead his voice cracked as he whispered out, "I want to go home."

Huon Arrahl was silent for a moment. Around them, the congratulatory bustle began to lessen as Nyx and Alkira left to find the Aru Elen a new home, away from their former masters. Ila and q'Orha left to see to the securing of the Warrens now that moisture had returned to the ground. Kaia and Ythen also slipped out, leaving Rata and Ydelle speaking across the room in low tones about the fate of the trampled and burned-out plains.

Eventually it spoke, its voice playing lightly across Callum's mind like a breeze igniting a long-cold ember.

There may yet be a way. The Keepers do not know it, but I have been a part of Tranthaea for ages past, longer than these Keepers have served as guardians, and longer than the Keepers before them.

The vine tightened its grip on Callum's shoulder.

If you wish to go, listen well.

Callum's vision blurred. Suddenly his mind was bombarded by a seemingly unending series of images, feelings, smells, and sounds. The information threatened to overwhelm him, but was held in check by Huon Arrahl, who was letting him see through its eyes.

Letting him see the past.

Images and memories burst across Callum's mind, like sparks igniting a wildfire. He saw a bare hill overlooking a quiet world. He smelled the dirt as the seasons cycled around him and a forest grew beneath him. He watched as cities and nations rose and fell. Flashes passed of peoples and creatures, long lost or extinct. Landscapes unseen by any other living eyes unscrolled before him.

Battles were seen from a distance. They were fought, won, and lost. A great duel raged over Tranthaea, and was ended. The world changed.

Powers came and went. Centuries passed.

The grandeur and minutiae of life lay before Callum, captured by the many eyes of the oldest being alive.

And Callum watched, and Callum learned.

Ythen stepped carefully over the charred remains of a spear as he climbed the side of the ridge. The bodies had long since been cleared away from the battlefield and buried or burned. Each culture of Tranthaea had conducted a service of some sort last night, upon returning from the northern sea. The Keepers had not attended any, instead choosing to hold a vigil in honour of Jera and his sacrifice. Jingwei had attended that, while Ythen had honoured the Daevyn dead with a massive funereal cremation ceremony.

This was the first time he'd been alone with Jingwei, newly renamed Kaia, since their time together on the beach and he found himself struggling to express his thoughts.

Kaia walked beside him, uncharacteristically quiet and patient as he tried to form his thoughts into words. She was clothed in shining aqua-coloured robes that floated gently around her as they had her predecessor, and they shimmered as if covered in pinpoints of dew. Her eyes shone with a fervour that both exited and intimidated him, making what he had to say all the more difficult to get out.

Finally they reached the peak of the Barricade and Ythen knew he had to speak.

"Kaia?" He paused for a response, but she just looked up at him and waited for him to continue. He turned away and gazed along the peak of the ridge to the blue sky beyond.

"This is difficult to say. I think you know... I mean, I am sure that you are aware of how I feel towards you." He risked a glance at her and saw that her face now held a slight grin and her eyes twinkled as she watched him suffer.

He sighed. "And I believe that you feel the same way towards me..."

Kaia laughed aloud, her cool demeanor vanishing as her brash personality returned. "You'd better believe it. I don't just go around kissing every boy on the beach, you know."

She grinned widely, but her smile faded as she saw that he wasn't joining her in laughter.

Ythen's face became grim. "There is a problem, Kaia." He swallowed once and rushed through what he had to say, desperate to get it out. "You are a Keeper now. You live in a different world than I do." He ignored Kaia's ironic snort and continued. "It would not be right for us to be together. It has never been before. The Keepers are different, their lives cannot be shared or understood by the rest of us. I have learned that over these last few days. What a Keeper must face is more than any one regular person can handle."

He fell silent, awaiting the tongue-lashing he was sure would follow.

It followed.

"You idiot!" Kaia leaned forward and smacked Ythen's chest, causing him to yelp as she jiggled his freshly-healed ribs. "So, it was ok when I was just a lowly Human? Then we could be together, but now that I'm a Keeper, you feel too..." she searched for the word, "inadequate?"

Kaia smacked him again and then just as quickly rose up on her toes and kissed him on the cheek. "You idiot. You think you can get rid of me that easily? Have you been paying attention? I don't give up on what I want. Besides, who says you have any choice in the matter?"

Ythen just shook his head and sat down in the dirt. Kaia looked down at him, confused. Her smile started to drop as she realized that he wasn't swayed.

"Wait, are you serious?"

Ythen spoke quietly, hating himself for every word. "I cannot. We are too different now, you and I. You belong on a higher level than me. I know you think of our ways as old-fashioned, but you are a Keeper of Tranthaea. Our ways are now your ways." He looked up at her again, his face a mask of regret.

"I'm sorry."

Kaia couldn't believe it. After all they'd been through, all the sacrifices they'd made. To be rejected now, just when everything seemed to be perfect...

"What if I give it back?" Kaia could hardly believe what she was saying. All her life she had been trying to be different, to be noticed, to be a powerful, strong, independent woman. Now that she had finally achieved her dream, was she really willing to give it all up to be with the man she loved?

So it would seem.

"What if I give the power back? Tell them I refuse to be the Sea Keeper. Can I do that, make them give it to someone else?"

Ythen resolutely shook his head. "No. Even if it were possible, I would not permit it. This is who you are, who you were always meant to be. I cannot allow you to give it up just for me."

Kaia cocked her eyebrow, and Ythen was suddenly reminded of the girl that had appeared in a scorched circle of dirt on the plains less than a week ago.

"You know, for a lesser being, you're awfully good at telling me what I can and can't do."

Ythen blinked. She had him on the ropes with that one.

A voice from behind her interrupted them.

"You don't have to give anything up."

Callum climbed the last few steps up the Barricade's slope and stepped around into her field of vision. He walked past her and right up to Ythen. "Here."

He leaned down and grasped Ythen's forearm, gripping it tightly. When Ythen did the same, Callum closed his eyes and breathed out slowly.

Kaia watched as a spark appeared on Callum's arm and danced down its length, circling both it and Ythen's arm in a tight helix. The spark landed softly on Ythen's skin as if testing it, and then circled their arms once more before disappearing again. Ythen watched it vanish in surprise, and then his eyes widened in shock. He looked around expansively, his head swinging up and around as if he were seeing the world for the first time before his gaze settled on the giant pillar of ice that was stabbed at an angle into the Barricade beside them, its core still pulsating with energy.

Callum released him and stumbled back before catching himself.

"Alright, Ythen?"

Ythen tore his eyes from the icicle and looked at Callum with wonder in his eyes. "But... it's not possible..."

Callum grinned. "Best get used to that feeling. All hail the new Spark Keeper." He turned to Kaia. "You'll have to make sure he picks a good name—"

He was interrupted when Kaia flew at him, slamming into his body and wrapping him up in a crushing hug.

"How? How did you...? Thank you, Old-Timer." She whispered.

"Don't mention it, Junior."

She released him and watched him clasp Ythen's hand, giving it a firm shake while he addressed the new Keeper.

"She's the only family I've got. You take care of her."

"I will." Ythen fixed his eyes on Callum's with great seriousness. "You have my word."

"Hey, fellas. I'm standing right here." Kaia poked her head in between them and looked back and forth in mock annoyance.

Callum ignored her and grinned. "And don't let her boss you around."

Ythen released his hand and pulled Kaia close in to him. "That, I cannot promise."

All three of them laughed. Once the laughter died away, Kaia had to ask, "So, what now?"

Callum adjusted the cap on his head. "Now s'time for me to go back home." He waved away their objections. "No, no. Your places are here, mine's there."

"But how?" Kaia felt herself tearing up and wiped her eyes with her sleeve.

Callum smiled down at her. "Huon Arrahl. That forest's been around for a long time. And knows well more than you might expect."

Kaia filed that information away and stepped forward, pulling Callum's head down and kissing him lightly on the cheek.

"Goodbye, Callum."

"Goodbye, Jingwei. And thanks."

With that, Callum stepped back. He closed his eyes for a moment, then suddenly opened them again as if remembering something. He reached into a pocket, pulled something out and tossed it to Ythen, gave the Daevyn boy a solemn nod, and threw one last wink at Kaia before closing his eyes again and raising his face to the sky.

A white bolt of lightning shot down from the clear sky and smashed into him, sending dirt and dust exploding into the air.

The shock wave forced Kaia back into Ythen's chest. She lifted her arm to shield her eyes from the blazing light and the dust.

When the afterimage on her retina faded, Callum was gone.

Kaia swiped at her eyes again with the hem of her cloak and put her arm through Ythen's. He was looking down at his hand, which held a burnished bronze Firedart canister decorated only with a delicate engraving; a thin circle surrounding two overlapping triangles.

Ythen looked up to meet her eyes and shook his head disbelievingly.

"That rotten little thief." He laughed as Jingwei slapped at his chest and playfully pulled her closer to keep her from hitting him again. She put her arm around his waist and swivelled to stand beside him. He quieted as they looked at the place where Callum had been standing and together wished him a silent, but heartfelt, farewell.

After a moment, they turned towards the towering city of Yshaar in the west and stared out at Tranthaea. Flocks of Aru Elen were spiraling out from the camp into the sky above them. On the plains below, the slow-moving green mass of Huon Arrahl was heading south in waves, while the Daevyn packed up their camp and rode west to Yshaar. Behind them, the gru'Esh were scuttling into their tunnels at the base of the mountains, already planning to rebuild their cities beneath the surface.

Kaia took in a deep breath. The thick air of Tranthaea filled her lungs with the life she'd always hoped for.

"Right." She turned and led the way down the ridge. "We have work to do."

Epilogue - Part One:
The Return
{Los Angeles, USA; 2012}

Callum stumbled slightly as he hit the pavement. All around him, shining carriages sat resting on their thick, black wheels. Beneath his feet, the ground was hard, but crumbled and blackened by the force and heat of multiple lightning bolts.

In front of Callum, a young man was lying on his back, his eyes wide with shock. He let out a small scream when he saw Callum appear and scurried backwards on his elbows, his body tensed with fear.

"You Hunter?" Callum stepped forward calmly. "Hunter Wells?"

The boy on the ground blinked at the sound of his own name and nodded slowly, taking in the old-fashioned clothes that Callum was dressed in.

Callum reached forward and grabbed Hunter, helping him to his feet. Hunter shied away from his touch but ended up standing anyways, his hands shaking, his ears still ringing from the double lightning bolts and accompanying thunder claps he'd witnessed.

"W-w-w-who are you? What happened to Jingwei?"

"Oh, Jingwei's tops," Callum said casually, brushing some loose crumbs of pavement off of Hunter's shoulder. "Same as ever. Speaking of, I've actually come on her behalf, though I'm sure she'd go mad if she knew I was here." He patted Hunter on the shoulder and steadied him, and then quickly stepped back and let his eyes flick down to the ground.

Hunter's shoes burst into flame.

He shrieked and began to panic, running in circles, leaping off the ground as if trying to escape the flames attached to his feet.

The fire quickly licked up Hunter's legs until it reached his waist, and then vanished in a puff of smoke, leaving the boy dancing wildly around the parking lot in only his underwear.

Eventually Hunter noticed the lack of flames and collapsed to the ground in shock, his mouth gaping open and closed like a fish out of water. His pants, socks, and shoes were gone, reduced to piles of ash on the pavement, but his legs were unburned.

Callum cocked his head at the sound of a bunch of boys noisily nearing the entrance to the parking structure. He looked down at Hunter with an overly-stern expression.

"Let that be a lesson to you. I don't like bullies."

He raised his hands and face to the sky before glancing down once more.

"Oh, and save the trees, yeah? Cheers."

The bolt crashed down swiftly and departed, taking him away from Los Angeles in 2012 and back to London in 1882, leaving behind a befuddled boy sitting on the ground in his underwear and a black scorch mark in the middle of the parking lot.

Epilogue - Part Two:
The Amulet

Yriel blundered blindly through the darkened passages of Kala's palace on the plateau of the Mountains of Du Garrah. She knew she didn't have much time before they figured out where she'd vanished to, and she had to find her prize and be gone before they arrived.

She'd been resigned to her fate in the newly created Council Hall when suddenly the bars to her cell had dissipated. Unsure of and uncaring as to why she'd been freed, Yriel had taken the opportunity and slipped out of the tent, making her way through the deserted camp until she arrived at the base of the black cliffs.

There she had found Wrem. The Aru Faylen Delevate had kept scouts circling high over the allied encampment and her escape had been reported to him. He had gone to meet her to offer her help in exchange for news, and while Yriel had little to tell him, he had been willing to bring her to the palace upon the promise of repayment at a later date.

Now, as she limped through the black corridors, favouring her wounded leg, Yriel began to panic. Upon Kala's death, the rivulets of molten rock that had always lit the halls had stilled and cooled into the same smooth black stone that made up the rest of the palace, and the halls were dark and almost impossible to navigate. Even Yriel, who had been there so many times before, felt lost.

But she had to find the amulet. Without it, she would always be at the mercy of the Keepers and their vengeance. With it...

Yriel's mind swirled with possibilities. Kala had always kept the medallion hidden, and had been furious when Yriel had snuck into the vault where it was kept. That had been years ago, and the one-time Quencher had forgotten all about it, until her dream, a few nights ago. Then, not only had she remembered, but she had understood.

The amulet was true power, more than even Kala had been able to handle. The Spark Keeper had kept it out of any and all hands, too afraid of sharing power to use it. Her selfishness had been her undoing; Yriel was sure that the events of the last week would have gone differently had she had the use of the amulet the whole time. It was a mistake *she* would never make.

Up ahead there was a change in the darkness. The black sheen of the rounded tunnels glimmered with a violet light. *Finally.*

Yriel fumbled for the wall and felt her way to the room's entrance. She turned the corner, her eyes slowly adjusting to the low level of light.

There, in the centre of the small room was a black stone plinth. And on the plinth...

Nothing.

The amulet was missing. Yriel almost screamed in frustration. Kala must have moved it after she caught Yriel snooping in the dream.

But where would she have put it?

The soft purple glow still filtered into the room, but it was dimmer than Yriel remembered it. In fact, she was sure that had the walls still been lit by flowing lava, she would not have noticed it at all.

And so in death you reward me, Kala. A pity I waited this long.

Yriel followed the glimmering light to its source. It was sneaking out into the room from a series of cracks in the otherwise solid stone wall: cracks that framed a removable block, and behind that block...

The amulet.

Yriel didn't waste any time. She scooped up the circular purple medallion and hung it around her neck. Then she was out the door and moving swiftly down the tunnel, the dim glow of the amulet lighting her way. She quickly reached an exit from the palace and hurried out onto the wide plateau.

Behind her, the land of Tranthaea was blotted out by the massive black walls of the cliffs as Yriel carefully picked her way down the steep slopes to the east.

Epilogue - Part Three:
The Other Side of the Mountains

Kaia stepped back, plucking a bead of sweat from her face and spinning it about her head, dividing it, stretching it, and flattening it until it spun like the blades of a fan, creating a breeze to keep her cool.

A few metres away a work team of Daevyn were meticulously taking apart the last Collector that sat on the plains and removing the water tank beneath it. So far they had found more bodies than Kaia cared to think about; would-be Keepers that had not survived Tranthaea's call, thanks to the First Flame-Bearer and Kala.

A blond young man separated himself from the others and walked over to Kaia. Ydama had changed since he had taken on his new name and position. In the months since Callum had left, Ydama had started to grow a beard that was patchy at best, and that tickled Kaia whenever she kissed him, but she didn't mind.

He stopped next to her and reached his hand out to the fan, making Kaia pull it away from him.

"Hey! Will you not cool me down, too?" He growled in mock frustration.

Kaia smiled sweetly and let the fan dissipate into the air. "You have enough sweat of your own, thank you very much."

Ydama made a big show of lifting his arm and taking a big sniff underneath. "Are you trying to tell me something?"

Kaia laughed and stepped back just as she released a downpour of rain onto him, drenching him completely from head to toe.

"Nope. You smell fine to me. *Now.*" She raised her hand to ward off a playful attack and he swooped in to kiss her unguarded cheek.

"That will teach you." He turned from her and headed back to the Collector, where the final water vat was ready to be emptied and removed.

Kaia sighed and looked away. Her part was coming up, and it was never a pleasant one. With each container she couldn't help but imagine what would have become of Tranthaea if any of those bodies had survived. Would Kala have been stopped before she had accidentally created Kano Aradat? Would the peoples have been saved from such a costly and devastating war? Would she and Callum never have been brought here at all?

Ydama called to her. She pivoted on her heel and walked up the hillock to the Collector.

She needn't worry about what might have been. There were enough problems to deal with as it was.

Far behind her, a lightning bolt arced down and struck the ground on the other side of the mountains.

Acknowledgements

I know that there are many aspiring writers out there who secretly doubt that they could ever actually write a book all by themselves. Well, if there is one thing I've learned as I've worked on this project, it is that there is no such thing as writing a book all by yourself. All writers are surrounded by support teams that encourage, editors that critique, and innocent bystanders who inspire. Here are a few of mine:

Thank you to...

The two most patient and valuable members of The Writer's Enclave trio, Nick Durbridge and Holly Barr, for being the solid walls off which I bounced so many ideas.

Kevin, Mitchell, and all the friends they represent, who helped inspire and instruct, whether knowingly or not.

Ron & Heike Vikse, who constantly struggle against the parental impulse to say "I love it because *you* wrote it," and have instead given me some of my greatest and most helpful critiques.

And most of all, to my incredible wife, Krista. Your support of me and my work is at worst, enabling, and at best, nothing short of miraculous. I, and my readers, owe you everything.

About the Author

J.R. Vikse is a Canadian reader-turned-author who, in a bold attempt to escape writer's block, currently lives in Melbourne with his wife, Krista. When he isn't writing he can be found treading the boards and chewing the scenery as a theatrical director and performer. *Playing with Fire* is the first book in his new trilogy: *The Keeper Chronicles*.

He is also the author of *The Lazy Postman*.

To see what he's getting up to next, you can find him at www.jrvikse.com.